BRAXTON'S PLAN
The Journey To The Cure Continues

Stephen R. Marks

The TYPE 1-YOU'RE DONE Project

"In the summer of 2012 Type 1 diabetes knew no cure
— but it had not yet faced off with Jonathon Braxton"

To The Type 1 Diabetes Community

May my words make a difference

somehow, someway

May the cure be upon us

tomorrow if not today

STEPHEN R. MARKS

WELCOME TO

BRAXTON'S
AM🏳️‍🇪RICA

Two Diseases
Type 1 Diabetes
U.S.A. Cultural Decline

One Cure
Jonathon Braxton

What Is The Type 1-You're Done Project?

Our effort to bring BRAXTON'S AMERICA to a screen near you.

Why?

The cures for type 1 diabetes and our country's cultural decline are out there.

By raising awareness through the power of storytelling,
we hope to harness the energy of our universe in their direction.

How?

Join our community and lend your voice to our mission. Stay in touch with us. Visit
our website often for updates on what's happening in the real world of diabetes
research and with our efforts to help speed it along.

To help us influence studios/networks/actors, email us expressing your interest to
have the story of Jon and Angela Braxton,
and the reality of life with T1d, told to the world.

steve@stephenrmarksauthor.com

Prologue

A s I pen this opening for my second novel, BRAXTON'S PLAN, on December 13, 2023, it is still unfortunately true the medical research community has not yet determined the cause of Type 1 diabetes. Nor developed a cure.

Millions around the world currently suffer from this autoimmune system disorder, and hundreds of new cases are diagnosed daily. The torment within this community of patients, caregivers, loved ones, advocates, and medical researchers is immense. As is the pursuit of the cure. Many dedicated medical professionals and researchers work tirelessly every day to understand why, at any point in time, a person's immune system begins attacking and killing properly functioning pancreatic cells within an otherwise healthy body. An attack which continues until all such cells are unable to produce the life-preserving hormone, insulin.

A human body unable to produce insulin is a body which will suffer and prematurely parish unless manufactured insulin is administered via injection into the bloodstream. Injections for a Type 1 diabetic which attempt to simulate the functioning of the human pancreas when administered with the proper amount of insulin at the proper time. In other words, an impossible task. It's just not that easy to simulate a miracle.

While the quality of life and the management of blood sugars for Type 1 diabetics improves every day, thanks to the ever-improving treatments and therapeutics constantly being developed by dedicated medical researchers, a Type 1 diabetic's quality of life is nowhere near as good as life is with a healthy, functioning pancreas.

The human pancreas is a marvel which seamlessly manages the conversion of the food we consume into energy to power our bodily organs. The fact it does this so elegantly, considering the variety of foods we consume, and the complexity involved in powering the human body to function in a healthy state, is nothing short of miraculous. We recognize a properly functioning human pancreas as a miracle because of the difficulty the medical research community has in replicating it.

But there is a cure out there, and we will find it. It's just taking a little longer than any of us would like. And the road to the cure may have to be navigated from someone outside the medical research community. Someone perhaps with a skill set better suited to overcome the obstacles in the way: obstacles of money, politics, and big pharma interests.

My story of Jonathon and Angela Braxton in ***BRAXTON'S TURN, BRAXTON'S PLAN,*** and ***BRAXTON'S MIRACLE*** is the story of two such people. It was born in fiction but lives on in the hope it one day will prove itself part of the reality of a cure.

— Steve

Contents

1. Go Ahead Jamey   1

2. Hello Mr. President   3

3. Uncertainty   9

4. Nacho Cheese   22

5. CURE IT NOW   33

6. KJ   47

7. Blackberry   65

8. Day ONE   75

9. Getting Down To Business   94

10. That's Right   104

11. Let's Fix It   114

12. Jackrabbitt   134

13. Fix Our Culture   140

14. Thirty Million Vials?   152

15. The Plan of Attack   159

16. We're Good   171

17. Lie Down, Mr. President   185

18. Spin Cycle   191

19.	You're Fired	203
20.	Fix Our Well Being	212
21.	Good Luck Sidney	234
22.	Food Fight	243
23.	Not Now Wil	248
24.	Who Is This Gorgeous Creature?	255
25.	Leave Your Bias At The Door	265
26.	Let's Stay In Our Lane	274
27.	Battle Lines	291
28.	Oh Canada	311
29.	It's How He Rolls	324
30.	Diabetes Diplomacy	332
31.	Do What You Need To Do	343
32.	Perfectly Understandable, Jack	354
33.	Setback	365
34.	Personal Policy	378
35.	Christina	389
36.	'Soulidarity'	398
37.	Call A Fireman	415

Chapter 1

Go Ahead Jamey

"Go ahead Jamey."

"Thank you, Sandra. I'd like to ask you about the President's plans for reelection. During his campaign in 2016, he consistently stated, should he win, he would likely serve only one term. And for the first two years of his presidency, President Braxton often reaffirmed it was unlikely he would seek re-election. But for the last year he has had little to say on the matter, and we do not know if he plans to keep his, shall we say, commitment. Since we are inside one year to the 2020 election, can you comment on what his current plans are? The American people have a right to know."

Suddenly, the door leading from the West Wing corridor to the White House press briefing room flew open. Jon, dressed in a dark blue suit, light blue button-down collar shirt, and orange tie, confidently strode in. He gave a brief nod to the surprised journalists and then looked directly at his trusted White House Press Secretary, standing at the briefing room lectern. Sandra Seracin returned his look with a slight smile and then returned her eyes to face the now re-energized White House press corps.

"Another good question from you, Jamey. You must have had your Wheaties this morning. Let's have the President address it."

Jon made his way to where Sandra was standing. She moved back and to his left. The room was now his. He turned to face the familiar faces of the press whom he had addressed at this spot on thirty-eight occasions over the first three years of his presidency.

"Jamey, as usual, a thoughtful question," remarked the President. "One which must have been keeping you up at night for at least a week. But since you raised the matter of the 2020 election, let's dive in. You're right and believe me, it took all my willpower to admit it."

The White House press corps erupted into laughter. Even Jamey DelaCosta from CNN managed a smile. He and Jon had sparred on repeated occasions in the White House press briefing room during the first three years of the Braxton presidency. It never ended well for DelaCosta, as Jon usually exposed his biased questions and corrected his misjudgments on Braxton administration positions. But did so in a way which had DelaCosta entertained and always coming back for more.

"The people of this country are entitled to know our plans for 2020. And we are going to tell them our plans one month from today. Right here at the same time. Jamey, I trust you'll be able to make it? And, by the way, I suggest you look up the definition of the word commitment and then get back to me if you felt we ever made one regarding re-election. Now, I've got fifteen minutes. Anyone else with questions on all the less important matters were dealing with?"

Chapter 2

Hello Mr. President

Two weeks after the 2016 Presidential election, with a scheduled break in the building of his administration, Jon Braxton returned to Thousand Oaks. It had been eight weeks since he checked in with Abby. He surprised her secretary, Roberta, when he walked into the Spectre executive office lobby area unannounced at nine a.m. on what would have otherwise been an ordinary Tuesday morning. He saw the door to his old office closed.

Upon seeing Jon enter the lobby, Roberta sprang to her feet and scooted around her desk to greet him, hugging and squealing. "Oh, Mr. Braxton, it's so great to see you and congratulations on everything."

"Thank you, Roberta. It's great to see you too. Everything going well in your life?"

"Yes sir. Very well, other than we won't be seeing much of you anymore."

"Unfortunately, it will be the case."

"Well, if we have to give you up, to do so for you to be the leader of the free world is a small sacrifice."

"Assuming I can do a decent job. Let's hope you're right."

"I have no doubts. You're going to be great. What brings you in today, Mr. Braxton?"

"Abby. She busy?"

"Never too busy to speak with you. I'll let her know you're here."

Roberta skipped back to her desk and hit the intercom button to gain access to Abby's speakerphone, unable to contain her excitement. "Mrs. Martin, the next President of the United States is here to see you."

A second later, Roberta's intercom buzzer came alive with Abby's voice. *"Does he have an appointment?"*

Roberta looked at Jon sheepishly, embarrassed. Jon smiled and shook his head with an *'it's OK, Roberta'* expression.

Before a word could pass between them, Abby bolted out from behind her desk, blew open her office door and rushed into the executive offices lobby to greet her boss and mentor. She fast-walked directly to him, arms outstretched for a long overdue hug. The deference lasted only a moment as they detached, still holding each other's hands and grinning at one another.

"Well, well, if it isn't the Mr. President-elect himself? One might think you'd be out in the wilds stamping out global warming or manifesting world peace by now. Surely, you're not in Thousand Oaks to eliminate world hunger or global poverty." She looked around to see if anyone else was nearby. "And shouldn't you have some kind of detail for protection, your highness?"

"I'm certain there will be plenty of time to work on those matters. And I do have new friends who like to follow me around these days." He motioned for Abby to look out the window behind Roberta's desk overlooking the Spectre parking lot where she could see the government GMC Yukon SUV and the two secret service agents standing beside it in surveillance mode. "And there's two more in the lobby downstairs."

"Why your majesty. You now have your own royal guard? Isn't this special?"

"Thought you'd be impressed, but I do have official President-elect business to discuss with you. Can we chat for a little bit?"

"Of course, sire. Step into my office."

They proceeded into Jon's old office, now the official domain of Abby Martin, Chief Operating Officer of Spectre Systems. The office was furnished and decorated similarly to how it was when Jon abdicated for Washington, DC, and Congress three years earlier. Abby did, however, add her own feminine touches.

There were now conspicuous potted plants, two in large-floor standing pots straddling the couch on the wall opposite Abby's desk. And three more shelf-standing pots on the bookshelf immediately to the left of her office chair. The more masculine desk accouterments had been replaced by those a bit more ladylike. There were pictures of husband Mark and her children on her desk. To the right of the bookshelf, Jon noticed old friend Captain Crunch still hanging on the wall, the dartboard looking completely comfortable with Abby's décor changes.

She noticed Jon's fixation on his loyal old friend. He sensed her stare and turned to look at her. She tilted her head toward the dartboard while maintaining her gaze at him. "If you must know, the Captain and I have I've been talking about his transferring to DC so he can hang out in the oval office with you, no pun intended. He's OK with it."

"Good to know. I have a feeling I'm going to need the captain's insights once I get there. Been thinking about carving out a 'senior administration official' role for my trusted confidant."

"I'm sure he would serve you well in a senior advisory capacity. OK, do you want a Spectre briefing? I'm not prepared since I didn't know you'd be coming in, but I can wing one for you."

"Let's save it for later. I only have ten minutes and there was something important I wanted to discuss. Felt it was better to do it in person."

"Thank God. You're firing me. Finally. Now I can pursue my Starbucks barista career. I've been waiting far too long. Thought this day would never come."

"In a way, yes, I am firing you. But before I tell you why, I want you to know I have tickets for you and Mark for the inauguration. I will not in any way accept you not being there. Schedule a trip to our East Coast offices, expense everything to the company and plan to stay in Washington for a couple of days."

"I wouldn't miss it for the world, Jon. Thank you. And I need to stay in Washington. Why?"

"The day after the inauguration, you have meetings in the White House."

Abby tilted her head to the left and tapped her left ear with her left hand. "Sorry Jon, something must be wrong with my hearing. I thought I heard you say I had meetings in the White House the day after your inauguration. Isn't that YOUR first day on the job?"

"You heard me right. The day after the Inauguration, you're interviewing in the White House with Heather, Lance Reibus, and Nikki Haley for an Assistant Secretary of State position. If you're hired, you'll be working for Nikki, as I'm nominating her to join the Cabinet as our State Department Secretary. And Lance is going to be my chief-of-staff."

"Jon, seriously, I think something must be wrong with my hearing."

"No, Mrs. Martin. You heard me right. I had Heather brief me from her experience as Secretary of State what the requirements for an Assistant Secretary were. And I asked Nikki to tell me what she would be looking for. After getting both their feedback, I had no second thoughts you would be perfect for the job. I'm going to need someone I can trust to help me build bridges with Vladimir Putin, Kim Jong-un, Xi Jinping, and all the rest of the new foreign friends I'll soon be making. I can't imagine anyone better than you to help me. You'll have both Heather and Nikki to mentor you if the interview goes well and you decide to take the job. Nikki's looking forward to meeting you."

For only the second time Abby could remember in Jon's presence, she did not know what to say or do. The first being after hearing of Luke's diagnosis. Jon knew it would take her time to gather her thoughts, and he waited. Abby had proven herself repeatedly over the years she could manage, efficiently and effectively, anything he threw her way. He had one hundred percent confidence in her abilities and judgments. He knew there would be considerable foreign policy challenges to deal with as the current state of U.S. foreign relations was teetering from a fragile Obama policy agenda under the leadership of John Kerry since Heather's resignation to pursue her presidential aspirations. A handoff which led to a significant decline in relations with trusted U.S. allies, and unfathomably culminated in Heather's selection as Jon's Vice-President choice.

"I need to talk with Mark. Can I have the rest of the week to digest everything?"

"Of course. And if you decide you don't want the position and want to stay here, it's perfectly OK and I would understand. I am asking you for way more than I should. The choice is yours and I'm behind you either way. OK? But as far as attending the inauguration,

I won't take no for an answer. And another thing to know to factor in your decision, it's likely Spectre will be acquired in the next few weeks before we take office. We have a couple of attractive offers on the table. I'm leaning toward Larry Ellison's Oracle offer. There's no doubt you'd be offered a significant position in an acquisition, but you'd certainly have new people to answer to."

Jon stood. Abby did as well and rushed over to him for another hug.

"I'll call you in a couple of days," Abby said with out-of-character uncertainty and doubt. She smiled at him warmly, shaking with the thoughts of moving from the friendly confines of Spectre Systems to an explosive world stage.

Chapter 3

Uncertainty

F ollowing his meeting with Abby, Jon and his entourage made their way twenty miles north to Oxnard. He had scheduled a meeting with Connie McIlroy and had asked Earl Gregory, the former Congressman and current Win-the-Day board member, and Rob Wiley, Jon's current California Congressional chief-of-staff, to meet him there.

The specially equipped Secret Service GMC Yukon, and the second secret service-occupied 'wingman' SUV pulled into the Win-the-Day parking lot at exactly two p.m. Earl and Rob had already arrived and were standing next to Earl's car. Jon had not seen either of them since the election four weeks earlier, though Jon had spoken with Earl the previous evening and advised him of his plans for Connie. He asked Earl to fill Rob in.

Jon stepped out of the SUV after clearance from his detail and approached the man he had replaced in Congress in 2013 and his trusted California Chief-of-Staff. He warmly embraced them both.

"Mr. President-elect, it's great to see you," Earl bellowed with his finest ex-Congressional delivery.

"Thank you, Earl. It's great to see you. You're looking fit and healthy."

"I'm feeling great these days. Working here with Connie is therapeutic and energizing."

Rob hadn't spoken with Jon since before the election and chipped in. "JB, congratulations. What a wipeout! Unbelievable."

"Thanks Rob, we've got much to discuss, but let's get this meeting with Connie out of the way. Did Earl fill you in?" Rob nodded.

Earl was curious. "Do you think she'll accept?"

"Only one way to find out." Jon replied with uncertainty. He looked at Rob.

Rob was confident. "I think she'll go for it."

"OK, let's see what she says." The three of them, followed by half of Jon's Secret Service detail for the day, purposefully approached the Win-the-Day lobby and entered the building.

Connie was notified they had arrived and made the way from her office to the lobby to greet them. After she collected her visitors, the four of them strode down the hallway in the former Oxnard Middle School administration building the twenty yards between the lobby and the facility's familiar conference room. Connie had taken Jon by the left arm and wrapped both of her arms around it as they walked. "Oh Jon, it's so good to see you again. I miss our talks and am finding the last three years hard to believe. And now here you are. Should I be calling you Mr. President-elect?" She asked with an affectionate smile.

"Connie, you call me whatever you want. And should I be calling you Madam Secretary? OK, don't answer yet. Let's go sit down in the conference room." A moment later, they were seated.

Connie started filling Jon in on the recent happenings with Win-the-Day. It had been four months since they spent more than three consecutive minutes talking. There was a presidential campaign and election which kept getting in their way. The beginning of the fall session started in September and there was a lot of catching up to do. Both Connie and Earl had volumes of information to pass along and took forty-five minutes to communicate everything. Once they completed their update, Jon popped the question.

"Connie, do you ever have any thoughts about going back into public education?"

"No. Why would I? I'm incredibly happy and satisfied with the work we're doing here. But I am curious about how the new fifth-grade curriculum you enacted with STYLE is working in the public education space. I've been wanting to ask you about the progress but I know you've been a little preoccupied lately," Connie asked innocently, not realizing she was going exactly where Jon was hoping to take her.

"Have you ever been to Washington, DC, in the springtime?"

"OK, Mr. President-elect, what's on your mind?" Connie stared directly at Jon with a slight look of mystery on top of a cursory smile.

"Well, when we have our Cabinet meetings, I've been thinking about who should be sitting in the Department of Education's secretary's seat."

Connie moved her eyes to Earl's. He forged a huge smile and when their eyes met, he nodded as if to say. *'Yes, he means it, and yes, you should accept.'*

Jon gave her a moment to digest. Then, in as good of a serious tone as he could muster given the long-standing familiar relationship between the two and the conspicuous smile on his face, he delivered his message. "Mrs. McIlroy, I'd like you to join the Braxton Administration Cabinet as the Secretary of the Department of Education. And then you'll get to know everything you're curious about. But better yet, manage everything you're curious about. And, whether you decide to take the job or not, I'd be honored if you attended the inauguration."

Connie was rendered speechless by the offer. Jon recollected he had never seen Connie flustered in the seven years he knew her. He was amused yet uncomfortable witnessing her dithering.

"Connie, I'm sorry to come from left field on this, but I wanted to wait until I could ask you in person. I realize the tremendous sacrifice I'm asking of you, and I wouldn't be requesting you to come and work with me if there was anyone else I felt could better serve in this capacity. And I can't. The job is yours if you want it. And if not, and you wanted to stay here and continue running Win-the-Day, I'd completely understand."

The meeting broke up shortly thereafter, with Connie promising Jon she'd attend the inauguration and would provide him her answer about accepting the offer to be the Secretary of the Department of Education in a few days.

Jon was looking forward to getting back to his Thousand Oaks home for the afternoon and evening.

He had only been home and slept in his bed four days over the previous six months. When he was home, he was in campaign mode, barely connecting at a personal level with his family. He had been looking forward to the prospect of a family dinner with Angela, the kids, and his in-laws since election night. Angela, Luke, and Darla, as well as Tanoro and Taka, had been with him in Thousand Oaks sharing the momentous event. But the next day it was back to Washington for meetings with Lance Reibus and the RNC. He had not been home since. Being in the family home with everyone and having Angela cook his favorite chicken cacciatore with artichoke hearts and vermicelli was a treat he had been craving for weeks.

The swiftness of the events of the last six months had not offered Jon much time for reflection. All his conscious thinking since the visit in July from Carlton and Cornelius Hale to offer the VP position on the ticket with Tony Jacobs was about being in the moment. On reflection, he was sensing himself detaching from reality. He knew he needed one-on-one time with Angela and his kids to check in with them. All their lives were soon going to be disrupted to an unimaginable degree, and he needed assurances they had no misgivings. Though it was a bit late, if so, to do anything about it.

Jon took solace in knowing improving Luke's quality of life, as well as all the others who were living with Type 1 diabetes, was his primary motivation for seeking the highest office in the land. But doubts were starting to creep in. Was this all really true? Were all the sacrifices he was making for an uncertain outcome worth it? His left brain was busy doing risk analysis. His right brain was struggling to ascertain just exactly how was he going to do this job. Had he lost sight he had become what he had always preached to himself to never be? Was he truly doing the right thing for the country in pursuing, acquiring, and assuming the job of commander-in-chief, given he had no experience in foreign affairs or the military? Was he acting in the country's best interests when his primary motivation was finding the cure for Type 1 diabetes, given the large majority of the country was not affected by the disease?

His escalating doubts notwithstanding, Jon craved assurance this unbelievable and improbable journey, one in which he had innocently embarked on only three and a half short years earlier and was now depositing him onto the world stage as the leader of the free world, was not a mistake which could jeopardize the wellbeing of billions of people. In the art of business, Jon Braxton was unquestionably a master. In the arena of politics, the gradation of bureaucracy, and the dispensing of diplomacy, he was a neophyte. No one saw this intricate, composite picture more clearly than Jon himself. It was a picture he was having difficulty putting into focus. A fuzzy picture becoming indelibly inscribed on his consciousness.

Jon was grateful Tanoro and Taka were joining the family dinner. He enjoyed their company and always felt forever grateful to them for their belief in him, their support of his relationship with Angela, and for their help in his acquiring Spectre. They had filled a huge void in his life, left by the loss of both his parents at the age of four.

Tanoro opened a bottle of 2015 Zinfandel from Sonoma County and filled Taka's, Angela's, and Jon's glasses. Angela brought all the food to the table, and they were ready to enjoy. Before anything could be served, Tanoro asked all to join hands and bow their heads for a moment of silent prayer and gratitude.

When the prayer was completed, Tanoro raised his wine glass. "Jon, allow me to propose a toast. I would like to toast myself, as I am the proudest father in the world."

"Daddy!" Angela thought her dad's humor might have been a little displaced.

"Tanoro, show some respect!" Taka commanded.

"Wait. I am not finished you two. Hold on a minute. If I may, I would like to toast myself as also the proudest grandfather and happiest husband in the world."

"That's better, daddy," Angela said, looking at him sideways with a hint of a smile.

"Good save Dad," Jon laughed as he raised his glass. "Let's drink to your quick thinking."

The dinner conversation was lively with Jon and Tanoro doing the bulk of the talking. Tanoro kept firing questions about Jon's experiences over the last few months. He wanted to know how Anthony Jacobs had approached him to be his running mate. He was curious about the conversations with Neil Hale and Lance Reibus about him being selected over Ted Cruz to be the nominee following Jacobs' death. He was fascinated with Heather Carrington and how she decided to blow up her career and subject herself to a lifetime of ridicule from the Democrats and the media. And he was in disbelief at how his son-in-law convinced her to be his running mate with Washington's head exploding from all the unprecedented bombshell news of her leaving the race and endorsing him.

"What did you say to her to convince her to join you? I would have loved to be a fly on the wall for that conversation."

"Well dad, I'm sure you don't remember this, but you once dropped a Japanese proverb on me when I was struggling in the early days of Spectre. *"Koketsu ni irazunba koji-o-ezu"*

"You remember well, son. If you do not enter the tiger's cave, you will not catch the cub."

"Actually dad. It wasn't hard to convince her. I just laid the cards out."

"As you always do," Tanoro responded.

"My goal is to bring this country back together so we can make better choices in government. I'm sure a majority of Democrats will demonize Heather. But the fact remains, she has millions of loyal followers. There is nobody better positioned to help us bring the parties, and the nation, together. I also told her I was only going to be a one-term president. If she wants to run for the job in 2020, I won't be in her way. I'm sure my interest in only one term made her decision easier."

"What makes you think you'll be able to quit and not run for re-election in 2020? Political offices are filled with multi-termers who never saw themselves as career politicians. The forces pulling on you to stay in the game will be stronger than you can imagine. You must draw a line in the sand you are unwilling to cross if you are serious."

"The only thing which will cause me to reconsider and run again is if we are not on the runway to the cure for Type 1."

Luke was compelled to interject. "Dad, you and I will make sure this won't happen. From what I've already seen and heard, we need to be done with Washington by 2020."

Tanoro grinned and put his arm around his grandson. "Kino mi-wa moto-he otsuru."

Jon smiled. "And?"

Angela provided the answer. "The fruit of a tree falls to its root, Mr. Braxton."

"Did Heather say she would want to run in 2020 if you don't?" Tanoro was still curious.

"She didn't say one way or the other. But she made it clear she did not want the job right now. She likes my vision for the future and wants to do what she can to help see it through. It's obvious she's been doing serious soul searching over the past few years. When I offered her the slot, she accepted immediately. Didn't need time to think about the repercussions. Didn't want time to discuss with her husband. I certainly wasn't expecting an instantaneous response."

Tanoro was not satisfied. "Speaking of her husband, how is he sitting with all of this? He strikes me as one who would be disappointed, if not angry, it is you and not his wife being inaugurated. I would be very watchful of him, son. He has, I believe, motivation for you to fail. And fail quickly. Be mindful."

Tanoro sensed he had changed the mood in the room and looked over at Luke, who was busy devouring his mom's cooking. He changed course. "Now, what about diabetes research funding? What will change with you in the White House?"

"Well, Dad, pretty much everything. The way Washington works, everything is about tradeoffs and compromises. These rarely lead to effective decisions but until we get different-thinking people in government, it's the way it is. People in Congress will have their own agendas to move forward, and they will need the Executive branch in its corner. We should be able to trade our way to the funding within the first year. Then it will take about two years to evaluate the hypotheses on pluripotent cells as a cure. If any hypothesis can be validated, we can hopefully see a clearer pathway to the cure being cultivated by 2020. Sooner if we can change the more frivolous and restrictive FDA regulations which hamstring medical research and protect the interests of entrenched corporate interests. And along the way learn more about what flips the immune system so we can develop preventative protocols or a vaccine."

"And son, other than diabetes research, what will be the primary premise for your term in office? What one higher-level purpose will you hold your administration accountable to?"

The question left Jon silent. With the volume of details needing his attention and, as of yet, the lack of meeting time with Heather, Lance Reibus, Paul Ryan, or anyone else he was thinking of inviting into his inner circle, Jon had lost sight of the big picture.

"Dad, I haven't had the time to give it any thought. But you're right in asking it. I need to give you the answer."

Tanoro's question snapped Jon back into the realm of self-awareness and doubt. The welcomed family dinner was but a brief respite. Jon was again staring face-to-face at the daunting uncertainty.

Dinner was all but consumed when Tanoro asked Jon and Angela to excuse him and Taka as they wanted to start their two-hour commute back to Torrance in early evening L.A. traffic. "We will miss you all when you move to Washington. But the country and the world need your spirit and your wisdom, Jon. Taka and I will see you for the inauguration and come to visit often. Go with our best wishes. And be sure to make the time to take care of your family."

The Aoki's left. Luke and Darla returned upstairs to their bedrooms. Jon and Angela headed to the kitchen to finish the clean-up. As Angela was finalizing the drying and putting all the dishes away, Jon headed to the living room. The fireplace was ablaze with warming flames. Jon sat on the floor with his back against the front of their white leather sofa and in front of a glass coffee table, his legs bent and knees pointing up, arms wrapped around them. He stared into the fire.

"Honey, when you're done, will you join me?" he shouted to Angela in the kitchen, louder than he needed to.

"In a minute."

She then joined him, carrying two cups. One, his favorite after dinner drink, a cappuccino, and two, her wind down drink of choice, hot black tea. She put the two mugs on the coffee table in front of Jon and sat next to him in the same position, taking his left hand in her right.

"Thanks for making dinner for all of us tonight. I've really missed these things lately."

"OK Jon, what's wrong? Something's bothering you."

"Why? How can you tell?"

"May I remind you, Mr. JB-son and President-elect, I know you better than you know yourself. And I can tell when that brilliant mind of yours is off center. Something's been bothering you the last few days. Let's talk it out. What's up?"

"Angie, try to put everything we've experienced over the last four years out of your mind. Clear your cache. Think of our lives before Luke was diagnosed."

"OK."

"OK, so forgetting everything about the last four years, jump to where we are now. In six weeks, you are going to be the First Lady of the United States. You are going to have tremendous responsibility and you are going to lose most, if not all, your privacy. You are going to have Secret Service agents following you everywhere. You will be unable to do what you want when you want. Your life is going to become highly regimented, and you will be forced to constantly be with people you may not like or trust. You will have to watch everything you say and everything you do. You will be living under a powerful microscope in a strange house and there will always be people around. And then there are your kids. Just look at how their lives are going to be affected. They will be in a constant spotlight. They're going to read and hear and see terrible things written and said about their mom and dad. They will lose their friends. Their lives will be in constant turmoil."

"Jon, seriously? Enough. You're right. Everything you've said is true. But guess what. It's already baked in. You don't think Luke and Darla and I know what we're in for? Well, don't underestimate this family of yours. We've got this. We know what you've done, and we know what you're about to do. And we are not feeling sorry for ourselves. No, we are not. Because we are in this fight with you one hundred percent. Just like Heather, we believe in the mission, and we are honored to serve. Do not doubt yourself for one minute. Do not take your eye off the prize. We are on your team, and we are looking for your leadership. So, lead us, Mr. Braxton, the man of my dreams and the love of my life. You put this country on your back, and you carry it forward to a better place. And your family will always be with you to help in whatever ways we can. Got it?"

Jon looked at her. Bowed his head for a moment. Then looked at her again. "Thank you, honey. You have no idea how I needed to hear you reassure me. This country is soon going to learn something I already know. You will be a great First Lady. Now, will you excuse me for a couple of hours? I need to go to Spectre to take care of a few things."

"OK, but no more than two hours, Mr. President. You can't be late for the meeting I scheduled for our bedroom this evening."

Jon smiled, nodded, and leaned over to kiss her on the cheek. He stood, slipped on a pair of loafers. After making his way to the garage, he pulled out into the cold and rainy mid-December evening in Angela's Lexus RX350. He headed slowly away from the house on his way to Spectre. The Secret Service detail stationed in a black Dodge Challenger across the street from the Braxton residence took notice and radioed into command as the President-elect pulled out. They followed.

Heavy rain was pouring down. The Challenger's worn-out windshield wipers were struggling to keep the visibility of Angela's Lexus fifty yards in front. The wipers moved sluggishly and were doing more water spreading than clearing. Squeaking to the left and swooshing to the right. Squeak, swoosh. Squeak, swoosh. Left, right. Left, right.

Adding to the annoying wipers was the sound of heavy rain pelting the Dodge at an increasing rate. Rat, tat, tat, tat. As were the splashing sounds of the Challenger's wide tires slogging through the increasing water level on Thousand Oaks Boulevard. The level of rain-induced sound inside the Challenger's cabin made the citizen's band radio call from the secret service vehicle almost impossible for Command to hear.

Click. Static. "Lion King is on all fours and has left the den." Static.
Click

Click. Static. "Make sure you join him, Simba. He loves your company." Static. Click.

Click. Static. "Roger that. Later." Static. Click.

Click. Static. "Copy." Static. Click.

After the ten-minute drive, Jon pulled into the empty Spectre parking lot. He pulled up to the curb adjacent to the front door and parked, bypassing all the handicap spaces. He jumped out of the car in his raincoat and hastened to the doors leading to Spectre's entry way. Using all the requisite keys, badges, and alarm codes, he made his way to the empty executive offices lobby on the second floor where he met Abby and Roberta earlier. Huge raindrops were drilling the windows of the lobby. Suddenly, a roar of thunder shook the building, and a flash of lightning illuminated the lobby at the moment Jon was putting his key into the lock of his old office.

He entered and turned on only a single table lamp. Heavy rain continued to pelt the windows, and flashes of lightening were illuminating his old office with increasing frequency. Jon walked over to the credenza to his right and opened the top left-hand drawer, fully expecting everything to be in order. It was. He opened the waiting cigar box and grabbed his eight darts. He closed the drawer and walked over to the wall directly opposite Captain Crunch and turned to look at his trusted advisor. The eight darts were in his right hand. He took one with his left and lifted his left hand to a point three inches from his open left eye. He extended and then retracted his left arm, moving the dart forward and backward to line up his toss.

Under his breath, the President-elect muttered, "Hello again, old friend. Let's have a chat, shall we?"

Chapter 4

Nacho Cheese

The gunfire was systematic, on point, and deafening.

Ten rounds were fired in perfectly timed rapid succession, each firing two hundred milliseconds prior to the next. Each round found its target with keen precision, leaving a gaping hole at the center of the body outline connected to a retrieving line thirty yards from the shooter bay. The perfectly executed shooting was accompanied by eardrum-shattering volume.

Mark Parker, a highly decorated Army Ranger, and the previous Chief-of-Staff for Heather Carrington during her tenure as Secretary of State from 2008 through 2015, was sharpening his skills at the Machine Gun Nest indoor shooting range in Frederick, MD. His tool of choice for this session—a 357 Magnum handgun. There was no mission for which he was practicing. His professional sharpshooting days had long passed. This session was simply to remind himself where he had come from and for what he was made. His years in the Washington federal government bureaucracy had dulled his memory.

Mark Parker was a true Democrat party loyalist. He started working at State in a lower-level capacity in 1996 while the Carrington's were in the White House and Madeleine Albright was the Secretary.

He attracted Albright's attention with his passion for the work and loyalty to her agenda. When Heather accepted the Secretary position in 2009, Albright gave Parker her highest recommendation to serve as her chief-of-staff. He was the only chief-of-staff Heather employed during her seven-year tenure.

Parker served Heather Carrington with a tenacity equal to the precision, technique, and discipline which molded his marksmanship abilities. His loyalty to Carrington and the Obama agenda were unquestioned, as was his consistent loyalty to the Democrat party. As such, in hindsight, it was not a surprise after Heather resigned; she kept her distance from Parker. While deciding to quit the race and the party and join the other side was far distant from her consciousness at the time, something held her back from fully embracing Parker upon her resignation. Their last conversation was during her going away party from State when she lukewarmly thanked him for his service and wished him well. She fully understood his loyalty to the party and knew despite their long and successful relationship, the thoughts and insecurities rolling around inside her head at the time would not sit well with the former Colonel.

Parker emptied his magazine and turned to walk into the sound-proofed locker room, leaving the tattered target with an enormous gaping hole where a heart could have been drawn. He took off his noise and eye protection, then packed his bag with his accessories and his firearm and made his way to the parking lot.

As he approached his car, his cellphone rang with '*CallerID unknown*' on the display. He answered cautiously. "Hello?"

"*What cheese does not belong to you?*"

Mark recognized the voice of the former president, Wilton Carrington, but as was his custom followed protocol to a tee while hysterically laughing to himself. It took all his willpower to answer the botched security handshake question with a straight face and a serious voice.

"I'm sorry. You have the wrong number."

Mark hung up, assuming the former president would find the correct security handshake question and call back. He decided to wait for the call before leaving.

Wil had called from the security of his study in the Carrington's DC residence. It would be another few weeks before they officially moved into the Vice President residence. With the call disconnected and the former president flustered, he began fumbling with his Blackberry looking for the notes on the current security handshake questions in use during the current quarter. He found what he was looking for, shook his head in disgust, and redialed Parker. Mark's phone again rang with *'CallerId unknown'* on the display. He again answered cautiously.

"Hello?"

"What cheese is not yours?"

"Nacho cheese," Parker responded with regimented seriousness.

"Hello Mark. It's good to hear your voice again. Did you really have to hang up on me?"

"Hello Mr. President. It's critical we follow our established security protocols to the letter. It's for our own security and protection. And always good to hear from you, sir. What can I do for you?"

"Mark, meet me tomorrow on Roosevelt Island. Fifteen hundred. There's a park bench on the east side of the island near the dock. The opposite end from the footbridge. Be discreet. Head covering. Sunglasses. I'll do the same. Look for me in an Orioles baseball cap. If you see anyone who can see us, we abort. No one sees us together, got it?"

"Yes sir. Tomorrow, fifteen hundred. Roosevelt Island, east side. Discreet. Confirmed."

Sidney Rosenberg was home in his Upper East side Manhattan apartment when his Blackberry rang with *'CallerID unknown'*.

"Hello?"

"What's your favorite color?"

"Gold Jerry gold!"

"Hello Sidney."

"Hello Wil." Rosenberg had long since dispensed with any formalities regarding the former president.

"Sidney, I need to come to New York and see you. Can we meet at your place next Wednesday evening around seven?"

"What's going on Wil?"

"Not over the phone. We have important matters to discuss."

"Regarding your wife?"

"No. Regarding the price of cheese in Slovenia."

"Their cheese pairs nicely with the 'Cab' I'm drinking. Bring some with you. I'll make it a point to be home."

"Fuck you, Sidney. Utmost discretion and security protocols."

"Understood."

Theodore Roosevelt Island sits in the Potomac River between Washington, DC and Arlington, Virginia. Its eighty-eight acres were donated to the federal government by the Roosevelt Memorial Association in 1933 in honor of the twenty-sixth president. The RMA had recently acquired the then-called Analostan Island from the Washington Gas Light Company, just two years prior, to create a living memorial to Teddy Roosevelt under the management of the National Park Service.

The island was used for a variety of purposes over the years, including use during World War Two as a training site. And had been thrashed. After the war ended, the park service decided the island should be returned to its natural forest and small bird and animal sanctuary state. It was also decided the island would be closed to automobiles and built out with footpaths. A foot bridge was constructed to provide island access from the Potomac bank in Arlington.

The dark and frosty winter day provided the perfect discreet meeting place in early January, 2017. The chill in the air was profound and the heavy dark gray cloud cover hung over the island like a collapsed shroud, assuring there would be little if any foot traffic on the island, particularly on the farthest end from the footbridge.

Wil arrived first and was sitting on a secluded park bench. It was below freezing. He had on a long black trench coat, a heavy blue scarf, a Baltimore Orioles baseball cap, and conspicuous dark glasses given the darkness of the late afternoon winter day.

A moment later, Mark Parker approached, wearing a brown leather unadorned bomber jacket and a black woolen knit skull cap pulled down over his ears. When he crossed the footbridge and noticed the darkness which had befallen the island, he dispensed with the sunglasses believing they could be considered suspect should anyone notice. He saw Wil and walked toward him while scanning all the viewpoints to the bench. He didn't see anyone and moved in his direction. Mark sat while looking in the same direction as Wil, straight ahead. They avoided any eye contact.

"Hello Mark. It's been a while. I hope you and your family are doing well. Last I heard, you left State shortly after the election. Have you landed anything yet?"

"No sir. Still evaluating offers but enjoying the time off and spending it with my family."

"From what I hear, Braxton is going to nominate Nikki Haley for Secretary. Do you know her? Any chance she can find a position for you?"

"Yes sir, I do and heard of her potential nomination as well. I did contact her. Unfortunately, she advised she didn't have anything for me."

"Mark, you should know Heather always had the highest respect for you and your loyalty. She felt you could be trusted with any information and any task. And it's an admirable reputation to hold. But I'd like to find out from you what your loyalty is attached to. I'd be surprised to hear you say to Heather given the way she abandoned you when she left State. And now she's changed sides, which I think will be temporary. Once the shine wears off Braxton, I think she'll come to her senses. But until such time we should be on guard against the possibility Braxton can be successful with any of his crazy ideas. So, Mark, for a variety of reasons, I need to know where you stand. Can I ask you a few direct questions and have you answer them candidly? And have your assurance this all stays strictly between the two of us?"

"Yes sir. I completely understand. You have nothing to worry about. What do you need to know?"

"You must be bitter with the way things have transpired. When was the last time you spoke with Heather?"

"The last conversation I had with her was at her going away party at State."

"Really? It's been two years since you've spoken? Not a single conversation since then?"

"No sir. Have not spoken with her since."

"Kerry never needed you to reach out to her for any information?"

"No sir. Any time Secretary Kerry needed information from Heather, he had someone else in the Department make contact. My understanding was this was at her request."

"Hmmm. Seems odd. You two had such a close working relationship for all those years. What do you think the reason was for her letting go?"

"I'm not sure. Always felt we had a strong working relationship. I know she left to focus on her campaign. All I can think is she wanted to move forward and not look back."

Wil was surprised at how cleanly Heather had cut the cord. "When she made her decision to quit the race and endorse Braxton, she didn't reach out to you to offer you any kind of role or position? I mean, you two worked so well together for such a long time. I'm surprised if she didn't."

"No sir. Nothing."

"Why do you think she ghosted you, Mark?" the former president asked inquisitively, looking for a specific answer.

"Honestly sir, it's probably because she didn't believe I would follow her. She knows my politics and my loyalties."

"What do you think of what she did?"

"Well, sir, in the spirit of being perfectly candid, I was tremendously disappointed. I felt she betrayed the party and the country."

"Mark, I know you might not believe it, but I am glad to hear you say this. Again, between you and me only and not to be shared with anyone, I feel the same way. Now what about Braxton? Any thoughts on him?"

"Nothing good, sir. He doesn't have the experience to do the job. By all rights, Heather should be the President. And if I may be so bold, Heather made a tremendous mistake with her decision. And I'm concerned our country may pay a heavy price."

"Why do you feel this way?"

"Well sir, from the perspective of the State Department, the remnants of John Kerry's agenda have placed us in dangerous situations throughout the world. To my thinking, Kerry made several miscalculations. We discussed those that concerned me, and it was clear we did not see eye-to-eye frequently. Needless to say, my influence at State diminished after my first few conversations with Kerry. Today we have potential hotspots smoldering in regions all across the globe. And now we have a President with zero foreign policy experience to deal with everything. From what I know of Braxton's thoughts on those matters, he seems very naïve. Diplomacy and dealing with foreign leaders and cultures differs from negotiating business deals with his peers. His choice of Heather for VP was smart for him, but who knows how much he will listen to her. Our adversaries, I'm sure, are ready to make their moves. The time is short before the fireworks start."

The directness of Parker's opinion jolted the former president and, at the same time, strengthened his resolve.

"Very insightful Mark. I agree with you the country with Jon Braxton at the helm is in a precarious situation. And I, like you, wonder just how much influence Heather will have on his thinking. To change course a bit, do you know Sidney Rosenberg?"

"Yes sir. I met him three or four times when he came to State to meet with Heather and sat in on two meetings with them. He certainly had his finger on the pulse of the political winds. Seems to know what he's doing and does his job well."

"Mark, let me get to why I asked you to meet with me. I agree with you, Braxton is not fit for the job and Heather should be the President. Sidney shares this belief as well, and we are meeting next week to discuss. I hope to enlist his support to develop a plan to, shall we say, make things right. Once we get our plan dialed in, would you be willing to help us?"

"What is it you'd like me to do?"

"I'm not sure yet, but once we have something to work with, I'll let you know. What I need to know at this point is if we craft a good plan, can we count on your involvement?"

"Yes sir. If your plan is to help the country, then by all means."

"Great to hear this, Mark. Thank you. And there is one other thing I've been thinking about asking you. I remember Heather telling me you were skilled with electronics and surveillance techniques. Is this the case?"

"Yes, sir, in a way. I don't work on the electronics myself, but I have a buddy from the army who's a magician and would help me with some creative surveillance activities while at State. I'd give him the landscape and the objective. He'd give me the tools."

"Is he discreet?"

"As quiet as they come."

"Good. Keep his contact info handy."

The former president had his driver take him from Washington, DC, to New York City to meet with Sidney Rosenberg, the former lead political consultant for both Carringtons. Rosenberg instrumentally steered Wil's campaign to the 1992 Democrat nomination and subsequent election to the Presidency. He was planning to do the same for Heather in 2016 until the train jumped the track. Rosenberg was in his nineteenth-floor penthouse apartment in the luxurious Manhattan House building on east sixty-sixth street curiously awaiting the visit from Wil Carrington.

Sidney answered the doorbell dressed casually in a black designer sweat suit and blue Nike tennis shoes. The president stood alone.

"Hello Wil. It's been too long. Welcome back to New York. Come on in."

The two exchanged pleasantries as Sidney moved to the wet bar and poured both a single malt. They moved to a large formal living room overlooking the southern Manhattan skyline and settled into two grayish plush accent chairs.

"I forgot how great your view is. No wonder you like to stick around the city."

"I love it here, Wil. Whenever I have to leave, I'm always glad to get back."

"Sidney, what the fuck happened?"

"I'm assuming you're talking about your wife?"

The former president smirked. "Didn't you see it coming? Couldn't you stop her? Talk her down? Reason with her?"

"She shut me down around March after a visit with Claymore. After she saw him, I never heard from her. And she didn't return any of my calls."

"So, you heard nothing from her since last March? You had no idea what she was planning to do?"

"No, I didn't. But you live with her. Didn't you notice the self-doubts she started having? I started sensing them in 2014 and questioned her numerous times if she had the desire to run. She always assured me she did. But I did sense her heart wasn't all in. Especially after Charlie's death in Yemen."

"I saw doubts creep in, but always thought her ambition was strong enough to overcome them," the former President concurred. "But to jump the party and join the Republicans? And attach herself to a neophyte like Braxton? Shit. Never in a million years. Looks like we were both blindsided."

"Wil, I feel as if I should have shared my observations with you when I first became concerned. I'm sorry. Looking back, I don't know why I didn't."

Wil was dismissive. "Right. Now what's your take on Braxton?"

"Well, what he's done thus far is impressive. You've got to hand it to him. But he won't last long with his goodie two-shoes agenda. The honeymoon will be short. Washington will eat him up and spit him out. The media, once they realize what he's all about and the threat he poses to their influence, and to the country's security, will crush him. Even Republicans in Congress will resist, particularly on campaign finance reform. He's a flash in the pan and will fail quickly."

"Let's hope you're right. When Braxton does hit the skids, what happens to Heather?"

"Depends on how closely she attaches herself to him and his shenanigans. If she lays back, she might come out the other side as a savior. If she dives in, she's collateral damage."

"This is what we need to discuss, Sidney. How do we take him out and move Heather in?"

"Without going to prison?"

"C'mon Sidney. Don't get overly dramatic. We're talking about a political maneuver. Not an assassination. Though I must say the thought has crossed my mind. We have the media to work with. Congressmen from both parties to work with. Obama executive branch bureaucrat remnants to work with. I know we can concoct something if we put our minds to it. You're the best in the business. Give it your attention. I'll be in touch."

Chapter 5

CURE IT NOW

T he set was ready.

The stage lights were ablaze.

The cameras were all in their places. Wallis Kriss' hair was coiffed immaculately. The production crew readied with eager anticipation for the production to start, as did this morning's seven million viewers. They were all awaiting Jonathon Braxton's first televised appearance on Big News Sunday in nine months. A span which included Braxton's selection by Tony Jacobs to be his running mate in May. The tragic death of Tony Jacobs in June. The highly improbable nomination of Jonathon Braxton as the Republican Party presidential nominee in Cleveland in July. The bombshell proclamation of Heather Carrington in September, and the election of Jonathon Braxton as the forty-fifth President of the United States in November.

The historic events of the previous one hundred and fifty days prior to the November 6, 2016, presidential election were unlike any other election cycle the country had ever experienced. Events which culminated in the improbable election of Jon Braxton, the party-uncommitted and acknowledged enemy of all things politically conventional, as the forty-fifth president. And the installment of Heather

Carrington, a lifelong Democrat and presumptive Democrat nominee with a history of presidential aspirations as Braxton's Vice President. The same Heather Carrington, who had the 2016 Democrat nomination in hand but left the race, quit the party, and threw her support behind her opponent. A political suicide attempt she somehow survived.

Now, after a most unlikely inauguration culminating the previous ten months of mind-bending political theater, the nation was ready for normalcy. They were ready for Wallis Kriss and Jon Braxton sitting at the bar, drinking their beers and talking shop. The nation was ready for the latest edition of Big News Sunday. One group in particular anticipation was the Type 1 diabetes community. Hope for those in the community that the cure for T1d was finally a dream ready to come true, had never been higher.

"Good morning from Washington. It's February 26, 2017. I'm Wallis Kriss and welcome to Big News Sunday. The first time we interviewed our newly inaugurated forty-fifth president was in August 2012, when he was a private citizen with not the slightest interest in a political career. In pursuit of lobbying the federal government for more medical research funding resulting from his son having contracted Type 1 diabetes, Jon Braxton was given a prime time speaking slot at the 2012 Republican National Convention. He delivered a speech which launched him on a most improbable journey. The next time we interviewed Jon Braxton in early 2013, he had just been elected to Congress in a special election to replace Earl Gregory, the sitting Congressman from his district who had recently retired.

"Over the course of just three short years in Congress, Mr. Braxton became the first first-term Congressman to author and pass joint, bi-partisan legislation, introducing what came to be known as the STYLE Act of 2013. Legislation which has successfully transformed the arc of public education in this country. In 2015, he again introduced historic legislation. To reform election law and campaign financing abuses, Jon Braxton authored the ELECT Act of 2015. Also known as the ELECTION LAW EVERYONE CAN TRUST Act. And in 2015, House Speaker Paul Ryan appointed him chairman of the powerful House Ways and Means Committee.

"In June 2016, Republican presidential nominee Anthony Jacobs tapped Jon Braxton to be his running mate. The unfortunate death of Jacobs shortly thereafter led to Jon Braxton being nominated to be the Republican Party's candidate for President despite his not being a member of the party, nor having earned a single primary election vote. To cap off his most remarkable journey, Braxton won the 2016 election in a landslide unprecedented in American presidential politics. And along the way convinced his Democrat opponent to join him on his ticket. His three-and-a-half-year journey has been like no other in history. Ladies and gentlemen (pause), the President of the United States (pause), Jonathon Braxton."

The TV cameras panned out to a shot of both Braxton and Kriss sitting at a counter facing one another at a 45-degree angle with the Big News Sunday set backdrop in full view. "Welcome back, sir."

"Thank you, Wally. It's great to be back."

"Sir, in the past, you had asked me to address you as JB. Since you're now the President, I'm not sure it's appropriate. In deference to the office, may I address you as Mr. President?"

"Wally, do you know what is inappropriate?"

Kriss smiled. "No sir, I don't, but I'm sure you are about to tell me."

"It's your tie Wally. For chrissakes, a turquoise tie with a yellow shirt? Who dresses you, your parakeet?" Laughter could be heard on set from the production crew.

"No sir. My wife actually. I'll let her know you question her taste."

"Never mind. I'm starting to like it. By the way, you are grandfa-thered in on JB. It will be my first Executive Order. And we're still two guys at the bar, shooting the breeze."

"OK JB, uh...sir, a Guinness it is. I might have a little trouble with the JB thing on occasion. I hope you'll forgive me."

"Of course, Wally. What's on your mind today?"

"Well, I think the question our television audience is most interest-ed in is what's on YOUR mind. We got a glimpse of your domestic and foreign policy objectives during the campaign, but everyone is curious to hear more details."

Jon interjected before Kriss could get rolling. "Wally, did I mention to you I was going to have a friend join us for our chat today? I think she just arrived."

Kriss could not formulate a response before Heather Carrington appeared on set, walking behind a stage hand, bringing a chair for her, which he placed to Jon's right. She seated herself, patted Jon's right arm, and stared piercingly at Kriss.

"OK, uh JB, you did not mention the Vice President would be joining us, but she is more than welcome. Madam Vice President. Congratulations on your victory and welcome back to Big News Sun-day."

"Why thank you, Wally." Kriss was slightly peeved Heather adopted Jon's nickname for him. "Yes, it's been eight years. Did you miss me?"

Kriss' mood shifted. The banter with Jon he could tolerate. The same coming from Heather Carrington, who Kriss had not favored for years, disturbed him. Kriss had thrown his support behind Barack Obama in the 2008 campaign after he and Heather had enjoyed a warm relationship during her tenure as First Lady from 1992 to 2000. Following the 2008 election and Heather's appointment as Secretary of State, Kriss asked her on the show a dozen times and was repeatedly snubbed. He decided the banter was over and it was time for some heat.

"JB, Madam Vice President, with you both being here, I'd like to cover a few specific foreign policy issues your administration is facing. One of the more pressing being the terrorism being conducted by Muslim extremists all over the world. It's clear the Obama administration's efforts to curb terrorism, with six of those years under the leadership of the Vice President as Secretary of State, have proven ineffective. What will you and the Vice President do differently? Is it your plan to reheat Mrs. Carrington's ineffective terror-containment policies?"

Jon and Heather looked at one another, each sporting a small grin. They anticipated Kriss' question, almost verbatim. "This is your baby. Do you want to take it?" Jon asked her.

"No Jon. Please. Have at it."

The President accepted her offer. "OK Wally, nice shot. You've been target-practicing, I see. To your question, as you know I do not have foreign policy experience, it's only prudent we depend heavily on the experience and expertise of the Vice President. But one structural intelligence change I've tasked her with is identifying and eliminating the collaboration barriers which currently exist between our various intelligence agencies. There is too much tribalism amongst these agencies, prohibiting the effective sharing of information. When we select our Director of National Intelligence, this person will have shown they understand these collaboration obstacles, and they will be accountable for identifying and implementing solutions to resolve them. We will do whatever we can to rectify our security agencies' tendencies to withhold, rather than share, important national security information.

"This will be a strict prerequisite for the position. The Vice President has narrowed her list to four individuals as potential choices for the DNI role, and we will begin final interviews for the position next week. This improvement-in-collaboration objective will be a critical one for the new DNI. If they make no discernable and demonstrable progress on this objective within ninety days, we will make a change. We will not wait for progress. The DNI will review each agency and will have full latitude to make the requisite changes within each agency to improve collaboration."

Jon continued. "Terrorism is a threat to Americans living all over the world. At the top of our foreign policy agenda is to take appropriate steps to eliminate terrorism to the degree possible. The American people have my word on this. The second thing we are doing is making a structural change to how we fight this war on terror. Currently, we are fighting it from an expensive and destructive offensive posture. We have American forces and tremendous amounts of military equipment on disparate battlefields. It's an enormous investment. If we measure the return on our investment by the reduction of terror attacks and by the capture of terrorist leadership, our ROI is poor, and innocent people are being killed in the process. We are going to make a change, whatever the political fallout. We will not use political calculations in this equation. In fact, eliminating political calculations from our policy formations will become foundational in our executive branch operating methodology.

"Our current methodology emphasizes capturing and or killing the fighters. We are going to shift our emphasis to capturing and or killing the leaders. We are going to do this by shifting funding of these battlefields from manpower, logistics, and military arsenal to bounties. Internally, we are referring to this program as 'talking money.' The 'talking money' program will utilize a systematic approach to motivate informants within terrorist groups with offers of money, safe and anonymous passage to another country in the region, housing, and education, in return for operable information to take out terrorist group commanders. According to the Vice President, we currently offer bounties, but not in a systematic and structured fashion where it's consistently effective.

"Our current unstructured bounty system is not providing informants with the things they need to give up their leaders. Namely, the safety and security of their families and the offer of a better life. Many of the fighters in these terrorist organizations, like ISIS and Al-Qaeda, are not idealogues. They serve out of fear, not out of belief. We feel these people can be convinced to provide valuable information if we provide the right kinds of incentives. Heather, given her experience, will lead this program. She is currently developing the 'talking money' framework. We're optimistic this initiative, along with creating better intelligence collaboration internally, will turn the tide for us. Any thoughts on this Wallis?"

"Mr. President, er JB, how will you convince other countries in the region to accept these terrorists turned informants? Doesn't this policy present a risk to those countries which take these people in?"

"Actually, Wally, there's a simple fix. It will be a condition to their receiving continued foreign aid from the U.S."

Kriss countered. "How does the State Department feel about it? The use of foreign aid is a valuable tool to advance our foreign policy agendas. They are going to object to your prioritizing aid for your agenda."

"Oh really? If giving aid is a useful tool, what about withholding? That should work too, right? If we have people at State who can't see that, then we need to find new people."

"Very well JB. Madam Vice President, anything you'd like to add?"

"Wally, you're right. There are entrenched silos in the State Department. I know this for a fact, as I constructed more than my share of them. Now it looks like I, with the help of Secretary Haley, get to tear them down. It's important nothing stands in the way of the President's agenda. He was elected with 63% of the vote. It's Braxton time.

"Now, allow me to go back to the change in strategy on fighting terror. First, let me say the two initiatives President Braxton just summarized are both his ideas. It is this kind of innovative thinking Jon has exhibited for the four years I have known him which attracted me to the ticket and to accept his offer to serve with him.

"The 'talking money' program will be effective in fighting terrorism. At its core, it serves to reduce the loss of life of innocent people. Instead of the brute force efforts we currently employ to fight terror, we will use instead more strategic and surgical maneuvers. And turn the tide of hate. We will reduce the loss of life and the destruction our forces are inflicting in fighting terrorism and instead replace it with a system where we reward people to help us take out the terrorist leaders. We feel this program will change the entire dynamic of fighting terrorism and in a way where we reduce cost, reduce loss of life, reduce destruction, and increase hope for the people living in fear of these extremists. From my experience in working with the nations in the Mideast, I believe this program will be well received."

Kriss nodded approvingly but skeptically responded. "It sounds promising. We'll look forward to having you back to the program to keep us updated on your progress. Now JB, on domestic matters, we heard from you on the campaign trail your continued interest in federal office election reform. But your efforts to advance your ELECT 2015 resolution proved unsuccessful and generated tremendous animosity towards you on Capitol Hill. With you now occupying the White House, what will be different?"

"Actually, Wally, nothing will be different other than the passage of time. Most promising ideas don't take root immediately. They need to marinate a bit and then they taste better. When you open an aged bottle of wine, what do you do before you drink it?"

Kriss thought it was a rhetorical question and remained silent, waiting for Jon to finish the thought.

"Wally! I know you like to drink good wine. What do you do when you open a fresh bottle? C'mon, don't be shy."

"You let it breathe?"

"Exactly, you let it breathe. It's what we are going to do with our ideas for election reform. Our ideas are in alignment with what is best for this country. We will continue to make our case and we believe the public will come to realize the value in what we are espousing and embrace it in time. And they will put pressure on their federal elected officials to adopt this mindset.

"These reforms will manifest themselves first in current lawmakers who will sense the public's sentiment and start rejecting the overtures of lobbyists. And then the manifestation will continue as people with different motivations choose to run for public office. People with the motivation to govern better and who understand that to govern better, they must reject the overture of those seeking to influence policy which is not in their constituent's best interests. Or, in the nation's best interests.

"We are going to brand our efforts '**Better People—Better Governance.**' For the most egregious offenders, those who are the biggest profiteers from dirty money, we will shine a light on their activities. But we're hopeful we will not have to do this for them to change their ways or retire.

"One initiative we will launch to aid in this effort will be to remind members of Congress who they work for. This effort will be spearheaded by a new website—*www.heresmytwocents.us.* An effort to be managed by the Executive Branch. We liken it to checks and balances on steroids. We'll use this website to poll the American people on their opinions of legislation before Congress. On this website, we will allow our citizens to read and express their opinion of each piece of legislation before Congress votes on it by giving it a ranking of one through ten. A rank of one for strongly opposed. A rank of ten for strongly in favor. Any vote in between will measure their level of satisfaction or dissatisfaction. We will outline all aspects of each piece of legislation, including all spending appropriations. We'll calculate the average score results for each piece of legislation sorted by state and by congressional district and deliver this information to our legislative branch colleagues. All members of Congress will have input from their constituents how they feel about the legislation they are voting on, including all the pork. Hopefully, this will lead to some pulled pork.

"To prevent fraud and abuse, each citizen will include their name, date of birth, county, and state of residence and last four digits of their social when they log in to read a summary and rank a piece of legislation. The database will be constructed to eliminate any unverified or duplicate entries. The outcome we're striving for is for each member of Congress will know how their constituents score the legislation they vote on. If a member of Congress votes out of alignment with their district, they do so under full transparency. We believe this effort will help remind members of Congress who they work for. Currently, we vote for our candidate choices on election day, and they go from there to propose and vote for legislation. We'd like to add citizen voting for legislation into the mix. Ideally, it provides a better method for the voters to hold their elected officials accountable to their will."

Jon sat back to let everything he had shared settle. Kriss was having difficulty forming a response or a question. Heather sensed his difficulty and saved him.

"Wally, I've spent more years in Washington than I care to recount, and the President's assessment is spot on. There is a swampiness in this city. Money and power become irresistible over time to those who serve in office at the federal level. Legislators are constantly presented with opportunities to leverage their position and profit by peddling influence. Even those who run for and win office for the right reasons, over time, lose perspective. Some maintain a desire to serve and do right by their constituents, but they realize they cannot stay in office to complete their mission unless they raise money to win re-election. They often justify their shady money-raising efforts as doing it for the right reason and in the process trade favors. These people may not be as brazen in their corruption but contribute to the swamp, nonetheless.

"Wally, you haven't yet asked me the question of what motivated me to quit the race, leave the party, and join Jon's ticket. I know you'll get to it but let me answer it for you now since we're on this topic. In 2015, I started to recognize I was an example of what Jon was referring to when he introduced his ELECT resolution. I entered public service in 1976 for the right reasons. In 2014, I started having doubts about running again for the Presidency. I realized I was not running for the right reasons. My campaign was already rolling out, and I was not enlightened enough to come to grips with my emotions. I kept campaigning, hoping the right decision would come to me. But I was also having conversations with someone to help me sort out my thinking, and I started watching Jon.

"In 2015, Jon's message with ELECT and striving to have better people run for public office, people who would run for the right reasons, started weighing on me. I realized I had lost the motivations I had earlier in my career. And had developed new motivations which I came to realize were in no one's interests but my own. This realization eventually led me out of the race. I realized people in government who thought and felt as I did were doing this country a tremendous disservice. With the right messaging and the public's active involvement in issues via the *heresmytwocents* website, I believe the more principled lawmakers will conclude as I did and make a move away from dirty money. Not all will, but if our efforts lead them to an early retirement, we will have accomplished our goal.

"We in the U.S. can make the world a better home for the human race. The U.S. already contributes a disproportionate share of resources to eliminate poverty and promote freedom throughout the world, but our influence is diminishing at a rapid rate. We see it here internally with the growth in political indifference and racial discord. And we see it world-wide in the rise of socialism, terrorism, racism, and a host of other isms. Jon is exactly right. The way to turn this tide starts with electing the right kind of people to public office. People committed to public service and serving the needs of their constituents. Not idealogues or people addicted to dirty money, but problem solvers. Four months ago, I came to see this clearly and decided to take my name out of nomination. I realized the potential election of Jon Braxton was an opportunity for the country to step onto the right path. When Jon asked for my help, I couldn't say yes fast enough."

Kriss did not anticipate Heather's transparency. He wanted to confront her, but at the moment had trouble crafting his next question. Jon did not give him the chance.

"Wally, may I take a moment and address your viewers directly?"

"Of course, Mr. President."

Jon turned his head to move his gaze away from Kriss and directly into a head on camera. "Good morning, everyone. As you can imagine, my administration will be faced with daunting challenges over the next four years. But there is one challenge which stands above all the rest for me. And I will make it a high priority for my administration. You know what it is. I told you consistently during the campaign my primary motivation for seeking this position is to do what I can to enable our medical research community to find the cure for Type 1 diabetes. And find it fast. To those of you in the T1D community watching this morning, you should know I have not forgotten my commitment to you.

"We talked about this constantly during the campaign. But the campaign is behind us and the time to stop the talking is now. It's time for the do. Tomorrow, the First Lady will be holding a news conference at the White House to announce the formation of the **'CURE IT NOW'** task force. It will be directed by Mrs. Braxton, and I will be by her side. Angie's job is to coordinate the medical research community's efforts to find the cure. My job is to come up with the money.

"Angie will announce a four-day meeting in the White House next month where any company with viable and realistic technologies, research, intellectual property, or concepts, which can be a component for a cure, will be invited to present. From those presentations, she will collaborate with a team of diabetes medical advisors, whom she is currently assembling, to evaluate the information presented and look for opportunities for these organizations with correlating or complimentary intellectual property to partner and share information.

"We have dozens of organizations in the country today doing solid research towards a cure. Unfortunately, most operate in silos, unwilling to share their work. They seek to protect their investments and their investors. They all want to be the ones to find the cure and apply for the patents. Secrecy is their collaboration model. And it is not the model to find the cure in the shortest amount of time. Angie will break down these barriers to enable and motivate the right combinations of companies to work together. Our goal is to identify the avenues of research which have the best chance to lead us to a cure. And to put together the relationships and partnerships to get us there the fastest.

"We know it's going to take money. I'm a business guy, remember? I know these organizations need to be compensated for the potential loss of revenue and opportunity from sharing their work and their intellectual property. It will be my job to figure out how to organize the funding. I've got a little leverage now and we will figure this out. There's too much suffering to alleviate around the world to let a few dollars get in the way. Do not lose hope. Please plan to watch the First Lady's news conference tomorrow when she will present her plan to drive the medical research community to the cure for Type 1 diabetes."

Kriss realized his hour-long show had run its course. "Mr. President, Madam Vice President, thank you for joining us today. Again, congratulations on your monumental victory and all the best to you in the coming four years. And to our viewers, please join us next week when we will have the former president and the current Second Gentleman, Wil Carrington, with us for the entire hour. It should be interesting to gain his perspectives on what the next four years will hold. Until then, from Washington, DC, good day."

The cameras switched off. Kriss looked at Heather smugly. She had no forewarning Kriss had been talking to her husband. She looked at him with contempt.

Chapter 6

KJ

The Rock Creek jogging trail in Washington, DC, was a favorite of the former Secretary of State and current Vice President of the United States. Since her inauguration eighteen days ago, Heather Carrington's jogging security detail had expanded to twelve secret service agents.

The early Sunday morning winter air had a chill which illustrated clouds of heavy breathing from the lungs of the sixty-five-years-old Vice President. And from the huffing and puffing of the six secret service agents jogging along in front, with, and behind, the Vice President. The other six members of her detail were surveilling the park from various vantage points away from the trail.

The Vice President was also accompanied by her government issue Blackberry mobile phone. It was resting comfortably in the front left pocket of her dark blue tracksuit jacket when a call came in. She felt the vibration and pulled the phone out without missing a step. She viewed the display and halted. Her detail stopped in unison. The clouds of heavy breathing wisping from their lungs did not.

"What is it, Marcie?" the winded Vice President asked. The call was from Marcie James, her former executive administrator at State. Now serving in the same capacity in the Vice President's office.

"Sorry to bother you on a Sunday, Mrs. Carrington. But thought you'd want to know immediately. We just took a call from the North Korea Foreign Minister expressing urgency. He's asking to speak with you now if possible and is standing by. What would you like me to do?"

"Patch him on. I'll hold."

Heather heard the familiar voice of the North Korea Foreign Minster, Ri Yu-Song, speaking English with a heavy Korean accent. He had placed the call while at a conference table in their presidential palace with the North Korea dictator and supreme leader, Kim Jong-Un, sitting silently at his side. "Madam Vice President, congratulations on your return to the White House."

"Hello Ri. And thank you, though technically I do not live in nor work from the White House. Wil and I enjoy our residence at the U.S. Naval Observatory and my official office is in the Eisenhower Executive Office Building next to the West Wing. I do, however, appreciate the sentiment. Now Marcie mentioned you had an urgent matter. What is it this time Ri?" Heather asked, annoyed with his urgency posturing to which she had become all too familiar while at State.

"After speaking with our Supreme Leader yesterday, as a matter of preserving our peace, I felt it important I discreetly speak with you. Please understand I could be imprisoned for treason if this call were to become known by him. Your utmost secrecy is requested."

"Well Ri, seems like old times. Urgent calls on Sunday. Wish I could say what a surprise. But we've been down this road too many times, you and me. You should be speaking with Secretary Haley these days.

She is now your touch point for communications. But for old times' sake, what are we concerning ourselves with today?"

"Madam Vice President. Our Supreme Leader has doubts about your new President Braxton. I called you since it is you who knows him well. He has been in office for many weeks now and we have yet to hear anything about his perception of the relationship between our two nations. This is our concern."

"You have no reason for concern, Ri. You will be hearing from Secretary Haley's office shortly."

"Nonetheless Madam Vice President, our Supreme Leader believes your President Braxton does not understand the strained and complex relationship between the USA and the PRNK. Your President has only a brief history of public statements and actions in government and seems only to be interested in a domestic agenda. Our Supreme Leader is concerned your State and Defense Departments may seek to advance their own agendas, which could be detrimental to the security of the People's Republic of North Korea. As such, the PRNK feels it necessary to put your President under duress to gauge his reactions. I felt you should know it is the plan of our government to start a new round of weapons testing. Next week, we will test our latest intercontinental ballistic missile system and test your new President. The reason for my urgent call and the request for discretion is to provide you with a notice of our intentions to dissuade your government from doing anything irrational."

"Minister Ri, you should know this is not the best way to start the PRNK's relationship with President Braxton. These actions will not be viewed favorably by the new administration. In fact, I will frame these actions to the President as an act of aggression. I suggest you advise Kim as such if he is not listening in on this call."

Kim and Ri looked at one another, astonished Heather would know.

The following day was Monday, February 19. At 8:30 a.m. a Lincoln Towncar pulled up to the security gateway entry point leading into the west wing of the White House. Abby Martin, now an assistant Secretary of State, exited the back seat with her shoulder bag and purse. She walked up the few stairs to a magnetometer situated just inside the doorway which preceded the security entry point to the west wing. She placed her bag and purse on the belt.

Abby walked through the x-ray scanner and then retrieved her shoulder bag and purse and began her walk to the Oval Office. As she turned a corner, first lady Angela Braxton, sans bag or purse, appeared in the hallway and walked in stride and purposefully towards the Oval with Abby. They acknowledged each other with a brief glance and a silent nod.

The two ladies then turned another corner and came upon the Vice President. She joined the two ladies, without speaking, in lockstep on their march to the Oval. White House staffers in their path, upon noticing the three determined ladies marching side by side, steered clear. They reached the Oval Office receptionist seated outside the President's door.

"Good morning, ladies. Go on in. The President is expecting you."

Without missing a step, Abby opened the door to the Oval. Heather and Angela walked in, followed by Abby closing the door behind her. Jon was seated on a sofa facing another where Jim Mattis, the nominated Secretary of Defense and Nikki Haley, the nominated Secretary of State, were seated. On the coffee table between the two sofas were satellite images of North Korea intercontinental ballistic missile movements. Angela and Abby took seats next to Jon. Heather sat with Mattis and Haley.

Jon looked at Heather. "Looks like the North Koreans are moving assets around. What's Kim up to?"

"It's why I asked for this meeting, Jon. I took an urgent call from their Foreign Minister yesterday. He warned me they would be test firing missiles next week."

Mattis was concerned and turned to look at Heather. He then looked directly across the table at the President. "From these images, these missiles don't look similar in nature to any of their weapon systems we're familiar with. We can't be sure of their capability. We'll need to go on full alert."

Mattis turned his head back to the left to look at Heather. "Did Ri give you an indication why they're doing this and why he would contact you with this information? It's not like the North Koreans to be this forthcoming."

Heather looked at Mattis and nodded. She then looked across the table. "This is all about them not knowing anything about you, Jon. They're using this maneuver as a means of building a profile on our new President."

Mattis was undeterred. "Not a smart move on their part. We're going on full alert and will assemble our threat response forces in the region."

Jon responded. "Hold off Jim. Not so fast. Heather, what is it they want to know?"

Heather again flashed a concerned look at Mattis and then returned her focus to Jon. "It's standard in the intel community to build psychological profiles on adversaries. They play a key role in policy decisions. They want to gain insight into how you would react in a time of crisis."

"I see. I imagine we have a thorough profile on Kim, Madam Vice President?"

"We do."

"How long before it's on my desk?"

Jon had scheduled standing dinners in the President's residence with Heather every Wednesday and Friday evenings when both were in Washington and their schedules permitted. Angela was also on the list when she was available, though her presence was not required for the President and Vice President to conduct their dinner meetings.

"Why isn't Angela joining us tonight?" Heather asked as they were served their dinner salads on a Wednesday evening in the presidential residence dining area.

"You've heard of taco Tuesdays? At the White House, we now have karate Wednesdays. My lovely wife and daughter are giving martial arts lessons to any White House staffers who care to partake. She has twenty students in class tonight. And she let me know she has twenty more signed up for next week. Her big picture is to have everyone in the Administration armed with the mental skills, physical moves, and discipline of a ninja warrior. Good luck to anyone in three months who wants to enter this place without a hall pass."

"Maybe I should sign up. I'm getting bored with jogging."

"Of course, why not? Everyone else will be slinging samurai swords around this place in no time. Why not the Vice President?"

Heather smiled and proceeded to change the subject. "I'm sure you've reviewed the Kim Jong-Un profile by now. Any thoughts?"

"Many thoughts. The most important being you and I are going to solve this country's North Korea problem starting tomorrow."

"Oh, really Mr. President? Just like that? No administration has made any progress with Kim or his father since the Korean War and we change this tomorrow?"

"You're a good listener."

"Right. And just exactly how are we making this happen?"

"I assume as Secretary of State you spent some time with Kim's profile?"

"I did and know it well."

"Then tell me under what circumstance will Kim launch a pre-emptive missile strike."

"Only one circumstance. If he feels in jeopardy of losing his rule."

"Right. And is any nation, including ours, currently threatening his rule?"

"No, but he doesn't know that."

"Has anyone tried to tell him?"

"We have, but he has a serious mistrust of us and our allies. He doesn't believe anything we say."

"Now let me get this straight. It's been sixty years and we've yet to end the Korean War. We have tens of thousands of troops stationed in South Korea, and we've made no progress in deterring the North's nuclear ambitions. In the meantime, they are a pariah nation, and their people are dying a slow death from starvation. How would you classify the effectiveness of our policy?"

"It's a policy of containment, Jon."

"Oh, how rich. We're containing Kim from doing something our profile says he won't do. And, in the process, contributing to the devastation of twenty-five million innocent lives. And were doing this because we believe he does not understand the attitude of his adversaries?"

"Unfortunately, all correct. And we can't improve the lives of the people of North Korea. Only Kim can do it. And he doesn't want to. He's more comfortable murdering them than feeding them."

"So, we sit back and wait for Kim to die or be killed and hope the next guy to take over isn't as delusional? Do we have a profile on the next Supreme Leader, which tells us he or she won't launch?"

"I see your point, Jon, but we've evaluated all our options, and the one we're pursuing is best."

"I'm sorry Heather. I know you and Wil have had your hand in our North Korea policy for a long while, but I don't agree with the rationale behind it."

"All right, then starting tomorrow, what will we be doing differently, Mr. President?" an annoyed Heather questioned.

"Pack your bags. You're going to pay Kim a visit. And you're taking Nikki, Angela, Abby, and Luke with you. We'll be telling Kim we're changing our tune and inviting him to dance. We'll give him time to get on the dance floor with us and if he instead chooses to sit it out, we'll put the old music back on and go to Plan B."

"You're not serious. We're taking Luke to North Korea? Jon. OK. Look. I know you're number one and I'm only number two, but I've got to call you on this one. With the backdrop of a nuclear holocaust, we can't be playing patty-cake with Kim Jong-Un. It's too dangerous."

"I see it the other way. It's too dangerous not to."

Secretary of State Nikki Haley called the North Korea Foreign Minister the following day. At the instruction of the President, she informed Ri Yu-Song of the satellite imagery the U.S. had illustrating the movement of unfamiliar nuclear missiles near North Korea missile launch sites. She asked the PRNK to delay any missile testing for two weeks. In return, she offered to send a delegation from the

United States the following week to Pyongyang to discuss the current U.S.-North Korea relationship.

Kim was reluctant to take the meeting but agreed on the condition Air Force One deliver the delegation to Seoul, South Korea. From there, the U.S. delegation would be flown into North Korea on a PRNK airliner. Kim did not trust Air Force One in North Korea airspace. After assurance from Heather and Nikki their safety was not in jeopardy, Jon approved Kim's request.

Air Force One was two hours out of Seoul and a serious card game of Hearts was underway in the cabin. The game was being contested by the five Americans sent by the President to achieve a diplomatic feat which had escaped U.S. executive branch administrative efforts for over sixty years. While the members of the delegation were being delivered their third hand of cards, courtesy of Luke's shuffle and deal, Heather took the opportunity to do a little coaching for their meeting with the North Korea Supreme Leader scheduled for the following day.

"When we meet with Kim, we'll be in the same conference room I was in for a meeting in 2014. My experience tells me there will be only three North Koreans—Kim, Ri, and a translator. We'll all have earpieces to hear Kim's translation. Ri will speak English, and...."

Suddenly, without warning, Air Force One's video conference system came alive, answering a call from Jon in the Oval. His face appeared on the large monitor situated six feet from the table where the hearts game was taking place. He laughed at the sight of the five of them with playing cards in their hands.

"Luke, I expect you to come home with all the money. Don't let those crafty ladies' team up on you."

"Not a chance, dad. And FYI, we're playing Hearts, not Poker."

"You're not practicing your poker faces?"

"No need, dad, we're good. And we're ready," responded Luke confidently.

Jon nodded his approval. "So, everyone's clear on what we're doing tomorrow?"

Angela assured her husband. "Don't worry, Jon, we've got this."

The Presidential complex in Pyongyang, also known as the Central Luxury Mansion to differentiate it from Kim's multiple properties, is located in the Ryongsong District. It is a sprawling, luxurious property replete with exquisite amenities, including poshly accoutered horse stables and riding areas, spa, sauna, shooting range, running track and athletic field, and luxurious lushly landscaped grounds. The twelve-building complex features an elaborate security infrastructure, including an underground nuclear radiation-proof wartime headquarters, electric fencing, and minefields.

The five Americans arrived at the complex at two p.m. Pyongyang time and were immediately escorted into the large conference room Heather had detailed. There was no one in the room as they were directed to their five seats at one end of a thirty-foot-long ornate cherry wood conference table. In front of each seat on the table was a wired earpiece on a small plate, an antiquated table-mounted wired microphone, a pitcher of ice water and an eight-inch-high drinking glass. To the left of the table, mounted on the wall, was a darkened seventy-two-inch video conference system monitor. The Americans took their seats.

Heather had instructed her team to not say anything until they were in the presence of their hosts, as they would be monitored while they were alone. The North Koreans hoped to pick up any inside information while the U.S. team was left amongst themselves. They were disappointed, though not surprised given Heather's experience, none was forthcoming.

The only thing to transpire in the conference room of interest to the North Koreans, as they secretly surveilled the American delegation was Luke pulling out his test kit, pricking his finger, and testing a drop of blood. Then proceeding to give himself a shot of insulin. Kim Jong-Un was unaware of Luke's condition and had limited knowledge and understanding of Type 1 diabetes. He was curious and fascinated by Luke's actions. He asked Minister Ri about the President's son's condition. Ri had experience with T1d and provided his Supreme Leader an overview.

After giving the Americans forty-five minutes alone to spill intelligence about the purpose of this visit, Kim, Ri, and a young North Korean female translator silently entered the room. The five Americans stood, as coached by Heather, as a sign of respect. The three North Koreans moved to their seats at the far end of the table, leaving twenty feet of distance between them and the Americans. Ri and the translator waited for Kim to take his seat and they, as did the Americans, followed his lead. The three North Koreans put their earpieces in. The Americans followed suit. The translator was first to speak, in English.

"Welcome to the People's Republic of North Korea. We are grateful for your visit. Madam Vice President, please introduce us to your comrades."

Heather leaned forward and turned on her microphone. "Mr. Chairman, Minister Ri, thank you for receiving us today. We are here to introduce you to our new United States executive branch administration. Of course, you know me from previous visits. I'd like my colleagues to take a moment to introduce themselves with your permission." She then leaned forward to turn off her mic.

The translator spoke Heather's words in Korean for Kim, but the translation was not audible to the Americans. Only to Kim and Ri. Kim said nothing, and without a facial expression extended his hand out in a 'proceed' gesture.

Heather looked to Nikki Haley and nodded. Nikki turned on her mic and proceeded. "Mr. Chairman, Minister Ri, I am Nikki Haley, and have been nominated by President Braxton to be the United States Secretary of State. I recently served for six years as the Governor for one of our fifty states, South Carolina. I was born in the United States in 1972. My parents were born in India and migrated to Canada in 1966. They then migrated to the United States in 1969. Upon my nomination's confirmation, I look forward to working with you. I have been studying our joint history and understand the complexity of our relationship. My goal is to improve the relations between our two nations to where we no longer consider ourselves adversaries." She turned off her mic.

The translator was fast and kept pace. She finished her translation of Haley's words within five seconds of the Secretary concluding. Kim nodded, again without any words or facial expression. Heather looked at Abby and nodded.

Abby turned on her mic. "Mr. Chairman, Minister Ri, my name is Abby Martin. Upon Mrs. Haley's confirmation, I will work for her as an assistant Secretary of State. Should we be successful today in beginning the improvement of relations between our two nations, our primary purpose for requesting this meeting, I will be the point person for implementing the initiatives we will be proposing. I've known President Braxton for fifteen years, serving as his executive assistant for eleven years prior to his entering politics." She turned off her mic.

The translator swiftly translated Abby's words for Kim and Ri. Again, the translation was inaudible to the Americans. Kim said nothing while nodding. Heather and Luke made eye contact. She nodded to him. He began to speak forgetting to turn on his mic.

"Mr. Chairman, Minister...."

Kim interrupted him loudly in English, his harsh voice booming throughout the room. "Turn on your microphone, please."

Luke was shaken by the North Korea dictator admonishing him sternly. Heather and Nikki were surprised to hear Kim speak English.

Luke turned fearfully to look at his mother. She returned his look and smiled slightly. She then slowly took her right hand and held it perpendicular to her forehead and lowered it to the bottom of her face. Luke understood his mother's instruction to calm and center himself. He regrouped instantly, turned his microphone on and looked directly at Kim.

While still a bit unsure Luke started over. "Mr. Chairman. Minister Ri. I'm Lucas Braxton. President Braxton is my father. I'm sixteen years old and I'm sure you're wondering why I'm here. We know you have a diabetes problem in your country. And we have a similar problem in ours. I know this first-hand as I am a Type 1 diabetic. Among the many things my father would like to collaborate with you on is finding a cure. If you followed his campaign for the presidency..."

Luke paused. He was distracted by Kim, who had shut off his mic, put his hand over it and leaned over to whisper into Ri's ear. Ri nodded and looked assuredly at the U.S. side of the table. Kim straightened back up and turned back to the U.S. delegation. His English had a heavy Korean accent. His tone was muted from his last words to Luke.

"Continue Lucas."

Luke, again unnerved by Kim interrupting and addressing him, quickly regained his composure and felt confidence beginning to build.

"If you followed my father's campaign for the presidency, finding a cure for Type 1 diabetes is one of his primary agenda items. Currently, he is working closely with Congress to allocate significant sums of money to research and clinically analyze a promising pathway to the cure. When my father speaks with you, Mr. Chairman, he will detail how he would like our two nations to work together to find the cure for Type 1 diabetes."

Luke shut off his mic and looked at his mother. She turned her mic on and looked at Kim.

"Mr. Chairman. Minister Ri. I am Angela Braxton and have been married to Jon for twenty-five years. My husband is aware you are unfamiliar with him, as he has only been in the public eye since 2013. He asked me to join this delegation to allow you to get to know him through my eyes if you choose. You can ask me any question about him you like."

Angela looked at her watch. "But it's now time for our scheduled......"

The video conference system in the room rang and a second later, Jon appeared on the monitor seated at his desk in the Oval Office. He was alone and sitting upright with his hands clasped. He was relaxed and smiling. His demeanor was calm.

"Mr. Chairman, Minister Ri. It's an honor to meet you. I trust you have met our delegation." Jon paused for a response. There was none as Kim stared at him with distrust.

Jon continued. "If I may, I'd like to provide my thoughts and vision for the relationship between our two nations going forward. May I?"

Kim answered in Korean, and the U.S. delegation heard only the translator through their earpieces. She spoke in expert English but with a moderate Korean accent.

"Please proceed President Braxton."

"Mr. Chairman, allow me to say first, I know you have no reason to trust the sincerity of my words. Our nations have been at odds for far too long. In light of our history, I will not ask you for anything today except consideration. Our conversation will only be about what the United States is prepared to offer you and the People's Republic of North Korea over the next twelve months. I will let time be your guide as to whether you wish to work with me. And as to whether you can trust me.

"Understand, while I do not have any requests of you today, I do have expectations over time. My reason for embarking on this path to improve the relationship between our two countries is to improve world security. Nuclear proliferation makes the world a less safe place. My hope is that as you and I work together, over time you will come to believe drawing down your nuclear arsenal is in your best interests. We will demonstrate our good faith intentions by inviting the PRNK back into the world community of nations for a period of time. We will work to make the positives of a nuclear drawdown more favorable to you than your continued development of nuclear weapons. I know our chances for success are small, but considering the potential consequences of continued nuclear proliferation, this path is worthy of our time and effort."

Jon unclasped his hands and leaned back in his chair, waiting for Kim's response.

Kim responded in Korean, which the translator delivered to the Americans in English. "Mr. President, you say period of time. What do you mean and what are the consequences of time passing without your objectives being met?"

"Mr. Chairman, we are prepared to work with you to do important things to advance the lives of the people of North Korea. We'd like to work on these objectives in a manner which helps you build better lives for your people. To this end we will be, tomorrow, lifting many of the economic sanctions which have been imposed on your country. We will reopen banking channels to enable the PRNK to take advantage of trading with the U.S. And we will discuss with other countries following our lead. We will do this without requesting any reciprocal actions on the part of the PRNK."

Jon continued. "As for time, we consider this defrosting to be temporary, with hope it becomes permanent. Whether it does will be up to you. It is our hope you will favor this new reality more than the current one and will decide to move in the direction of our expectations. After twelve months, should we see no interest on your part in collaborating with us towards our expectations, we would return to the status quo."

Kim turned off his microphone, put his hand over it, and leaned over to speak softly in Ri's ear. Ri nodded as he looked at Luke. Kim finished his comment to Ri, straightened up, and turned his microphone back on. He again spoke in Korean, audible to only Ri and the translator. She then relayed his words to the Americans.

"Your son mentioned our countries working together to help our people who suffer with diabetes. What do you propose on this matter?"

Jon responded. "I'll let my son elaborate. Luke?"

Luke leaned forward and turned his mic on. With his father now in the room and taking control, he had shaken off his intimidation and spoke confidently.

"Mr. Chairman, we know your country currently imports a tremendous amount of insulin from China, and we know what you pay for it. We also know the quality of Chinese insulin is poor and is not highly effective in addressing the suffering of North Koreans afflicted with Type 1. Starting tomorrow, we will begin efforts to make the highest-grade U.S. insulin available for export to the PRNK. And we will sell our insulin to you for one half the price the Chinese currently charge you."

"Second, we wish to invite a team from your medical research community to the United States to collaborate with our researchers and clinicians to educate them on effectively treating the disease. And to share our work with them on what we are doing in the development of a cure. We would like to work with North Korea on conducting clinical trials, allowing your team to be at the world's forefront of medical research into the cure."

Luke switched his mic off. As did Kim, who again put his hand over it. He again leaned over to Ri, whispering in his ear. As Kim whispered to him, Ri starts to laugh and nod his head while looking down at the table. Kim straightens up and looks at the monitor. The translator turns her mic off. Kim speaks in English with a heavy Korean accent.

"Mr. President, thank you for your generous offers. We will consider them and get back to you if we decide to accept. Also, I wish to commend you on your son. He is a most impressive young man. Your relationship with him reminds me of the relationship I enjoyed with my late father. But I do have one question. What, Mr. President, is a luke? Or did you mean to say nuke?"

Jon laughed. Heather frowned with concern.

"Mr. Chairman, Luke is my son's nickname. It's short for Lucas."

"I see. Are these nick...these nicknames common in your country? Does everybody have one?"

"They are somewhat common. But no, not everybody has one."

"I see. Do you have one President Braxton?"

"As a matter of fact, I do. I acquired one on my first job in the tech industry. My boss started calling me JB, and it stuck."

Sidney Rosenberg was lounging comfortably in his Manhattan apartment on a Monday afternoon. In between his daily routines of walking in Central Park, hanging out in his favorite coffee shops to read current political news stories and op-eds, and meeting with friends for games of chess and backgammon, he was doing the bidding of the former president, Wilton Carrington. His mission—find information or an angle to take down and take out Jon Braxton.

He stood to move to his wet bar to pour a glass of Cabernet when his cell phone rang with *'CallerId unknown'* on the display. Sidney answered cautiously.

"Hello?"

"Boom chakalaka," the former president offered.

"Chakalaka boom boom," Rosenberg responded.

"Hello Sidney."

"Hello Wil. Heather back from North Korea yet?"

"Got home yesterday morning."

"And?"

"Appears were now playing cake-patty with the North Koreans. While she was groggy and half asleep, she told me we're unilaterally taking off sanctions, opening bank channels and inviting Kim back into the world community."

Sidney laughed at the former president's dyslexic transposition. "What are we asking for in return?"

"Apparently not a damn thing for now. Oh, and one other thing to know. Kim wants Braxton to call him KJ."

Chapter 7

Blackberry

On the grounds of the U.S. Naval Observatory in Northwest Washington DC, at Number One Observatory Circle, two and a half miles from the White House, sits a nineteenth century two-story house which serves as the official residence of the Vice President of the United States.

The house was constructed in 1893 for the observatory superintendent. The idea of a national observatory was proposed in 1825 by President John Quincy Adams when, during his first 'annual message' to Congress, he proposed his vision for the United States. One element of his vision included a national university and naval academy and *'connected with the establishment of a university, or separate from it, might be undertaken the erection of an astronomical observatory, with provision for the support of an astronomer.'*

This decree was not surprising given Adams' fascination with the stars, though Congress never approved this piece of Adams' vision while he was president. But he continued to advocate for its establishment while serving in Congress following his presidency.

In line with Adams' vision, the then U.S. Secretary of the Navy, John Branch, in 1830, established the U.S. Depot for collection and housing of the Navy's navigational equipment and charts. Its initial purpose was to restore, repair, calibrate, and rate navigational instruments. In 1842, Congress officially established the depot as a national observatory. In 1844, its mission evolved and the observatory was funded for construction in Washington's Foggy Bottom district overlooking the banks of the Potomac River near the White House. Its new mission was to conduct scientific experiments related to astronomy. In 1844, it was designated the U.S. Naval Observatory.

In 1870, Congress decided the observatory should be moved because of the unhealthy living conditions in its vicinity—numerous cases of malaria were contracted by its staff from the banks of the Potomac. And gas lantern light pollution from the city hampered their telescopes. The facility was moved to higher ground on hilly terrain northwest of Georgetown, which, at the time, was outside the city limits. In 1893, the observatory was moved again to its current location on Massachusetts Avenue in Northwest Washington, DC. At the time, also outside the city limits. The new construction approved included a superintendent's residence at Number One Observatory Circle.

In 1928, deciding the house built for the observatory superintendent was too beautiful to be occupied by one occupying such a 'lowly' position, the then Chief of Naval Operations (CNO) kicked him out and moved himself in. From this point until 1974, the home served as the primary residence for the person serving as CNO, the most senior naval officer assigned to serve in the Department of the Navy.

Historically, Vice Presidents had maintained their own private residences. With the cost of securing these rotating private residences growing, Congress, in 1974, decided it was prudent establish an official Vice President residence. The house at Number One Observatory Circle on the grounds of the U.S. Naval Observatory was selected.

In 1977, then Vice President Walter Mondale became the first VP to occupy it.

The current Vice President and her husband, the Second Gentleman, were ready to be served their dinners. Heather had been sleeping a good part of the twenty-four hours since her return from Pyongyang. They had a brief casual conversation when she returned, and Wil was waiting patiently to speak with her in more detail about her visit with Kim Jong-Un. And to dig around to find out how Jonathon Braxton was performing behind the curtain. He felt the two of them alone at their dinner table would give him the opportunity. In planning for this dinner, he decided there would be a slight change for the dinner table. The usual pitcher of iced tea would be left in the kitchen.

The two were seated at the dining room table when their housekeeper delivered their mushroom barley soup. "Well honey, welcome back to the living. How did you sleep?"

"I slept great. How have you been, my darling husband? What kept you busy while I was away?"

Wil started to fish. "You know, the usual. Keeping active. Still waiting to hear from Barbara what my official duties and travel will be. I forgot to mention to you before you left, I ran into Mark Parker. He told me to say hello and wish you well in your new position."

Hearing Mark's name jolted Heather. She had successfully buried the sense of remorse for the way she treated him on her departure from State. Wil's words brought her uneasiness back to the surface. She didn't even think to ask her husband how or when he crossed paths with Parker. "Was he pissed? He has reason to be. I wasn't very gracious towards him when I left State."

Wil wanted to know more about Heather's and Mark's relationship and the fallout. He felt the more he knew, the better he could manage Parker for what was to come. "I think he'd like to hear from you. Maybe give him a call? He said he hasn't heard from you since your retirement party. Which was when, two years ago? Given how closely you two worked together, I was surprised to hear you two don't speak."

Heather was regretful. "When I decided to leave, I was confused as to what I was going to do with the campaign. I couldn't talk to Mark about it knowing how loyal he was to the party and how disappointed he would be to hear of my insecurity. I knew how much he was looking forward to the opportunities my being president would present to him. At the time, considering everything, I felt it best to just cut the cord. For his sake and for mine."

Wil dismissed her excuse. "Call him and talk to him. You owe him an explanation. He may not agree with your decision, but it's done and there's nothing he can do or say to change it. At least it will give you a chance to clear your conscience. At best, you might rebuild the relationship and have a new ally and resource to work with. Invite him over to have dinner with us next week." Wil hoped Heather's rekindling her relationship with Mark would provide useful intel and made their reconciliation a priority.

Heather considered her husband's words. "You're right. I will."

"Good. Now tell me, how's the little bastard, Kim?"

Heather was annoyed with Wil's tone, feeling he was minimizing the importance of her visit to North Korea. He's doing just fine."

Wil was uncomfortable being in the dark on the visit. He was unaware of the call Heather took from the foreign minister and unaware of Kim's threat of more missile testing. He realized something consequential must have happened for Braxton to send a delegation, which included his wife and son, to visit a nuclear adversary. The fact

Heather had only shared a few sanctions were coming off, and that Kim wanted Jon to call him KJ, frustrated him.

"Seriously, honey, what happened? Did you go because Kim is doing some saber rattling?"

"It's all fine, Wil. We accomplished what we set out to do."

"Which was?"

"My darling husband, this is classified for now."

"Come on, honey. Why won't you talk to me?" Sarcastically. "You know I have a little experience with North Korea and on these matters."

"Not tonight, Wil. I'm still a little jetlagged. Can we just enjoy a nice, quiet dinner?"

Wil capitulated for the time being. "Of course, honey. More iced tea?"

Heather had emptied her glass. "Yes, thank you."

He collected both their glasses and walked into the empty kitchen. He refilled both with iced tea, and to hers added a small vial of light blue powder.

Wil waited until the sleep-aid he had slipped into Heather's tea had time to put her down. She was fast asleep when he entered their bedroom. He tiptoed to the dresser to the right of their bed and unplugged her Blackberry cell phone from its power charger cable. He put her phone in his leather coat pocket. It was just past eleven p.m.

The former President, and now Second Gentleman, was dressed in all black, including a black knit skull cap, as he nimbly walked down the stairs to the back door entrance. He maneuvered himself outside the residence without being noticed by the three secret service agents on duty. Wil made his way from the house covertly through the property's landscaping to nearby Massachusetts Avenue. He then proceeded, walking at a brisk pace, north the two miles to the parking lot of the Saint Nicholas Orthodox Cathedral.

He covered the two miles in thirty-five minutes and found Mark Parker waiting for him in a blue Ford sedan parked in the far southern area of the Cathedral's parking lot away from any overhead lighting. As the former president approached the car, he nodded at Mark and got in. Mark proceeded slowly out of the parking lot with lights off and turned right onto a mostly deserted Massachusetts Avenue. Mark switched the car lights on, and they began their twenty-minute drive to the Martin Industrial Park in Edmonston, Maryland.

They arrived at the sprawling industrial park at midnight. Mark pulled the car to the side of an alley which crossed the front of Unit 3B, a small space with a steel entry door and a rollup loading door. He switched the lights and motor off. Wil handed Heather's cell phone to Mark, who then exited the car. "I'll be back in sixty minutes."

"Sooner, if possible," Wil answered nervously.

He watched Mark cross the alley and approach 3B's entry door, to which Wil had a clear view. Mark knocked. Seconds later, the door opened and a tall and muscular Asian man wearing a black sweatshirt, black sweatpants, and dark wrap-around sunglasses answered. The two men shook hands and Mark entered. The Asian man closed the door behind him.

As Wil waited for Mark's return, his mind resumed focus on his master plan. A plan with a defined objective but not yet the roadmap. Wil was having difficulty outlining what needed to be done to force Jonathon Braxton from office and have his wife installed as the forty-sixth President of the United States. He did not have the patience to wait until 2020. He was not confident Braxton would not run for reelection, nor confident his wife would choose to run if he didn't. Wil's anxiety and impatience to return to the White House were growing.

He tried to sit still and focus on his thoughts. He liked Sidney's idea of using Heather's cell phone as a covert listening asset. And he welcomed Mark's idea and resources to make it happen. But the anxiety remained. He was confident if Mark's plan worked, they'd soon have a wealth of inside information. He was not as confident he could use the information in a way which would not tarnish the reputation of his wife.

After forty-five minutes, he could not continue containing his apprehension. He pulled out his cell phone and dialed his co-conspirator. The display on Sidney Rosenberg's phone, perched on the nightstand next to his bed, lit up with *'Caller ID unknown'* as the phone vibrated.

Sidney slowly opened his eyes and shook the sleep. He reached for his glasses and the phone. He answered cautiously.

"Hello?"

"Twinkle, twinkle little star."

"Jesus fucking Christ Wil. It's almost one a.m. What is it?"

"Aren't we supposed to be following security protocols?"

Sidney wanted to tell his former boss to stick his security protocols where the sun doesn't shine but decided against it.

"Twinkle, twinkle little star? Help me find the nearest bar. OK, now what the fuck is it?"

"Just wanted you to know we're going through with your idea and rigging Heather's phone. Should be done here shortly."

"Great Wil. Couldn't you have waited until tomorrow to tell me?"

"Yeah, you're right. Sorry. Go back to sleep."

It was almost two a.m. when Mark Parker walked out of Unit 3B. The winter night temperature had dropped below freezing. Parker's hands were buried in his coat pockets and his shoulders squeezed to buttress himself from the icy wind. He reached the car and got in on the driver's side, then pulled the phone from his pocket and handed it to Wil along with a piece of paper with handwritten instructions.

"When you get inside the residence, turn the phone on but don't dial any numbers," Mark instructed. "Then from your computer log onto a website listed on the paper. The site is set up to build a secure tunnel when anyone connects with one of the two passwords on the sheet. The top one is yours. The bottom one is Sidney's. After you login, launch the audio player. Then just start talking. The Blackberry will pick up your words and you should be able to hear yourself talking from the audio player on the website with a three second delay. If you do, then we know it's working from the residence. Make sure you test this somewhere in the house where no Secret Service agents can overhear you. Always wear headphones when logging into the site as another precaution. This way the conversations won't be inadvertently heard through the computer speakers. Also, always clear your browser history when you log off. It's all on the paper. We've set up you and Sidney as the only ones with monitoring access. Your logins are on the sheet. If everything's working properly, then you should be able to hear any conversations taking place in the same room as the phone. And when she's on a call, you'll be able to hear both ends of the conversation. All audio the receiver in the phone picks up and transmits to the server will be recorded and time stamped, enabling you to go back in time to listen. Let's test and see if it works from the residence tonight. If it does, we'll let Heather take it into the White House tomorrow and see how we do."

"Your friend, the Asian guy who did this, you're sure we can trust him?"

"Rayban? Yeah, he doesn't know whose phone it is. He's discreet. He doesn't ask, and I don't tell. It's how we operate. The less he knows, the better it is for him. And he's not operating the monitoring website. I have another asset taking care that. Everything is encrypted and my agreement with Jokester is he blocks himself from access."

"Rayban?"

"He lost an eye in Iraq. Prefers the shades over an eyepatch."

"How does the audio get to the server?"

Parker was impressed the former president would think to ask. "It's our only weak point. The phone's transmitter will open a secure VPN tunnel to a satellite network using an unlicensed frequency. Unless White House airspace monitoring security has been updated since Braxton moved in, we'll be OK. With the right equipment, it would be possible to jam transmission, but the White House has never been outfitted with gear to do so. If somehow our signal was intercepted, with the encryption were using, it would take fifty years to decipher what's being said."

"And Jokester? Who the fuck is he? And how can we trust him not to listen in or have any knowledge of what we're doing?"

"The server we're using is buried at State. So is Jokester. He's got maximum security clearance. He wrote the code and created the security where the only access to the recordings is with the two passwords on the sheet. And I'll change the passwords tomorrow and let you know the new ones. My people on the inside installed the code behind heavy access security. There's no way Jokester can get to the server and listen in. The front door is heavily fortified, and there is no back door. Rayban and Jokester have bullet proof plausible deniability. They have no knowledge of you or Sidney. They only know me, and I trust those two dudes with my life. Memorize everything on the instruction sheet and then light a match to it."

It was two-thirty a.m. when Mark dropped Wil off on Massachusetts Avenue, a half mile from the residence. Wil made his way back to the property and into the residence undetected. He was anxious to see if their plan was going to work and went directly into his study. He switched the phone on and then opened his laptop and attempted to sign on. It took him four tries between forgetting his password and 'fat-fingering' the correct one, and he grew more frustrated with each failed attempt. Finally, he successfully booted up his computer and plugged in his headphones. He opened a Google chrome browser and logged into the monitoring website. And per his instructions, launched the audio player.

"Testing 3-2-1."

The audio player repeated Wil's count two seconds later.

Chapter 8

Day ONE

A sizable portion of the White House staff was banged up and bruised, yet in a highly enthusiastic mood. The bangs and bruises were remnants of an intense and physical martial arts session the night before. The fourth such session conducted by the First Lady. The enthusiasm amongst the staff was for the day ahead.

Angela Braxton would be stepping out and showing the world what she was made of. A composition already well understood and admired by the people who worked in and around the White House. The First Lady's toughness and grace, beauty and humility, energized the White House staff led her to become a favorite of all who crossed her path. A cadre which included Kim Jong-Un who sent Angela three dozen roses and a personal note shortly after her return from North Korea. A note which read.

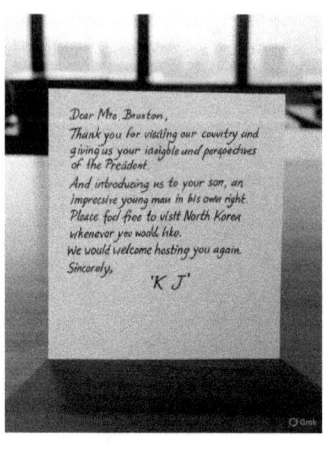

Jon, Angela, Lance, Heather, Luke, Secretary of State Haley, and Press Secretary Seracin met early in the Oval. Wil Carrington was also attending, though undetected and out of eyesight. Nonetheless he was listening to every word spoken, thanks to the ingenuity and resources of Mark Parker.

In three hours, the world would be introduced to Project **TYPE 1-YOU'RE DONE** and the **CURE IT NOW** task force via news conference from the White House East Room. The White House staff set the stage to give Angela Braxton the platform to win the world over to the cause of fighting harder to find the cure for Type 1 diabetes.

In attendance from the U.S. political world would be both the Speaker of the House, Paul Ryan, and the minority leader, Nancy Pelosi. The Senate majority and minority leaders, Mitch McConnell, and Chuck Shumer. And five senior members from each body.

At the behest of Vice President Carrington and Secretary of State Haley, selected foreign dignitaries would be in attendance. A list which included the Prime Minister of Canada, Justin Trudeau. The Prime Minister of the U.K., David Cameron. The Prime Minister of Australia, Malcom Turnbull. The President of Mexico, Enrique Nieto. And the Prime Minister of Israel, Benjamin Netanyahu. It was not terribly difficult to garner their agreement to attend. They all knew the importance of this initiative to the new American President and the personable First Lady.

One foreign dignitary would be in attendance without any need of persuasion from Heather or Nikki. Ri Yu-Song from North Korea was encouraged by Kim Jong-Un to be in the East Room for Angela's world stage debut if he wanted to keep his job.

Also in attendance would be celebrities and sports personalities afflicted with Type 1 diabetes. From the entertainment world, actors Hallie Berry, Vanessa Williams, Elizabeth Perkins, and Mary Tyler Moore. Singers Nick Jonas and Brett Michaels. From the sports world, athletes Jay Cutler, Brandon Morrow, Max Domi and Adam Morrison.

Also afflicted with Type 1 and in attendance would be United States Supreme Court Justice, Sonia Sotomayor. And soon to be British Prime Minister, Teresa May.

From the Jonathon Braxton fan club would be Pastor Jeffrey Claymore, Carlton and Cornelius Hale, Abby Martin, Earl Gregory, Rob Wiley, the recently confirmed Secretary of the Department of Education Connie McIlroy, and Taka and Tanoro Aoki.

But the most important individuals in attendance in the mind of Angela Braxton were the ninety representatives of thirty companies and research organizations from around the world engaged in the quest for the cure. Companies and organizations each with their own hypotheses, intellectual property, and processes. Individuals and organizations in search of what would be the treatment, or the regimen, or the shot, or the pill, or the serum which would finally end the suffering for millions of people around the world, many of them small children, as the result of their body's inability to produce insulin.

The individuals and organizations included,

Sean Kramer - CEO Diabetes Research Institute Foundation – Miami, FL.

Dr. Douglas Melton - Stem Cell Research - Harvard University

Michael Yang - President and CEO of ViaCyte - San Diego, CA

Dr. Jonah Shapiro – Canada Diabetes Research Institute (Canada-DRI) - Edmonton, Alberta

Dr. Denise Faustman- Director Immunobiology Massachusetts – General Hospital - Boston, MA

Dr. Francisco Leon- Chief Scientific Officer Prevention Bio - Red Bank, NJ

Doug Langa- Executive VP North American Operations Novo Nordisk - Denmark

Dr. Hong Jiang- Founder and Chief Scientific Officer Avotres – Cedar Knolls, NJ

Gregory Oakes- President and CEO Landos Biopharma – Blacksburg, VA

"Luke, have you got your words ready?"

"Yeah dad. And I even wrote them down."

The reference to Jon's aversion to write out his thoughts and speeches brought smiles to everyone in the room. Not however to the former President clandestinely listening from his basement office. Wil bristled at the thought of Braxton being able to deliver his speeches without written words or a teleprompter.

"Good job Luke." Lance Reibus, having twice been conjoined to Jon's unwritten and unprompted Republican National Convention speeches, couldn't resist.

"And we're all OK going without the teleprompters?" the President asked. "Luke, Sandra, Angie?"

They all nodded in affirmation.

"Good. So, we're ready?"

"Jon," his press secretary had a thought. "I think we should have Luke lead things off. It will have more impact. Everyone already knows my face and my voice. If Luke were first to address everyone, it would add to the moment."

Jon looked at his son, not saying a word. Luke had watched Sandra make her point and then looked down at his hands folded in his lap. He quickly processed whether he was up to the task. He then looked up and moved his eyes to his father. "I can do it dad. Just give me ten minutes to make some changes."

Angela chose the East Room in the White House to be the setting for the rollout of Project **TYPE 1-YOU'RE DONE.** A rollout soon to be witnessed around the country and around the globe. The room seemed the perfect setting to the First Lady. It was large, open, and modestly adorned. It measured eighty feet by thirty-seven feet. The ceiling was twenty-two feet high. The East Room had served to host the most solemn and most joyous events connected to past President's lives and deaths. Five President's daughters had been married in the room. Eight Presidents who died in office were laid there in state, including the last to die in office, John F. Kennedy. Dwight Eisenhower took his oath of office in the room in 1957.

The East Room, situated on the State Floor of the White House, is considered to be the most prestigious for notable events, though its size was the ultimate determining factor for Angela. Attendance at the news conference was by invitation only from the First Lady. In addition to the one hundred forty-five friends, government officials, foreign dignitaries, diabetes research industry leaders and celebrities, were sixty members of the press. A contingent which included numerous foreign networks and journalists.

At nine-thirty a.m. the room was full, and the buzz was loud. But it silenced immediately when the four members of the Braxton family made their entrance at the end of the room where a speaker's podium was set up. The front of the podium was adorned by the new **TYPE 1-YOU'RE DONE** logo Angela had designed. There was no music nor fanfare for the Braxton's entrance. Nothing accompanied their look of silent resolve. Four chairs were set behind the podium, off to the left. Jon, Angela, and Darla went straight for their seats. Luke went to the podium. Like his father, he had no notes. There were no teleprompters. In his left hand he was holding a small medical bag containing a blood glucose testing kit which he placed on the podium when he reached it. He stood silent for a moment looking at the seated guests. He noticed Pastor Claymore in the front row and flashed a look of confidence towards him. He saw Ri Yu-Song, the North Korean Foreign Minister. When their eyes met, Ri held up both fists to his shoulders and shook them to convey a sign of confidence. He saw Taka and Tanoro. His grandmother beamed. His stoic grandfather granted one nod. There were still lingering murmurs and coughs as Luke began, nervously.

"My name is Lucas Braxton. I'm sixteen years old and I'm a Type 1 diabetic." The room immediately silenced itself.

"I wasn't always. I used to be a normal fun-loving, carefree twelve-year-old. But everything changed in July of 2012 when my immune system decided the cells in my pancreas which made insulin were diseased and needed to kill them."

Luke unintentionally paused briefly to collect his thoughts and steady his nerves. These seconds of silence added to the impact of the moment.

"Insulin is the bodily hormone which converts the food we eat into glucose. Our bodies need glucose. It is the fuel which powers our organs. Without glucose our organs begin to shut down. Without a properly functioning pancreas our bodies cannot make insulin. When we cannot make insulin, we start to die. On July fourteenth of 2012, I started to die."

Jon and Angela were stunned by Luke's frankness and looked at one another in an exchange of jet-fueled emotion for their son and the power of his first words.

"Thankfully, my mom and dad wasted no time. Once they realized I was having symptoms of glucose deficiency, they immediately had me diagnosed. I'll never forget the time when I woke my mom up in the middle of the night to tell her I wasn't feeling right. She asked me to describe what was wrong and then went online to figure out what might be going on. When she realized I was experiencing symptoms of glucose deficiency, my parents rushed me to the doctor where we learned about my condition.

Since July of 2012, my life includes, every day, the monitoring of my blood sugar levels and the injection of insulin when my blood sugars are too high. My life includes monitoring my carbohydrate intake. I have to be aware of everything I eat. And if I plan to consume carbohydrates, I either have to inject insulin before or test my blood sugar soon after. Sometimes my body over-reacts to insulin which causes my blood sugars to drop to dangerous lows. That's when I hit the orange juice. If I go too low before ingesting something high in sugar content, I go into a condition called hypoglycemia, or as we know it in the community, insulin shock. These highs and lows randomly come and go even when I'm managing my blood sugar and taking insulin when I need to."

Luke was slowly gaining confidence. He paused speaking and thought back to his interchange just three weeks prior with Kim Jong-Un. How he had been terrified when Kim feigned outrage when he forgot to turn his mic on. His thoughts turned to how his mother coached him with her centering gesture to regain his composure. A calm came over him.

"Until six months ago I took insulin by giving myself a shot in the stomach. At least once a day, sometimes twice or three times. Every day. Six months ago, thanks to advancements in the field of treating the disease, I started wearing a new device. An insulin pump. Thank God, no more shots."

"Amen," Jeffrey Claymore said in a voice loud enough for Luke to hear. Luke made eye contact with Jeffrey who smiled at him.

"My insulin pump enables me to take insulin through a tube in my stomach connected to the pump. We call the tube a 'site.' The site is OK for about a week and then we have to change it. Let me show you."

Luke moved out from behind the podium, took off his blue suit coat and his gray tie. He turned around and walked over to his surprised sister and handed them to her. Jon and Angela looked at one another again, not knowing what to think or say or do. Before they could finish their thought, Luke had relocated back to the left side of the podium and unbuttoned his shirt. He pulled it back to expose the left side of his abdomen, and the insulin pump attached to the site with Velcro. He gave everyone in the room a moment to see the pump.

"If anyone in the back wants to get a picture take it now."

The press cameramen in the back obliged. The clicking sound of the cameras permeated the East Room. Shortly, those pictures of a pump attached to the abdomen of the son of the President of the

United States would be transmitted around the world creating a viral internet furor no one could have imagined.

"Now excuse me for a moment. I haven't checked my blood sugar yet today."

Luke walked back behind the podium where he had placed his test kit. For all to see, he took out a needle to prick his finger, extracted a drop of blood, and placed it on a test strip. He then slid the test strip into a glucose monitor and read the display.

"Looks like I'm a little high. I'll dial in a few cc's of insulin from my pump."

He moved back out from behind the podium to his left and turned the dial on the pump for everyone in the silent room to see. He then returned the five steps to the podium, put his supplies away, buttoned up and tucked in his shirt. All eyes in the room were glued on Lucas Braxton.

"Speaking for the millions around the world who suffer from this disease, we have days when we feel good and some days not so much. While we have the tools to manage our blood sugars, we can't do it as well as nature does no matter how closely we follow the protocols. The human pancreas when it's functioning normally is almost perfect. We cannot come close to managing our blood sugar as well as it can. We try but sometimes things don't work out. We can do everything right. Eat the right foods. Drink the right liquids. Monitor our levels. Limit our carb intake. Correctly measure our insulin intake. Exercise. And still have imbalances which leave us feeling like we're about to die. But today is a good day for us no matter how we might be feeling. No, make it a great day. It's a great day because it is day one of Project **TYPE 1–YOU'RE DONE**. Today is the day we begin to look forward to the time when it is Type 1 dying, and not us.

"I'm sure you all know the story of my dad. The man who once hated politics and politicians." There was muted laughter from the guests. Most were not ready to give up the surge of empathy and emotion Luke had generated.

"Then I got sick, and my dad decided he was going to find the cure. Pretty funny for a computer nerd who knew nothing of the disease or any of the science behind finding the cure. But my dad decided nothing would stop him and here we are. Who you may not know is my mom. My dad says he wouldn't be anywhere without her. I'm not sure that's the case. But my mom is special too. When we won the election, my mom told my dad she was taking over the job of finding the cure, so he could concentrate on the rest of his job. As for Project **TYPE 1-YOU'RE DONE**, she told him he only had one task, get us the money.

"My mom has a plan to find the cure for T1d and find it fast. You're going to hear about it shortly. Time is not our friend. Millions of people, many of whom are young kids, are struggling to live with this disease. You are here today to hear her plan. And hopefully after you hear it, you will give her and all of us living with this disease your support. Thank you."

Luke walked back to the open seat between his sister and his mother. The room sat in stunned silence but for sporadic camera clicks. Not only did Jon and Angela not know what to do or say next, neither did any of the seated guests nor the standing members of the press. Luke sat and Darla handed him his suit coat and tie. She leaned over and kissed his cheek. The silence was profound, and it was now Angela's turn to speak. She stood, leaned over to kiss Luke, and made her way deliberately to the podium, now unsure the words she had were right for the moment. There was no sound in East Room but for a few coughs which had supplanted the camera clicks. Angela took her place facing an audience waiting in silent anticipation. The words she had planned to deliver to start her presentation now seemed an afterthought. Instead.

"How blessed am I to call Lucas Braxton my son?"

Her show of humility ignited the room. A loud, respectful, and soon standing ovation erupted. She moved to the side as Luke was acknowledged. He didn't know how to respond. It was just as well. Any response from him could not have been more dignified than his decision to simply bow his head. His mother stood aside to let the room express its affection for her son.

Angela returned to the podium and began what she considered to be the most important moment of her life. She knew her words might well determine if her son could look forward to a life without both the short- and long-term ill effects of his condition. A life free of the stress of acutely managing blood sugar. She knew if her son were to see a cure in his lifetime, it would be because of the talents of the people now seated before her. It was time to say the right words in the right way to motivate these people to take actions which could be against their best interests. The standing ovation for Luke had concluded but the residue of his words persisted as Angela began her presentation.

"When I was a young girl, I was very stubborn. I knew everything. No one could tell me anything I didn't already know. No one could tell me what to do before I had decided for myself to do it. One day when I was being particularly obnoxious my father said to me '*i no naka nokawazu taikai wo shirazu.*' Loosely translated, he told me that a frog in a well knows nothing of the sea."

She paused briefly then continued. "Over the last month I have met with you here from the medical research community individually. We met because I wanted to know your challenges, your outlook, and your confidence. Your confidence in your hypothesis being proven successful. To date, I have not shared what you shared with me during those enlightening conversations with anyone other than the President. Let me now share with the world what I learned from you.

"The first question I asked when we met was what was standing in your way of successfully developing a cure for Type 1 diabetes? And from you all I received remarkably similar answers. You all cited it was money and time standing in your way. Money and time. Jon and I know more money is needed to expand your research efforts, to purchase materials and fund the resources you need to successfully explore the science, conduct your clinical trials, and fully test your hypotheses.

"My husband has never lied to me in the twenty-five years I've known him. And I don't expect him to start now. He has promised me he will expand our government funding into your research to the levels you need, under the right circumstances, to develop the cure. In other words, scratch money off your list of obstacles. It will be there.

"In reference to time, I asked should your organization have the money it needed tomorrow, then how long? What would be the length of time you need to complete your research, fully evaluate your hypotheses, and if your hypotheses were proven to be accurate, successfully formulate a cure to submit to the FDA for approval? I asked for the answer in a yearly range. Remarkably, your answers were again similar. The shortest estimate was six years. The longest was fifteen. The consensus was between eight and twelve years.

"Third, I asked you how well you understood the research of the other organizations represented in the room today working to find the cure for T1d? Again, your answers were similar. The consensus was you were not well versed in the research of your peers. Three of you mentioned familiarity with others, but only marginally so.

"Lastly, I asked you all what stops you from working more closely together? What keeps you from sharing information and research to accelerate the development of the cure? It was a question I knew would make you uneasy and your answers reflected your discomfort. We know you have responsibilities to your shareholders and stakeholders. We know you all have invested considerable time, substantial amounts of money and your careers in this endeavor. We know there will be fame, notoriety and return on investment for the individuals or organizations credited with the development of a cure. Perhaps even a Nobel Prize. We understand the pressures you are under and the inclination to not share your work with whom you might consider your competitors.

"It is not our intent today to understate the level of your commitment and your sacrifices. We understand the intensity of your devotion. I speak for all in the Type 1 community when I say we are grateful and indebted to you for all your sacrifices which yield continuous improvement in treatments and therapeutics for the community. But ladies and gentlemen, eight to twelve years? We refuse to wait that long without attempting to change the dynamic which has you saying you need so many more years. You all know what the Type 1 community endures day after day. Every day, scores of young children around the world are newly diagnosed, adding to the millions already living with what amounts to a day-to-day fight with their own immune system. A fight which for many leads to serious medical consequences. Yes, we have better treatments today for those in the community to fight the disease. But the scars of battle remain and over time the human body becomes more susceptible to consequences of the continuous onslaught on its pancreas."

The distinguished guests from the medical research community squirmed uneasily in their seats. It had long been a discussion point in the T1d community that organizations searching for the cure seemed to work slowly. There was an understanding in the community re- search efforts were underfunded, but it didn't mask the disappoint- ment prompted by continuous missed timelines and failed testing efficacy. The medical research community had been saying for the last fifteen years the cure would be developed within five. As time moved forward the community was losing its patience and its hope.

The First Lady continued. "Money and time. As you are now aware, money will no longer be an issue for you. We are prepared to spend the money it will take to fund your research to develop the cure. We are supremely confident you in this room today possess the knowledge and the expertise and the dedication to make the cure a reality. We have no doubt at least one of you will succeed.

"But it's imperative we deal with time. Time is now our biggest ob- stacle. Unfortunately, we cannot change time. It has and will continue to operate as it always has. One second after another. One minute after another. And as time passes the millions of people currently diagnosed with T1d will continue to suffer. And the millions of new people who will be diagnosed in the future will soon know the suffering."

The First Lady paused and scanned the rows of chairs on which the members of the medical research community were seated. "A frog in a well knows nothing of the sea. Yet it is in the sea where we will find our answers and find our way to bring the cure to the world within three years. It is in the sea of cooperation, the sea of collaboration and the sea of communication where we take control of utilizing time in a manner to achieve our objective to quickly eliminate the current and future suffering of the people in our community."

The press immediately recognized the significance of the First Lady's proclamation. Cameras were snapping, journalist notepads were opening, and pens were clicking. The East Room, silent for the last thirty minutes as Luke's and Angela's words anesthetized all in attendance, suddenly was abuzz. The First Lady had just challenged the T1d medical research community to deliver a cure within three years. The ninety members of the T1d medical research community in attendance realized the First Lady had just laid out a new reality attached to U.S. government funding. Yet none in the room foresaw a pathway to take them from where they were today to their hypotheses being fully researched, evaluated, and proven safe, in three years. There was considerable consternation among the researchers in the room as illuminated by their squirming in their seats and their muted murmuring. Yet feelings of hope and promise reverberated from everyone else.

Amid the buzz Angela continued. "I mentioned earlier there will be money made available to all of you to expand and accelerate your research. But there will be strings attached. Simply providing more money only to wait for eight to twelve years is not a viable option in our minds. Jon and I believe the fastest path to the cure is dependent on your willingness to work together. Working together is the key factor for accelerating our timelines and, as such, it will be the key factor for receiving grant money. We recognize there will be those of you who will view this as being coerced to work against your own best interests. You should know we view it differently. Your best interests are important. But to the millions of us in the patient and caregiver T1d communities, they are not as important as relieving the suffering of millions in the shortest period of time possible. We hope you will come around to our point of view and choose to join with us in the **TYPE 1–YOU'RE DONE** Project."

Angela paused and the clicking of cameras and journalist pens restarted. An aura of excitement among those in the room other than the medical researchers was building. The buzz was considerable as they realized history was in the making. Jon Braxton had campaigned on a promise to the T1d community he would bring them the cure. Today Angela Braxton had begun sharing exactly how it would be done. Millions from the T1d community around the world were watching on the internet and live television. Their hopes for better lives were building. Angela continued.

"I mentioned earlier the formation of the **Cure It Now** taskforce. We are in the process of building a team to manage and monitor the efforts of Project **TYPE 1-YOU'RE DONE.** The first order of business for the taskforce will be to review the current research of all the organizations represented here today for the purpose of aligning your organizations into teams. You will be grouped with other organizations which possess complimentary research, intellectual property, and processes. It is our intent to organize four teams among the organizations here today. Your organizations will be asked to join forces and share your research, your IP, and your processes to accelerate the timeline for the cure."

Angela paused to let those words settle. The uneasiness among the individuals representing the medical research community was unambiguous. The First Lady was now asking these organizations to cast their lot with a team of their competitors, potentially abandon their hypothesis, share all their intellectual property, and give up their ambition to be credited with the cure. And if they chose not to participate, abandon all U.S. federal government funding. Angela continued.

"It is our objective to change the course of your research by increasing your efficiency. Our plan is to transform your thirty underfunded solo-flying hypotheses, into the most promising four. And in support of those four, eliminate funding as an issue. We will strive to motivate collaboration, cooperation, and communication amongst the brightest and most talented diabetes researchers in the world. This is how, ladies and gentlemen, we will have the cure in three years. This is our first step to leave the well and head for the sea."

Sidney Rosenberg's cell phone lit up with *'CallerID unknown.'* He answered cautiously.

"Hello?"

"What up my brother?"

"You have the wrong number. I'm an only child."

"Hello Sidney," the former President offered.

"Yes Wil, I was watching."

"Any thoughts?"

"We shouldn't mess with the First Lady. How many black belts does she have again?"

"Very funny. Now what's the status on our plan?"

"I'm still working on it."

Wil couldn't hide his frustration. *"What about sabotaging this idea the Braxton's have about pulling the rug out from under these medical researchers? I'm sure there's going to be animosity towards the White House. And if this plan is a dud, we can use it as a springboard to take him down. I know high-ranking people in a few of these organizations. We can ensure this project fails."*

Dinner in the First Family's White House residence following the Project's rollout was a celebration. The Braxton's invited the Vice President, Angela's parents, Pastor Claymore, and Abby Martin to join them. Not invited but among the guests in audio attendance were Wil Carrington and Sidney Rosenberg courtesy of the compromised government Blackberry in Heather's purse.

The mood was joyous even though the feedback from the medical researchers after Angela's speech was not all positive. The Braxton's were not expecting the First Lady's plan to be embraced immediately, but they were all pleased with how well Angela and Luke had delivered the message.

"They'll come around," Jon assured Tanoro as everyone had been seated for dinner. "Once an organization realizes they'll lose their government funding if they opt out and their competitors who do join the Project will be highly funded, their thinking will change. Think about it. Say one organization is the furthest along the road to the cure and is receiving government money. They think they can get home on their own and choose to opt out. Their government funding is now gone. Their closest competitor opts in, and they're now partnered with four other companies with complimentary IP. And the team is highly funded. The horse race has changed dramatically. One broadcast with Kriss should galvanize public opinion. We're good."

Tanoro was still thinking of his daughter's presentation. "Angie, I didn't think you remembered my words to you when you were five. I was surprised to hear them today."

"Dad, I remember everything you taught me," she replied to her father.

"Luke, I'm so proud of you. You killed it today." It was Abby.

The President chipped in. "Yeah man, you had your mother and I on the edge there for a minute. We didn't know where you were going. And how much of your clothes you were going to take off."

"Jon. Really?" Angela feigned disgust. The table shared a laugh. A television was on over the fireplace on an adjoining wall. The volume low and not audible to the table. Wallis Kriss appeared. He had Bridgett Masterson on set with him. Heather took notice and asked the table. "Should we hear what Wally has to say?" They agreed and Luke went for the remote and turned up the sound.

Kriss had just started the interview. "Well Bridgett. You're thoughts on the First Lady's performance today."

"Quite remarkable really. We didn't have any idea about Mrs. Braxton's public speaking talents before today. But she looked like a natural leader. Composed, dynamic, charming. If I remember correctly, President Braxton has expressed his intent to not seek re-election in 2020. I can't help but thinking we were watching our next President in the East Room earlier today."

Luke and Darla were startled by Bridgett's comment. They both raised their eyebrows to the top of their foreheads and looked at one another. Heather turned her head to look inquisitively at Angela.

Angela returned Heather's glance with an emphatic, "No way."

Chapter 9

Getting Down To Business

"Good morning, everyone."

The cheerful greeting to his Cabinet clearly signaled the President was in a good mood. He was relaxed when he entered and smiled warmly at the gathering of seventeen. Thirteen executive branch department secretaries, the Vice President, the Attorney General, his Press Secretary, and his Chief of Staff. All were seated awaiting him in the Cabinet Room, a meeting room adjacent to the Oval Office in the West Wing of the White House, for the start of their first official Cabinet meeting. And clandestinely listening in thanks to the electronics installed on Heather's cell phone were Wil Carrington and Sidney Rosenberg.

"Hope everyone enjoyed watching my wife and son yesterday," Jon said in a playful mood as he slid into his seat.

The Secretary of the Department of Education was first to comment.

"You must be tremendously proud, Jon," remarked Connie. "For Angela to rise to the occasion so brilliantly. And Luke. Oh my God. He was incredible."

"Thank you, Connie. Anyone else going to attempt to make me cry before we get started?"

Next was his Chief of Staff. "Jon, the messaging we have been receiving from around the world from foreign officials just from yesterday and this morning has been off the charts positive. Everyone wants to work with the First Lady. She's started something big."

"Thanks Lance. She certainly struck a chord. Though she might call it plowing her hand through a stack of boards. And Luke's been updating me on what's been happening on social media. Appears he now has girlfriends in ports all over the world. Amazing what a teenager showing off his abs can accomplish."

The room shared a good laugh.

"OK, let's get down to business. Let's go around the room quickly because I've got a lot I want to share today. Keep your summaries to five minutes. Jim, let's start with you."

The Secretary of Defense, Jim Mattis, was ready. As a military man, he could not bring himself to address the President by name as Jon requested from his inner circle. "Sir, we are seeing significant increases in ISIS activity in the Middle East since the inauguration. We believe they believe your administration will maintain the posture of the last administration. They are continuing to consolidate their efforts to bolster their caliphate in Iraq, creating ongoing instability. And they're not encountering any opposition from the Iraqi government to speak of. They're also operating freely in Syria. Assad doesn't seem to want any part of them either."

"Heather?" Jon wanted her input.

"It's a mess Jon. If we want to shut ISIS down, we're going to have to get serious. We couldn't get a consensus to take a more forceful posture in the last administration. What we're seeing now is the result of the lack of a more aggressive policy."

The former president was listening in and had Sidney Rosenberg on his speakerphone. "Heather's spot-on Sidney. I always told her Obama was being too soft on terrorism."

Jon went back to Mattis. "Jim, we discussed three weeks ago your submitting a plan to address ISIS centering on our 'talking money' initiative. Let's move quickly. When can I expect it?"

"It's almost ready, sir. We should be ready to present next week."

"OK, let's table any further discussion on the Middle East until we have your plan. What else have you got?"

"Sir, for good news, we can talk about North Korea. It appears Kim has taken direct efforts to draw down his nuclear ambitions. We're seeing the dismantling of launch sites and the personnel clearance of reactor sites. We're also hearing chatter they are slowing down their uranium purchases from Pakistan."

"Another accomplishment of the First Lady and her sidekick, Luke?"

"Yes sir. I think so. Back to more troubling news, Russia is stirring the pot in and around Ukraine. Ground intelligence is telling us they are stoking insurrection in the Dombas. It's heavily populated with separatists wanting to return to Russian rule. The Ukrainian government has its hands full there and we're seeing an increase in heavy combat operations."

Jon was not familiar with the history of the region. "Jim, what side are we on there? Do we have any reason to support one side over the other, or should we stay clear and let it play out?"

Mattis responded. "Sir, the danger for us is continued Russian aggression and where it will end. We did nothing to stop them from taking Crimea. If they annex the Dombas without opposition from outside Ukraine, Putin will be emboldened and go for the Baltic states next."

Jon went for more perspective. "Do the Ukrainians have the ability to stop them in the Dombas?"

"We're not optimistic they do. Their fighting forces are capable. But there's so much corruption in that country it's hard to know how loyal their military leaders are. We can ship arms into the region but, without a significant presence there, we have no way to control what makes its way to their soldiers and what makes it onto the black market for sale elsewhere. And they don't want any operational assistance from us."

"Heather?"

"It's another hot mess Jon. Jim and I have been talking about putting more conditions on any more aid. But we have an issue in Congress. The Ukrainians have done a solid job lobbying key members of the House and Senate. We'll have difficulty imposing anything too restrictive on our foreign aid packages to them."

"Really? You're saying our own congresspeople, the stewards of our offers of foreign aid, our lawmakers who swear an oath of office to dutifully work in the best interests of this country, do not want to have assurances of how our money is spent once we hand it to the Ukrainians?"

Heather and Jim looked at one another, not knowing who should answer or what to say. Heather took the bait.

"You have a lot to learn about Washington, Jon. When you view things in a vacuum, they often don't make sense. When you view them from a broader perspective, they do. The Ukrainians do a lot for us in the region. And they're shrewd. They ask us for things in return for their loyalty. When transacting with our foreign allies, we frequently have to compromise a value or two to make tough judgment calls."

"You know Heather. I'd like to believe it. But I can't. For the sake of argument, let's say your logic, what they were doing for us in the region was worth our sending big aid packages without any oversight or accountability. If this is the case, then the question in my head is, would the good people in Congress make the exact same decision if they weren't being, how do we call it, lobbied? In other words, would the quality of the deal hold up if there were no backroom or sidebar deals?"

Jon continued. "You know my feeling on these kinds of matters. We've discussed it often. For the rest of you, take note I am not a huge fan of how our government operates. And this scenario is a prime example. Just because this has always been the way we've done things, is not the reason to continue to do them in the same fashion if the results from those decisions are suboptimal. Our decisions need to work in the best interests of the country, and I'm afraid they often do not. From my brief time in Congress, it's become apparent to me most decisions in Congress are made in the interest of re-election."

Eight of the Department Secretaries in the Cabinet Room had served in Congress during their careers. They knew Jon was right, but could not bring themselves to acknowledge agreement. He continued. "OK Jim. Let's not burn any more time on this today. We'll get our intelligence team together soon to go deeper. Get me your plan to address the ISIS situation quickly. Make sure it includes a definable pathway to a desired outcome. OK. Let's move on. Tom, you go next."

Tom Price, a Republican from Georgia, had just recently been confirmed by the Senate as Jon's Health and Human Services Secretary. Jon had twice interviewed Price before he was nominated and confirmed. They were closely aligned. Both felt the Affordable Care Act, now the law of the land, was not an efficient solution to increase the opportunities for affordable health care to the greatest number of citizens. Both felt increasing competition and reducing regulation would enable free market forces to provide more affordable options across a greater swath of the population.

"Jon, we're getting volumes of information requests from patient advocacy and health care organizations all over the country. They are aware of your position on the ACA and feel you will be working to weaken the legislation. We need to establish baselines about what our position on the ACA will be and how we will be enforcing it. There's been confusion ever since the law was enacted and the botched rollout and the website debacle certainly contributed. Now with you in office, the uncertainty has been magnified."

"I agree Tom. Let's have HHS create 2017-2018 baselines. But come at it from ground level. Establish your guidelines on what we discussed in our meetings. It is the position of this administration to strengthen patient-doctor relationships. Improve competition for medical supplies and services. Enable insurance to be sold and delivered across state lines. Break down artificial barriers which limit the abundance of goods and services which lead to higher prices. We can make these points without ever referring to the ACA or obstructing its provisions. It's the law of the land. Let's respect it but not necessarily cater to it. When you respond to these organizations, let's not refer to the ACA or its provisions. Lead with your baselines and plant seeds with these advocacy groups were going to promote free markets more than our predecessor did. I'm not sure it will reduce suspicion, but it may detour organizations from fully launching their ACA-based services, giving us an opening to push free market solutions to fill any voids. What else you got?"

"I have a meeting with the First Lady later today to discuss how HHS can support her initiative with the T1d research community. We haven't yet heard from any of the organizations which were in the East Room yesterday, but I suspect we will. I want to understand from the

First Lady what she might be expecting from us and how we should respond to any objections."

"Thanks Tom. As a heads up, you should know I want to collaborate closely with you on mental illness, drug addiction and homelessness in this country. I include all three in the same breath as they are linked. You should know this administration is going to be highly focused on solving this issue. I'm giving you a heads-up. You and I will work closely together on this. Please start formulating your thoughts for our next conversation. OK. Connie, take it away."

Over the next ninety minutes, Jon gave all his department secretaries and the Attorney General five minutes each to put on the table what they felt was most important for the President to hear this day in the very brief time they were allotted. Jon knew five minutes each was not enough time to have a substantive dialogue with the people leading the important departments of the Executive Branch, but he wanted to reserve enough time to outline his vision to his cabinet for his term in office. An outline on his mind since Inauguration Day, but not ready for delivery until he had experienced enough time in office to have at least a faint idea of how he wanted to run the country.

"OK. Sorry for the lightning round discussion. I wanted to hear from all of you today and will collaborate with you one on one as time permits. But today I wanted to reserve some time to give you my thoughts about how, at a high level, we work together going forward. Let me start with the tough stuff. Budgets. This administration will have a strong focus on budgets. A key word you should expect to hear in context with focus is efficiency. Expect to hear this word often. I'm asking all of you to give Lance within two weeks your plan to cut your department budgets by twenty percent. Only one exception, Defense. Jim, you're welcome."

Jon knew this wouldn't be received well in the room, and he was right. No one knew it was coming. Not the Vice President. Not the Chief of Staff. Not the Secretary of State. There were grumbles of dissatisfaction, but none of the secretaries were ready at this moment to fight this battle. Jon anticipated their discomfort.

"It's a tall order. I get it. But do what you have to do. Everywhere I turn in this government, I see inefficiencies. It's not fair to the taxpayers to foolishly spend their money on waste, abuse, fraud, and mismanagement. I have no doubt you can all run your departments with eighty percent of last year's budget. My view is you can run your departments better with eighty percent because when inefficiency is baked in it spreads like a disease. And I'll venture to say all our executive branch departments are sick."

"Heather, you ran State for six years. What did you see? Could you have cut twenty percent if you had no choice?"

"If I had no choice, yes. It would have required shifting priorities and could have affected our effectiveness."

The President countered. "I'll grant you the point, but where would you draw the line? If with more money you could be more effective, then where would the funding stop? With more money, it becomes harder to be efficient. Throwing more money at a problem or a bureaucracy is not an answer to inefficiency. Just because this has always been the way we've done things is not the reason to continue to do them. The prescription for efficiency is effective leadership. As department heads, I'm referring to your effective leadership."

Jon was now in high gear. He had been building his vision on how to run the country. Now, for the first time, he was hearing his thoughts.

"You are all just starting out in your jobs. Be effective leaders, not bank managers handing out money. We have a brand-new administration. It's the perfect time to disrupt with the least amount of disruption. Chart your courses starting now. Transform your departments into lean and mean execution machines. Evaluate your personnel and shed the people you feel are not up to the task. The country will continue to operate even with unoccupied desks in your department. Things will fall through the cracks, but your top performers will pick up the slack. They'll find new and better ways to get things done. Find your good people and give them latitude. I've seen it work in my business. It will work in yours. Challenge your people to be effective leaders. Challenge the status quo of our government. Get Lance your plans detailing your budget cuts. Two weeks. Any questions?"

There were none. Jon continued.

"OK next. Another favorite word of mine, as you might have gathered, focus. Impossible to focus while working in government, right? Too many distractions, too many crises, too many curve balls, too many narratives. Dealing with the press. The opposition party. Your own party. Lobbyists. Constituents. Focus? Yeah, probably not. I'm not going to task you to be overly focused. Instead, I want you nimble. In running your departments, you need to be elastic. Pliable. As for me, I'm going to be laser focused. There are five things I want to accomplish while I'm here, six if you count developing the cure for T1d. Angie's got that one. I'm taking the other five.

"I've been studying how my predecessors approached this job. And by the looks of it, they spent valuable time and energy on political events, ceremonies, state functions, campaigning, public relations. Figurehead stuff. All things you would expect the leader of a political party to do. But I don't see myself as a political party operative. I see myself as a problem-solver and I'm here to work with all of you to solve our biggest ones. Wish we could solve all our problems over the next few years, but it's not realistic. I believe solving five is optimistic, and

I'm not yet sure Washington is ready for what I have in mind. I may be lucky to solve only one. But I'm going to take on five."

Jon continued. "Heather, for you, this means I'll be leaning on you to take on a majority of the tasks and duties my predecessors occupied themselves with. I don't want to be sidetracked by them. You've been here before. I have no doubt you can do a much better job than I with those tasks. In many respects, I expect you to function as a co-President.

"As for the rest of you, short of my occasionally sharing a big picture view with you, you are going to have considerable latitude in running your departments as you see fit. Just remember the part about cutting your budgets by twenty percent. Most of my communications with you will come through Lance. Get the information you need from the White House through him. From the big picture perspective, here are the guiding principles I'll expect you to abide by. The first is remember who you work for. You don't work for me. You work for the country.

"Second, remember what your primary job is. It is not to oversee your departments. It is to make life better for as many American citizens as you can. Let that thought guide you and your actions.

"Third, execute your duties in a manner to make your mothers proud. Don't be unduly influenced by politics, lobbyists, money, or ambition. Instead, be influenced by the trust and hope the people in this country have for you to make their lives better. Okay ladies and gentlemen. Let's wrap this up. Questions?"

Heather had one. "Jon, what will be your five priorities?"

"Make sure to catch Wally this weekend."

Chapter 10

That's Right

T he black limousine pulled into the garage of Sidney Rosenberg's Manhattan residence at half-past six. The former President exited and was escorted by one of his secret service detail into the parking garage elevator and up to the nineteenth floor. They walked together in silence to Sidney's door. Once Wil Carrington was safely inside, the secret service agent retreated to their car.

"Hello Wil."

"Hello Sidney. Thanks for agreeing to see me on such short notice."

"I hope you didn't make the long drive here for nothing. Like I told you, I don't have anything yet."

"The fact you don't have anything yet is the reason I'm here. Let go in and sit down."

Sidney made a quick to stop at his wet bar. "Macallan, three fingers, one ice cube?"

"Yes, and pour one for yourself," replied the former President.

Sidney complied and walked over to Wil, who had already made himself at home in a plush high-back velour chair facing the southern Manhattan skyline. The two men sat silently for a moment as they each enjoyed a taste of their scotch.

"You know Sidney, I used to have complete faith in your capabilities. But I'm starting to have my doubts. We've been listening in on Braxton for three weeks now. Among other things, we've learned Braxton's appeasing North Korea potentially creating a national security crisis. We've heard him extort companies in the pharmaceutical and medical research businesses to share their intellectual property with their competitors or lose government funding. And now we know he's going to back away from the traditional responsibilities of a President so he can play around with a small handful of pet projects. How bad does it have to get before you can come up with a plan to nail this guy?"

"Come on Wil. You're letting your ambition cloud your better judgment. Everything you mentioned is tracking towards positive outcomes. The only possible angle I can see is an effort to rally Big Pharma and all their cronies in Congress to stand up to his diabetes agenda. Diabetes is big business. If Braxton is successful in bringing in a cure for Type 1, it could have positive outcomes for fighting Type 2 as well. Depending on the solution, it could mean huge drawdowns in corporate profits. But it's a risky proposition for the companies and their supporters in Congress because of the public sentiment on Braxton's side. He and his wife and kid are doing an impressive job building ground swell support. Any company which chooses to fight the battle could get battered in the arena of public opinion. As far as North Korea goes, he has Kim drawing down his nukes. You sure you want to hammer him on the progress he's making? As far as his five pet projects are concerned, let's find out what they are before we waste any energy figuring out how to use those against him. And don't forget, what he's proposing will give Heather more power than any VP in history."

Wil contemplated Sidney's words. "Well good. At least we're talking about something now. Let's play the Big Pharma angle out a little bit. Can we find out how much the top twenty companies in the industry pull in from diabetes-related products? If it's a big enough number, we might have something to work with."

"I'll start working on it tomorrow. Should have something for you next week."

The camera was focused on the show's venerable host as the broadcast started.

"It's Sunday April 23rd, 2017. From Washington, I'm Wallis Kriss and welcome to today's edition of Big News Sunday. Today will be a first for this show as we dedicate the entire hour to the man and woman now taking up residence in the White House. For the first half of our show today we are honored to have with us the First Lady of the United States, Angela Braxton.

"Mrs. Braxton made her debut on the World Stage from the East Room in the White House earlier this week when she introduced the TYPE 1-YOU'RE DONE Project to a worldwide audience. She presented her plan to bring the world the cure for Type 1 diabetes within three years. A most ambitious goal considering the current state of the research into the cure and the difficulties the medical research community is having in identifying the underlying cause of the disease.

"We have many questions for the First Lady about her plan and the controversy it has created among firms in the industry and members of Congress taking issue with the White House's heavy-handed approach linking government funding to the sharing of intellectual property. The First Lady graciously accepted our invitation and here she is."

The camera panned out to capture both Wallis and Angela seated at the show's glass table. It had a ninety-degree corner, and their chairs were set for them to face one another.

"Welcome Mrs. Braxton."

"Thank you, Wallis. It's time we finally met. You've been sharing beers with my husband for what now? Over three years? This meeting is long overdue."

Kriss had a thought to himself. *'I've seen this movie before.'* "You're right Mrs. Braxton. Way overdue. We'll make sure this won't happen again."

Suddenly, a stagehand walked onto the stage with a glass vase containing two dozen bright red roses. He set them down next to Angela. She was surprised and amused. "Wallis, you shouldn't have."

"Uh, I didn't. They're not from me. At least not to my knowledge. But I see a card. Very sweet of the President."

Angela picked the card from the roses and opened it. "Well, they're not from the President."

"No," Kriss responded with surprise.

"They're from Kim Jong-Un."

"Ah, I see. I heard he also sent you roses shortly after you returned from your recent visit to North Korea."

"He did, but these are even more beautiful."

"Well, Mrs. Braxton I didn't plan to speak with you about North Korea this morning but since we are now on the topic, please tell us how you and your delegation were able to defrost the deep freeze resulting in Kim Jong-Un's beginning to dial down his nuclear ambitions?"

"We were all pleasantly surprised at the swiftness of the positive reactions emanating from our meeting with Kim. We were all expecting something quite different. Looking back, I think the primary reason for our success was Kim taking a liking to my son. I wasn't sure what the President was thinking when he included Lucas in our delegation, but Jon has a knack for always constructing a formula for success. Also, Jon's proposition. The President gave Kim an offramp for ending development of nuclear weapons and an on ramp into the brotherhood of nations attaching attractive and common-sense concessions. No posturing. No politicking. Just a straight-forward dialogue with a realistic time limit. I think Kim appreciated being spoken to in a straightforward manner."

Kriss responded. "You and your son are a formidable team. It was certainly on display in the East Room this past week. We all heard your presentation, but I think our audience would like to hear from you how you arrived at your plan. And what you think the realistic chances are to accomplish your three-year timeline objective. It seems overly optimistic."

"Well Wallis, as you and your audience know, Jon was clear in his campaign the quest for the cure for Type 1 was his number one agenda item. He has been fighting for the cure since Luke's diagnosis in 2012 and when the opportunity arose for Jon to pursue the White House, tragically from the death of Tony Jacobs, there was never a thought of him changing his priorities. Especially after meeting Tony's niece, Lauren Woods, who, like Luke, is also a Type 1 diabetic. After the inauguration, we both realized an asymmetrical focus on T1d was incredibly naïve because of all the responsibilities the President has, so I went to Jon and told him I was going to take on this mission so he could focus his attention on running the country. And he agreed it would be best."

Kriss felt compelled to ask. "You told him?"

"That's right."

Kriss wanted to explore. "It was your idea to take the lead on what the President contended was his number one agenda item? And he agreed?"

"That's right. And I had no idea how to get started, so I invited my friend, Abby Martin, from the State Department, to spend a weekend with me at Camp David to mind share an action plan."

Kriss asked. "Abby Martin? Wasn't she the President's executive administrative assistant in his tech company?"

"That's right. And she now works in the State Department for Nikki Haley, and she was part of our North Korea delegation. We've always worked well together, and she always has great ideas."

"OK. What came out of your talks with Mrs. Martin?"

"After a girl's weekend of karate workouts, wine tasting, and serious mind-bending, we decided we would invite the top thirty organizations in the country involved in Type 1 diabetes research to meet with us individually at the White House. They all accepted our invitation and over the course of the next four weeks, we had two hour meetings with each of these organizations. In these meetings, we asked them all to share with us what they were working on and what the current state of their research was. And as you know from our news conference, we also asked them what they needed to move more quickly; how long it would take to fully prove their hypotheses valid; and if they were aware of or were partnering with any of the other organizations in search of the cure."

For the benefit of those in his audience who had not witnessed the First Lady's news conference, Wallis reviewed what she shared in the East Room.

"And from what I understood from your news conference, each organization responded to move more quickly they needed more money to further their research. Even with the money they needed being available, each felt they needed somewhere between eight and twelve years to complete their research. And these companies were not working together on any joint initiatives. You referred to them as frogs in a well."

"That's right."

"And from this information, you developed your plan?"

"That's right," Angela replied confidently.

"As to your plan, can you give us your thinking behind it? I'm sure you're aware of the controversy surrounding it which links future government funding to these organization's willingness to share their intellectual property with competitors. Property which certainly required considerable capital to create and whose return on those investments could be compromised."

"Yes. We're aware of what we are asking and believe we have the moral high ground and the common-sense reasoning to do so."

"Mrs. Braxton, your husband has always expressed a preference for free markets and capitalism. Yet your plan is weighted with government intervention. How does your husband reconcile this apparent contradiction?"

Angela was ready. She answered with a smile on her face and charm in her voice.

"He reconciles conundrums the same way as I do. In this case, we see our son and Lauren Woods both living with a life-threatening condition. And we see millions of others around the world, a sizable percentage of whom are young children, also living with this condition because we do not have a cure for T1d. We considered the current state of the research for a cure. We considered the millions of dollars the taxpayers in this country have already invested through government grants to these organizations to find the cause and the cure for Type 1, only to have these companies, during our interviews, ask for more money and eight to twelve more years."

Angela paused to give Kriss a chance to respond. He did not and she continued.

"At the same time, we see the incredible brilliance of these organizations and their dedication to solving an extremely complex human physiology problem. We see the difficulties they face in researching the disease, and the considerable expense involved in conducting their research while following FDA guidelines. We also learned from our interviews with these organizations, with the help of our Cure It Now task force, their hypotheses are similar to others in their field. And their research methods are complimentary. Once we compiled all these data points, a picture began to form for Abby and me. We saw by putting these organizations into teams based on complimentary factors, their research could proceed faster, and they could scale their efforts more efficiently. Is this making sense to you, Wallis?"

Kriss was noncommittal. "It sounds reasonable."

"Good, we thought so too. These organizations have significant obstacles in their path. It quickly became clear to us by establishing joint development partnerships, we could shorten the timeline and potentially reduce the overall expense required from this point forward to develop the cure. After our interviews, we saw the problem more clearly, and this recognition led us to our plan to bring the cure to the world faster. We saw our plan as a pathway to increased efficiency and expediency while potentially reducing costs. If the solution needs a little nudge from the White House for these organizations to work more closely together, Jon sees it as a worthwhile utilization of his office. What was it Obama said? Elections have consequences?"

Angela paused to take a breath and awaited Kriss' comeback.

"All well and good Mrs. Braxton, but you are also asking these companies to potentially work against their monetary interests. It's possible one of them might be on the verge of finding the cure and be sacrificing the financial gains associated with a discovery or a patent."

"Wallis. Come on. Think clearly here. If one of these organizations is, as you say, on the verge, they don't have to join the project. We're not mandating them to do so."

"But then they won't be eligible for government grants. You're penalizing them," Kriss retorted.

"Really? Where is it written one of our federal government's responsibilities is to give these organizations taxpayer dollars? And continue to give them money when their progress is slow and expensive. These organizations have been receiving grant funding for years and are on record saying they're still eight, ten, twelve years out. And we're being unfair because we want to spend the taxpayer's money more efficiently to help reduce the suffering of millions of people? And our unfairness is we don't want to continue to invest in organizations which have spent millions in taxpayer dollars but, by their own words, need more money and more time and want to continue going in the same direction? Are you serious, Wallis?"

It was time for a commercial break. Kriss was grateful for the pause. He wasn't confident he could counter the First Lady's arguments. But he did want to get one more question in. When they returned from the break, he fired it off.

"Mrs. Braxton, Wall Street Journal opinion editor Bridgett Masterson was on the air with me the night of your presentation in the East Room. She mentioned you looked, shall we say, presidential. We know your husband has intimated he will only be a one-term president. And it has been assumed Heather Carrington will be a presumptive nominee in 2020, though we're not sure of what party at this point.

Should the President decide not to run for a second term, will you comment on whether you might have any presidential aspirations should your husband decide not to seek re-election?"

Angela looked at Kriss. Her emotion was somewhere between admiration for asking the leading question and disdain for the same reason. She responded firmly. "No."

"No, you have no aspirations. Or no, you do not care to comment?"

"That's right."

Chapter 11

Let's Fix It

It was time for the second half of Big News Sunday. The stage lights brightened and the cameras came alive showing Wallis and Jon sitting at the same table as the previous segment with Angela. Their chairs were again placed directly facing one another. To the left of the President on the glass table were five footballs, each placed on a kicking tee standing upright. There were also two frosted mugs with a dark colored liquid topped by a half-inch of foam. The red roses from Kim Jong-Un were gone.

"Mr. President, welcome. What's with the footballs?"

Jon stood and took one of the frosted mugs and placed it next to Kriss. He then returned to his seat. "Wally, again so formal? Thought we were going to be tailgating today."

"Uh yes sir, uh JB. Right. Tailgating. I assume we're at a football game? But my contract doesn't allow me to drink alcohol during the broadcast."

"We're not at the game. We're in it. The game started on Inauguration Day, and we have four quarters to play. Since I'm the President, as you just reminded me, I thought I'd bring my own balls. And root beer."

Kriss recognized he was woefully unprepared for this interview. "Right. The football game has started. How are we doing? Are we winning?"

Jon was confident. "It's early in the first quarter. It's still zero-zero, but we have the ball and we're marching down the field. We have a good game plan and if we execute, we will be victorious."

Kriss nodded. "Might I assume these footballs, each noted with markings which I can't quite make out, are part of the game plan?"

"You might, Wally, but be wary of assuming. But in this case, you are correct. These footballs are the game plan for my administration."

Kriss picked up his mug of root beer and raised his glass. The President raised his glass, and they both took a swig.

Kriss smacked his lips and set his mug down in front of him. "I see, Mr. President. Care to share more with us?"

"This last Tuesday we held our first full official Cabinet meeting at the White House. Our primary agenda item was to discuss the details of how our administration will operate during my term in office. First thing for you and your audience to know is Vice President Carrington will be assuming a larger role in our administration than is traditional for a Vice President. This should surprise no one considering my lack of and her abundance of experience. I've decided in the interest of maintaining my focus, the Vice President will have primary responsibility for conducting many affairs typically the domain of the President. Official meetings, politically oriented tasks, foreign dignitary and policy meetings, and all ceremonial events. Undoubtedly, I will participate where my absence would be conspicuous, but the Vice President will be front and center. For many intents and purposes, she will be the face of this administration."

Kriss was not surprised. This detail of the Cabinet meeting had been leaked to him by the New York Times by way of an 'anonymous'

Sidney Rosenberg. Wil and Sidney saw Kriss as an ally in their mission to discredit the President. They were forwarding him inside information they felt Kriss could use in their effort through a political ally at the Times. Kriss couldn't resist the opening.

"In the interests of focus? What exactly does this mean and what will be your role in the Carrington administration?" Kriss snidely remarked.

"Not so fast there, Wally. It's still the Braxton administration since it's my butt on the line. And as a hallmark of the Braxton administration, we are going to be less focused on the ways of the past and on outdated traditions. And more focused on solving this country's biggest problems. One practice which always served me well in business was placing people in positions where they would have their best chance to succeed. Put aces in their places was how one author I read put it. Another practice which served me well was focus. If you want to solve a problem, apply focus. The more difficult or complex the problem, the sharper the focus need be."

Jon continued. "My decision on the role of the Vice President in the Braxton administration accomplishes two objectives for us. One, she's better at being a politician than I am. She has the experience in office and the knowledge of Washington to be more effective at these tasks than I would be. The ace is in place. Second, my best chance for being successful and winning this football game is putting myself in a position to have the time to do what I believe I do best. Solve problems. Having her address the time-consuming tasks a President ordinarily is involved with frees up my time for me to do what best serves the objectives of solving our problems.

"I've been on the job now for twelve weeks. During this time, I've been introduced to and studied our nation's most pressing issues. We have a full plate. More problems than we could ever hope to solve in one term. But some are more critical than others. They're bigger and more impactful on the well-being of our citizens. And they require sharper focus. I've identified what I believe to be our five most pressing issues. What I will be focusing the majority of my time on during my term in office. As for the other issues the Executive branch is responsible for, those will be the primary domain of the Cabinet.

"Our Cabinet secretaries will have a wide lane of autonomy to run their departments. While I fully intend to set the higher-level objectives for each agency, I don't plan on being involved in each Secretary's tactical efforts. Hopefully, we will have hired the right people for the job. If not, we'll make changes quickly.

"The five issues I intend to focus on I see as the country's most pressing. These five are the ones our country needs to address to make everyday life for Americans better. And the lives of future generations of Americans better. As the President, I feel focusing on these five will be the best use of my time. By doing so, we will enable our administration to be as efficient and impactful as we could hope. I recognize it's not a good strategy for being a popular politician and I'm leaving myself wide open to scrutiny, but that doesn't matter to me. I'll let Vice President Carrington fight those battles."

Jon leaned back to let Kriss get a question in. He obliged.

"If I understand you correctly, the Vice President will take on the duties traditionally the job of the President. Your Cabinet secretaries will have considerable autonomy running their departments. And you, sir, you will contain your focus to five issues. Is this a good summary?"

"A great summary, Wally. But let's say concentrate my focus on rather than contain. What do you think?"

Kriss snickered. "I think it will differ from what we're used to. Has your team run any opinion polls on how the public might react to their

President abdicating on traditional responsibilities? The people in this country might not like the idea of you limiting your involvement to your five issues. They might view it as being highly self-serving, particularly since you've communicated often your primary reason running for office was to help your son by leading the effort to find the cure for Type 1 diabetes. Now you're adding five pet projects and that's it? And you're asking the Vice President to take on tasks the people in this country would expect you to be involved with? They voted for you to do the job. The voters might think you're not taking the job seriously."

"Those are good points, Wally. Let's cover them. First, on the matter of working for the cure for Type 1, the First Lady will run point. She's got a brilliant plan for accelerating the timeline to the cure and knows how she wants to execute it. Other than finding the money we need; I'll stay out of her way unless she requests my involvement. As for the five issues I will concentrate on, let's air them out and see what your viewers think about our plans after they hear them."

"Ok Mr. President. What's number one?"

Jon stood up and reached for one of the five footballs. He flipped it the six feet separating him and Kriss, who caught the ball awkwardly. Kriss spun the ball around until he could read the words written next to the laces. He repeated them, "FIX OUR CULTURE."

Jon couldn't resist. "Sounds good, Wally. It's exactly what I was thinking we should do."

Kriss burrowed his forehead and sounded surprised. "OK? Fix our culture. What's broken and how do you propose to fix it?"

"Wally, do you remember much about your childhood?"

"I do. I remember it fondly."

"Do you feel you're in the same country today as you were during the time of your childhood memories?"

Kriss shook his head. "No, not really. Life seems tremendously more complicated today. I see it in my kids. Life seems harder for them than I remember it being for myself at their age."

Jon concurred. "I feel the same way. As I review the state of this country today in 2017, a thing which strikes me is how directionless we are as a nation. I feel too many people living in this country go about their daily lives without a sense of purpose. The meaning of life and living a good life for too many is buried under the weight of a declining culture. Too many people, especially our younger generations, live without direction. They live without hope for a better future, without goals, without pride. They live uninspired lives. Wally, how old were you in 1980?"

"Let's see. I was seventeen."

"We're you a sports fan?"

"No. Not really."

"Do you remember the 1980 Winter Olympics in Lake Placid?"

"A little bit. Weren't those the Olympics when a young U.S. ice hockey team was a huge underdog to win anything, and they defeated the older, more experienced, World Champion Russian national team for the gold medal?"

"They had to defeat Finland for the gold. The memorable game against the Soviets was a semi-final. No one gave them a chance in you know where to defeat the Soviets. They had played an exhibition game against them in New Your City just before the Olympics started and were humiliated ten to three. But then the games started, and things changed. Did you happen to watch?"

"No. I didn't see it," Kriss responded, slightly embarrassed.

Jon pressed him. "Have you ever watched any of the documentaries about the game? They're all over YouTube."

"No, Mr. President. I have not seen those either."

"Too bad Wally. I recommend you check them out. I was nine when those games were played. The memories of watching the players and the crowd and the emotion of the moment are still with me. It fascinates me to this day. It was only a hockey game. Yet the reaction winning that game kindled not only for the people in the arena but for the nation overall was amazing. We were in a bad place as a country at the time. High inflation. The Iranian hostage situation. Economy in recession. High interest rates. Stagflation. Gas shortages. The malaise of the Carter administration. There was no way we should have won that game, but we did, and the spirit of the entire country was uplifted by the efforts of those kids. The entire outlook of the country changed. Winning against the improbable odds generated tremendous hope in the country. Hope better days were ahead. Those kids won the game, against all odds, because their coach convinced them to be proud to represent their country, win or lose. And with pride came hope. And with hope came an improbable victory."

Jon sensed Kriss wanted to fire in a question. He paused to give him the chance.

"The game was played thirty-six years ago. What does it have to do with 2017 and your administration?"

Jon picked up his root beer mug and extended it towards Kriss as if to toast. Kriss did the same, and they both took a swig.

"In 1980, this country was not in a good place, and today we are not in a good place. It's not a malaise like it was then. The heat's up too high with all our divisiveness. But we are in a funk, nonetheless. We are not the nation we could be. We are not the nation we should be. Our citizens are constantly fed a steady diet of unwelcome news, misinformation, and reasons for self-doubt and pessimism. An attention starved broadcast media and the unrelenting stream of negativity and hateful messaging from social media has bred a degree of hopelessness and contributed to our cultural decline. Too many cultural norms which played a large part in our country growing to be the most prosperous and generous country in the history of the planet and contributing to an overall standard of living unmatched by any other society, are disintegrating. In response, over the next four years, one of my primary areas of focus will be fixing our culture. We will do this by rebuilding pride. Pride in ourselves. Pride in our families. Pride in our communities. And pride in our government.

"Wally, do you know anyone in mainstream America who can say without hesitation they are proud of their country's government? You'll be hard-pressed to find the shrinking number who do. The Braxton administration will fix this. We will build a government which operates in a manner to restore the confidence in Americans that their government is working to serve them and not serve lobbies and special interests."

Kriss countered. "An interesting thought, Mr. President," Kriss was still uncomfortable addressing his guest informally, "but is this what you feel the people who voted for you want you to do? To work on our culture? It seems invasive. You have always subscribed to limited government."

"Wally, I believe people voted for me because they want solutions to the country's problems. And I passionately believe many of the problems in our society today are tied to our cultural decline. Whether its drug addiction, alcohol addiction, obesity, crime, disease, racial discord, corruption, poverty, the fracturing of the family, dependence on government. All these issues are symptoms of an unhealthy culture. I want to minimize the symptoms and treat the root causes of our decline. By establishing this as an area of focus for myself and not a bureaucracy, I'm hoping to bypass the dysfunctional influence of politics. Is this the type of work the people of this country want their president doing? We'll find out soon enough. Two years from now will be here tomorrow and the mid-terms will answer your question.

"In the meantime, we have ideas on how to rebuild our culture. How to restore purpose and pride within the American psyche. When we have our ideas fully baked and ready to implement, I'll come back on your show, and we'll discuss them."

Jon stood and motioned to Kriss to toss him the ball back. Jon replaced it where it was and picked up a second ball. He tossed it to Kriss, who again caught it awkwardly.

Kriss read the markings aloud. "FIX OUR POLITICS? If I recall, we've had conversations on this topic over the years. What do you have in mind now?"

"If we're going to fix our culture, we've got to bring the federal government into alignment. The Executive branch can get the ball rolling, but what I have in mind will also require the Legislative branch. To succeed with this agenda, laws will need revamping and our spending norms will need re-prioritizing. We will have to spend on new initiatives. Initiatives not normally a priority in Congress. Unfortunately, the people in Congress today don't always have the best interests of their constituents in mind and often stand in opposition to fixing our problems because it conflicts with their agenda. To expedite this effort, we will reintroduce the ELECT legislation we proposed in 2015."

Kriss wanted some of this. "Legislation which failed miserably. And your opposition was bipartisan," he was eager to remind Jon.

"Only bipartisan if you count along party lines. If you count along moral lines, our opposition was completely partisan."

Kriss ignored the comment. "Will you be amending your proposals or reintroducing them as they were written two years ago?"

"We'll have changes, but the emphasis and the purpose will be the same. We're going to get private money out of federal elections and eliminate influence peddling to the degree we can. We'll eliminate special interests and lobby money funding campaign war chests. We'll create an environment where the best problem solvers in the country will want to run for public office and serve. Our aim is to move out the career politicians responsible for so many of our problems and move in people who have the proper moral fiber and pragmatic decision-making abilities."

Kriss was unconvinced. "Mr. President, you know as well as I this is easier said than done. You know you will again have considerable opposition on Capitol Hill. They will not sit idly by and authorize legislation which gets in the way of their careers. I'm sure a considerable number of your colleagues watching today feel you're pointing the finger directly at them. You may be creating a landscape where it may be difficult for you to work with Congress in any manner."

"I like you chose the word careers to describe what our colleagues in Congress are out to protect. But the fact is, being in Congress should not be a career. It should be a public service excursion with a finite time limit. The longer these people are in office, the more susceptible they become to not representing their constituents and instead those who contribute to their campaigns. Fixing our politics could be the issue which galvanizes the American people. Let's go back to our discussion of pride. Is it possible the people of this country are not proud of their government because they are aware of the abuses of power by so many elected officials and feel powerless to do anything about it?"

Kriss countered. "I suppose this could be the case, sir, but along the way you're going to generate tremendous ill will from your colleagues."

Jon dismissed the notion. "I understand it perfectly. Ill will from politicians I can live with. Ill will from the American people, I can't."

Kriss received the toss of Jon's third football and read the marking aloud. "FIX OUR FINANCES. Tell us about this one."

"What are your thoughts on prosperity, Wally?"

"Prosperity? Always good to have."

"If you had to guess, what percentage of our population would consider themselves prosperous?"

"I think it would depend on how you defined the term."

Jon wanted an answer. "OK, how would you define it?"

Kriss was never comfortable when his guests started asking the questions. "I'm not sure. I've not given this a thought in this context. I sense you have, though. Let's hear your thoughts."

Jon was ready. "We are the most prosperous country in the world, yet too many of our citizens have fewer than one thousand dollars in savings. A large majority of people in our country live paycheck to paycheck. In totality, our country is prosperous. On average, our citizens are not. How should we fix this? Should we even try to fix it? We are a capitalist society and there is tremendous opportunity for anyone willing to work hard. Those who want to achieve prosperity can. So why try to fix it?"

Kriss was confused and felt the need to interrupt. Why was Jon questioning himself? "Surely, sir, you are not considering more of a welfare state or redistribution of wealth or universal income to reduce income inequality. These are not concepts I would expect to be endorsed by the Jonathon Braxton I know."

"I'm still the man you know, and I would never advocate those misguided governmental means to a bitter end."

"Then what, sir?"

"Wally, you play poker?"

"A little when I was younger, but not for many years."

"You familiar with the game Texas hold 'em?"

"Somewhat familiar," Kriss responded, confused.

"If you play the game, you know it can be cruel. You can have a great hand at the flop and if the price were right, you stay in the game to see if you could make it to the river. But the other players in the game put pressure on you to drop out by betting and raising. You've got a good hand and good prospects for a positive outcome, but the other players at the table with big stacks of chips and often working in conjunction with one another to take you out, make it too costly and risky to stay in. They bet and raise you until you fold. The heavy bettors are at the table working together to separate you from your chips."

"OK, sir, what does poker have to do with our country's finances?"

"I see our taxation system as a game of Texas hold 'em. All our taxpayers are sitting at the table. The big stacks of chips are across from where they sit, stacked in front of the wealthy and special interests. The wealthy and special interests have acquired those chips by way of tax loopholes and designer deductions. Every new tax year they're ready for the next hand and the opportunity to separate industrious Americans from more of their chips. The playing field is not level. The end result? The tax burden to finance this country is shouldered in large part by industrious middle America. The playing field needs better landscaping."

Kriss smiled. "I remember your interview with Todd Chuckman in 2013. You were talking about flattening tax rates and eliminating and minimizing deductions. He had a bit of a meltdown, if I recall."

"Yes. He had quite a meltdown. He told my staff I'd never be invited back on his show, and he's been true to his word. But if I were to go back on his show." Jon turned his gaze from Kriss to the camera. "Todd, you there?" Jon turned his eyes back to Kriss. "I'd tell him I'm going to do everything in my power, and I have a little more than I did when we first met, to do what I said I'd like to. Wally, you balance your checkbook?"

"Frankly no. Mrs. Kriss does."

"Good. At least someone in your household does. Not so in the U.S. Congress. If your household controlled its finances the way this country does, you'd be in one of two places. Either in prison or in debt up to your neck and on a bus heading there."

Kriss picked up his mug and took a swig of root beer. "Would you like to call Mrs. Kriss? She could help you balance the country's books."

"I'm sure she would do a better job than the people who have been doing it. And thank you for your offer, but we're going to try to do this without Mrs. Kriss. First, let's address a question which undoubtedly will be asked by those who disagree with us. They'll ask why we should do it. Why should we cut government spending and focus on balancing our budget when we've been doing the opposite forever? Deficit spending is the norm for most governments today as it is for us, and we're managing. Why take on the pain we would endure if we went down the road to balance our federal budget?"

Kriss interjected. "And Mr. President, you must acknowledge those are valid concerns. Reducing our federal deficit in any kind of accelerated manner would create tremendous hardships for the people of this country."

"I don't doubt it, Wally, and we can thank the weak and feckless leadership this country has been burdened with, particularly since 2008 when our debt to GDP ratio jumped from sixty-eight percent to eighty-two percent in one year. The bailouts of the finance sector combined with the recession which followed set us on a path of irresponsible fiscal policy we're still traveling on. And unfortunately, we're picking up speed. In 2016, our debt to GDP ratio jumped from one hundred percent to one hundred five percent."

Kriss countered. "Sir, we've heard these statistics before, but to most people in this country, they're meaningless. The statistics don't intersect with people's lives."

"And for how long will this be the case? Indefinitely? How long can we continue at our current pace before our foundation cracks and our nation's credit worthiness collapses? We had a great run from the beginning of the internet era in 1993 until 2000. What happened in the dot com space in 2001? We had a great run with real estate from 2002 through 2007. What happened to real estate values in 2008? Today, the numbers are larger and the institutions at risk are an embedded component of our social fabric. Social security, subsidized health care, pensions. In 2001, we lost investments in internet companies. Painful, but not unbearably so. In 2008, we lost financial institutions and real estate values. Considerably more painful. And given how our government responded to those crises with short-term and short-sided responses, and the results we experienced, we have to ask what's next. The bubble is significantly bigger today, and it's tied to everyone."

Kriss countered. "Mr. President, anyone listening to us is no doubt is starting to get concerned. You must realize the impact of your words on the public. Are you not concerned what the result could be of what you're suggesting?"

"Of course I'm concerned. But the American people have the right to know the truth about the fiscal health of their country. They have the right to know how the current executive branch of their government is assessing the situation. They have the right to know what we are prepared to do to address the situation. And the right to know what to expect should the course not be changed."

"All right, sir. You've painted a troubling picture for us. What are you planning to do?"

"Detailing all our plans would be a lengthy conversation we don't have time for now. But let me share a few insights. Our federal budget consists of two primary components. Revenues and expenditures. To lower our federal debt, we either increase revenues, or decrease expenditures, or do both. In the Braxton administration, we will do both. To increase revenues, we're going to fix our taxation system, starting with personal income tax. We're going to push for a flat tax rate system and eliminate all but five personal deductions. And deductions will be capped at a percentage of income. This will cause pain for some, no doubt. But those affected will be larger income earners who have long benefited from deductions not available to most taxpayers. If you look at the allowable deductions in the federal tax code, most are in place to support a special interest. They made it into the tax code because of lobbying and influence peddling. These deductions are in large part what ail us. They are like a cancer. To get better, we must cut them out."

"Mr. President, in your previous statements, you floated a seventeen percent flat income tax rate and an annual cap of deductions at fifteen percent of income. Are those still your numbers?"

"They are and before you go down the road Chuckman did, know we have the data showing our proposals will increase annual federal tax revenues by twenty-five percent, all from higher income earners who have taken advantage of loopholes and deductions. In parallel, at seventeen percent, the tax burden on lower and middle-income earners who do not enjoy the advantage of most deductions will be reduced. The bottom line? Increased revenue, less opportunity for the wealthy and special interests to underpay, and fairer distribution of the burden."

"And expenditures? What is your plan there?"

"We took our first step at our cabinet meeting earlier this week. I informed all our cabinet secretaries, except for the Department of Defense, we are instituting a twenty percent reduction in budget allocation for all Executive branch departments for this coming fiscal year. For too long, our government has normalized waste, fraud, and abuse in allocating our budgets. We have grown a culture of spending without questioning efficiency or efficacy. No more. The time has come to turn the tide, and this is just the beginning. We're looking at other creative ideas all designed to reduce the insatiable appetite our government has for wasteful spending. Will this be painful? No doubt. As painful as accepting the status quo? I think not. Wally, I know we're running out of time. Let's move on."

Jon motioned for Kriss to toss the 'FIX OUR FINANCES' football back and then tossed him the fourth football. Kriss caught it and spun it around to read the marking. "FIX OUR WELL BEING?" he read as a question.

"You're unsure of the meaning or surprised it's included?" the President asked.

"I think a bit of both. Tell us what you mean."

"Wally, we are an unhealthy country. Both physically and mentally. For one to live their best life, they need good health. Why, as a nation, are we so unhealthy? Do you realize eighteen percent of our GDP was spent on health care last year? Three-point-three trillion dollars. Mostly dollars spent after we get sick. Only a fraction spent on preventative care. In the Braxton administration, our focus will be acting on the prevention of illness through the promotion of well-being.

"Our studies into health and well-being show there are two primary causes of illness. One is our environment. We are constantly exposed to toxins, eat unhealthy food, undertake unhealthy habits, fail to exercise, live with high degrees of stress. Each of these factors has been proven to lead to illness and disease. The second primary cause of illness, and this may surprise your viewers, is our own mind as manifested by our perceptions and our subconscious. Or stated differently how we perceive the world around us and how we react to it. I realize this is an unconventional statement from an elected official, and we are still working through our investigation, but we have enough evidence to conclude the human mind and how an individual thinks have considerable influence on an individual's health and well-being. In many cases, more influence than drug treatments. And I'm certain the pharmaceutical industry will take issue with our conclusions. We're talking about their profits here. So be it."

Kriss was uncomfortable with Jon targeting the pharmaceutical industry. The industry which represented his show's largest sponsors.

"That's most unconventional indeed. Do you believe you can influence Americans to accept these theories?"

"These are not theories. There's an abundance of analytical and anecdotal data to consider these concepts anything but fact-based. When people live without pride and purpose, they tend to neglect their well-being. We're going to take steps in our Administration, on top of helping people find pride and purpose in their lives, to help Americans improve their well-being through a series of initiatives designed to focus on helping Americans improve their physical health and improve their mental health."

"Can you share a little about what those initiatives will look like?"

"Again, we've just started working on our game plan, so we don't have everything compiled yet. But in terms of physical health, we all understand how important diet and exercise are. We also know which segments of our population struggle most staying physically fit. One area we will focus on is working with influencers popular within those segments to carry public service messaging forward. We are going to message being physically fit as a popular cultural trend. A key area of our focus will be on healthy food. Educating our population and ear-marking federal grants and low-cost funding to businesses which can provide more healthy food choices, particularly in areas where they are limited. In the Braxton Administration, we will focus on promoting well-being lifestyles. Of primary importance will be education about, availability of, and affordability of healthy food."

Jon continued. "To improve mental health, our mission is more challenging and the solutions more nuanced. Again, we have not yet completed our analysis, but there are promising avenues we will re-search to improve mental health and well-being. To the dismay of our friends in the pharmaceutical industry, the avenues we're considering do not utilize medications or pharmaceuticals. Our efforts will target natural healing therapies. One natural healing concept in particu-lar which fascinates us is the use of natural psychedelic compounds. When administered in micro-doses within a clinical therapeutic envi-ronment, these treatments show tremendous promise. This therapy is showing efficacy in helping mentally ill persons reduce their suffering from addiction and depression resulting from trauma.

"Trauma experienced in an abusive childhood, or an abusive adult relationship. Or from poor self-esteem. Or, with our military veterans who suffer disproportionately from post-traumatic stress syndrome as the result of witnessing the horrors of war. Trauma experienced at a conscious level, then buried into the subconscious as a means of coping. Unfortunately, burying those experiences leaves behind guilt and shame, and leads to destructive behavior. Mentally ill patients, connecting with their subconscious mind in a structured therapeutic environment, confront their trauma. With this connection, they can begin a transformation to better understand their behavior and start forgiving themselves. The first step in addressing mental health."

"Sir, where are you drawing these conclusions from? I'm not aware of this research."

"Wally, sixty years ago in this country, there was no shortage of well-documented studies from reputable medical institutions showing promise using these natural compounds to alleviate the effects of addiction and depression. Unfortunately, Richard Nixon shut down all this research in the late 1960s to fight a war on drugs and classified these natural compounds as illegal substances. The Braxton administration will support restarting this research with funding and legislative support. We hope our efforts will lead to effective treatments for mental illness using naturally available compounds instead of dangerous drug and narcotic therapies."

Jon motioned for Kriss to toss the ball back. Wally put his hand on the football as if a quarterback might. He turned the ball around in his hand, admiring his grip, and then confidently flipped the ball back to Jon who caught it, and placed it on its tee. He then reached for football number five and flipped it to Kriss.

"FIX OUR FUTURE? We have only a moment left, Mr. President."

"Wally, we believe a byproduct of the plans we are working on to fix our culture, our politics, our finances, and our well-being will mean a better future for future generations of Americans. But only if the decisions we make take the future into account. We must understand the ramifications and unintended consequences of what we do before we do it. If we decide to solve a problem, but the decision creates other problems counterproductive to our intentions, then it's the wrong decision. Washington is not good at assessment or considering unintended consequences. Too often, decisions are made for political expediency or short-term pain-relief. In hindsight, they prove to be bad decisions. To fix our future, we need to undertake better decision making. Going forward, every policy decision we make will be heavily weighted by anticipated future outcomes. Our policy decisions will be influenced to a greater degree by longer term desired outcomes rather than shorter term political gains."

The hour for Big News Sunday had concluded. Kriss saw the signal from his producer to close the show. The 'FIX OUR FUTURE' football was sitting on the table in front of him. He reached for it with his right hand and again gripped it as a quarterback would. He again looked admiringly at his grip and then at Jon. "Mr. President, as usual, a most provocative conversation. Thank you and please thank the First Lady for joining us."

Kriss tossed the football to Jon, then turned to the camera to address his all-time high nine million viewers. "To you at home, from Washington DC, welcome to Braxton Time. We wish you a pleasant Sunday."

Chapter 12

Jackrabbitt

The opulent Dassault Falcon 900LX corporate jet, property of Costello Labs, the world's largest pharmaceutical corporation, crossed into Illinois airspace. There was a crew of five aboard to serve a passenger list consisting solely of one former president. The immaculately accoutered vessel, customized to carry twelve passengers in utmost luxury, embarked from Martinsburg Airfield in Northern Virginia at eleven a.m. eastern standard time. One hundred and ten minutes later, it began its approach into DuPage Airport, thirty miles west of downtown Chicago.

The landing was smooth, and the Falcon taxied into a nearby hangar. As the jet came to a stop, the hangar doors were closed before the exit door from the jet was opened. Wil Carrington exited with no one in view. Also discreetly parked in the hangar was a black Cadillac Escalade with overly tinted dark windows. The former president made his way down the aircraft's exit stairway and into the vehicle.

The Escalade left the hangar and began its fifty-mile northwest drive towards a luxurious private residence on the western bank of Lake Michigan in Glencoe, Illinois. The home of Jackson Raymond Abbott, the CEO and Chairman of the Board of Costello Labs, affectionately and not-so-much, known as 'Jackrabbit.' Costello Labs enjoyed the distinction of being the world's largest producer of insulin and manufacturer of diabetes therapies and testing equipment.

Meeting at Jackrabbit's secluded private estate insured no one would know of this reunion between the former president and one of his most vocal supporters during his tenure in the White House. Support which included significant campaign contributions before and during Wil's time in office. And serious donations to the Carrington Charitable Trust and the Carrington Library Foundation thereafter.

The Escalade pulled into a secured garage where the driver exited and circled the vehicle to open the door for Wil. A moment later, the former president entered the residence through a service door and was escorted into the vast library. Waiting for him was a monster of a man, standing six foot seven and weighing close to three hundred and fifty pounds. He was dressed in white tennis shorts and a blue polo shirt. On his head was nothing but a clean-shaven scalp, shining illuminate as if it were a spotlight atop a large lighthouse.

Abbott approached Carrington to shake his hand. "Mr. President! How great to see you again! How long has it been?"

Carrington never genuinely enjoyed Abbott's company but always treated him with the respect a large financial donor to a president was due. He held out his hand. "Hello Jack. It's good to see you. I think the last time we saw one another was in 2003."

Suddenly, two extremely large and upset adult Doberman pinschers raced into the library from the adjoining sitting room. They were barking and snarling and in attack mode as they raced straight for the former President.

"HEEL," Jackrabbit boomed.

The two dogs stopped abruptly at Jackrabbit's side, not six inches from Wil's crotch. They sat but were still snarling and growling with all teeth now presented. The former president was in a state of shock.

"NICE," Jackrabbit commanded. On cue, the two Dobermans transformed into mild and well mannered puppies. They both stood and whimpered and nuzzled their snouts into each of Wil's hands, petitioning for affection. The former President, still in shock, allowed himself to breathe and gently patted the heads of the two dogs who, but for Abbott's commands, would have mauled him to death.

"OUT," barked Abbott and the dogs merrily left the way they entered the library.

"I'm sorry Wil, I had no idea my babies were in the house. I apologize for your discomfort and imagine you could use a drink. Macallan, three fingers, one ice cube?"

Wil was still too shaken to speak. He nodded. A moment later Abbott's butler entered the room with a silver tray holding two goblets, each containing three fingers of forty-year aged Macallan scotch. They both grabbed their drinks.

"Let's go out onto the veranda. We've got a magnificent view of the lake today. Are you hungry? I can have Claude cook us up a couple of steaks?"

Wil was starting to regain his composure after staring down an untimely and uncomfortable death at the hands of Jackrabbit's babies. "No thanks Jack. The drink will do me."

Abbott laughed at the former president's unease. "Come on, let's go sit down."

The two settled into a comfortable setting overlooking the banks of Lake Michigan. It was mid-afternoon, and the sun was shining brightly, enhanced by a cloudless, deep blue sky. Abbott's drink was empty a moment later and Claude brought him another. Wil was still nursing his, not yet completely recovered from the episode with Jackrabbit's sweet little puppies.

"Wil, the question I've been dying to ask you since Heather left the campaign is, what the fuck happened? I mean, you had one foot in the White House and the other crossing the threshold. You were so close. We were so close. So close to being back in business together, and then what? What happened?"

Wil traveled to Chicago at Abbott's request, though the former president had him on his short list to enlist for his mission, eventually. He was keenly aware of the power and influence Abbott and Costello wielded in Congress. Abbott's invitation was timely, and Wil accepted it as an opportunity to vet his former 'colleague' while not divulging anything of consequence. When he stepped off the Costello private jet three hours earlier, he was optimistic Jackrabbit would be a valuable asset to the cause. The last half hour in his home, and the interlude with Jackrabbit's monsters, had introduced doubt. He decided he would play his cards close to the vest. And under no circumstance divulge he had compromised Heather's Blackberry.

"Jack, I have to say I don't know what the fuck she's doing. And she doesn't confide in me. Sometimes it seems like she's really committed to this asshole and his cockamamie agenda. And then sometimes I look at her and I'm not sure this isn't a grand scheme she's concocted to take power."

"Come on, Wil, you can't be serious. If she wanted power, she had it. She was right there. The election was hers."

"Not according to a lot of the polling I saw," Wil lied. "It's possible Heather felt she was truly going to lose, and it would be the end of her career. And by doing what she did, she could somehow live to fight another day."

"OK, then how did she know Braxton would tap her for VP?"

"Only thing I can think of is Jeffrey Claymore. He had the ears, eyes, and hearts of both. He introduced them in 2012. And was in the middle counseling them both all the way to the election. He was in the house the night Heather told Braxton her plan to leave the campaign."

"Sonofabitch. Is your wife really that crafty? Holy shit."

"Yeah, the thing is, Braxton has already announced he's only in for one term. So worst case, she's the nominee in 2020. For which party, your guess is as good as mine. Best case, Braxton decides he doesn't want the job and resigns, or he fucks up and gets himself impeached and we move in earlier."

"Frankly, Wil. I like the best case better. The longer this guy stays in office, the more of a threat he is to my business. The more he will become addicted to power. And the greater the chance he will run for re-election."

"I feel the same, Jack."

"Good. I imagine you're aware of HHS reaching out to us. They're interested in buying significant amounts of our insulin."

"I expected he would come to you once I heard about his deal with North Korea."

"Yeah. And it's a shit deal for us. He wants our insulin at six percent margin and there's no quid pro quo. And at the same time, he's funding other companies who could kill our market with their research. Just who the fuck does he think he is?"

This precarious position the Braxton administration had placed Costello Labs in was openly apparent to Wil. Abbott and Costello stood to lose billions of dollars in diabetes related revenue if Angela was successful in her efforts to find the cure. Wil knew his interests were in alignment with Abbott's. Now he only need ascertain if he and Jackrabbit could once again work together.

Abbott continued. "Sounds like you're in a pickle, Wil. What are you thinking these days? I think the best-case scenario could be helped along with a good plan, help from our friends in Congress, and some old-fashioned Wil Carrington execution. You?"

"I don't have anything in mind right now, Jack," Wil lied again. "It's early. I'm still working to get deeper into Heather's head and to see how Braxton steers the boat. But I will welcome your help down the road if we decide to put something into action. I assume you'd be onboard to help us?"

"Of course, Wil. Tomorrow is too long for this guy to stay in office. If you have a way to move him out, I'm with you. The sooner the better. I can line up lots of senators and congressmen to join us. In fact, I have an idea to run by you if you promise you won't run it by Heather. Not sure I trust her."

"OK. Shoot."

"Let's say we reach a deal to sell Braxton insulin for North Korea. And let's say once the insulin gets there and gets into the bloodstream of the North Koreans, it doesn't quite work out too well and people start getting sick. How would this blow back on Braxton?"

"What are you suggesting, Jack? Tainting the insulin? It would never work. All your product will be sampled, evaluated, and certified by the FDA before it's cleared for export. If it were tainted in any way, it wouldn't be certified. It would never leave our shores."

The moment those words left his mouth, Wil realized the true magnitude of what Jackrabbit was advancing. The number of innocent people who would be harmed or killed if Jackson Raymond Abbott had his way entered his consciousness.

As Wil processed Abbott's words, the CEO offered a gentle reminder. "Wil, I know you've been out of office for sixteen years and perhaps you forgot. I own the FDA."

Chapter 13

Fix Our Culture

"Jeffrey Claymore to see the President."

"Welcome Pastor Claymore. I'm Rosemary Barnett. The President is expecting you. How was your trip in from Philadelphia?"

"It was great, thank you, Ms. Barnett. I've never been on Air Force One before. It's a nice little ride."

"I know the President wanted you to be comfortable and is looking forward to meeting with you. He's out on the West Lawn and wanted me to show you the way when you got here. Please follow me."

Rosemary led Jeffrey to a doorway which led outside to the expansive lawn outside the West Wing where he found Jon and Luke tossing a football. Luke had just delivered a thirty-yard tight spiral the President caught with ease. As soon as he secured the catch, he noticed Jeffrey approaching out of the corner of his eye. Jon moved the ball from a cradle of his left arm into his right hand and walked towards the pastor with a huge smile on his face. The two men reached each other and embraced, with Jon still holding the ball in his right hand.

As they were doing so, Luke sprinted over. When he reached the two of them, the pastor let go of Jon and embraced his son. "Luke.

My main man. How are you doing, son? And how are you enjoying White House life?"

"It's cool Jeffrey. The food is so good. And the people are nice. I've got a cool bedroom and I love the work me and my mom are doing. I miss the beach a little, but it's OK. My mom promised me a surfing trip to Hawaii this summer, so I can live with a few months off."

Jeffrey laughed. "You are a special young man, Lucas Braxton. And yes, the work you and your mother are doing is so important. She invited me to meet with her this afternoon to fill me in. I assume you'll be there?"

"You bet."

"And I want to hear all about your new friends in North Korea."

Luke was excited to share his experiences with the Pastor. "Are you staying for dinner? We can talk about it then."

Jon responded for Jeffrey. "That answer is yes."

"Cool. Hey dad, I've got to get going. I have a conference call with mom and two diabetes researchers from Harvard. Pastor, I'll see you at three in my mom's office." Luke ran towards the same door Jeffrey had used for entry to the West Lawn five minutes earlier.

"Jon, he's getting so big and so wise. And he is growing into his role as the world's face of Type 1 diabetes effortlessly. You must be enormously proud, but tell me, how is his health holding up?"

"If you talk to Luke, he's fine. But the truth is his body does not utilize injected insulin well. His numbers continue to jump around all over the place even though he follows all the protocols to the letter, and he's great at controlling his carbohydrate intake. The doctors have shared a concern about his glucose level instability creating undue stress on his organs. They're seeing toxicity in his liver and are concerned his other organs may start reacting to stress as well. We're monitoring it closely."

"Oh Jon. I'm so sorry to hear this. We will all pray harder for him. And we will all pray harder for you and Angela to be successful in your mission to bring us the cure."

"Thank you, Jeffrey. Let's head back in and go into my office."

"Good. I'm curious why you asked to see me today."

As the two were walking back towards the same entry door Luke had just sprinted through, Jon flipped him the football he was still holding. The pastor snagged it and rotated the ball in his hands so he could see the three-word marking, which he read aloud as they were walking. "FIX OUR CULTURE. Hmm."

When the two made it back into the Oval Office, Rosemary buzzed his intercom. Jon and Jeffrey were already seated on a pair of matching eight-foot sofas facing one another in a sitting area adjacent to the President's desk. The President leaned forward and pressed the intercom button on the phone atop a coffee table which separated the two sofas.

"What is it, Rosemary?"

"Mr. President, the Vice President is running late on a call with the Japanese Prime Minister and said she would be here in fifteen minutes. She asked me to ask you not to wait for her and to get started with the Pastor."

"Thank you."

Jeffrey was grateful for her delay. "This is good Jon. I wanted to speak with you briefly without Heather in the room."

The Pastor was still holding the football. Jon stood and motioned to him to hand him the ball, which he then placed on an empty kicking tee sitting atop the credenza to the left of his desk. The 'FIX OUR CULTURE' ball had been returned to its place with the other four he had previewed on Big News Sunday three days earlier.

"OK, you've got your chance. What's on your mind?" Jon asked as he made his way back to the sofa.

"How much time have you spent with Wil Carrington since the election?"

"Nothing significant. Everything Wil knows, Heather knows, and she's great at informing me. And I don't think he particularly likes me. Wil hasn't really made himself visible around here."

"Does this concern you in any way, Jon?"

"No. Should it?"

"I've known Wil Carrington since 1987. I can only imagine how he is processing the sequence of events which took him from the doorstep of returning to the spotlight of the White House, to the obscurity of the Naval Observatory. The night in Heather's home when she informed you of her decision, I was observing Wil. And I came away with a distinct sense he would not be a friend of your administration. I felt I should let you know. My advice is to be mindful of him."

"My father-in-law had the same advice. And what about Heather? Need I be concerned about her intentions?"

"No. You do not. As well as I know Wil, I know Heather even better. I am confident she is one hundred percent with you. But I am also certain Wil's acrimony, hidden or otherwise, is creating significant difficulty for her. All I wanted to do by sharing this was for you to be aware he could pose problems for your administration. And for you to be aware, Heather could be under duress from the expectations of her husband."

"What expectations are those?"

"Being perfectly candid, that she occupy your office as soon as possible."

The intercom buzzed again, and Jon again leaned forward and hit the button. "The Vice President?"

"Yes," replied Rosemary.

"Send her in."

When Heather entered the Oval, she saw Jeffrey and rushed straight to him for an embrace. Jon stood as well. When the embrace had run its course, the three of them sat. Jon and Heather on one sofa facing Jeffrey on the other. And unbeknownst to the three of them, they were joined by Wil and Sidney, courtesy of Heather's compromised Blackberry she had just placed on the table between them.

"It's so good to see you, Jeffrey. Thank you for coming on such short notice. Since Jon's appearance with Kriss last Sunday, all he's been talking about is getting you here to help him."

"Well, here I am. What is it you'd like me to do?"

Jon stood and started pacing around the Oval. Jeffrey and Heather each followed him with their eyes. "Jeffrey, I think our country needs an intervention."

The Pastor concurred. "As a man who often speaks for God, I would certainly agree."

"Why am I not surprised," Jon mused. "Since I've been on the job, I've had the opportunity to look at the current state of this country from a different viewpoint. And I also have the pleasure of everyone I come into contact with providing me with their viewpoints as well. With all these lenses and given what my job is, I can't just look and listen. I have the responsibility to examine, to assess, and to respond."

"And knowing you the way I do, why I am I not surprised," Jeffrey mused in return.

"Touché," Jon responded.

"And once you're satisfied with your examination and your assessment, how do you plan to respond, Mr. President?"

"My dear friend, this is why you are here. I need you to put things in order in Philadelphia. Let Darby take over at Faith Central. Find a new pastor for First Pentecostal. Move to Washington. And take an office in the White House."

"Ah, I see. And just what is it I would be doing here besides spending more time with Luke?"

"You'd be doing what the nation's first Culture Czar needs to do to get this country back on better footing. And we need this desperately because from my examination and my assessment, too many people in this country have built and are living their lives atop a shaky foundation."

The pastor contemplated his response for a second. "I have my own reasons for believing what you are saying is true. And you know where I'm coming from. But I'd like to hear from you why you believe as you do."

Jon responded. "I'm concerned about the culture of this nation. It is degrading rapidly before us in full view. We have too much addiction, disease, depression, chaos, obesity, crime, poverty. We have too many people in this country leading meaningless lives. Lives without purpose or hope or pride. And unfortunately, no one here in Washington seems seriously interested in doing anything meaningful to change things. Everyone here sees this country's problems through political prisms. As a result, no one sees our problems clearly. Any reasonable or viable solution which makes its way into the legislative discourse passes a through a political process before it can be seriously considered. And the process is stunningly efficient in stripping out anything resembling reasonable or viable, especially when those solutions conflict with the interests of our politicians or our bureaucrats or those individuals and organizations supporting them."

"I'm not surprised to hear you say this, Jon. I watched you with Kriss last Sunday."

"Then you heard the Braxton administration wants to do something about it. And the first thing we need to do is to have you here with authority. And I don't mean just the moral authority you already have. I have ideas I want to put into play, and I want to run them all by you and get your feedback and your criticisms. And if my ideas are worthy in your eyes, your approval. I want the Braxton administration to start a renaissance in this country, and we need someone to be the face of this transformation. And I can't think of a better face than yours."

The Pastor and the Vice President laughed. "Of course, I'm willing to help Jon, and I understand your perspectives and agree with your perceptions. I see and fight these battles every day in Sharswood. But our ideas about solutions may not be in alignment. I would offer our society is in the condition it is because we are losing touch with God. If you want my help with solutions, God must be included."

"Jeffrey, you know we have a convention in this country of maintaining the separation of church and state. The country was founded on the idea of religious liberty. We can't do what I want to do and include a Christian God as part of our efforts. The country already protects the right of one to seek the spiritual path of their choice. There's no shortage of churches, synagogues, or mosques if anyone is so inclined. If people want help from God, it is already widely available. But what I want to do is put the weight of the federal government behind an effort to enable one to find help from a different source. A source within."

The Pastor nodded in partial agreement. "I'm not sure we're not saying the same thing. If someone wants help from within, the best avenue is God's love."

Jon had anticipated the Pastor's viewpoint and was undeterred. "I'm not smart enough to comment on that. But I can tell you what I want to do has to be secular. If it's attached to the federal government, we must maintain church and state separation. If not, the left will never let our ideas see daylight. We'll need Congress to partner with us. As it is, we're in for a dogfight, as we'll be exposing their policies as the root cause of many of our issues."

The Pastor agreed. "There's no doubt there, unfortunately."

"So?" Jon asked, knowing the question was vague.

"So what?"

"If we had a plan to help people in such a way which would help fix our culture and it was completely secular, would you move to Washington and work with me?"

"To anyone else, I would say no. I'm not negotiable on God." Jeffrey smiled. "To you, Jon, I would say, tell me more."

Jon was ready with his closing argument. "Let's help people lead better lives. Let's do it by founding a network of culture centers with storefronts in our inner cities. Let's make this organization a public private partnership so we can generate funding and support from both the federal government and the private sector. Let's develop a curriculum and provide resources to help people overcome the negativity in their lives with methods people can use to lead purposeful and meaningful lives. Let's work with colleges and universities to start an instructor program to train college students interested in public service to deliver our curriculum. Let's help our instructors establish a career in this organization to help people make profound changes. Let's develop a strong social media presence and let's develop a smartphone app to spread the word. Let's find the formula for helping any individual in this country who wants to live a better life, to do so."

"Sounds familiar Jon. It's a similar message to Win-The-Day's."

"Exactly Jeffrey, but instead of helping kids, we help people who have moved into adulthood and have not yet found purpose. What do you say? Are you willing to serve this country as its first Culture Czar?"

"I'm honored you'd consider me Jon, but I can't give you an answer right now. And as for God, we could put him on the sidelines, but his will is strong and we may not be able to keep him there."

It was three in the afternoon when Jeffrey Claymore was shown into the office of the First Lady. Angela was not there, but Luke was seated in one of the two guest chairs in front of his mother's desk. Jeffrey walked in and sat down on the other. "Where's your mom?"

"She's running late in a meeting. She said she'd be in here in fifteen minutes and asked me to entertain you."

"Good. We have a little time alone. I wanted to speak with you privately, Luke."

"Sure. What's up?"

"Tell me, how is your health? How are you feeling lately?"

"Most days I feel fine. Some days, not so much. But I'm OK."

"And how are you doing with managing your blood sugar levels? Are you following all your protocols?"

"Definitely. I'm watching the carbs and testing my blood three times a day. And when my sugars are high, I take a shot right away."

"Your father tells me your blood sugar numbers tend to bounce around and your body does not always manage your insulin injections well. He says your health is not as good as it should be."

"I know. But I'm doing everything I can."

"Are you?" the Pastor snapped back in a stern and forceful tone Luke had never heard from him before. He was taken aback.

"I think I am. What do you mean?"

The pastor returned to his calm, tranquil voice. "Luke, when I was seventeen, I was in prison for armed robbery. I stayed mostly to myself. Everything and everyone scared me. When I had out-of-cell privilege, I would often walk by a large, windowed room, which was where prisoners would greet and talk with their visitors. Now prison is not a happy place. The prisoners and the guards never laughed. Never smiled. But there was one prisoner who was different. He always seemed happy. The prisoner's name was Archie, and he had a regular guest. A priest. Every time I walked by the room when Archie was there with the priest, I would see them both smiling and laughing. I couldn't understand how and why Archie could smile and laugh while being incarcerated. One day I saw Archie in the exercise yard, and I approached him. I asked him about his visits with the priest. I asked him what they were always laughing and smiling about.

"He said he and the priest were comparing the conversations they were having with God. He said they would laugh at how similar and enlightening the conversations were. They laughed at how uncanny God's lessons were in helping them both see the world in a light which would provide them peace and happiness. They laughed at their good fortune God would talk to them. I'll never forget Archie and I'll never forget how his good nature in the face of the overwhelming darkness and depression of prison life changed the course of my life."

"What happened to Archie?"

"Two months later, he was released when a judge granted him a new trial. His lawyer had uncovered additional evidence and eventually all the charges against him were reversed. He had become a free man."

"Are you still in contact with him?"

"Not any longer, but six months after he was released, Archie sent me a gift." The Pastor reached his hands behind his neck and un-clasped a chain dangling a crucifix on his chest. He pulled the chain and crucifix from his neck and placed it in his left hand. "When I received this from Archie and put it on, my life changed its course.

Good things happen when you talk to God, Luke. When was the last time you did so?"

Luke was embarrassed and dropped his eyes. "Prayed? I don't remember."

"Look at me, son." Luke raised his gaze to meet the Pastor's. "God wants to hear from you. He has chosen you to do important things with your life. He loves you and wants you to be well. And he wants you to talk to him. Promise me you will do so."

"I promise."

Jeffrey extended his left hand towards Luke. "Please take this. I've been wearing it for forty-five years and it has served me well and it is time for it to move along. I can think of no one I know who deserves to have it more than you."

Luke extended his right hand and allowed the Pastor to place the chain and crucifix in it. Luke closed his eyes and bowed his head as tears formed. The door to Angela's office then burst open, and she blew into the room, excited to see and talk to Jeffrey Claymore, only to find both her son and the pastor sitting quietly in a somber state.

She was concerned as she walked from the doorway towards her desk. Jeffrey turned his head over his right shoulder and glanced at Angela with a reassuring smile. She relaxed a bit as she slid into her chair.

"Luke, are you OK honey?"

"Yeah, uh mom can you put this on me?" He handed her the chain and crucifix.

"Of course." She stood and looked at Jeffrey. "Come here," she said as she returned her eyes to her son.

He stood and moved around to where she was standing. She affixed the chain around his neck. She turned to again look at Jeffrey, not knowing what to say.

He did. "Well, Mrs. Braxton. When are you going to tell me about the **TYPE 1—YOU'RE DONE** Project?"

Chapter 14

Thirty Million Vials?

T he conversation at the White House dinner in the first family's residence that evening started as a recollection of Luke's, Angela's, Abby's, and Heather's visit to North Korea. A conversation which included the first details Jeffrey Claymore heard of the historic encounter. And the first details for Wil and Sidney, as they were listening in courtesy of Heather's compromised Blackberry resting comfortably in her purse next to the dinner table.

"I was so nervous and when it was my turn to speak, I forgot to turn my mic on. And Kim Jong-Un started screaming at me."

"Come on Luke. Don't be so dramatic," Angela quipped.

"Yeah mom, well he stood up and was talking loudly. And it freaked me out."

Jon, Darla, and the Pastor laughed heartily.

"And the veins in his neck. I thought they were going to pop out," Luke excitedly recounted.

"They were bulging quite a bit," Heather added.

"But all's well which ends well. Right Luke. Between Kim and Foreign Minister Ri, it seems like you've got some powerful new friends," said the President.

"You're right, dad. They've been great to me since our visit, and I'm really excited about how we're going to help them with better insulin. I'd like to go back to North Korea sometime."

"By the way," Angela interjected, "I received news late this afternoon on insulin. Heather, you're familiar with Costello Labs, I'm assuming?"

"Oh yes, highly familiar. Wil interacted with them quite a bit during his term. We both got to know their CEO, the pompous jackass Jackson Raymond Abbott, quite well," she responded with contempt. "Why do you ask?"

"With Costello being the world's largest manufacturer of insulin, we approached them with a proposal to help us with our North Korea commitment. Late this afternoon, we received a formal outright rejection. No counteroffer. No suggestion of negotiation. They slammed the door on us. Any ideas where we go with them?"

"Definitely sounds like Jackrabbit."

Angela chuckled. "Jackrabbit?"

"Your husband and Kim Jong-Un aren't the only ones with nicknames. What was the gist of the proposal?"

"We offered the federal government would broker a deal between Costello and the PRNK, where the PRNK would commit to buy thirty million vials over the next two years. We appealed to Costello's sense of patriotism aligning this purchase with our efforts to motivate North Korea to temper their nuclear weapons ambitions."

The Vice President was skeptical. "Knowing Jack Abbott as I do, I doubt the appeal of patriotism had any impact. Did you propose a price?"

"We did," Angela replied. "We did some research to estimate their cost to manufacture a vial of their various strengths of insulin and offered them cost plus a small markup."

"How much?"

"Twelve dollars per vial," Angela replied, questioning her judgment under Heather's line of inquiry.

Heather nodded and firmed her lips. "A three-hundred and sixty-million-dollar deal. That would bubble up to Jack's level. Your rejection was directly from the horse's mouth, no pun intended."

"What should we do?"

"Nothing," Heather responded confidently. "You'll hear back from them in a few days with a counteroffer."

It was later that evening when Wil Carrington's cell phone vibrated from an incoming call. The display read *'CallerID unknown.'* He answered cautiously.

"Hello."

"Do you know the way to San Jose?"

As Wil was typically the one making the calls dictating the need for verbal authentication, he rarely had to offer security handshake responses. And always had trouble remembering them, as Mark Parker changed them on a monthly timetable.

"Uh, I do, but we can live wait, uh. Shit, I forgot."

Sidney laughed to himself and dropped the call.

Wil had recognized his voice. "Goddammit Sidney," he yelled into the thin air shrouding his phone.

A moment later, his phone vibrated again with *'CallerID unknown'* on the display.

Wil answered. "It's the way to live another day."

"Not bad Wil. This time, it only took you two tries."

"What the fuck do you want, Sidney?"

"Were you listening in on Heather's two conversations with Braxton and Claymore today?"

"Yeah, interesting stuff. What about it?"

"After what we heard today, we may have something we can work with."

"For chrissakes, it's about time. Fill me in," the former president offered with a blend of frustration and relief.

"Last week I lobbed trial balloons to my associates on Capitol Hill and uncovered something which could provide us a pathway. Especially after what we heard today. Seems like your old friend Bob Krueger has been organizing a posse in the Senate to go after Braxton. He's got twenty-two other senators showing interest, and they've met three times in the last two weeks. And they also have one Jackson Raymond Abbott involved. To what degree my source couldn't tell me, but he knows Abbott has been in on the last two meetings. Given what we heard from the First Lady today, I thought you might find Krueger's efforts interesting. Since you used to pal around with Abbott, I figured you could find out what they're up to. And I'll work with my sources in the Senate to find out what Krueger's game is. Once we know more, we can figure out how we might assist them."

Wil was debating whether to fill Sidney in on his meeting in Chicago with Abbott. He decided to hold back for the moment. "Not surprising Senator Krueger, the senior senator from the great state of Illinois, and Jack Abbott are working together on this. They've partnered on quite a bit if of shadiness over the last thirty years."

Sidney was cautious. "If you do talk to Abbott, don't get into any specifics right now. Keep your questions general. We need to protect my source. Keep your distance from any details of their plans for a little while in case the shit hits the fan. Remember, you need to keep plausible deniability in your back pocket."

Wil's frustration was building. "And just how will I do this, Sidney? How do I ask Abbott what they're cooking up and then act uninterested to know any details?"

"Gee Wil. You're the former President of the Harvard Law School Alumni and of the United States. Thought you had skills in this area."

"And you're a fucking premier political strategist. This is what you're paid for."

The following evening at the Naval Observatory residence of the Vice President was dinner for two. Wil wanted quiet time with his wife to do fact finding. He was interested in understanding what the cabal of twenty U.S. Senators plus one gigantic pharmaceutical corporate Chairman of the Board might be concocting. He was concerned whatever deeds they were planning could potentially position Heather as unfortunate collateral damage. He knew Jack Abbott would throw her under an eighteen-wheeler without hesitation if it served his purposes. And Jack would unhesitatingly send his two Doberman babies for his crotch for the same reason. The former president had concluded his encounter with the Dobermans on the banks of Lake Michigan was anything but unintentional.

For Wil to claw his way back to the White House as the First Gentlemen, Heather had to be left unscarred. If the plan under formulation in the bowels of the Senate posed any risk to Heather's political career, it had to be stopped. There was always 2020 in play if they had to wait. Despite Wil's longstanding cordial relationship with Abbott, he well understood the possibility Heather had crossed a red line. Her decision to join Braxton and become a party to the policy decisions coming from the Braxton administration, toxic to the interests of Abbott and Costello, could well have left the both of them no road back to the good graces of Jackrabbit.

On the other hand, if the Krueger-Abbott plan did not put Heather in jeopardy, he reasoned it was all he had to work with at the moment. He concluded it was worth investigating. And joining their cabal if their plan would accomplish his goals. He rationalized assisting Krueger would give him visibility and potential control of any activities they may be crafting which could pose harmful to his wife's future opportunities. Tonight was for fishing for information which could prove valuable to the mission.

Wil decided an upbeat and cheery demeanor was in order. "How was your day today, honey? Anything interesting you can tell me about?"

"Jeffrey Claymore paid Jon and I a visit in the White House yesterday. It was great to see him."

"What a surprise," Wil lied. "How is Jeffrey? What was he doing in Washington?"

"He's doing well. Jon invited him. He had ideas he wanted Jeffrey's opinion on."

"Opinions about the ideas he discussed on Kriss' show last week?"

"Yes." Heather wasn't interested in sharing any details.

Wil pressed on. "Seems odd. Jeffrey is not really a policy guy, but I'm not sure it would phase Jon. What did Jon do? Offer him a job or something?"

Heather thought it curious Wil would ask and was uncomfortable confirming it. "No."

"Come on, honey. Share things with me. I'm sure I'll be able to help. What's the latest with North Korea?"

"Kim is behaving better. We're seeing evidence he's drawing down his nuclear weapon ambitions."

"That's great honey. Is this tied to the offer to help North Korea with insulin?"

The thought came to Heather to turn the tables and ask about Jack Abbott. Could she uncover any intel which would help Angela and the upcoming insulin purchase negotiations?

"I think yes, but we don't know for sure. As you know, Kim is hard to read. And about the insulin offer, Angela is shopping for a large quantity, and they've approached Costello. Have you had any conversations with Jack Abbott lately? Any chance you might help us in the negotiations?"

"Thirty million vials are a substantial number. You should have decent leverage. Glad to help. I'll poke around and see what I can learn."

Chapter 15

The Plan of Attack

L egislative power in the State of Illinois is executed by a general assembly consisting of elected officials from fifty-nine 'legislative' districts and one-hundred-eighteen 'representative' districts.
Each legislative district elects one representative to serve in the Illinois
State Senate, and each representative district elects one official to serve
in the Illinois House of Representatives.

Robert Krueger served tours of duty in both the Illinois state Senate
and Representative bodies before aspiring to the U.S. Senate in 1976.
He had always been a staunch liberal democrat and rode the wave
which swept Jimmy Carter into the White House, though his election
was assured given the strong democrat majority in his state. Once in
the Senate and armed with the knowledge and backing of Chicago's
political machinery, Krueger quickly rose through the ranks and assumed powerful committee chairmanships when the democrats were
in the majority. And influential minority leadership positions during
the few occasions they were not.

The pharmaceutical industry, with three of the world's largest
firms based in and around Chicago, was particularly fond of Senator
Krueger. Fond enough for the industry to be a continuous supporter

over the past thirty years building and maintaining a huge campaign war chest for their favorite son. A war chest Senator Krueger put to maximum use to maintain power and a lavish lifestyle for himself and his family.

In 2015, when Jon Braxton announced his ELECT resolution and its provisions to remove private money from federal office election campaigns, Bob Krueger felt a laser pointer squarely on his back. Since Jon's first public statement of his intent to reform federal office campaign financing, swiftly ending the political career of the then Congressman and now President became Senator Krueger's most important personal agenda.

In congruence with the Senator's disdain for the newly elected president, was the rage consuming Jackson Raymond Abbott. Jon and Angela Braxton's desire to speed up the development of the cure for Type 1 diabetes could prove financially devastating for Costello Labs should they be successful. Abbott and Costello profited handsomely from the disease, which prevented the Type 1 diabetic's body from producing insulin. By replacing this deficiency with lab-created insulin, produced in mass quantities at obscenely high margins, Costello earned billions. If through the efforts of the Braxton's, the bodies of Type 1 diabetics restarted internal manufacturing of the hormone replacing Costello's production lines, their profits would take an enormous hit.

Krueger and Abbott had a longstanding, mutually beneficial, and lucrative relationship, which predated Jonathon Braxton's entrance into politics by thirty years. Over the course of their enduring association, their 'modus operandi' had never been challenged. Now, in the presence of a common foe, their association took on added significance. They both agreed it was imperative they virtually stop at nothing to eliminate the threat now posed by the current president.

—◦◆◦—

The Chicago meetings between Abbott and Krueger were always on the down low. Always just the two of them. Always at Abbott's luxurious estate on the banks of Lake Michigan. Krueger requested this latest meeting after he tuned in to the Wallis Kriss show the previous Sunday and watched the President discuss his intent to relaunch his campaign finance reform plan. Krueger's motivation to eliminate the President had reached an apex. It was time to put a plan into action. The two were seated where Abbott and Wil Carrington had congregated five days earlier. Krueger was unaware of that meeting and Abbott planned to keep it concealed for the time being. Abbott was unsure how committed Wil was to taking Braxton out sooner rather than later and was feeling he may have opened up too soon by sharing his thoughts on tainting the insulin he would eventually agree to sell to North Korea.

"Another drink, Bob?"

His answer, "sure", was still crossing his lips when Claude appeared with another Bacardi rum and coke.

"What do you think it will take to get him to resign, Jack? And how long will it take?"

"Not soon enough," Abbott replied as he brought a tumbler filled with scotch to his lips. Krueger was comforted, though not surprised, to hear Abbott as motivated as he was. Abbott continued. "Our best strategy is to open multiple fronts. Your job, Senator, is to create as many legislative hurdles as you can to frustrate the hell out of him. Make it as hard as possible, if not impossible, for him to get anything done. Do your guys have the balls to go up against Braxton's momentum?"

Kreuger was confident. "We can throw up roadblocks. We've got twenty-two hard line Senators on board who want to see him fail. Nine are Republicans, and six of those are committee chairs. We can inflict severe damage to any legislation he wants to push or spending he wants to do, starting with his stupid 'fix the culture' crap. The Republican chairs for Appropriations and Health, Education, and Labor are in our camp. It's possible we can influence our like-minded colleagues in the House, and kill, reduce, or delay any funding he's looking for. Braxton made scores of enemies during his two terms on the hill. We can leverage the animosity his efforts generated. But I'm concerned about Heather Carrington. She's holding her friends in Congress. It will be hard to keep a lid on this thing."

"Let me worry about the Carrington's" Abbott assured him.

"OK, they're yours. You said multiple fronts. What others are you thinking?" Krueger asked.

"For one, we start efforts to dig up shit from Braxton's past. He went from obscurity to nominee so quickly as a result of Jacobs' death, he was never strongly vetted. We should also find ways to rip his family. Start germinating bogus death threats to scare him. I'm not sure what his panic triggers look like. We need to find out."

Krueger had another thought. "An important employee of his business is now working in the State department. Abby Martin. From what I understand, she was his executive assistant and then was promoted to COO when he ran for Congress. Was with him over ten years. Bet she knows everything about him."

"Was he sleeping with her?" Abbott asked hopefully.

"I don't know. Maybe. I know someone at State who might be able to dig it out. Handsome bastard. Could get her in bed and start some pillow talk."

"Go for it. Anything could help. And we should line up help in the media. So far, the press is handling Braxton with mittens. No one wants to lay a hand on him. We need to change the media dynamic.

They need to start hammering him. Anyone you know who could help us make it happen?"

"Yeah. We have friends at the Washington Post, the New York Times, and Atlantic Magazine. They'll print anything we feed them. They love the leaks from our anonymous sources."

"Good," Abbott replied. "I'll have our media team at Costello work on some juicy stories and get them over to you. The sooner we can get them published, the better."

"Jack, speaking of the Carrington's, I've been meaning to ask you about Wil and how he's feeling about everything. I imagine he's pissed. Have you spoken to him since the election?"

"I haven't" Abbott lied, "but I know the man well. I guarantee you he's pissed, and he'd love to see Braxton go down quickly, but his priority is moving Heather in. And moving her in means she stays clean. Not sure how we engineer Braxton going down and keep Heather pure, so we may have to do this without his knowing. He can't know of anything we're doing until we really know where he stands, which also means watching out for Sidney Rosenberg. That little fuck has eyes and ears everywhere."

As Abbott was listening to himself, he was also kicking himself for showing Wil his cards. He wasn't going to make the same mistake with Krueger.

Krueger reflected. "You know, Jack, on second thought, Heather has to go down with Braxton. We don't know what she'd be like once sworn in and occupying the Oval. Sometimes the late converts are the most zealous. We don't know how she'll respond in the wake of her new idol going down. Especially if she knew we had something to do with it. I don't like it. She has to go, too. I'd rather see Paul Ryan in the Oval. At least we'll know what we're getting."

Abbott was resigned to the thought. "Yeah, you're right."

That evening, the First Lady decided the Presidential bedroom would be her refuge as she needed alone time to prepare for her big news conference scheduled for the following day. Jon and Heather were at the Canadian embassy for an impromptu dinner meeting with Prime Minister Justin Trudeau. Luke and Darla were entertaining each other in Luke's room. She could be alone and concentrate.

A week earlier Angela had decided it was time to give the nation, and the world, an update on the progress of the **TYPE 1 - YOU'RE DONE** Project. She scheduled a news conference for the following week. She, Luke and the administration's Secretary of Health and Human Services, Tom Price, would host. Angela had achieved considerable progress in herding thirty organizations to start pulling in the same direction towards the cure. She had plenty to share to offer the world's Type 1 diabetes community hope. Angela was sitting upright in bed studying her notes when Darla ran into her room screaming frantically.

"Mom, mom, something's wrong with Luke."

Angela bolted from the bed and ran into Luke's room to find him unconscious on the floor. He and Darla had been in his room listening to music when he mentioned to his sister he didn't feel well and was going to the bathroom. He fainted after his first step.

"Honey, get me some orange juice from the refrigerator quick," she directed her daughter. There was a phone on the nightstand. Angela picked up the handset and dialed 211. She was immediately connected to the White House Emergency Services Department and told the operator she needed a paramedic and an EMT in the residence immediately. She also requested they contact the President and let him know his son was suffering an episode of insulin shock and was unconscious. The First Lady correctly assumed Luke's body had overreacted to the last infusion of insulin from his pump, and his blood sugar level had dropped to a dangerously low level.

Three minutes later, four first responders entered the residence and rushed to Luke's room. He was still unconscious. One of the paramedics immediately administered a shot of glucagon and Luke slowly regained consciousness as his blood sugar spiked from the injection. It was decided he would go to Walter Reed Hospital for stabilizing his blood sugar and observation. The President arrived just as Luke was being wheeled out in a wheelchair with an IV tube affixed to his left arm. He was still groggy when he saw his father. "I'm OK dad."

Jon and Angela accompanied their son to Walter Reed and stayed with him for three hours until they felt comfortable leaving him alone with the hospital staff. They made it back to the residence at half past midnight.

The world press was excited for the second round of Angela Braxton's cage match against a stubborn and resilient opponent, Type 1 diabetes.

They gathered early in the East Room for the ten-a.m. news conference start time. As they arrived, the journalists took their seats in chairs arranged theater style, facing a table with three empty chairs. The camera operators gathered in the area behind the seats, their cameras pointed at the table. They all focused their gaze on three name plates. Besides the First Lady, were plates for Tom Price and Lucas Braxton.

At ten-fifteen a.m., Angela and Tom Price entered the East Room and took their seats facing the reporters. The camera operators were snapping one photo after another, the snaps echoing throughout.

"To all members of the press in the room and to everyone watching from afar, thank you for joining us today." The reporters silenced their murmuring, and the camera operators their cameras as the First Lady began.

"It was my intent to have Luke with us today, as he has been instrumental in helping me with our efforts. Unfortunately, he will not be. He is at Walter Reed Hospital recovering from an episode of insulin shock he suffered last evening. I just spoke to him before joining you. His condition has stabilized, and he is feeling well. He'll remain at Walter Reed today as a precaution and come home tomorrow."

The First Lady's tone was firm. The press corps was silent.

"To those of you in the Type 1 community watching or listening, you know all too well what happens when the body of a Type 1 diabetic overreacts to injected insulin. To those of you unfamiliar, when blood sugars drop sharply, the body undergoes a partial shutdown. A sharp drop in blood sugar causes the body to go into preservation mode. The body senses a lack of available energy and begins to shut down organs and bodily processes when faced with what it perceives as an energy deficiency. The body is unaware of how long the deficiency will last and works to conserve what it has to work with. Last night, Luke was in his room with his sister when it happened. He wasn't feeling well and stood up to go to the bathroom and fainted. We tried to get him to drink some orange juice, but he slipped into unconsciousness before we could get it into him. Thankfully, White House paramedics responded within two minutes and administered a shot of a peptide hormone called glucagon, and Luke regained consciousness shortly thereafter. This is not the first time Luke has experienced insulin shock. While an overwhelming majority of Type 1 diabetics have no issues with injected insulin, some do. And Luke is in that minority."

With those words, Angela's disposition weakened, and her voice started to quiver. "We're grateful his episode last night happened in the presence of his family. It's uncertain what would have been the result had it not."

The emotion of the moment caused the First Lady to pause. She reached for a glass of water to take a drink. The press corps remained silent, stunned by the news explaining Luke's absence. A moment later, Angela regained her composure and began her presentation.

"Ladies and gentlemen, we invited you here today to inform you of the progress we're making in the search for the cure for Type 1 diabetes. As you recall from our last visit together, the intent of the Braxton administration is to bring together all organizations in this country which engage in research for a cure for T1D. We identified thirty such organizations and asked them to make a sacrifice. A sacrifice for the benefit of humanity. We knew what we were asking could be considered being in contrast to their personal and financial best interests. Nonetheless, we asked them to join in partnership with other like-minded organizations pursuing similar avenues of research. We asked them to collaborate in the interests of more quickly advancing their individual research and hypotheses.

"From our initial interviews with each of these organizations, we learned they all lacked sufficient funding and resources to advance their research more quickly on their own. And even with adequate funding, they estimated between eight and twelve years to validate a cure. We are not willing to wait eight to twelve years without attempting an effort to accelerate development. This effort has evolved into the **TYPE 1-YOU'RE DONE** Project. Our strategy is to align these organizations in a well-coordinated manner to facilitate collaboration, ensure their funding levels are adequate to commensurate with the research they're conducting, and accelerate the research for a cure."

Angela paused again for a drink of water. A few coughs from the press corps echoed. She continued.

"We are pleased to report to you twenty-eight of the thirty organizations we originally communicated with just six weeks ago opted to join the Project. In addition, we attracted four organizations from outside the United States to join our efforts, giving us thirty-two organizations participating. Thirty-two collections of brilliant and dedicated scientists and researchers, each with their own ideas, concepts, intellectual property, and hypotheses. Each with their own motivation to find a cure for Type 1 diabetes. Each willing to sacrifice potential individual gains in favor of participating in our project and advancing the cure on an accelerated timeline. Please join me in acknowledging them."

Angela led a round of applause, which quickly became loud and boisterous. When the clapping subsided, the press corps rediscovered murmuring and camera snaps. The historic significance of what the First Lady was communicating was rocking the East Room and the excitement could not be contained until Angela asked for quiet.

"We have grouped these thirty-two organizations into four teams, with each team engaging in a particular avenue of T1D research. Each team has a chief executive. The chief executive was selected by the member organizations within each team. We asked each member organization to vote for their choice for chief executive based on the one hypothesis each team would focus on. The hypothesis the team felt had the best chance to be successfully developed into a cure within an accelerated timeline. It is the responsibility of each chief executive to oversee the research within each organization on his team. To ensure each organization on his team is working cooperatively on the same hypothesis. And to uncover through collaboration, opportunities for improving chances for success and opportunities for maximizing efficiency of time, resources, effort, and money. It is also the responsibility of each chief executive to oversee the writing of a grant and research plan to be evaluated for funding by the NIH. The chief executive's responsibilities are enormous, but we are fortunate to have four of the most talented men and women in the science of endocrinology working in that capacity."

At this pause, the room needed no prodding to start another round of applause. Angela did nothing to settle them down. She was thankful for the time to regroup as her thoughts turned to Luke. After two minutes, the room quieted itself. The press corps sensed the world wanted to hear more from the First Lady.

"I mentioned we grouped our member organizations into four teams, with each team being involved in a particular avenue of research. The four avenues of research we are pursuing to find a cure are Islet Cell Transplants, Blood Stem Cell Transplants, Immunotherapies, and Vaccine Therapies. I encourage you all to visit the **TYPE 1-YOU'RE DONE** Project website for more details on each organization participating, the team they belong to, their collaboration efforts, and their individual accomplishments. The Project's website also includes details on ways you can become involved in our efforts. We have tremendous hope of bringing the most gifted minds in Type 1 diabetes research together in a coordinated and, thanks to President Braxton, well-funded attack on this disease to bring us the cure in the shortest amount of time possible. I'll now take your questions."

The first question came from Jamey Delacosta, the White House Correspondent from CNN. "Mrs. Braxton, of your four teams have any distinguished themself as being ahead in the race to find the cure? And can you share anything about their work?"

"Yes Jamey. There is one team which is on the verge of groundbreaking discoveries. I mentioned to you we had four organizations from outside the United States join our cause. One of those is from Edmonton, Alberta, Canada. The organization is known as Canada-

DRI, the Canadian Diabetes Research Institute. CanadaDRI is led by Dr. Jonah Shapiro. Dr. Shapiro's research involves using STEM cells from the blood of Type 1 diabetics and engineering them to be converted into insulin producing cells and then reintroduced into the patient's liver. The liver, and not the pancreas, for a variety of reasons you can read about on the project's website. This blood cell engineering process takes twenty-eight days and is extraordinarily complex. The promise of this research in using the patient's own blood and then reintroducing the cells into the patient's liver, serves to mitigate the threat of the immune system attacking them as foreign cells. To what degree we don't yet know. The research has a way to go, but preliminary results are promising. Dr. Shapiro has already written their grant document and business plan, and we hope to be funding this team shortly."

Chapter 16

We're Good

The preliminary success of Jon Braxton's efforts to end North Korea's nuclear weapons ambition led him to believe it was time to normalize diplomatic relations with the PRNK and open a United States Embassy in Pyongyang. The President hit the intercom button on his desk phone.

"Rosemary."

"Yes, Mr. President?"

"Work your magic and assemble the Vice President, Secretary Haley and Assistant Secretary Martin in my office at three-thirty today."

"Yes, Mr. President."

At three-thirty p.m. the three ladies and the President were seated on the Oval's two sofas facing one another adjacent to the President's desk. The President opened the meeting.

"Ladies, I'd like to get your thoughts on our normalizing diplomatic relations with KJ and North Korea. Including opening an embassy. Pros and cons. Heather, let's have your take first."

Vice President Carrington and Secretary of State Haley exchanged a concerned glance. Abby and Jon both picked up on it. Heather cleared her throat.

"Jon. A huge con would be Kim's most certain negative reaction. We are starting to build some trust, but it would be quite a leap to say Kim will view this favorably. My belief is he will see this initiative as provocative and a ploy for us to spy on them. Making this suggestion at this time could set him off and destroy everything we've built over the last few months. It's too soon."

Jon frowned. "Nikki?"

The Secretary of State responded. "Another large con would be the negative fallout from our allies in the region, particularly Japan and South Korea. They are not in lockstep with our appeasement efforts towards the PRNK. They don't trust Kim and feel he is playing you. Offering to normalize relations with North Korea at this time, and not including them in the conversation, would dramatically impact our other alliances in the region. It would make you look weak. We would be mocked by the rest of the world for capitulating. We haven't yet established faith in our allies in the region that our working to improve relations with North Korea is in their best interest. We need more time to lay that groundwork. I agree with Heather. It's too soon."

"OK. Abby, care to add anything?" the President asked his long-time trusted assistant, sensing defeat.

"Jon, I haven't been at this diplomacy gig for long, but what I would say to you from what I've seen and heard thus far is, are you freaking crazy? Obviously, you haven't conferred with Captain Crunch on this yet, have you?"

"Uh no Mrs. Martin. You're correct, I haven't."

"OK, well, there's no need because I'll spill those beans. Here's what the Captain would tell you. And that is you can't work with

Kim like you did with our customers and vendors at Spectre. You had a history and a reputation you built in the industry which put you into position to work your magic. But U.S. foreign policy is a different ballgame. Our people working for the State Department around the world put their lives on the line every day in dangerous situations. And now you want to place our citizens in one of the most dangerous places on earth? Are you out of your mind? Have you thought about their safety? The safety of their families?"

Abby continued. "You think Kim likes you? Likes Luke? Adores Angela? Well, maybe he does Angela, considering all the roses. I mean, what's there not to adore about your gorgeous wife? But listen Jon, this is a bad idea. Do your risk analysis. What do we stand to gain and at what risk? Normalizing North Korea at this time doesn't buy us anything. We're already on a good path to get there and making this move now is premature and could cost us dearly. It's too soon." She leaned back on the sofa and crossed her arms.

"OK, what are the pros?" Jon's half-hearted question was met with silence. "Good, we're all in agreement. It's a horrible idea. Thank you, ladies."

The following early morning, Jon was in the residence, dressed for the day and finishing a cup of coffee, when he picked up a copy of the Washington Post News.

He sat stunned as he glared at the headline. It took the President a minute to process what he was seeing before reading the article referencing a detailed description of the previous day's meeting with Heather, Nikki, and Abby, including their passionate objections. As he read the article, which quoted *'an anonymous source familiar with the White House agenda,'* his anger boiled over. He picked up the handset from a phone on a credenza next to the breakfast table where he was seated. He hit the speed dial button for his receptionist. She answered.

"Good morning Mrs. Braxton."

"Sorry Rosemary, you got it wrong. It's your real boss. I want Heather, Nikki, Abby, and Lance in my office NOW! No excuses. NOW!"

"Yes, Mr. President."

Heather arrived first but decided to wait for Nikki and Abby. She had already seen the Washington Post News headline and read the article. Expecting a blistering attack from the President, she thought it better to walk into Jon's office with cover. Nikki had already been briefed and was expecting uncomfortable moments ahead. Abby had been in an early morning phone meeting with India and was unaware of the headline or the article. The Secretary and Assistant Secretary of State arrived separately a moment later and gathered with Heather at Rosemary's desk. The President's receptionist cautioned them before they entered the Oval. "He's really upset. I've never seen him like this."

Jon was at his desk and didn't look at them as they entered. He was face down reading a national security report generated two hours earlier because of the Post News headline. His Chief of Staff was already in the room and reading the same NSA briefing. Jon barked at the three women. "Have you seen the front page of the Post News today?" Heather and Nikki nodded. Abby shook her head no. "Sit down, ladies."

They did so and waited for three minutes for Jon to finish judiciously digesting the five-page briefing report. He ignored their presence as he read the briefing twice, then stood. He moved to the front of his desk, leaned his rear end against the desk, and crossed his arms in front of his chest.

"Any ideas on who's talking to the Post News about our confidential meetings, or is it one of you?"

Heather answered for them. "Jon, you should assume the leak did not come from us."

"Thank you for the advice, Mrs. Carrington, but I'll assume nothing of the sort."

Abby couldn't hold back. "OK, what's going on?"

Heather answered. "You're not aware of this morning's Post News headline?"

Abby answered as she looked directly at Jon. "No, I've been on back-to-back overseas calls since five a.m."

Heather responded. "The Post News ran an article this morning detailing the discussion the four of us had in this office yesterday. Details of Jon floating the North Korea normalization idea and our pushback. It cast Jon in an unfavorable light and has started a firestorm with our allies in the region."

Jon was annoyed. "Madam Vice President, thank you for running interference for your two colleagues, but I'd like to hear from them for myself. Nikki, how did this leak?"

"Jon, I have not mentioned anything about our meeting yesterday to anyone. What you're suggesting is squarely against protocol. I have written down any notes or thoughts. I promise you the leak did not come from me or my office. No one in the State Department except Abby knows anything about our discussion."

The President wasn't satisfied. "Well, everyone knows about our conversation now thanks to this dishrag of a newspaper. Mrs. Martin, who did you tell?"

"Jon. You're kidding, right? You're accusing me? You've known me for fifteen years. You know this is not my style. You, better than anyone, know how discreet I am. So, Mr. President, you can choose to believe me or not, but I did not say anything to anyone about our conversation."

Jon was highly agitated. "OK, so we're back to where we started when you walked in. We obviously have a serious leak somewhere close to this office and we have no clue who or where. Isn't that special? Heather, Nikki, what can you tell me about Rosemary? Can I trust her?"

"Jon," Heather answered, "can I speak to you alone for a few minutes?"

"Why?"

"After I tell you, I think you'll understand."

Jon thought back to his conversation with Jeffrey Claymore and his cautionary comments about Wil. He also recollected Jeffrey's comments about Heather.

"OK. Nikki, Abby, Lance, give us ten minutes, but stay close."

With the three of them out of the room, Heather stood and walked to the back of the Oval. Jon was still leaning against the front of his desk. He had uncrossed his arms and now had the palms of his hands to his side, pressing against the desktop. She turned around and looked at him. "My husband has mentioned things to me over the past few weeks he should not have known. Things you and I discussed in this office and in the residence. Things I never discussed with him."

"Like what?"

"The day after Jeffrey was here, I had dinner alone with Wil. He asked me about my day. I told him you had invited Jeffrey to the White House, and it was great to see him. He asked me why you had, and all I said was you wanted to talk to him about the things you talked about on the Kriss show. That was all I said. He then made a comment he didn't see Jeffrey as a policy guy and was wondering if you offered him a job. I didn't connect it to our conversation with Jeffrey. I thought it was simply a lucky guess on his part. I then had a thought to ask him about Jack Abbott. If he had seen or talked to him recently. I was just fishing to see if Wil could help Angela with the insulin negotiation. And he said thirty million vials over two years should give her good leverage. How could he have known that detail?"

Jon questioned her. "You think someone in the White House is leaking to Wil? Whoever it might be, how could they know any details about a job offer to Jeffrey or the insulin negotiation? We first heard the details of the insulin deal from Angela on the night of Jeffrey's visit. Wait, it couldn't be Jeffrey, could it? He knew about the job offer and the details of the insulin buy."

Heather reminded him. "He wasn't in the room for the North Korea discussion."

Jon's rage was growing. "Let me get this straight. Your husband knew about the job offer to Jeffrey and he knew the details of the insulin negotiation. And now someone, maybe your husband, learns the details of our North Korea conversation and they show up the following morning in the papers? To make it to press on time, the story had to have been relayed within an hour or two after our meeting. It's like someone is listening in real time. I trust you're not wearing a wire, or are you Madam Vice President?"

She understood how Jon could make the accusation, but her anger was not directed towards him. She was apologetic. "No Jon. I am not a party to this. I understand how upset you must be. I'm not wearing a wire and I am not doing any leaking. If I were, would we be having this conversation? But believe me, if my husband has something to do with this, I'll be the first one to kick the shit out of him thanks to the karate moves your wife has taught me. And there is something else."

The President was not amused. "Go on."

"I can't see how it's related, but there's something wrong with my Blackberry. For a new phone, I don't have much battery life. No more than two hours now before I have to charge it. And sometimes the phone starts hissing and crackling while I'm not using it, like static on a bad phone line."

"Hissing and crackling when you're not on a call?" The President was skeptical.

"It will hiss and crackle just sitting on the table, not being used."

"Let me see it."

"I don't have it with me. It's in my office charging."

"Go get it."

Heather nodded and went to the door. Before she could open it, Jon made a request. "Shut the phone all the way down when you take it off the charger."

Heather returned in three minutes with her Blackberry. When she entered the Oval, there was a White House staffer whom she did not recognize sitting across the desk from the President. He stood when she entered the room.

The President brokered the introduction. "Heather, this is Ben Wade. He's an IT genius who worked with me at Spectre for ten years.

I offered him a change of scenery with a move to Washington and he now works in the White House." The two shook hands.

"It's an honor to meet you Madam Vice President," Ben offered.

Heather answered nonchalantly. "I suppose you want this," she said as she handed him her Blackberry. He took it and sat down. Heather followed suit.

Ben looked closely at the phone case, turning it around in every direction, looking for anything out of the ordinary. "I'm going to power it on, but based on what the President told me, let's all remain silent while I check a few things out." Heather nodded. Jon pursed his lips, closed his eyes, and shook his head a skosh in disgust.

Ben powered the phone on and used customized Blackberry backdoor entry commands, which were developed by Blackberry's parent company, Research in Motion, specifically for U.S. government use. After five minutes of investigation, Ben powered the phone all the way down. "There seems to be suspicious code embedded in the operating system. I need to connect it to a computer to fully analyze what it might be. Mr. President, I'd like to run tests on your phone as well. And I think it would be prudent, until we understand more, to have all government employees refrain from using their government-issued Blackberrys until we assess everything. It could be a widespread breach."

"How long will it take you to do your analysis?" The President's angst was still heightened.

"Should be no more than two hours."

Shortly after the Washington Post News headline surfaced, Jackrabbit called Senator Krueger's office in Washington. He wanted to congratulate him on the Post News story and ask if any of it were true. He reached him at his desk at ten the same morning.

"Well done on the Post News story this morning, Bob. How did you get it? Or should I ask who made it up?"

"Wish I knew Jack. It wasn't us."

Abbott was puzzled. "Seriously, nobody from your posse was involved? You sure?"

Krueger was confident. "I've already taken roll. No one knows anything about it."

Abbott was smug. "Well, isn't that interesting? Could be coming from within. Seems the White House is starting to spring leaks. I like it. Now we get to see how Braxton starts dealing with the shit hitting the fan."

At eleven that morning, Ben Wade was back in the Oval with Heather and the President's Chief of Staff, Lance Reibus.

"OK Ben. What have we got?"

"Mr. President, we opened the phone casing and found foreign circuitry. Someone had installed a microphone and a transmission device. We also verified the presence of foreign code in the operating system. This code controls the mic and the transmitter. It's activated when the phone is powered on. In the lab, we powered the phone on and simulated a casual conversation between two people in proximity to the phone. We observed the microphone pick up the conversation and the the transmitter generate a stream from the phone to an IP address. The stream used heavy encryption and we can't yet determine what's being transmitted. Our guess at this point is it's the conversation being relayed. We identified multiple IP addresses the transmission is being directed to, but they appear to be a group of proxy addresses. The algorithm is exceptionally sophisticated. Every block of data is routed to a different proxy IP address. My guess is the algorithm then forwards each block back to an aggregation server where the algorithm reassembles the stream for playback. We can't yet determine what or where the aggregation server is, but we should be able to within twenty-four hours. Oh, and one other thing, the code initiates a secure Virtual Private Network tunnel to a satellite for the first hop. We've identified the satellite as one of ours."

The President couldn't contain himself as he looked squarely at Heather. "Shit. It's an inside job, Ben?"

Ben confirmed. "Yes, sir, it appears to be."

"And what about my phone?"

"It was unaltered and still secure, Mr. President."

Jon was beside himself with anger. "OK Ben, I think I know what you're going to suggest, but why don't you spell it out for Mrs. Carrington and Mr. Reibus."

"Well, we only assessed two phones. Since we don't know who or how the Vice President's phone was compromised, we don't know how widespread this breach is. My recommendation would be, as painful as it is, to recall all Blackberrys issued for government usage and distribute new ones. But before we distribute any new ones, we will work with RIM to have better anti-hacking tools implemented so we can get pre-emptive notice and visibility when or if it happens again."

"Lance, can you make the recall happen with as little fallout as possible?" Jon asked his Chief of Staff.

He assured the President. "We can ask all our people to stop using their phones and power them all the way down, as we have discovered a potential security threat with them. That's all we have to say."

"OK, put a detailed plan together on how you will do this. Have it on my desk within the hour, without fail. And gather up at least thirty phones from different executive branch departments and get them to Ben. Let's see how badly we've been fucked."

Lance nodded, stood, and left the Oval.

"Thanks Ben, you can go. Let me know the moment you have any more info. Mrs. Carrington, stick around."

When it was just the two of them, Jon started grilling the Vice President. "Given everything we know and everything we just heard, should we presume your husband is behind this?"

Heather sat stoically. "I guess it's possible, Jon. At this point, I don't know."

"You guess it's possible? You're the one with the suspicions. You know what it means if it's discovered he's behind this. He could go away for a long time."

"Yes Jon. I've been agonizing over that possibility since I saw the headline this morning. But I don't know what to think or do at this point."

"What you should be thinking about is what side you want to be on. If all roads point to your husband, you'll have to choose. That is all Mrs. Carrington."

The Post News headline would reach the Korean peninsula shortly. Jon knew he needed to get ahead of the impact. He asked Nikki Haley to find out where Foreign Minster Ri was and schedule a call with him as soon as possible. He was grateful to hear Ri was in Washington and had Nikki invite him to the White House for lunch. Ri had a request for attending. He wanted Luke to join them.

They gathered in the intimate dining room adjacent to the Oval Office. It had just been swept to verify there were no foreign listening or watching devices. Ri had already seen the headline, read the article, and spoken with Kim. The impact in North Korea was not anything close to what Jon was fearing. Kim assumed the article was not a fabrication and perceived Jon's raising the possibility of normalizing diplomatic relations as a positive. And he saw the pushback of the idea by Jon's team as 'on point.' He was not yet ready to trust Jon, but he was sensing they could work together. And the fact Jon's team was counseling him it was too soon to put a U.S. Embassy in Pyongyang was an opinion shared by the PRNK's Supreme Leader.

When Minister Ri was ushered into the dining room, Jon, Luke, Angela, Nikki, Abby, and Lance were already seated. Heather was not invited. They all rose to greet him. Ri approached Jon, and they shook hands. He did so with the First Lady as well. When he approached Luke, the handshake was replaced by an embrace. Ri's first words in the room were, "how are you, Lucas?"

The luncheon started with discussion of the **TYPE 1—YOU'RE DONE** Project. The Foreign Minister was pleased to hear the First Lady's ideas of coalescence and collaboration among the organizations involved in researching a cure were yielding positive results. And he was excited at the prospect of a North Korea medical delegation being involved in the research for the cure. Angela briefed Ri on the latest developments of the four teams and on her efforts to negotiate the sale of thirty million vials of high-quality American insulin to be delivered to North Korea over the next two years. She also discussed what North Korea needed to do to get ready to receive, store and distribute the insulin once it was received. Once the salads were served, Jon took the lead on the conversation.

"Minister Ri, I'm assuming you've seen the Washington Post News headline and article this morning?"

"Yes, Mr. President, I have, as has Supreme Leader Kim."

"I'd like to offer you and your country a formal apology on behalf of myself and my administration. It was a careless lapse in security on our part for this information to be made public. We will do everything we can to minimize any negative impact this may have on the People's

Republic of North Korea. We are already discussing the matter with South Korea and Japan to insure they do not take any provocative action."

"Thank you, Mr. President. Supreme Leader Kim asked me to ask you a question."

"Please."

"Mr. President, the details of your meeting in the article. Were they all accurate?"

"Yes, Minister Ri. All the details discussing what transpired in my office in that meeting were one hundred percent accurate. What I cannot confirm are the reactions from Japan and South Korea."

"In that case, Mr. President, let's consider the matter closed and move on to more productive discussions. Your meeting showed your interest in normalizing relations with our country, which we appreciate. And your team counseled it was too soon to be considering it, which we agree with. So, as you might say in your country, we're good."

Chapter 17

Lie Down, Mr. President

As the luncheon with Foreign Minister Ri was concluding, an aide to Lance Reibus entered the Oval Office dining room and approached her boss. She leaned over and whispered words into Lance's left ear. Lance stood and strode out of the dining room with his aide by his side.

A moment later, Lance reentered the dining room with a White House photographer. He wanted a photo of the President and the North Korea Foreign Minister shaking hands. He didn't need to ask or stage it, as the two men were already doing so. Lance asked them to hold it for one minute and allow the photographer to get the shot. While Ri was saying his goodbyes to Angela and Luke, Lance approached the President. "Kelly (John Kelly, Secretary of Homeland Security) asked you head to the situation room. Massive tornadoes are hammering Texas and Arkansas. There's been significant loss of life and property damage."

"OK, let's go," Jon said as he transitioned from diplomat to Chief Executive. "Minister Ri, thank you again for joining us on such short notice. You'll have to excuse me now. We have another disaster to attend to." He started out of the room after kissing Angela on the cheek and shaking hands with his son.

A moment later, the President and his Chief of Staff entered the main conference room of the five-thousand-foot area on the ground floor of the West Wing of the White House known officially as the Situation Room. Secretary Kelly and four of his staffers were watching a variety of disturbing video feeds coming from Texas and Arkansas. The videos showed massive amounts of devastation. Homeland Security had not yet quantified the loss of life, but it was certain to be extensive.

"Should I call the Vice President?"

"No," Jon snapped back to Lance. He hadn't yet let go of his sense of her betrayal. "Secretary Kelly, what's your assessment?"

"The loss of life and property is going to be extensive. The quantity and intensity of these tornadoes are unlike anything we've seen before. We're still working to reach the governors, but they're up to their asses in alligators. I'm sure we'll hear from them soon. We've already started the groundwork to declare all the counties affected as federal disaster areas once the formal request from the states come in. FEMA is in route to both states. We're lining up large shipments of aid. Food, water, medicine, clothing, portable housing. We're readying the National Guard for deployment. Preliminary estimates predict two hundred thousand homeless. And two million without power. For how long we can't be sure."

"John, what specifically can I do to help you do your jobs?"

"As for now, Mr. President, authorize us to respond quickly to any requests for declarations which come in. And help raise awareness and provide moral support. The people in the region impacted are going to have it tough for a while. We can provide the basics, but whatever you can do or say to give these people hope is what they need from you."

"Keep me up-to-date, John. I'll be in my office. Lance, walk with me."

They started the walk back to the Oval. The President was walking briskly and looking straight ahead as he asked his question. "How well do you know Wil Carrington?"

Lance was struggling to keep up. "Not well Jon. We're from different planets."

"He's from Arkansas, right?"

"Yep."

"Think he'll be willing to take a trip down there with me to lend some moral support to his home state?"

"I'm not sure, but I would hope so."

"And what planet is the Vice President from?" Jon couldn't shake the thought she was a participant in the North Korea leak. Or at best, she unknowingly enabled it.

As Jon and Lance reached Rosemary Barnett's desk, she let the President know Ben Wade was inside waiting for them. "Mr. Wade said it was urgent, so I told him it was OK to wait for you. I hope it's OK sir."

"It's fine Rosemary. Thank you." Jon brushed past her without a glance or hesitation. Lance followed and gave Rosemary a look of condolence.

"What have you got, Ben?" Jon asked as he bounced into his desk chair. Ben was sitting in of the two guest chairs opposite Jon. Lance took the other.

"Mr. President. We've examined the thirty phones Mr. Reibus gathered for us. None were tampered with. We can't yet be sure, but thus far, it appears the Vice President's phone is the only one compromised. Also, we could partially decrypt portions of the transmissions. As suspected, the transmissions relay the voices picked up by the microphone in real time."

Jon looked at Lance. "What planet did you say she was from?"

Lance was befuddled. "I don't know Jon."

"What else, Ben?"

"We're working to find the end destination of these transmissions. Since the satellite the phone is communicating with is one of ours, we located and parsed its logs to look for the IP addresses the satellite was relaying the transmissions to. They're all Proxy server IPs and they're spread all over the world. It's likely these relay servers are all compromised so we don't know the end point yet, but because of the components of the compromise we can safely say the breach was orchestrated by people close to the U.S. Government with intimate knowledge of our communication networks. It's likely whoever is behind this is connecting to the end point server and listening in or recording the conversations. Or both."

"Ben, let me have her phone." Wade handed Heather's Blackberry to the President, and he stared at it for a moment.

"Leave it with me. I have a job for it. You can go now. The minute you know anything new, let me know."

"Yes, sir." Ben left the Oval, leaving Jon and Lance.

"Anything else, Lance?" an irritated Jon asked.

"Permission to use the photo you took with Ri today with a story we'd like to put out about North Korea's appreciation of your interest in restoring diplomatic relations and their agreement with your team it was too soon."

"What does this buy us?"

"Makes everyone look good and calms Japan and South Korea down. And whoever is behind the leak to rethink things. Or better yet, flush them out."

Jon was disgusted with the whole matter. "Politics, what a shit business. Permission granted."

Sidney Rosenberg's cell phone vibrated. The display read '*CallerID unknown.*'

"Hello?"

The former president hesitatingly worded this week's opening security handshake line with a monotone delivery. *"There she was, just a walking down the street."*

Sidney laughed to himself, hearing the former president unemotionally mouth the words as he sang back the reply. "Singing doowah diddy diddy dum diddy do."

"Hello Sidney."

"Hello Wil. You should try singing the clues. Might help you remember them."

"Fuck you, Sidney."

"What's on your mind, Wil?"

The former president was troubled. *"I've been logged in all day today and haven't heard anything. I was hoping to hear Braxton and Heather discussing the fallout from the article. You think there's something wrong?"*

Sidney was exasperated with the former President's insecurities. "Gee, I don't know Wil. Maybe they didn't enjoy the opportunity to discuss it today with all the shit happening in Arkansas. Anyone from your family affected?"

"No, thank God. My sister and her family are all OK. But even if Jon and Heather didn't meet, I usually hear all of Heather's other meetings. But today, nothing."

"Not sure Wil. Give Mark Parker a call and see what he says."

As late evening descended on Washington, DC, an exhausted and exasperated President Braxton retreated to his bedroom. It was eleven p.m. He had concluded four hours earlier this was, by far, his most frustrating and disappointing day in office.

When he entered his bedroom, he walked into a room illuminated and scented by four strategically located fragranced candles. The mood lighting and soothing aroma were accompanied by soft music one would expect to hear in a luxury spa. Jon walked in and his stress level dropped by two standard deviations. A moment later, Angela appeared from the bathroom dressed in a sheer red teddy. The sexy lingerie highlighted her tall and slim, curvaceous figure. She was also wearing Jon's favorite perfume. Her long silky brunette hair was brushed down the length of her torso.

"Hello Mr. President. Don't say a word. Take all your clothes off and lie face down in our bed."

"Am I about to experience the magnificent bottom of your feet on my back?"

"Yes, among other pleasures."

Chapter 18

Spin Cycle

The Vice President made the call to her secretary early in the morning from her residence office at the Naval Observatory. "Brenda, I won't be in my office today. Please reschedule all my appointments."

"Yes, Madam Vice President. Does anyone need to know where you'll be?"

"No. But should anyone ask, I'll be back in my office tomorrow."

"Yes, Madam Vice President."

As she placed the phone handset back on its base, there was a knock at her office door, followed by her husband's entrance. "Good morning, honey. Thought I'd bring you a cup of coffee. You didn't say a word to me last night when you got in. Is everything OK?" the former president asked in an innocent, placating tone.

Heather, still freshly processing the idea her husband may have initiated a spying effort against her, was annoyed by his presence. She did her best to not give him any idea there was anything out of the ordinary on her mind. "Everything's fine, Wil. Thanks for the coffee. Now please excuse me. I'm extremely busy."

"Come on Heather. Talk to me. How can I help you?"

"By leaving me alone, dammit."

Air Force Two is the call sign for any United States Aircraft carrying the Vice President of the United States. Today it would be the usual. A Boeing C-32 variant of a Boeing 757. This morning's soon to be AF2 was resting comfortably in a hangar at Andrews Air Force Base, a thirty-minute drive from the Vice President's residence. At ten a.m., it awaited her arrival. The flight plan to Philadelphia had been filed.

At eleven-fifty a.m., Air Force Two entered New Jersey airspace in route to McGuire Air Force Base, thirty miles northeast of Sharswood, PA. The landing was uneventful and fifty minutes later, the Vice President was sitting alone in the congregation area of Jeffrey Claymore's First Pentecostal Church. It was Heather's first visit in a year.

She was only alone for five minutes when Jeffrey entered the worship area. He saw Heather sitting in row fifteen, staring at the pulpit, looking defiant. Her demeanor differed completely from her last visit one year prior when she sought Jeffrey's guidance on what to do about her candidacy. For that visit, she had her eyes closed and head bowed when he first saw her. Her demeanor this day was exactly the opposite. The pastor noticed immediately.

"Hello Heather. It's wonderful to see you again. I'm sure you have much to tell me. What has brought you to Sharswood?"

Heather turned her gaze from the pulpit and into Jeffrey's eyes. Her look was one of coolness, as if her visit to Jeffrey was a formality. "It's my husband," she said indifferently.

"I see." He stopped there to prod her.

Heather obliged. "I don't know for certain, but I have evidence which leads me to believe he's done something unforgivable. And I'm not referring to another bimbo this time. It's possible he's done something illegal. Potentially treasonous."

"You say you don't know for certain, yet you have suspicions. What can you tell me?"

"No specifics. For now, it's classified. I'm not here because of what we believe he's done, but because I'm uncertain what I should do about it. And how I should feel about him. For all the philandering he's done over the years, I've always found it within me to forgive him. On this one, I'm not sure I can."

"We believe he's done?"

"Yes, Jon is aware. I shared my suspicions with him because if Wil has done what I believe, there are national security ramifications."

"I see. Is your husband continuing to do what you suspect of him? Is there an ongoing national security threat?"

"I don't believe so. We believe we found the tool he was using. He no longer has access to it. Sorry to be so cryptic. I owe it to Jon to be discreet. And for good measure, it's classified."

"I understand. Have you confronted Wil with your suspicions? And what are Jon's intentions at this point?"

For the first time in the conversation, Heather showed remorse. "I don't know Jon's intentions," she replied in a distressed manner. "He's not interested in speaking to me about the situation. Or any matter recently. I sense he's lost trust in me."

"When did the two of you last speak?"

"It's been four days."

"Does Jon have a reason to not trust you?"

"I'd say he does. I've never really discussed my relationship with my husband with him. It's reasonable for him to be concerned I may have a hand in what my husband is doing."

"Do you?"

"Jeffrey!"

"How else would I know if I didn't ask? I don't even know what we're referring to. Have you expressed the same sentiment to Jon?"

"I did briefly when we first discussed it, but he was upset with the situation he was placed in because of what we believe my husband may have done. I'm not sure he heard a word I said, let alone believe me. Now I'm in the middle and I can't stay there. There is no middle ground. Jon made it clear I must move to one side or the other." Heather turned her gaze back to the pulpit and Jeffrey followed her lead. They sat in silence for a moment.

"Heather, I should caution you. I might be to blame for Jon's explosive reaction."

"Really?"

"Yes. I expressed my concern about Wil's ambition to Jon when I was in Washington for our last meeting. I told him I believed Wil was more displeased with your decision to leave the race and give up the opportunity to be the President than he led you to believe. And it was possible he would prove to be a distraction. From the little detail you've shared, it appears he may be something more problematic."

"This explains Jon's reactions when I related my suspicions to him."

Jeffrey attempted to reassured her. "I know Jon. And I believe his reaction to you was not because he does not have faith in you. As you well know, Jon disdains politics and if what your husband may have done was a political maneuver, then Jon reacted as I would expect him to. Give him a little time to think things through. I'm sure he will see things more clearly."

Heather attempted to clarify. "My concern is not my relationship with Jon. I know with a little time he'll realize it was I who brought this to his attention. If I were a party to my husband's deeds, I'm sure he realizes I would not have gone to him as I did. I'm just disappointed he hasn't made the connection yet."

Jeffrey inquired. "What else was happening when you had the conversation? Was he under duress? Was it just the pressures of the day which clouded his thinking?"

"You're probably right. But what's more troubling to me is coming to terms with what my husband may have done and what to do about it. This could play out with Wil going to prison. On one side, he's a former president and what he did has been contained and there were no serious repercussions. But if we uncover proof, I'm not sure what Jon will want to do. And frankly, I'm not sure what I will want Jon to do. Jeffrey, help me understand."

"Heather, unlike last year when you were truly unsure of what path to take with your candidacy, I believe this time you know exactly what you need to do. You just are not comfortable with it yet. The comfort will come with time and working with Jon. He'll help guide you on this one. Promise me you will reach out to him and discuss everything."

Heather nodded in agreement. "I promise."

"And one other thing. When you talk to Jon, let him know I'm accepting his offer and I'll be ready in three weeks to move to Washington. Can you recommend a good realtor to help me find a place to live?"

After saying her goodbye, Heather moved to the reception area of First Pentecostal and linked up with her secret service detail. As they were walking in the church parking lot towards the Chevrolet Yukon SUV to ride back to the airport, Heather's new cell phone rang. She answered cautiously.

"Hello?"

"Heather, it's Jon. Please meet me in my office at seven thirty to-morrow morning. I need to apologize to you."

After hanging up with Heather, Jon hit the intercom button to his secretary. "Rosemary."

"Yes, Mr. President."

"Reach out to Wil Carrington's office and ask his secretary to have him call me."

"Yes, sir."

As Heather moved through the White House the following morning on the way to the Oval, she noticed an unusual number of staffers in a state of discomfort and moving slowly. As she approached Rosemary Barnett's desk, she noticed the bandage over the President's receptionist's left eye.

Despite the appendage, Rosemary was in good spirits. "Good morning, Madam Vice President. And good call missing the First Lady's martial arts class last night. It was brutal."

"Yes. I can appreciate that and see the bandage. What happened?"

"The First Lady had us in pairs doing full contact combat drills. I had the unfortunate experience of being paired with Abby Martin. Whew, that girl can kick."

"Did you get any good licks in?"

"Not really. Did I mention she is an animal on defense?"

"You didn't, but I've seen her skills in earlier sessions. Just bad luck for you she was your sparring partner."

"Agreed. The President's expecting you. Go on in."

Heather entered the Oval to see Jon alone, sitting on one of the two sofas adjacent to his desk. He was nursing a cup of coffee and reading the morning's edition of the Wall Street Journal.

"Good morning, Heather. Thank you for coming in so early."

"Good morning, Jon."

Jon was quick to the point. "Come in and sit with me." She moved to the sofa across from Jon and took a seat. "OK, let's clear the air. First, I'm sorry for the way I acted towards you the other day. I was frustrated with the leak and had no right to disrespect you the way I did. Please accept my apology."

"Apology accepted."

"Good. Second. I know you were not involved in the tampering of your Blackberry, but we're now certain your husband is behind it."

"You are? What did you find out?"

"We located the endpoint server online which was receiving and storing the aggregated voice streams. Ben hacked it and remotely installed tracking code on the server to give us visibility of the communication logs. In one of the logs, we found two IP addresses which had been connecting to the server frequently over the last six weeks. One address was traced to the residence at the Naval Observatory. The second to an apartment in Manhattan leased to one Sidney Rosenberg. We understand Rosenberg worked for your husband as a consultant for his presidential campaigns."

"And he worked for mine," Heather felt compelled to add.

"Yeah, we know."

"All right, Mr. President. What now?"

"Good question. Was hoping to get your input."

Heather was uncertain of Jon's intentions. "Given the serious nature of his actions, aren't you planning to notify the DOJ? You discovered he was spying on a sitting president and leaking confidential conversations. He was violating federal law, and his actions could be considered acts of treason. I don't think you have a choice."

"Do you want me to make the call? He could end up in prison for a long time."

"Honestly, Jon. You're putting me in an uncomfortable position."

"Then we agree. I don't want to see him accused or convicted, either. So far, no harm has been done and we've shut down his little enterprise. Let's figure out what else we can do with the information we have. Somehow use it for the good of the country. If not now, then maybe sometime down the road. Are you OK if we keep this in our back pocket?"

"Only if you are," Heather replied with mixed emotions.

"I am, but I am going to confront him. Let him know we know. This should stop any further leaks he might be planning with any other conversations he has recorded. This should contain his interest in me taking an early retirement. And should make things a little easier for you."

Heather was reserved. "Your good intentions are appreciated, though I'm not sure I deserve them. You should know I visited Jeffrey yesterday. He told me about his conversation with you regarding my husband and his apparent ambitions to undermine you. I want you to know I never considered him a threat until he made those comments to me about Jeffrey and the insulin. Now knowing what he's done, what he's capable of, and understanding his motives a little better, I feel I should offer my resignation."

Jon dismissed the notion. "Your husband and I do agree on one thing; you will make a great President in 2020. Yes, Jeffrey warned me about Wil. And he was prophetic. And no, I do not think it's a good idea for you to resign. You'll be wasting your time because I won't accept it."

Heather smiled faintly. "For the record, I didn't give Jeffrey any details of what Wil was up to. I only mentioned he had done something I'm uncertain I can forgive him for."

"Good. If we're going to let your husband skate on this, we've got to contain it. I spoke to Wil yesterday afternoon. Any issue for you if your husband comes with me to Arkansas tomorrow?"

"No. Are you going to let him know what you know during the flight?"

"Yep. I'll take your old Blackberry along and we'll talk about it. When we touch down, we'll have him do some morale boosting and fundraising to take his mind off things as we show solidarity and commitment on the part of the federal government. It's his home state. He can't turn me down, can he?"

"He better not, the son of a bitch."

Jon was already aboard when Wil was ushered onto Air Force One. As he stepped into the fuselage, the former president looked around as if reminiscing. "God. I miss this plane," he uttered as he reconnected with the internal workings of his former sky-based office.

Jon stood and greeted him as he saw Wil walking down the center aisle towards him.

"Mr. President, welcome aboard," Jon chirped with an upbeat tone.

"Hello Jon, thanks for inviting me along," Wil answered, reluctant to greet the current president properly.

"Good idea Wil. Let's work on a first name basis. Get settled in. We're taking off in twenty minutes."

The President offered the former President a drink. He was poured a scotch and water by the cabin attendant. Jon had a club soda with lime.

The two exchanged pleasantries as Air Force One left Maryland airspace and pursued a course for Little Rock, Arkansas. Fifteen minutes later, Jon changed the course of the conversation.

"Wil, I wanted to talk to you about a threat the White House network security team had uncovered recently. As a former president and husband of the Vice President, I felt you should know. And I'm hoping you might have insight how we might respond."

Wil was surprised at Jon's frankness, and unsure of it. He had no reason to suspect the voice recording scheme had been uncovered, but he had been feeling uncomfortable over the last four days, as no new voice streams had appeared on the server.

"I'm glad to help, Jon. What's going on?"

Jon pulled Heather's old Blackberry out of his carry bag and placed it on the table between the two of them. He watched Wil's response intently. Inside, Wil was terrified at the thought they had uncovered his scheme but maintained his composure. He looked up at Jon, puzzled.

"Do you recognize this phone, Wil?"

"It looks like a standard government issue Blackberry."

"It was your wife's phone. We took it out of service four days ago. We found it had been sabotaged. Not only was there foreign code installed, but the hardware had been altered as well. A secure microphone and transmitter were installed inside."

Jon picked up the phone from the table and feigned examining it. He had it in his right hand and turned his hand in every direction to examine every inch of the case. Wil was stunned into silence.

Jon continued. "For a period of time, we don't know how long, Heather's voice conversations were being recorded, encrypted, and relayed via satellite link to a server on the internet. Whoever is behind this was listening in on your wife's conversations whenever she was in the same room as this phone. Whoever is behind this had access to the phone for an extended period to install the electronics we found. Do you have any idea who might be involved? Anyone who could have had access to her phone long enough for the foreign hardware to be installed without her knowing?"

Though now picturing himself in prison garb, Wil somehow kept his fears concealed. "No Jon. I don't. Do you?"

"There is one individual who appears to have been involved, but we don't believe he's the mastermind. There is reason to believe Heather's former political strategist, Sidney Rosenberg, has something to do with this." Jon intentionally did not disclose why Rosenberg was fingered. He wanted to reserve the smoking gun to use in the future. And he was hoping to build a separation between Rosenberg and the former President. While the IP address evidence pointed only to Wil and Sidney, Jon was concerned there were others involved.

Wil went on defense. "I know Sidney Rosenberg extremely well. I highly doubt he would have either the motive or the fortitude to stand up an illegal wiretapping scheme against the Vice President. Sidney has known Heather for twenty years. They were close. He was her chief political strategist for both her 2008 campaign and last year's. What is the information leading to Sidney? This has to be a mistake."

"I'm sorry I can't give you any details. Classified. But I'm willing to give him the benefit of the doubt. Do you think he'd willingly come in and meet with me?"

"Meet with you, Jon? You're leading the investigation?"

"For now, yes."

"Why?"

"To protect your wife. If she's going to take over when I leave, then I'd like to see this matter settled discreetly. Especially if the responsible individuals included someone close to her. Wil, you've been around Washington a long time. Am I being too naïve? Should I just refer the matter to the DOJ and let them oversee it?"

"The DOJ does not know about the scheme," Wil asked hopefully and wishing it to be the case. "What about the FBI? Secret Service?"

"No, they don't. Only a few staffers in the White House know. And of course, your wife."

"You're not being naïve whatsoever, Jon. You're being smart. You're absolutely right, it's best to contain it. The fewer people who know, the better. If word were to get out, it could prove to be an enormous embarrassment. Not only to Heather, but to the entire Braxton administration."

Jon played along. "Thank you, Wil. It's reassuring you agree with the way we're managing the matter. Would it be OK if I briefed you occasionally on our progress? Tap into your expertise?"

Wil felt it was now the right time to show a bit of respect for the office. "Of course, Mr. President. Whatever you need."

Chapter 19

You're Fired

B eethoven's fifth symphony reverberated loudly from six strate-gically placed professional quality stereo speakers. The per-fectly chilled Chardonnay filled an expensive and exquisite Williams Sonoma etched wine glass. Both the music and the wine were being enjoyed to their fullest in the Upper Manhattan luxury apartment of the former President's chief political strategist, Sidney Rosenberg. He was in a deep, closed-eye trance when the doorbell rang. Sidney opened his eyes, stood slowly, and moved to the door, wineglass in hand. He looked through the peephole and felt a blend of surprise and annoyance at unexpectedly seeing the former president standing impatiently at his doorstep with his right index finger pressed against his pursed lips.

Sidney cracked the door and before it was open three inches, he heard 'shoosh.' Without saying a word, Wil motioned Sidney into the hallway. He led him thirty feet down the hall towards the elevator he had just traveled up. Wil turned and looked down to face the six inches shorter Rosenberg. His hushed voice was barely audible. "Where can we go and talk privately?"

Sidney was confused. "Uh, how about my apartment?"

"Can't take the chance. I'll explain when we go somewhere else where there's no risk we're being monitored."

"What?"

"We've got issues OK. We need to go somewhere we can talk privately."

"There's a wine bar nearby," Sidney offered. "There's a backroom table. I know the owner. She can keep us secluded."

"Good. Go grab your coat. Don't say a word. I'll wait here."

Ten minutes later, Wil and Sidney were alone at the backroom table of Amelie's, near Washington Square.

"I just got back from a trip to Arkansas with Braxton and learned some troubling things."

"Yeah, I saw you two on the news. You and he looked chummy together."

"Well. We're not. He knows."

"Knows what?"

"About Heather's phone and the recordings. And he knows you're involved."

"Shit Wil. You're kidding me. What exactly does he know?"

"I'm not sure, but he mentioned you specifically. And he had Heather's phone."

"What? How could they have suspected anything about her phone? Thought Parker had this all locked up tight. And what about you? Is he aware you're involved?"

"He only mentioned you. Asked me questions about you. Said he's going to invite you to the White House to discuss."

"Why would he tell you all this unless he suspected you?"

"He said it was because he wanted me to know someone was spying on my wife and he asked for advice on how to respond to it. He wants to tap into my experience."

"You believe him?"

"Shit Sidney. I don't know, OK? All I know is he knows someone has been listening in on Heather's conversations. Whether he suspects me or not, I have no idea."

"But he's fingering me," Sidney responded apprehensively. "Appears I'm screwed Wil. I know I shouldn't have jumped into this with you."

"OK, look Sidney. We're going to figure out a plan to get out of this."

Sidney was unconvinced. "You know I could go to prison for a long time. Do you think Braxton knows more than what he told you? Is he going to offer me a deal to disclose what I know, like who else is involved? And how would you expect me to respond? Are you thinking I would take a fall to protect you?"

"Hold on Sidney. You're getting too far out in front of your skis. We don't know if he was serious about calling you in. We don't really know exactly what he knows. He just might be fishing."

"Well, he knows something if he brought my name up. Is the DOJ or the FBI engaged?"

Wil decided to hold that card back. "I'm not sure. I haven't figured him out yet and Heather has not been sharing information with me lately."

Sidney was confused. "It's curious Braxton told you he wanted to speak with me. Why would he involve himself in investigating?"

"Remember, he's still a political neophyte. It's the way he did things in business. Tackled issues head on. It's better if he's going to do this himself. You can outsmart him. And remember, lying to the FBI is a federal offense. It's a good thing if you go to Washington and don't have to talk to them."

Sidney's apprehension returned. "What else did Braxton tell you? Anything else I should know before I'm administered my last rites?"

The former president felt obligated to answer. If Sidney were facing a stint in prison because of his misdeeds, Wil sensed the need to share information Sidney could use to protect himself. "His team opened the phone and found the foreign hardware installed. They also hacked into the phone's operating system and found the code Rayban installed. They know the phone was recording conversations and then sending them out to the internet."

"What about Heather? What does she know?"

"I'm not sure. Like I said, she doesn't talk to me anymore," Wil responded distraughtly.

"When did the silent treatment start? Maybe when she and Braxton became aware of what we were doing? When she became aware you were spying on her?"

Wil was exasperated and shook his head. "It's possible. I guess anything's possible at this point."

"Well, Mr. President. I seem to be royally fucked here. Did you come here with any brilliant ideas for me? Or are you here to say sayonara?"

"I'm here because you need to know what's going on so you can protect yourself."

"And you Mr. President? What will you be doing to protect yourself? Blame everything on me? If you are, you should know it won't work out well for you."

"No. We're not blaming anything on anybody. We're going to figure a way out of this. You get paid handsomely to provide consulting services. Come up with something."

—◦✦◦—

"Mr. President?" It was Rosemary's voice on the intercom.

"Yes, Rosemary."

"Commissioner Barnhardt to see you."

"Send him in."

Stanley Barnhardt made his way into the Oval Office to find Jon sitting at his desk. The President stood and motioned him to one of two guest chairs across from him. Jon coolly extended his hand in a show of disconnected formality. The Commissioner of the United States Food and Drug Administration had never met Jon and took no notice of his emotional detachment. He shook the President's hand with great enthusiasm.

"It's an honor to meet you, Mr. President."

"Let's see if you feel the same in fifteen minutes," Jon responded tersely.

Barnhardt furrowed his brow. "Is there something wrong, Mr. President?"

"There is Stanley. But perhaps I'm misguided, so let's have a discussion, shall we?"

"Yes sir. Of course."

"Stanley, I trust you're familiar with the biological product provisions in Section 351 of the Public Health Service Act?"

"Yes, Mr. President."

"Good. Summarize those provisions for me." The disdain in Jon's voice hovered over his words.

"Well, sir, Section 351 refers to the treatment of new biological and drug products and equipment. It stipulates pre-market approval processes and post-market compliance requirements for any new products in those classifications seeking FDA approval."

Jon responded instantaneously. "And those pre-market approval processes and post-market compliance requirements are quite difficult and extremely expensive to navigate I've been led to believe."

"Yes, sir, intentionally so. Our charter at the FDA is to protect people in this country from health-related products which are not adequately evaluated for safety and efficacy."

"I see. And I trust you're also familiar with Section 361 of the Public Health Service Act."

"Yes sir. Section 361 regulates the use of human cells, tissues, and cellular related products. Human organisms and cellular-related products are subject only to limited FDA oversight focusing on how securely these human-based products are collected, processed, stored, and distributed."

The President was growing impatient with Barnhardt's pretentious tone. "And I presume, correct me if I'm wrong, products subject to the regulations under Section 351 rather than 361 encounter many more obstacles and far greater expense, making their way into clinical trials and eventually into the marketplace."

"Yes, sir, again by design. Manufactured inorganic products are subject to greater regulation coming onto the market than processes and procedures utilizing organic materials."

"I see. Stanley, as you know, the Braxton administration is highly focused on finding the cure for Type 1 diabetes."

"Yes sir. I'm well aware of the work the First Lady is doing. We stand by her one hundred percent."

"As I would expect of you, Stanley. It would be unfortunate if you were somehow standing not by her, but in her way."

"Sir?"

"Stanley, explain the difference to me between pancreatic auto-islet cells and allo-islet cells."

"Well sir, pancreatic auto-islet cells are pancreatic cells extracted from the pancreas of a patient and then reintroduced into the same patient. Allo-islet pancreatic cells are cells extracted from a donor pancreas and then transplanted into a patient who is deemed to be a genetic match."

"And Stanley, is it your understanding that in most cases it is not practical to harvest pancreatic cells from a Type 1 diabetic since the cells have already been compromised, if not already destroyed? And realistically, the only hope for a Type 1 diabetic to take advantage of the advancements in the field of islet-cell transplantation is to have allo-islet cells from a matched donor transplanted?"

"Yes sir. This is unfortunately the case."

The President cut Barnhardt off from elaborating. "The advancements in allo-islet cell transplantation are quite remarkable would you not agree Stanley? And this area of study could hold the key for eliminating the suffering of millions of people around the world. Would you agree on this point as well?"

"Yes sir, to both."

"Good, we're in double agreement. Now, since both auto-islet and allo-islet transplantation procedures consist of the transplantation of organic material, as you call it, then I would presume both allo-islet and auto-islet cell transplantations are regulated under the less restrictive Section 361. Am I correct Stanley?"

"Uh, no, sir. That is not the case."

"It's not?" The President feigned surprise. "Explain please."

"Auto-islet cell transplantation is regulated under Section 361. Allo-islet cell transplantation is regulated under Section 351."

"Why the difference Commissioner Barnhardt?"

"Well, sir. I am not sure. These regulations have been in place for quite a while. I haven't studied the thinking and the circumstances behind them."

The President was finding it more difficult to contain his rage as the conversation progressed. "I find it curious, Stanley. Our allies around the world don't have the burdensome regulations we do on transplantation procedures, which have proven to be effective in helping Type 1 diabetic patients. Europe. Japan. Canada. They don't have a Section 351 for allo-islet cell transplantation. And they are performing these procedures regularly. Yet in the United States we are not. And the only reason is outdated and illogical FDA regulations. Is this your belief as well, Mr. Commissioner?"

"Again, sir. I have not studied this."

"Why not?"

"We have many responsibilities at the FDA. We can't get to all of them as quickly as everyone would like."

"Stanley, talk to me about the pharmaceutical lobby. Are they involved in the execution of your responsibilities? With our FDA putting health care products and procedures under regulations which impose immense capital requirements to bring life-saving propositions to market, I would think this hinders competition and facilitates an unlevel playing field. And limits our ability to take advantage of new and innovative therapies and potential cures. I can't imagine our FDA would do this intentionally."

"Sir, as you might imagine, we have many parties attempting to influence our policies and our decisions."

Jon was doing his best to control his anger, his best not being enough to contain his unequivocal contempt. "I see. And I would also imagine you can see past those influences and make your decisions based on the best interests of our citizens."

Barnhardt was stunned by the President's words and tone and did not answer.

Jon continued. "I've been informed auto-islet and allo-islet cells are isolated using the same methods, technologies, and regimens. By the same personnel, in the same facilities. And the characteristics of the resulting cells are the same. It seems to me regulating the transplantation of allo-islet cells under Section 351 while regulating all other organ transplantation efforts under Section 361 is effectively restricting access in this country to this therapy. This despite studies by our own NIH showing this therapy to be safe and effective. What's your opinion on this Stanley? Is it flawed thinking restricting our citizens from accessing this therapy, which stands to benefit them? Or is there something more sinister in play, like politics or the interests of the pharmaceutical industry?"

Barnhardt sat stoically, unwilling to answer.

"Mr. Commissioner, how long have you been in your position?"

"I was appointed in 2009, Mr. President," Barnhardt answered indignantly.

"You've been in your role eight years and during your tenure you have not reviewed nor evaluated nor amended Section 351 as it relates to Type 1 diabetes treatments using islet-cell transplantation. And your reason is you can't get to it?"

The President slapped his two palms on his desk in frustration, stood, and walked to the Oval Office door leading to Rosemary's desk. He opened it and turned to look at Barnhardt.

"Stanley, this meeting is over. And your tenure as the Commissioner of the FDA is over. You're fired."

Chapter 20

Fix Our Well Being

"Good morning from Washington DC. I'm Wallis Kriss and welcome to Big News Sunday. Today, we have a special show for you. We're pleased to have three quests from the White House joining us. During our first segment, we'll talk with one of our favorites, the First Lady, Angela Braxton. There have been significant developments within the **TYPE 1-YOU'RE DONE** Project, and the First Lady is excited to bring our audience, and the world, up to date. During our second segment we'll be interviewing the country's recently appointed Culture Czar, Jeffrey Claymore. Mr. Claymore, now six weeks into his role, will discuss his appointment and what his agenda is shaping up to be. And for our last segment, we'll be welcoming back for his first appearance in over two months, the President himself. He'll be discussing with us how he views the job he has been doing, what his current priorities are, and what lies ahead. It should be an interesting and informative sixty minutes. Please stay tuned and we'll be back with the First Lady after a word from our sponsors."

When the broadcast resumed, Angela was sitting in front of a glass top desk at a forty-five-degree angle from Kriss and directly facing a camera stage right. Kriss stared into the camera stage left as the red light went on and addressed his growing multi-million strong viewership.

"Welcome back to Big News Sunday." He turned slightly to his right to face Angela. "And welcome back to you Madam First Lady. We're grateful to have you back on the show. I know you only have a short while with us today, as you have meetings taking place this weekend at the White House. But we'll take whatever time you can spare. The feedback from our listening audience for your last appearance was overwhelmingly positive. You are quite popular."

The First Lady radiated a captivating smile. "Thank you, Wallis. It's nice to hear your audience approves of what we are doing and I'm happy to be back. Especially with the exciting news we can share about the developments taking place within the **TYPE 1-YOU'RE DONE** project.

"I won't be standing in your way, Madam Vice President. I know better. Please tell our viewing audience what's happening with the project."

"Wallis, we are more confident than ever we will meet our goal of seeing a cure for Type 1 diabetes within three years, Recent developments are driving our enthusiasm and our expectation we will accomplish our objective."

Kriss was impressed and upbeat. "Without being overly technical, can you describe what those developments are?"

"As we shared with your viewers the last time we were here, we have four teams working in four distinct areas related to different pathways for preventing and curing Type 1 diabetes. Within each area, the leading medical research organizations in the country specializing in those pathways, thanks to the President's restructuring of NIH grants, are now collaborating. With the collaboration now taking place within each team, the pace of advancement and testing of multiple hypotheses is accelerating significantly. And one team has achieved what we consider a significant breakthrough, our Blood Stem Cell team. Stem cell therapy has always offered promise as a potential cure, but an issue difficult to maneuver around is the Type 1 diabetic's immune system. Their immune systems see newly implanted cells as foreign material and begin an onslaught to destroy them."

Wallis jumped in. "So even though you're seeing advancements and promise in stem cell transplantation therapy, these cells also come under attack by the patient's immune system? Just as the patient's own insulin-producing cells did with the onset of the disease?"

"That's right Wallis. The immune system of a Type 1 diabetic detects newly donated blood stem cells as foreign and attacks them much in the way the patient's immune system attacks their own pancreatic insulin-producing cells. Because of this, transplantation therapy has to be accompanied by immune suppression therapy. Today, our only immunotherapy suppression options are pharmaceuticals, and these drugs all have negative side effects. This reality has been a major obstacle in scaling out transplantation cell therapy as a viable cure for most patients. But our Blood Stem Cell team has recently achieved a historic breakthrough."

"Sounds promising. Tell us more about the breakthrough."

The First Lady tempered her enthusiasm to offer Kriss' audience a clinical explanation. "Thanks to the efforts being led by Dr. Jonah Shapiro from CanadaDRI in Edmonton, Alberta, we are on a path to successfully utilize a patient's own blood cells transformed into insulin-producing cells, as opposed to using cells from a donor. This breakthrough could help us overcome an obstacle presented by the patient's immune system. Dr. Shapiro is expanding on the findings of Dr. Shinya Yamanaka, the 2012 Nobel Prize winner in the field of medicine, who discovered a process for reverting an adult's blood stem cells back to a pluripotent pre-embryonic stem cell state. Once in a pluripotent state, these cells can be reprogrammed to become insulin-producing with a reduced risk of coming under attack from the patient's immune system. Another significant aspect of this breakthrough is using the patient's own blood cells eliminates the restrictive supply limitations of using donor pancreatic cells."

"This sounds fantastic, Madam Vice President," Kriss added enthusiastically.

"It is extremely exciting, Wallis. If you remember my husband's address to the Republican National Convention in 2012, he discussed the promise of pluripotent cells but also the moral dilemma their use presented. The idea of harvesting embryonic or pre-embryonic material for medical research was disturbing and unethical for many. With the promise of the findings of Dr. Yamanaka and the research being led by Dr. Shapiro, we eliminate the moral dilemma associated with harvesting native pluripotent cells. We mitigate the tendency of the patient's immune system to attack donor transplanted cells. And we overcome the shortage of donor pancreatic cell supply. The successes of our initial results are giving us all optimistic hope we will see a cure within three years."

"Truly amazing, Mrs. Braxton. It sounds as if your strategy for building more collaboration and removing funding obstacles is delivering the results you expected. Remarkable. The work of you and your colleagues is to be commended. What's next in the process of evaluating the Blood Stem Cell team's hypothesis?"

"The team is only working with lab animals at this point, but if we continue at our current pace, we should be ready to start human testing and then clinical trials by early next year. The team is currently studying what would constitute the most sensible group of volunteers to consider for phase one. Age would be one factor for consideration.

Length of time with Type 1, another. Insulin sensitivity, another. In expectation of advancing to the next stage, the team is already collecting blood samples from potential phase 1 candidates and exposing those samples to Dr. Yamanaka's protocol. In the coming weeks, the team will evaluate these reverted blood cell samples for pluripotency. If the reversion protocol proves successful, those cells will be gene-edited to transform them into insulin-producing cells. We hope by the first quarter of next year the research will be far enough along for phase one clinical trialing where we will transplant these newly reprogrammed cells back into the individual from which they came. Then we monitor their ability to produce their own insulin and monitor their immune system for any problematic responses. And now, Wallis, you'll have to excuse me. We have important project business being conducted today and I should get back to the White House. But I hope you will invite me back soon so I can share our progress with your audience."

"Of this you can be certain, Madam First Lady. Again, congratulations on your progress and thank you again for taking time from your busy schedule to join us." Wallis turned to face the camera stage left. "We'll be right back with the country's first Culture Czar, Jeffrey Claymore, right after these messages."

This was Jeffrey Claymore's first appearance on any broadcast media since his appointment as the country's first Culture Czar. Thanks to his forty-plus years of standing in front of God, and the last four years watching Jon Braxton spar with Wallis Kriss, he was well prepared for what he expected to be tough questioning from the often-confrontational host of Big News Sunday. Jeffrey was calm, cool, and collected. And dressed for the part in a modest dark gray business suit, light gray shirt, and solid blue tie.

"Welcome back to Big News Sunday." Kriss was staring into the camera stage left. "We're now pleased to be joined by Jeffrey Claymore. Pastor Claymore, as he is commonly known. He is the nation's first Culture Czar, as appointed by President Braxton six weeks ago. Good morning, Pastor. Welcome to Big News Sunday."

While Claymore's religious affiliations had been played down to the media on all press releases and discussions of the position coming from the White House communications team prior to and following his appointment, Jon and Jeffrey discussed the likelihood Kriss would bring it up immediately to put Jeffrey on the defensive. He did not disappoint. Wallis Kriss wanted first-time guests to his show back on their heels. This was his show, and he would set the tone. Or so he thought.

"Thank you, Wallis. I'm excited by the chance to tell you and your viewers what we have in mind to cure this country of what ails it. And please just call me Jeffrey, as the President does."

"Out of reverence, sir. I'd prefer to call you Pastor Claymore. OK with you?"

"No," Jeffrey responded politely and with a smile.

Kriss was expecting a different answer, and one with more than one word. Jeffrey's engaging smile made the show's host uneasy. There was a brief awkward silence before Kriss recovered. "And why not, sir?"

"Wallis, you served in the U.S. Army for six years as I understand it. And I believe you had attained the rank of sergeant. Is my information correct?"

"It is, sir. What is your point?"

"Would it be appropriate for me to refer to you as Sergeant Kriss at this time?"

Kriss squirmed. He wasn't comfortable when guests, particularly first-time guests, would reach for the upper hand. "No, it would not.

I'm no longer in the army and my rank has nothing to do with my show."

"Exactly. I agree. It is not appropriate. And it is not appropriate for you to refer to me as Pastor Claymore today. My religious affiliation has nothing to do with the job I've been hired to do, nor how I will approach it. And has nothing to do with the reason for me being on your show."

Kriss felt an urge for a second to engage in a sparring match with Claymore but quickly dispelled the thought. He decided to concede this skirmish and keep the interview going in a positive direction, at least until he saw another opening for confrontation. "Very well Jeffrey, please give our viewers a little background on yourself and how you came onto the President's radar for this role."

"Of course. What's important for your viewers to know about me is I am a businessman. I'm in the business of making people's lives better. I've been in this business for over forty years and have thousands of satisfied customers. The majority of customers I've served were young kids from the streets of Philadelphia, where I first met them. And I've continued to serve them as they have grown into adolescence and adulthood. As for how I came to know Jon, it was an introduction made by Carlton and Cornelius Hale in 2012. The Hales were investors in my business and introduced us, as they believed Jon could help me solve a difficult personnel problem. We met, and the Hales turned out to be correct. Jon solved our problem quickly and efficiently. As you now know, having seen Jon in action in Washington for the last four years, he's rather good at problem solving. Wouldn't you agree, Wallis?"

Kriss loathed it when his guests started asking the questions. He responded half-heartedly, "I certainly would."

Jeffrey continued. "After our initial interaction, Jon and I became close friends. When Jon made the decision to enter politics in 2013, we spoke often. Mostly about Jon's challenges in Congress and how he should navigate the swamp. But we also often talked about public policy. We talked about what the role of government in people's lives should be. What should be its primary objectives? How far should government intrude into a person's life? Jon remembered all those conversations, and after four months being the President, he decided a focus of his administration would be to seek ways to make people's lives better while striking balance between intervention and personal autonomy. He's asked me to lead this measured cultural revolution, and here I am."

Kriss saw an opening and sought to regain the upper hand. He pushed back hard. "Sir, it seems a classic example of government overreach into people's personal lives. A cultural intervention and a Culture Czar? You have to admit this will not sit well with those on the right who favor smaller government and less intrusion into people's personal lives. Frankly sir, without knowing specifics, this effort seems to me an unneeded exercise in futility. It seems overly idealistic and completely unrealistic. For your mission to have any chance at success, you'll have to make your case to the country. Is this is a worthwhile investment in time, money, and effort? You'll need to explain to the country exactly why we need a cultural intervention. Exactly why we need a Culture Czar."

Jeffrey smiled again, to the chagrin of Kriss, who was hoping to see him buckle under. His smile was from his recollection of a conversation with Jon when he predicted Kriss' bullying attempt to the word. "I agree completely, Wallis. Let's get started with those explanations, shall we?"

Kriss was frustrated he couldn't ruffle Claymore and was angered at having to field another question. "OK Jeffrey, get us started. Tell us what you're proposing and why the country needs you and needs your plan."

Claymore maintained an upbeat tone and was eager to accommodate. "Before I address your questions, let me address one I mentioned earlier. When Jon was in Congress, he and I often talked about the role the federal government should play in people's everyday lives. Let me answer by describing what Jon and I feel the role of the federal government should not be. In no way should our government take on a role of dictating anything when it comes to people's personal choices on how they live their lives. First and foremost, we both believe in respecting the right of our citizens to make their own choices, even if they are poorly formed and harmful to their health, happiness, or success. Instead, we believe the most useful role the government can play is providing accurate, truthful, and actionable information to help people make better choices for themselves. But the choice should remain with the individual. For the individual, we value personal liberty and freedom. For the federal government, we see its role being to help our citizens make better choices by providing them the information and the tools to do so."

Kriss could not contain his skepticism. "You said the President believes the country needs a cultural intervention. I'm having trouble accepting his conclusion. It's a strong term, and it suggests a belief the country is in cultural decline. Is this your belief as well, Jeffrey? Is our country in a cultural decline, and given all the other issues facing us, does this effort deserve the intense focus from the White House to appoint a czar and to perform, as you refer to it, an intervention?"

"Wallis, let me share relevant information with you and then you can tell me if you think the country might need what we're working to provide. Immediately after my appointment, my team set out to validate the President's assumptions. We reached out to five polling organizations and polled ten thousand Americans. Each organization conducted a poll asking a cross section of two thousand Americans questions about how they perceived their quality of life. We asked for the responses to be given as a number from one to ten, with one being a strong no and ten being a strong yes. We chose five polling questions. One, are you leading a meaningful life? Two, do you have a purpose which guides your life? Three, how happy are you with your life? Four, do you have specific goals and objectives you are striving for and are you on a path to achieve them? And five, if you had an opportunity to go through a learning experience to improve your life, would you take your time to go through a free program? We now have the results. Would your viewers be interested in hearing them?"

Kriss was dismissive. "Of course. What did you learn?"

"We polled ten thousand Americans. Remember, we asked the responses to each question to be a number from one to ten, with one being a strong no and ten being a strong yes. On question one, are you leading a meaningful life, the average response was 2.5. Question two, does your life have purpose, 2.4. Question three, your degree of happiness with your life, 3.2. Question four, do you have goals and are on the way to achieve them, 2.9. And question five, if there was a free program to help you discover ways to lead a better life would you attend, 8.7. These results tell a story, Wallis. The President was right. And my job is to get the numbers up on questions one through four."

Kriss could not focus on the numbers. He had already decided to counter everything Jeffrey would say. "And what were your conclusions?"

Claymore sensed Kriss' detachment and decided to change course. "Can I ask you something?"

"You can ask, but I'm not sure I'll answer. I'm the host and it's my role to ask the questions."

Jeffrey ignored his reply. "How do you define yourself?"

"What?"

"After your role as a husband and father, how do you define your-self?"

"I'd say as a political commentator and talk show host."

"Why?"

"Because it's what I do."

"OK, it's what you do. Are you good at it? Do you like doing it?"

"I believe I'm good at it. And I love doing it."

"If you were asked our questions, on the first four where we asked Americans about the meaning of their lives, their level of happiness, their direction, what numbers would you have responded with?"

"Probably eights or nines," Kriss responded nonchalantly.

"From our polling, most Americans answered two or three. Can you describe what your state of mind would be? What your level of happiness would be? Or what your outlook on your life would be if you could only respond to those questions with a two or a three?"

Kriss did not answer immediately. Jeffrey's question had struck a nerve. After three seconds, he replied with uncertainty. "I'm not sure."

"You're not sure because you don't live the life a large majority of Americans live. You're not feeling the gradual decline of our culture. Our polling results tell me Jon's intuition is right. It tells me a large majority of people in this country lead lives with little meaning or direction or satisfaction. You say an effort to change this, to offer the citizens of this country information and tools they can use to add meaning, direction and satisfaction to their lives is overly idealistic and completely unrealistic. I would counter, what better role is there for government?"

"OK Jeffrey. Your job as the country's Culture Czar is to improve people's everyday lives. Just how do you propose to do so?"

"We're going to conduct our poll again in two years. The President has tasked me to get the average responses on questions one through four, up from twos and threes to over five on each question. To accomplish this, we're going to develop and roll out a nationwide program to help our citizens add meaning and purpose to their everyday lives. Because we see more need for our tools and information in larger urban areas, we're going to start our efforts in the country's twenty largest cities."

Kriss returned to skepticism. "This sounds like a tall order. What's this program going to look like?"

"We're establishing a public-private partnership we're calling the Lead A Better Everyday Life Foundation. Otherwise known as the LABEL Foundation. Our plan is to repurpose unused properties in each of the cities were targeting and build out LABEL campuses. We're starting an outreach to private companies in these cities to join the partnership and help with funding. We're confident we'll get significant buy in as these companies will see our efforts enhancing their labor pool. We're formulating a curriculum to include learning tracks to teach information and mental exercises to help people develop better thought patterns and behaviors, which we know will lead to greater personal happiness, purpose, and direction. Our efforts are being modeled after Jon's private sector Win-The-Day Foundation and his public sector STYLE education reform legislation. Both programs have proven extraordinarily successful in helping school age young people add meaning and purpose to their lives. We hope to accomplish comparable results by teaching similar concepts to adults. We've started working with universities and state colleges to establish instruction tracks for these principles. It's an enormous task in front of us to create the curriculum and train educators to deliver it. But so far, the response from everyone we've approached to work with us has been positive."

Kriss' objections were fading and his tone and attitude towards Jeffrey shifted. "What kinds of things will be taught in these learning centers?"

"There are numerous avenues we will be pursuing. And to describe them in any detail would take hours. But let me summarize a couple. One avenue is occupational guidance. We feel helping people choose a line of work which matches up with their personality would enhance personal satisfaction. You mentioned earlier, Wallis, you love your work. Most people do not have the same affection for the work they do. Many tolerate their work, but most begrudge their jobs. They only do the work they do because they need to pay their bills. Would you say you do the work you do because you have to? No, you do it because you want to. This plays an influential role in your satisfaction with your life. One program the LABEL Foundation will focus on is personality assessment. We will help people determine which professions best match up with their personalities and preferences, and we will work with public and private sector employers to provide opportunities for these people in areas where their assessment concludes they will be the most satisfied and productive."

"We have just another two minutes, Jeffrey. Describe one other area on which you'll be focusing?"

"Thanks Wallis. One thing I've learned from my forty-plus years of working with young people is how fulfilling artistic expression is. People leading unfulfilling lives will benefit immensely from an opportunity to express themselves through art forms. We see our campuses providing people an opportunity to be exposed to different art forms, with the intent they find one to invest time and effort in. We'll offer lessons in music, acting, painting, sculpture, and glass art, among others. Another area we'll focus on is nutrition. Many lead unfulfilling lives because they are not adequately nourishing themselves. We will offer classes on food choices, nutrition, and cooking. We will reinforce the connection between proper nutrition and personal happiness and success. These are examples of the things we will focus on. I hope this gives your audience an idea of how we plan to create an improved cultural landscape in this country, particularly in our inner cities."

When the broadcast resumed, Jon was seated in the guest chair fronted by the glass desk. The camera stage left showed a closeup of Kriss. "And we're back now for our last segment with the President. Sir, welcome back to Big News Sunday."

Camera stage right panned out to show both Jon and Wallis facing one another. On the table in front of Jon was a pitcher of a dark colored liquid, two frosted mugs, one football seated on a kicking tee and a vial filled with a gray powdery substance.

"Wally, ready for a root beer?"

"Of course, Mr. President. You buying?"

"Indeed." While remaining seated, Jon filled the two mugs and handed one to Kriss. They both leaned towards each other, clanked their mugs, and took a swig.

Kriss was half-laughing as he addressed the President. "I see you've brought items for us to work with today. The football I think recognize from our last visit."

Jon took the football from the tee, placed it into his left hand and tossed it softly six feet to Kriss, who caught it without effort. He spun the ball around to read the marking aloud. "FIX OUR WELL BEING."

"Wally, how are you feeling today?"

Kriss replied while looking at the football and working on his grip. "I feel good, sir. How about you?"

"I feel good as well, but we cannot say the same for millions of Americans. There is a pandemic of poor health in our country and a vast majority of people in this country simply don't often feel well. Many suffer from physical conditions, my son, as an example. And many suffer from what's commonly called mental illness. Both can devastate a life and devastate a family. Couldn't or better said, shouldn't the people elected to lead this country champion relieving suffering from illness, both physical and mental, as an area of focus?"

"Certainly, a noble task, sir, but we already have an industry in this country focused on health care. I know you're an advocate of the private sector and a free market economy. There are tremendous advancements made every day, every year, in the field of medicine and therapies. Isn't the health care industry better positioned than the federal government to deliver health care solutions?"

"Wally, do you watch any television, particularly the network your show airs on?"

"Yes sir, I watch the Big News channel regularly. I enjoy the work of my colleagues here at the network."

"Good, then you're probably aware of what industry dominates the advertising on your network and on your program."

Kriss was uncomfortable answering with a feeling where Jon was going would not be welcomed by his show's largest sponsors. "I'm not entirely sure."

"It's OK. I understand your hesitation. But there's no denying the pharmaceutical industry is well represented on your list of advertisers."

Kriss was looking at Jon, but his peripheral vision caught the Big News Sunday show's executive producer off stage waving his arms to get Kriss' attention. When the producer saw Kriss' eyes move in his direction, he pointed his fingers towards his throat and moved them back and forth in a slashing motion. Jon noticed Kriss' eyes looking off stage and his change in facial demeanor.

"Wally, your producer should know what I'm planning to tell you and your viewers today, I'll also be sharing during a White House news conference this coming Wednesday. If you'd like to change the course of our conversation so I do not offend your advertisers, let me know and you can take the interview in another direction."

Kriss was frozen, but managed a response. "Mr. President. We're cutting away for commercial. We'll pick this up when we return."

Kriss unplugged and ran offstage to confer with his show's executive producer, during which time three pharmaceutical commercials aired.

"Jim, what do you want me to do?"

"Shit Wallis. I don't know. Why don't you just start asking him about Jeffrey Claymore? Take the conversation down another road."

"Yeah. I don't know about that, Jim. It will be plain as day we're censuring the President of the United States. We'll lose tens of thousands of viewers, and knowing Braxton, he'll make us regret it. And never come back on the show. Can we risk losing him as a regular guest?"

"OK Wallis. It's your show. But if we lose our biggest advertisers, it hurts us all. Be ready to take a pay cut come contract negotiation time."

"I know. But we can't lose our viewers. We can find new sponsors."

When the commercial break was over, Kriss was back in his chair, all plugged in. The broadcast resumed. He was never more uncertain about directing the course of an interview. He had a sense this was a defining moment for the future of his show, and potentially his broadcasting career.

"We're back with President Braxton and we're discussing the physical and mental well-being of Americans. The President has a plan to improve the lives of Americans by improving their physical and mental health. Sir, you say you wish to fix our well-being. Is it your belief our health care system is broken and needs fixing? It's common knowledge people throughout the world feel our nation's health care industry is second to none."

"Wally, let me answer you this way. Fixing our well-being has little to do with our health care industry. And more to do with convincing people to change their behaviors. Your statement earlier stating I'm a big advocate for the private sector and free market economies is correct. Your statement we have a health care industry focused on wellness I disagree with. I see them more focused on treatments. Thirty minutes ago, the First Lady shared with you the advancements being made in the search for curing Type 1 diabetes. Not to say these advancements would never have taken place outside of her project, but the fact remains, without her strategic intervention, we might be waiting another twenty years. Another twenty years of suffering. People in the Type 1 community have been promised for a long time the cure for T1D was just around the corner. But after twenty-plus years of involvement and hundreds of millions of government-funded investment dollars, we still have no cure. The First Lady has proven there is a positive role for government in a free-market capitalist system. A role in establishing priorities to guide a free-market economy. When we have a failure by an industry to solve a problem it's their business to solve, it's a result of their priorities not being in order. Or it's more profitable to maintain the problem than to solve it. So yes, we have a vibrant health care industry. They produce amazing products and provide valuable services. But the fact remains, we have millions of Americans suffering from physical and mental illness in this country. Now, not to be misunderstood, let me say this is not the fault of health care service and delivery individuals. The men and woman on the front lines who dedicate themselves to their profession and serve patients, often under extremely difficult circumstances, are genuine heroes. At issue is our systems, our health care regulations, and our health care bureaucracies. All of which are unduly influenced by special interests and lobby money."

Kriss was picturing the show's biggest advertisers pulling their commercials, but stayed in the moment. "You mentioned strategic direction changes. Can you share another one with us?" Kriss was still holding the football marked with 'FIX OUR WELL BEING.' He tossed it back to Jon, who placed it back on the tee, spinning it around so the markings faced the camera, and then responded.

"We have an industry in this country focused on health care. And the industry is booming. They have millions of customers and make billions of dollars. Good for them. But not necessarily good for their customers. A sizable percentage of their business comes from people who don't properly take care of themselves. And the result of this neglect is suffering and expense. Why is this, Wally? Why do people adopt behaviors which lead to their ill health? Jeffrey Claymore addressed this earlier on your show and as you now know, we'll be addressing why people make such poor decisions for themselves. What's our plan to fix our well-being? Quite simple, actually. We will start focusing on wellness care. We're going to educate people how to take better care of themselves. We're going to address their tendencies to make bad choices. We're going to educate Americans how to get better and stay well. We're going to promote wellness behaviors through public service announcements and campaigns. We're going to address the underlying causes of why people neglect their good health. We're going to collaborate with our citizens to give them reasons to take better care of themselves. This will be a focal point of fixing our culture. And we expect the private sector will follow our lead and bring innovative methods for healthy behavior modifications to the marketplace. This approach worked successfully against tobacco smoking in the 1960s. How many lives have been saved and how much suffering avoided by the significant reduction in smoking in this country?"

Kriss was thinking about his next career move while formulating his response. He felt it appropriate to toss his advertisers a bone. "Well, sir. I expect corporations in the health care industry will not be pleased with your plan. It will impact their businesses."

"I'm sure you're right, Wally. But on the other hand, we believe our focus will kindle new companies and new products in the wellness space. As for companies with legacy businesses which would be negatively impacted by our focus, I suggest they study the science of obsolescence. Old ways and legacy business models often disappear over time. It's the inevitable result of progress. Besides, I see their demise as a small price to pay for improving the overall health and wellness of Americans. I believe this should be the focus of our federal government, not the profits of the pharmaceutical industry."

"Sir, if I may change course a little bit, I see you have a vial of powder in front of you. Is there something else you wish to tell our viewers?"

"First, another root beer?" Kriss' mug was empty. He handed it to Jon, who poured him one and handed the mug back as he answered. "Wally, are you a student of the Vietnam War era?"

"Somewhat. I've interviewed dozens of military personnel over the years."

"Have you ever interviewed a soldier who came back from Vietnam with trauma? Or from any of our wars. Korea? Iraq? Afghanistan?"

"I can't say I have, Mr. President."

"How about our Veterans Administration? Ever done any investigative journalism on the VA?"

"No, sir."

"This may have been before your time, but did you ever have the chance to speak with Richard Nixon?"

Kriss was puzzled by Jon's line of questioning. "No, and you're right, sir. Richard Nixon was a bit before my time."

"Wally, I've been in office now for seven months and one thing which truly bothers me about how this country operates is how we treat the brave men and women in our military who make monumental sacrifices in service to our country. Some the ultimate sacrifice. They make these sacrifices not knowing the reasons behind why they are asked to do what they do, even if it cuts against their principles, their morals, or their beliefs. They simply do their job because it's how they are trained. They are trained to fight, knowing they could die or become incapacitated. And they do this because they believe they are protecting you and I."

Kriss was unprepared to respond. He sat still and stared at Jon, hoping the President would see he had nothing to say and carry the conversation. Jon picked up the glass vial containing the gray powdery substance. He held it up to the light and spun it around and then handed it to Kriss, who set it on the table in front of him. He stared at it, still speechless.

"Wally, if we want to be a better country, we need to take better care of the people in this country who are ill. Either physically ill or mentally ill. We spoke moments ago about how our people can improve their physical health by learning new behaviors. But we need also address the issue of mental illness where learning new behaviors is more challenging. And we should start with our military veterans and first responders. Wally, want to venture a guess on the number of our military vets who commit suicide every day?"

"Uh no, sir. I have no idea."

"On an average day, it's between thirty and fifty. Every day, somewhere between thirty and fifty of our nation's finest give up. They decide they can no longer live with their trauma. They decide they would rather stop living than continue to live with their nightmares and their guilt. And they decide to take their own lives and leave behind the ones they love. To my thinking, our nation knows no greater shame than the shame we deserve for failing these heroes."

Jon reached for the football marked with 'FIX OUR WELL BRING' sitting on the tee in front of him. He spun it in his left hand, so his fingers crossed the laces and tossed it softly back to Kriss, who caught it without effort and responded, "what are your ideas sir for addressing this injustice?"

"Wally, I'd like to ask all your viewers to do homework. May I?"

"Of course."

"Good." Jon turned his attention to the camera, stage right. "Because of the success of the First Lady and Project **TYPE 1-YOU'RE DONE,** I'm convinced we have the ability in our country to improve our wellness. To do so is a matter of applying the right focus and establishing the right priorities. I ask you all, please go online and do research on PTSD. And do research on the studies conducted in this country in the 1960s on the use of natural psychedelic compounds to treat trauma and depression. Studies which were showing amazing results and promise but were unfortunately halted because of Richard Nixon's war on drugs. Learn about the substances ibogaine, psilocybin, ayahuasca, mescaline, peyote, and 5-MeO-DMT. Educate yourself on how these substances are not pharmaceutical narcotics, but natural organic materials placed on this planet by whatever power it was which had the wherewithal to do so. Educate yourself on the legitimate clinical studies conducted in this country in the years prior to Nixon's ill-advised policies. Study the effects of these compounds on mental illness. Learn all you can and form an opinion. Join us and our administration's efforts to fix the mental health crisis in this country. Do so by becoming informed. And be ready to help us put an end to the suffering of so many."

"Mr. President, this vial of gray powder you handed me. Would you like to tell us about it?"

"It's psilocybin powder. Psilocybin is a natural organic material produced by over two hundred species of fungi. Mushrooms. The compound has been used in spiritual ceremonies all over the world for thousands of years. When your viewers start their own research, they'll see the number of therapeutic studies on psilocybin and other natural hallucinogenic compounds conducted in this country over the last sixty years. And the positive results generated by micro-dosing, administered in a controlled therapeutic setting. There's little doubt Wally the natural compounds nature provides us can be instrumental in improving the lives of so many people around the world suffering with mental illness when administered properly."

The hour was over. Kriss looked into the camera stage left. "Ladies and gentlemen. That concludes our show for today. Let's hope we get the chance to do it again. From Washington, I'm Wallis Kriss."

Chapter 21

Good Luck Sidney

The empty limousine pulled up to Sidney Rosenberg's Manhattan apartment building at eleven a.m. on a Wednesday morning. Sidney told Rosemary Barnett he would fly to Washington for the meeting requested by the President, but Jon insisted on a limo to minimize the inconvenience. And to ensure Sydney was alone with his thoughts for a significant while before they met. At eleven-fifteen a.m., the four-hour journey commenced.

Sidney was chauffeured directly to the Waldorf-Astoria Hotel, a half mile from the White House, where he would spend the evening. He arrived at five. The meeting was scheduled for the following morning at nine. He spent the evening in his suite with room service. At eight, shortly after he finished his dinner, there was a knock at the door. He answered to find no one there, and a sealed box at the foot of the door. Taped to the outside was a typed note requesting he visit Roosevelt Island following his meeting with Jon.

When Sidney arrived at the White House the next morning, given the briefing the previous week from Wil, he was uncertain what to expect. In parallel, Jon had been contemplating how to stage the meeting. He considered having Heather in the room to set Sidney at ease. He considered having Ben Wade in the room to explain their findings, with all references to Sidney's and Wil's involvement purposely excluded. He considered placing Heather's Blackberry, without explanation or reference, on the coffee table which would separate him and Sidney. After considering all, he decided on neither. It would just be the two of them.

It was nine a.m. when Sidney was ushered into the Oval Office. He found Jon standing in front of his desk to greet him.

"Mr. Rosenberg, welcome back to the Oval Office. No doubt you've been in this room on occasion. Is it still the way you remember it?"

"Hello Mr. President. It's an honor to meet you. And yes, I've been here once or twice," he answered sarcastically, "though not since President Carrington left office. And yes, it looks all too familiar."

"Really? Obama never invited you over?"

"That would be no Mr. President. We don't particularly care for one another."

"Ahh, makes sense. Well, I want you to feel comfortable and at ease. Can I pour you a cup of coffee?"

"No, sir. I've already had enough this morning."

The President nodded. "OK, let's sit down. I need your help with something urgent and would welcome discussing it with you. I appreciate your making the time to travel to Washington and apologize for any inconvenience. Please, have a seat."

Jon motioned Sidney to a place on one of the two sofas adjacent to his desk. He sat on the other, leaned back, and casually crossed his legs. Sidney sat back uneasily, leaving his feet planted on the floor. Jon waited for his guest to speak, hoping to gain an understanding of his level of anxiety. Sidney remained silent.

"How was your night at the Waldorf?" the President queried. "I hope the suite we arranged for you was comfortable."

"Yes, Mr. President. Wonderfully comfortable. Thank you." Sidney concluded he would let Jon show his hand first. He would not ask questions about why he was asked to the White House. And would not show any anxiety. He had moved Wil's words of warning out of his mind and would wait for Jon to explain the reason for his presence.

"Sidney, may I call you Sidney?"

"Of course, Mr. President."

"Good. Heather and I have been talking about you lately. She has extremely high regard for you. Says you're the best political strategist in the business. And I'll trust her judgment. The reason I asked you here is something has come up where Heather and I believe we can use your services." Jon paused to get Sidney's response.

"I see. Please tell me more. If there's a way I can help you, I certainly will."

The President nodded his approval. "We have had a serious breach of security in the White House. We could use your help to ascertain any risks this poses for our administration."

"Mr. President, I'm not a security analyst."

"I'm aware, but we believe the breach may have political undertones. This is why I wanted to speak to you. I'd like to brief you on what we have uncovered and get your perspectives on how we might address and respond. And hopefully, given your lengthy career in presidential politics, you can help us understand the threat landscape. And perhaps even give us an idea of who might be behind what we've uncovered."

"Sir, I must ask why it is you speaking to me about this. Normally, the way this place works, the FBI and the Secret Service would be the agencies to investigate a security breach."

Jon had a thought and decided to change tactics. He stood, walked to his desk, and opened the top right-hand drawer. He pulled out the compromised Blackberry. It was in two pieces, with the circuitry being exposed. He put it on the table in front of Sidney without saying a word and sat back down across from the now uncomfortable Rosenberg.

Jon studied Sidney's body language before continuing. "I recognize I am managing this unconventionally. After I fill you in, I believe you will understand why. But first I must ask for your word nothing we discuss in this office today be shared by you with anyone. Not the media, not your family, not your colleagues in government. No one. And whatever you may learn following our conversation will be discussed only with me. Is this acceptable? Will you agree to sign a non-disclosure agreement before you leave the room?"

"I think so. Not that I would consider doing so, but what are the ramifications of violating the NDA?"

"It would be a civil penalty. You would pay the U.S. Treasury five hundred thousand."

"I see. Am I being offered anything in return to accept this liability and the information you want me to share to have me help you if it's within my ability?"

"No."

"Mr. President. This is not a good deal for me. Five hundred thousand liability and no due compensation. Why would I agree to this?"

"Sidney, are you aware of my stated intent to only serve one term as president?"

"Yes."

"Who would you prefer to succeed me?"

"You know my preference. I've always believed Heather was uniquely qualified and should be the one to break the glass ceiling."

"I'm grateful she's your preference. Our problem, Sidney, is what we have uncovered could threaten her chance to succeed me. If the breach becomes known or any confidential information is leaked, there's a distinct possibility it will reflect poorly on Heather. If you can help us resolve this situation, you are helping her 2020 chances. Is this enough of a just reward for your services? If not, we can shake hands and part company."

Jon was succeeding in confusing Sidney. Wil's words of warning came back to him. If the President had evidence he was complicit, walking out of the Oval without signing the NDA was guaranteeing himself a long prison stay. On the other hand, he contemplated a scenario where Jon had knowledge of a breach but no real clues as to who was behind it. Was it possible Jon was really looking for his help? Maybe. Sidney concluded signing was the only reasonable choice.

"Mr. President, I agree to sign the NDA. If I can help Heather, I'm willing to agree to complete discretion."

"Great Sidney. I have it on my desk. Don't let me forget to get your signature before you leave. Now, what you see on the table was Heather's government issued Blackberry. We've taken it out of service because we believe around six weeks ago, it was compromised. Foreign hardware and software were installed which enabled the phone to record and securely transmit all her conversations. Not only her phone calls but also face-to-face conversations in proximity to the phone. We know the phone would establish connection to a satellite and relay communications from a face-to-face conversation or a phone call. We're assuming all of Heather's conversations were picked up and transmitted. To who, we don't know, Once we discovered Heather's phone had been compromised, we checked all the Blackberry's. They were all clean. It appears she alone was targeted. And we're trying to find out by who."

Sidney willed himself to not look at the phone and maintain his focus on the President.

Jon continued. "It's imperative we find out who is behind this and recover all the recordings. And any copies of the recordings. As you can understand, it's possible there is information in those conversations which could hurt Heather's chances in 2020." Jon paused. He wanted to hear Sidney's reply.

"Now I understand why you're managing this the way you are. Who else knows about this? And what ramifications have there been so far?" Sidney asked innocently.

"As of now you, I, Heather, Wil Carrington, and a White House IT person whom I trust explicitly are the only ones who know. As for ramifications, the only one to surface so far is the article in the Post News two weeks ago detailing a conversation in this room about North Korea. A conversation which was leaked shortly following our meeting and published the following morning. The disclosure turned out to be harmless, though there were anxious moments before we smoothed everything over with South Korea and Japan. Of course, we are concerned about any future leaks from conversations which took place before we discovered the issue with her phone."

"Wil Carrington is aware? How did he find out?"

"I told him. Felt he should know someone was spying on his wife. I was hoping he was aware of a political adversary who would be able and motivated to do so."

"I see. What did he say?"

"He had no idea who could be behind it. But he's been out of the game for a while, so I was not surprised. Heather felt you, with all your connections, might uncover something. Any thoughts so far?"

"Only questions at this point. How did you uncover what you know?"

"Can't share those details with you, Sidney. Classified. But I can share I'm only going to hold my cards for a few days. I'm really hoping between you and Wil and Heather you can find out who's behind this. If you do uncover who, try to convince them to come forward to me and give up all the recordings so we can nip this thing before it makes out to the media. Who knows what happens to Heather's 2020 chances if anything more is leaked? And who knows, I might offer an unofficial get out of jail free card if the people behind this turn themselves in before I give it to the DOJ next week. And now, I must excuse myself. I have another meeting in the East Room. The NDA is on my desk. Sign it, put it in an envelope and leave it in the upper right-hand drawer. Good luck with your detective work. Your limo is waiting to take you home. Rosemary will escort you out. Enjoy your ride back to Manhattan and stay in touch."

Abby's intercom buzzed. It was her secretary.

"Mrs. Martin, there's a Conrad Sterling from research asking to get on your calendar. He says he has information on North Korea you will be interested in."

"OK, Janice, book him late morning on Friday."

"Yes, ma'am."

Abby picked up the handset from her phone and dialed Nikki Haley's direct extension. She answered.

"Nikki Haley."

"Nikki, Abby. All good?"

"Yeah, if you don't count the normal bullshit around this place. What can I do for you, darling? How did your call with Ukraine go yesterday?"

"I'm writing up the notes right now. I'll shoot you a copy before lunch. Hey, do you know a Conrad Sterling in research?"

"Only by reputation."

"Which is?"

"*Lady's man.*"

"Yes, Janice."

"*Conrad Sterling is here for your eleven meeting.*"

"Send him in."

Abby had chosen an appropriate outfit for this meeting. It consist-ed of a gray, loose-fitting, high-necked thread-bare sweater over a plain white t-shirt. Loose fitting Capri pants. A pair of old tennis shoes, no socks. Unbrushed hair in a sloppy ponytail. Not a speck of makeup. The always stylish and attractive assistant Secretary of State looked almost homeless.

Sterling walked in. Abby, seated behind her desk, stood to give him a better view of her shabby attire. In contrast, he was dressed immaculately. Giorgio Armani plaid suit, gray. Canali flared collar dress shirt, blue. Red, white, and blue tie flawlessly knotted. Gold cuff links. Gucci lace up dress shoes, black. His longish blond hair was brushed with every strand in place, and his pearly whites radiated as he smiled. His clean-shaven face sparkled.

Sterling had been scoping Abby in the hallways of State for a week prior to requesting their meeting. He wanted visuals of his next con-quest. She was always well-dressed, and her attractive features always appropriately complimented. Sterling mentioned to Senator Krueger he was going to enjoy this mission. He had his approach thought out and his lines committed to memory. He thought it all for naught when she stood to greet him.

"Mr. Sterling. Pleasure to meet you. I'm Abby Martin."

"Hello Ms. Martin. Thank you for making the time to see me."

"Of course." She motioned Sterling to one of the desk guest chairs across from hers. He had a file folder in his left hand. He unbuttoned his suit coat with his right and took a seat. Abby stood and moved to the coffee service to his right. He now had a full view of the vagrantly dressed woman posing as an assistant Secretary of State.

"Mr. Sterling. Coffee?" She had his back to him. He was looking at her, trying to determine how to move this meeting where he wanted it to go. All his prepared lines highlighting Abby's attractiveness, his respect for her work, and his interest in knowing her better now seemed completely inappropriate.

"No, thank you," he offered.

She poured herself a cup and returned to her seat, avoiding any eye contact. She started moving papers on her desk around and stuffed them in a folder. With her intentional stalling task completed, she looked up at him and smiled faintly. "What have you got for me, Conrad?"

"Well, we have been doing research on North Korea's storage capabilities for the volume of insulin we've committed to send them. Thought you might want to review it." At that moment, he concluded he would abort the mission. "I'll leave it with you. You can call me if you want to discuss, but I have to cut this short. I got word from my boss before we started I was needed in a meeting."

"Thank you, Conrad. Appreciate your efforts. I'll give you a call if I need anything further."

Chapter 22

Food Fight

Sidney Rosenberg was delivered to his Manhattan apartment, courtesy of a U.S. government limousine, in the late afternoon following his uncomfortable meeting with the President. He had read Wil's note to meet him before he left Washington. After the conversation with Jon, he decided instead to head directly home from the White House.

He had not yet opened the package delivered to his hotel room the previous evening. Once he had changed into lounging attire and poured a glass of red zinfandel from California's Sonoma Valley, he razored the packing tape and ripped the box open. In it he found only a burner cellphone with operating instructions. He plugged it in to give it a charge. Five minutes later, the burner phone rang.

Sidney answered cautiously. "Hello?"

The former president responded. *"Sidney, where are you? Thought we were meeting on Roosevelt."* Wil waited for five seconds for an answer. *"Sidney, dammit, are you there?"* He wasn't.

Wil redialed. Sidney answered not so cautiously. "Go on."

Wil could not hide his contempt. *"Why did the chicken cross the road?"*

Sidney was equally perturbed. "He felt the need for feed."

"Sidney. These are burner phones. Why are we doing this shit?"

"At this point, Wil, I have no clue about anything except I'm probably going to prison for a long time, thanks to you."

"Why? What happened with Braxton?"

"He knows everything."

"What do you mean he knows everything? He knows I'm involved too?"

"You can bet your freedom on it."

Suddenly the realization hit the former President. The current president was toying with him. He replayed Jon's words about him asking for help. For tapping into his experience. The White House had tracked Sidney's IP address. He realized he was naïve to think they hadn't tracked his. His anger began to build but he could not verbalize it. Sidney could feel Wil's emotion.

"Ever play chess, Wil?"

"What the fuck does that have to do with anything?"

"It's time to lay your down your king."

"Jack. Thanks for returning my call. Are you in Washington, by any chance?"

"I'm heading to DC tomorrow, Bob. There's much we need to discuss. I assume you'll make yourself available?"

"Let's meet for dinner at my home tomorrow night."

The following evening, Jack Abbott arrived at Senator Krueger's Georgetown residence at seven. He was not in a festive mood. The Senator was of a like mind. A moment later, they were helping themselves to a variety of catered Italian dishes laid out on a serving table. As they sat at Krueger's dining room ensemble with their full plates, Abbott took a cloth napkin and stuffed it into his collar. He ate with a veracity sure to leave significant drops of marinara sauce on his tailored, expensive silk shirt, but not for the bib he had fashioned for himself.

"Where's Mrs. Krueger?" Abbott managed once his mouth received its first forkful of lobster ravioli.

"I told her it would be best if she were not here tonight. She hustled up a bridge game at one of her girlfriend's places."

"You watch Kriss and Braxton last Sunday," Abbott asked as he stuffed his face with an extra-large forkful of lasagna.

"I did. We need to get moving fast. I'm sensing a sentiment change on the Hill. Braxton's message is resonating with moderates in the Senate and new House members. He's building momentum. They see his popularity rising and they're reaching for his coattails. If we don't do something quick, it's going to get more difficult to take him down."

"Is your posse holding?" Abbott asked while spewing chunks of meatballs and peppers onto his bib and beyond.

"So far, so good. I polled them all yesterday. They're all concerned about Braxton's campaign finance reform agenda. As of now, we still have twenty-two on board for sure. There may be others, but I haven't found them yet. I'll get on it tomorrow."

Abbott's bald and shining head was face down to the table. He was lifting and shifting his fork back and forth from his quickly emptying plate to his ever-filling mouth. He nodded at Krueger's observation without his eyes leaving the disappearing mound of spaghetti and meatballs in front of him. Krueger watched the food fest with wonder.

"Jack, our resource at State, the guy who we wanted to get dirt from Braxton's ex-assistant. Well, he flamed out. Said he tried every seducement maneuver he knew, and she resisted everything. As if someone clued her in."

"Sadly unfortunate," were the words from Abbott's mouth, accompanied by fragments of veal parmesan being sprayed in all directions. "Did you discuss this maneuver with anyone? Is there a chance we have a mole in your cabal?" Abbott asked as he loaded up with another forkful.

The Senator could not help but stare at the spectacle of one of the most powerful corporate executives in the country, make a mockery of decorum as he continued to put the Italian delicacies away at a rapid pace. "Anything's possible in this town, but no, Jack, I don't think so. Everyone on our team has reasons to feel threatened by Braxton. But as of now, we're still floundering around without a strategy. Do you have any ideas about how we can go after him? Have you talked with Wil Carrington? I've got to believe he would help us."

Abbott finally had enough food. He swallowed his last mouthful and pulled the bib from his collar. He wiped his mouth with it and then set it on the table next to his empty plate. Abbott reached for his half-full glass of chianti, chugged it all down, and then let out a thunderous belch which filled the room with a new, not so pleasant aroma.

"Well Bob, I'm really disappointed. This is the first time I've ever seen you so helpless. So powerless. In all the years I've known you, taking out a political rival seemed second nature to you. But with this guy Braxton, you seem confounded. I'm not sure you and your team, or whatever it is you call them, are up for producing the shit show needed. So, I'm going my own way. I've got ideas I'm considering moving forward with, but I'm going without you. Hopefully, you'll formulate something new on your own and then we can rejoin our efforts and engineer his takedown. But for now, you'll have to go your way without me. And when I meet with the pharma big five next week, I'm going to recommend we review all lobbying and campaign contributions to everyone in Congress until you hit back against Braxton. Capiche, heir Krueger?"

Chapter 23

Not Now Wil

I t is not customary for U.S. Presidents to visit their cabinet members at their offices. When Jon personally phoned Department of Health and Human Services Secretary Tom Price to expect him in thirty minutes, it created a chaotic reaction within the walls of HHS. The Secretary quickly straightened up his desk and informed his staff of the President's pending arrival. Most in the department had not yet met the President, but his legend within had been growing since his appearance with Wallis Kriss and his introduction of 'FIX OUR WELL-BEING.'

The Hubert H. Humphrey Building at 200 Independence Ave. near the foot of Capitol Hill opened in 1976, as the headquarters for HHS. The fifteen-minute ride from the White House, in a backup nondescript presidential vehicle, was navigated southwest on Pennsylvania Ave. to Third St. At Third, the right-hand turn took the President and the three secret service agents accompanying him past Union Square to Independence Ave. A left on Independence and then a quick right into the HHS headquarters' secured parking structure left Jon to enter the building with two agents. The third stayed with the vehicle. An aide to the HHS Secretary greeted the President at the entrance from the parking structure before leading him to Tom Price's office.

"Mr. President. Welcome to HHS. I must admit I was surprised by your interest in visiting. And I'm expecting unprepared for whatever it is you want to discuss."

"No worries, Tom. I just decided yesterday to come over and see you. I hope I'm not creating too much of a disturbance, but there is something bothering me. And you and I both had flexibility in our schedules, so here I am."

"Of course, sir. Can I offer you anything?" Price asked as he motioned the President to a comfortable high-backed chair facing his desk.

"It's Jon, remember Tom. And no thank you, I'm good. I've only got thirty minutes, so I'll get right to it. First, I should apologize to you for firing Barnhardt without discussing it with you. But I won't. The man was standing in the way of improving the health and wellbeing of the people of this country. There was no reason for him to stay on the job one minute longer after my conversation with him. I'm guessing you're not happy with the decision and how I handled it, but I don't care. One of the primary missions of this administration is to make our people healthier. And since you're the Secretary of the Department of Health and Human Services, wherever you stand is ground zero. And since you serve at the pleasure of the President, the fact I felt Barnhardt was not one I could trust should be enough for you to support my decision. Do you?"

Price was stunned at Jon's directness. He stumbled with his answer. "Of course, Jon. His firing was completely your prerogative."

"Good. I'm glad you understand Tom. You should know one thing bothering me about Barnhardt was his candy-ass answer when I asked him about pharmaceutical industry influence. He answered in effect, it is what it is. Big pharma is just one of many influencers on decision making at the FDA. Do you agree with his assessment, Tom? Accepting and managing your bureaucracy with the presence of outside influence is just the way it is?"

"Jon, I know where you're coming from. It looks bad, I know. And it is bad. But we are working to clean things up. We have no shortage of initiatives in play to improve our decision making and reduce outside influence."

"No shortage? Reduce? Really? Tom, what kind of reduction are you shooting for? Ten percent? Twenty percent? Fifty percent? One hundred percent? You're an MD, right Tom?"

"Yes. I practiced orthopedic surgery before going into politics."

The President was unimpressed. "Did you ever let people outside the medical industry influence the decisions you made on behalf of your patients?"

"No Jon. I did not."

Jon shook his head in disgust. Price looked at him as a child would look at their father when he knowingly tells a lie. "All right Tom, who's in the lead to take over at the FDA?"

"We're still profiling candidates. We don't have anyone we would consider a leading contender at this time."

Jon was not surprised by the noncommittal answer. "I'd recommend you look at people from outside of Washington." The President offered. "And stop using private jets and government aircraft for your personal travel. That shit will get you fired."

Martin Roberts was an extremely ambitious bureaucrat who had served twenty years at the FDA. When Stanley Barnhardt was appointed Commissioner, he immediately tapped Roberts to head the Office of The Counselor to The Commissioner, considered to be the number two post at Food and Drug. He was also the personal choice of Jackson Raymond Abbott to replace Barnhardt, and a favorite on Jackrabbit's speed dial.

Prior to Barnhardt's firing, there were few occasions when Abbott needed to speak with Roberts. Barnhardt had Abbott's agenda under control, and the less communication about Abbott's agenda, the better. But things had changed, and Roberts was now taking regular cellphone calls from the CEO and Chairman of the Board of Costello Labs.

"Marty, just checking in. Any word on the FDA Commissioner job?"

"Nothing yet, Jack. Price has been playing it close to the vest since the President was here last week."

"What?"

Roberts was quick to provide the intel. "You didn't know? Yeah, Braxton was at HHS for half an hour last week."

"What did they talk about?"

"I haven't heard, although Price looked pretty shaken up after he left. One thing coming out of the meeting was Price revamping the department's travel policies. He made them much more restrictive."

"This is what Braxton's getting mixed up in now? Travel policy? Jesus. OK, listen Marty. You need to find out about the commissioner's job. Get a meeting with Price and just ask him straight up what your chances are. And find out who else he's considering. And then let me know. We've got to head off any other candidates. You've got to get the job."

"Will do, Jack."

The Vice President had been doing an astute job of avoiding her husband ever since it became clear he bugged her cell phone and initiated a spying operation which both violated her trust and reached into the Oval Office. Her visit with Jeffrey Claymore failed to facilitate an ability within to reconcile her emotions towards Wil. She vacillated back and forth between resigning, despite Jon's objections, and filing for divorce. Both actions would certainly end her political career. And during times of intense despair, she considered doing both during the same press conference to maximize her self-punishment. She had a path to leave her career intact by doing nothing but could not see a way to live with herself by simply accepting what Wil had done and carrying on as if it never happened. It was not an option in her mind, as Wil had thus far refused to admit his involvement despite a mound of evidence and Jon's well-played hints. She often thought back to the conversation with Jon when he called her out to choose a side. And she did by offering to resign. A resignation Jon then refused to accept, only adding to her confusion. She had thought about calling Sidney to gain understanding of both his and Wil's involvement, thinking he might add clarity, but had refrained at Jon's request. The President had reasons to continue the charade a bit longer.

Since Sidney's meeting with Jon and his briefing of the meeting to Wil, the former president was staring into a future adorned with an orange jumpsuit and metal bars, plates, latrines, and cuffs. He had faced dozens of inconvenient situations throughout his political career and always navigated around them. But this one was different. He was no longer politically relevant and his adversary, holding all the cards, was the current, and popular, President of the United States. The previous evening, he reached the conclusion Sidney was right. It was time to concede.

Heather was working from her office at the Vice President residence when there was an obligatory knock at her office door followed by the entrance of her husband. He walked directly to a guest chair opposite her desk and sat.

"Honey, I'm not leaving this room until you give me some time to talk to you."

"I'm leaving in ten minutes," answered an annoyed Heather.

"I'll take it. Shut your computer down, please."

Heather reluctantly complied without speaking a word. She closed the cover of her laptop and leaned back in her chair, staring at her husband. "Go on."

"I felt you should hear this from me. I have a meeting with your boss tomorrow morning."

Heather was only halfway listening. "Didn't know anything about it. What does he want?"

"There was no way you could know about it, as I just set it up with him a few minutes ago."

"OK. What do you want?"

Wil sighed. "The thing I want most is for you to forgive me. I know it won't be happening anytime soon, but there is something else. I want to find a way through this without hurting your career or your legacy. Sidney and I both believe the only way to accomplish this will be to tell Braxton everything."

"I don't know what everything is. And what makes you so sure telling him everything won't destroy me and everything I've worked for?"

"Jon told Sidney he would deep six everything if the offenders came clean to him quietly and could destroy all remnants of the operation."

"You believe Sidney's understanding was accurate, and that is Jon's intention?"

"I have no reason not to."

"OK fine, Wil. Do what you have to do to save your own ass."

Wil nodded, unsurprised by his wife's demeanor. "There is one thing I may need your help with to make this happen."

"I'm listening."

"At my request, it was Mark Parker who put all the pieces together."

Suddenly Heather went from casual listener to eyes and ears all on. "What do you need from me?" she asked anxiously.

"Braxton wants proof all the recordings have been destroyed and there are no copies. It's not something I can guarantee. From my understanding, everything is stored somewhere on a remote State Department server. Mark said he set it up so only Sidney and I had access, but I'm not savvy enough with the tech to know if that's the case. We can log in to the server and erase the files, but I can't say there are no copies anywhere. Parker holds the cards there and unbelievably, he's still loyal to you and I think you're the only one who can convince him to destroy everything."

"Funny way of showing loyalty, don't you think?"

"He only wanted what I wanted. Outside of me, he's the biggest Heather Carrington fan I know. Will you call him and tell him everything? And ask for his help?"

"You've got to be kidding me. Ask him for his help after what he's done? Yeah, I don't think so. You got him into it. You can get him out of it. Have your meeting with Jon tomorrow and figure out how to save all your asses. Now, excuse me. I'm running late for a flight."

"When will you be back?"

"Day after tomorrow."

"Where are you going?"

"Chicago. Angela and I are meeting with Jackass to discuss the North Korea Costello insulin deal."

"Yeah honey. About that."

"Not now Wil."

Chapter 24

Who Is This Gorgeous Creature?

The limousine carrying the First Lady was already parked outside the Vice President's residence when Heather exited through a side door. She approached the limo and bent down to enter the back seat, whimpering. "You know Angela, your martial arts classes are not very nice to my aging body."

"But your mind is enjoying them," responded the First Lady with a hint of a smile.

"You're right there. I do feel more present and alert the day after our workouts. Listen, there are things I want to tell you about Jackrabbit before we sit down with him."

Within a moment, they were on their way to Andrews Air Force Base for a date with Air Force One and a two-hour flight to Chicago. Angela was eagerly anticipating their upcoming meeting with Abbott and a team of Costello executives. The Vice President, having been mistreated to Jackrabbit's gross and boorish behavior on dozens of prior occasions, was less enthusiastic.

"If you're thinking of appealing to the bastard's sense of patriotism for this deal, stop. Only one thing appeals to him. It's whatever will serve his own personal best interests. I've only seen two ways to get

Jack Abbott to come around to another's way of thinking. One is to appeal to his ego. And two is to scare the living shit out of him. Wil was a master at both. Using logic or reason to change Jackrabbit's thinking is futile."

Angela countered, "Then we have two methods to motivate him. If necessary, we'll use both."

Heather acknowledged the First Lady's resolve. "OK, second. Negotiating for thirty million vials of his insulin is one thing, but knowing Jack the way I do, I'm certain he's not happy about the work you're doing with the project. I know he's calculating the hits to his business from any success you have reducing market demand for his biggest selling product. There's no doubt in my mind he will link the two. He'll see three hundred sixty million in low margin revenue as a small fraction of what he could lose in the bigger picture."

Angela was undeterred. "If he's busy with calculation, I'll be happy to remind him when we discover the cure, he's going to lose plenty of insulin business whether he collaborates with us or not. And if it becomes publicly known he refused us, well, we can't be responsible for any public opinion backlash, can we? If he believes we are on our way to success, if he's as shrewd as we believe, he'll look at his options. When we get close to our goal, I imagine he'll pivot. He'll lighten up investment in therapeutics and go big into the cures market, through acquisition if necessary. It's always possible the FDA could make his pivot difficult if he were to be unreasonable with us."

"My goodness, Mrs. Braxton, you have learned your lessons well. Another thing to factor into your thinking is Jack's powerful influence on Capitol Hill and in the government bureaucracies which oversee the markets he plays in. He's been around a long time and has built a staunch support mechanism throughout the city. Don't underestimate his ability to pull strings, especially with the FDA. I saw it up close during Wil's term and it's not pretty."

The four-vehicle motorcade, provided by the State of Illinois, transported the Vice President and First Lady into the parking garage at 55 Monroe St. in downtown Chicago. The home of the worldwide headquarters of Costello Laboratories, the world's largest pharmaceutical corporation.

Heather and Angela were escorted to the thirty-seventh floor and then to a glass-walled executive conference room along the east side perimeter. The east-facing outside view offered a magnificent view of Chicago's downtown skyline. The internal west-facing view through the glass wall offered a panorama of a honey-combed maze of cubicles, ringed along the perimeter of the thirty-seventh floor by exquisitely accoutered executive offices.

When Heather and Angela could see inside the conference room before being ushered in, they saw the Costello team awaiting them. There were four men: two Caucasians, one African American, and one Hispanic American, all sporting cleanly shaved heads. All heads radiated a reflection of the room's overhead lighting. Jack Abbott was sitting at the north end of the table, and his three deputies were seated to his left, facing west towards the low-walled cubicles. As soon as Heather and Angela were ushered into the conference room, Abbott rose, grinning broadly, and approached Heather with his head tilted and arms spread apart. Instead of enabling the fond embrace he was seeking, Heather extended her right hand for a shake. As did he, once he realized a hug was not forthcoming.

"Heather, it's been too long. How are you?" Abbott asked as he moved his left hand towards the top of her right to punctuate his faux pleasure to see her.

"I'm fine, Jack," she answered as she pulled her hand from the handshake to thwart his power move.

"And you look well. The Vice President job suits you."

"Thank you, Jack. You look about the same," she said flatly.

He laughed nervously. "And who is this gorgeous creature you brought with you?"

She was not in the mood for his act. "Mind your manners, Jack. This is Angela Braxton."

"Yes, I know." He grinned. "Mrs. Braxton. It is an honor to meet you. Welcome to Chicago and Costello Labs."

"The honor is mine, Mr. Abbott. Your resume and accomplishments are very impressive. I want to personally thank you for all the tremendous work you and Costello do in support of the Type 1 diabetes community. You should know my son takes Costello insulin and we are grateful for your organization producing a quality product to help people around the world."

Heather laughed to herself as she marveled at how well Angela was executing the ego-appeasement tactic they discussed three hours earlier.

"Thank you, Mrs. Braxton. You are too kind. Permit me to introduce you both to my colleagues." The three men stood. "This is our corporate legal counsel, Larry Lewis. Our Executive Vice President of Sales and Marketing, Mo Martinson. And our Executive Endocrinology Scientific Director, Diego 'Curly' Santana."

Each of the men extended their hands to both ladies. When all the handshakes were completed, they sat. Heather wasted no time setting the time boundary. "Jack, Angela and I have only two hours with you, so I'd like to dive right in to why we asked you for this meeting."

"Of course. Heather, Mrs. Braxton, we're interested to know the administration's thinking behind your request for proposal. As you must realize from our initial response to decline your request, we have significant reservations in tendering an offer. Your target price of twelve dollars per vial is so far below our cost to manufacture, we felt starting a negotiation would not be in either party's best interests. It would be an exercise in futility which would only create acrimony. An unnecessary waste of time and resources. This is why we elected to no bid."

Heather recognized Abbott's tactic. "Jack, I could be wrong, but I believe you just started a negotiation. You would not have accepted our meeting request otherwise."

Abbott decided well before this meeting started, he would work out a deal with Angela and partner with the Braxton administration to sell thirty million vials of Costello insulin to North Korea. He concluded successfully executing the deal would provide him with access to the inner workings of the **TYPE 1-YOU'RE DONE** Project and insight into how to sabotage it. And the opportunity to wreak havoc on the Braxton administration's efforts to use diabetes research to build better relationships with the country's political adversaries. He saw both initiatives as potential threats to Costello's insulin business.

But Abbott was going to posture disinterest as a means of obfuscating his true motives. His objective was to establish a position of plausible deniability should he be successful in delivering tainted insulin to North Korea to destroy any goodwill the Braxton administration would generate. And, in tandem, deliver a body blow to the credibility of the Braxton administration and, by association, the **TYPE 1-YOU'RE DONE** Project.

"Ah Heather, it seems your time out of the White House has not dulled your senses. We accepted your meeting out of respect for the new President and the First Lady. We are not interested in bad business, but we are interested in good relationships with important people. Mrs. Braxton, may we hear from you? We have watched your appearances with Wallis Kriss and your news conferences. You are most impressive, as is your husband. Please."

Angela complied. "Mr. Abbott, we are here because my husband has opened a door which we all hope will lead to a safer world for us, our children, and our grandchildren. Do you have any children, Mr. Abbott?" It was a question for which she already knew the answer.

"Unfortunately, no. My late wife was unable."

"Who are your heirs, if I may ask?"

"Mrs. Braxton, we are going off topic here. Can we get back to the discussion of the reason for your visit?"

"Of course." Angela moved to tactic two. "We have entered into a relationship with North Korea, which we hope will eventually lead to the quelling of their desire for nuclear weapons. Our first effort along this road is to help their government improve the health of their citizens who suffer with Type 1 by providing them with higher quality insulin at a lower price than what they purchase from China. We're counting on cooperation from all U.S. manufacturers of insulin. We've conducted research on all our U.S. companies with large-scale insulin production capacity. All, of course, being your competitors. We have calculated an estimate of the costs to produce thirty million vials for each insulin manufacturer and have tendered individual RFP's to all companies who possess the capacity to produce this quantity over the next twenty-four months, taking those costs into account. Each RFP has target price points inclusive of reasonable profit margins. This list includes you and five of your competitors. We're hoping one of the six companies will come forward and offer North Korea a proposal in line with our price points, which the United States will commit to stand behind and guarantee. Our insulin partner, whomever it turns out to be in this endeavor, will enjoy tremendous goodwill. We will be committed to helping our partner make up for any sacrificed margins through a massive goodwill campaign. Mr. Abbott, is Costello going to be our partner?"

Abbott listened intently to Angela's words. Inside, he smiled. She was making it difficult for him to say no, just as he had hoped she would. There would be no question what his motive would be in accepting her deal.

"But Mrs. Braxton, twelve dollars per vial? I'm not sure how you calculated our cost to manufacture, but your estimates are much too low. Should we decide to respond to your RFP, is it mandatory we accept your target price? Or is there an opportunity to negotiate? We'd be willing to open our books to show you our manufacturing costs."

Angela offered a short answer. She felt she had said enough, sensing she had Abbott on the hook. Which she did, but not for the reasons she presumed. "There's only one way to find out, Mr. Abbott."

"Yes, of course. Now, assuming we resolve the price issue to the satisfaction of both parties, there is another aspect of this deal of great concern to Costello's legal representation. May I address it with you?"

"Of course."

"As Chairman of the Board and CEO, I have fiduciary responsibilities to our stakeholders and shareholders. I must always keep their interests in mind. Entering into an agreement with a hostile enemy of the United States may not sit well with those to whom I owe such responsibility."

Angela interrupted. "Mr. Abbott, the U.S. government will guarantee the contract. There is no possibility Costello would not be paid. And we will guarantee each invoice for each delivery will be paid in sixty days. If North Korea does not make their payment, the U.S. government will."

"All very reassuring Mrs. Braxton, but the questions on the minds of our legal counsel and communicated to our board are of liability. We see many he potential issues and the potential for liability claims. We have no control nor visibility over North Korea's ability to safely store and dispense insulin. There's no history with North Korea doctors and their ability to accurately assess patients and accurately prescribe. We don't know the skill level of people in the North Korea health care system administering shots and managing pumps. Patients themselves, parents, caregivers. We know nothing of North Korea's ability to successfully administer Costello insulin. We do not know the motives of the North Korea government for accepting what would be a very generous offer from us. Would they somehow abuse our products to advance an unknown agenda? And finally, we have never heard of our product being consumed by any North Korea diabetics. We have never trialed our product in that country and cannot attest to our product's efficacy with anyone from North Korea."

"Those are all legitimate concerns, Mr. Abbott, except for your last one. It's patently ridiculous. You sell a large volume of insulin to South Korea, do you not?"

"I believe we do. Mo?"

"We do," Costello's chief sales and marketing, Mo Martinson, replied.

Angela was quick to respond. "Can you attest to your product's efficacy on people from South Korea, Mr. Abbott? Mr. Martinson?"

Jack was impressed with her command. "Uh, yes, I believe we can. Mo, how does our insulin do in South Korea?"

"They love it."

Angela was satisfied she had made her point. "Very good to hear, Mr. Martinson. Particularly since there is no difference in genetics between North and South Koreans. They are the same people, unfortunately separated by barbed wire and heavy artillery."

Abbott intervened. "Yes, you're absolutely right, Mrs. Braxton. We can eliminate genetics from consideration. But I'm afraid our Board will have trepidations around the other issues I mentioned. And I fully expect all our competitors will have the same concerns."

Angela had not considered liability issues in the RFP and was upset with herself for not doing so. She quickly determined discussions surrounding liability issues would be a negotiation for another day. She countered with the question she was determined to ask before the meeting concluded.

"What is it you are asking for, Mr. Abbott?"

"Mrs. Braxton, remember this is not coming from only me. Our Board members all share these concerns. You are asking for an extremely aggressive price against a backdrop of considerable risk."

Angela interrupted and dispensed with formality. "Jack, again, what are you asking for?"

"We would need a total waiver on all liability against any claims of substandard product quality or efficacy."

Later that evening, while Heather was being entertained by Illinois Governor Bruce Rauner, Angela was alone in her hotel room, scribing her notes and thoughts from her discomforting conversation earlier in the day with Jack Abbott. Though she had known the man for only six hours, it was long enough for her to dread the prospect of partnering with him. Knowing the exorbitant price Costello charged for insulin, the tremendous hardship it presented for the Type 1 diabetes community, and the regrettable fact many diabetics rationed Costello insulin because of the expense, her contempt for the man was extreme.

The **TYPE 1-YOU'RE DONE** Project was not working with Big Pharma, as Big Pharma was not in alignment with the project's objectives. There was too much revenue to be captured on treatments and therapeutics by the mega corporations that comprised the bulk of the pharmaceutical industry. After processing her first interaction with an executive from the industry, she decided she would add a secondary focus to the project. Reducing the cost of insulin in America. During the time it would take to bring the cure to market, she would coordinate an effort to ease the financial burden of treating the disease imposed on the T1D community by the likes of Jack Abbott.

With that contemplation, she put her thoughts away for the evening and clicked on the television. She tuned to the Big News Channel to see Wallis Kriss recounting the happenings of the day in Washington. Suddenly Kriss' broadcast was interrupted by a cutaway to the station's Los Angeles affiliate. The L.A.-based Big News correspondent reported over four dozen people attending an outdoor music festival on the Las Vegas Strip were murdered by a lone individual shooting out of a Mandalay Bay Hotel Room. It was the most deadly mass shooting event in United States history.

Chapter 25

Leave Your Bias At The Door

S he walked into a chaotic White House press briefing room. This October 2, 2017, session would be unlike any other she had or would face during her four-year tenure as the President's Press Secretary.

The room was pressure cooking as she made her way to the podium. Emotions were boiling over. Every member of the press corps was speaking loudly, mostly to themselves. No one was in listening mode. They were all talking rapidly, simultaneously, moving amongst themselves in a state of near frenzy, expressing whatever thought bounced into their mind about the tragic events of the previous evening to a comrade who happened to be the closest. They tried to console one another but didn't seem to know how. They were journalists energized by the story, and undeterred by the pain.

The mood in the room was complex. There was excited expectation for telling a story they recognized would captivate the nation. And it was compounded by an uncertainty about how they would express the appropriate magnitude of sorrow while objectively retelling the facts and adding the obligatory political commentary.

The press corps showed no signs of turning down the pressure valve until they realized Sandra Seracin had entered the room. The chaos quickly subsided as the journalists took their seats and tempered their hyperventilating. Seracin scanned the room, saying nothing, waiting for the last of the murmuring to stop.

"Ladies and gentlemen, there is nothing good about this morning, so forgive me forsaking my usual greeting to you."

The room was now completely silent but for a few coughs and throat-clearings. "The President has asked me to give you the details of what we know to this point about what happened last evening in Las Vegas. When I've finished, I ask you to hold your questions. For what you will likely ask, I will likely have no answer. The President will join us in ten minutes, so let me get started."

Seracin finished summarizing the information she learned in the Oval Office prior to the start of the briefing just as Jon and Jeffrey Claymore entered the room. She moved away from the podium, passing Jon who was moving towards it. They made eye contact, unemotionally. She took a seat to Jon's right. Jon reached the podium and stood before the familiar faces of the White House press corps. Jeffrey was standing behind him to his left.

"I have no words to describe what happened in Las Vegas last evening. I will leave the accounting and description for you and your fellow journalists to tell the nation. As you outline and draft your reporting to inform your viewers and your readers, I hope you will keep in mind the emotions of the friends and families of the victims. Draft your reporting as if you are writing to them. Show them, and the rest of us, your humanity, and your compassion. I ask that you save your viewpoints and narratives for another day. For another story.

Today is a day for you to take the high road. Tomorrow, will be a day for you to stay on it.

"As to why someone would find it within themselves to act upon whatever their motivation was to create such pain and heartache, we can at this point only speculate. The task before us now is to turn our speculation and investigation into informed conclusions. And to act. I asked Jeffrey to join me today because he will lead the effort of the executive branch to help the nation develop our informed conclusions and chart a path forward to take us to a better place. As individuals. As a society. As a nation."

The room was silent. Jon turned to look at Jeffrey, who was standing behind him. Their eyes met unemotionally. Jon returned his determined gaze to the press corps. He gripped both sides of the podium, using it to maintain his balance as his legs wobbled.

"Jeffrey will lead us as we look for a path to take us to a place where things like this can't happen. Won't happen. Unfortunately, the path from where we are today to where we want to go will be a long and difficult one. And along the way to our destination, that path will take us through additional distress and heartache. And painful introspection. There is no switch to flip to stop these events. There is only our resolve to learn and to act.

"As we all seek answers and understanding, our tendencies as human beings will be to cry for action to stop the pain. Unfortunately, that emotion does not always serve us well. Our pain is but a symptom of what ails us. The root cause disease cuts deeper than our pain. Treating the symptoms is not our best answer. If the disease is allowed to persist, we will only play whack-a-mole with the pain. Addressing the pain without addressing the disease is not the cure for what ails us. It is only a tepid response, not a solution.

"As we seek solutions to address the disease of the random, emotionless violence we suffer from, it is important we keep the idea of unintended consequences in mind. And keep in mind the events in Las Vegas last night were not an isolated incident. Our nation has been suffering with this disease for a long time. It is clear some kind of legislation is called for. And it is the job of the Congress to author and pass legislation. It is their job to weigh the arguments. Propose a medicine. Assess if the medicine will cure the disease or only stop the pain. And what the potential side effects in the form of unintended consequences might be.

"We can deliberate on legislation that addresses the pain. Or we can deliberate on legislation to cure the disease. I'd prefer the latter. Jeffrey and I will work together to craft a position which addresses the disease and deliver it to Congress. And we will expect our members of Congress will consider our position when drafting legislation to act. Legislation that I want on my desk before the end of the year.

"As you go forward to tell the story, consider today, tomorrow, and for as long as you can resist the temptation, are not days for rehashing the well-known arguments, positions, and talking points of both sides of the political spectrum relating to the private ownership of firearms. We all know what they are. You've used them at every opportunity. We've heard them over and over.

"As you in the press travel the high road today, tomorrow, and for as long as you can, in support of creating an environment in which sensible, realistic, and effective legislation for curing this disease can be debated, drafted, and delivered to the White House, I ask that you join me in not rehashing these all too familiar talking points. These arguments and positions are not prescriptions for curing the disease. They are only political talking points for our lawmakers to use to cater to their voting and fundraising bases. They do not serve the purpose of reducing random acts of violence. They're useful tools to fundraise and pontificate, but they won't put us on a path to a better place.

"I ask you, the esteemed members of the press, to not rehash the familiar arguments, positions and talking points of private ownership of firearms for another reason. These arguments and talking points serve to polarize and hog-tie our lawmakers, making them incapable to act. These arguments spread the divide and make it difficult for lawmakers to build the bridge for intelligent debate and sensible compromise. I ask the members of the press to be part of the solution and not part of the problem. You can do this by refraining from narrating your old and overused talking points. And instead foster an environment focused on curing the disease by reporting on the why and not the how.

"In order to begin the deliberative process to lead us to effective and meaningful legislation to address our disease, I am defining a role for the executive branch of our government in this debate. Our role will be to provide a voice for the middle ground. A voice not heard in Congress in the arguments of the political left or right. In response to an escalating level of random violence in this country involving firearms and mass casualties, the extreme positions of the Republican and Democrat parties unfortunately only serve their agendas but fail to solve our problem. Their extreme positions serve to excite their bases and assist in fund-raising, but fail to solve our problem. Their extreme positions serve to set the extreme boundaries of the debate and generate intense emotion but fail to solve our problem. We will offer a third position to bring our political parties together. Our position will not fit nicely in either corner. Our position will anger both sides. But we will make our case to the American people and see if they are in favor. Maybe someone in Congress will be listening."

Jon paused to let his points take root. The press corps was unsettled, yet motionless.

"Let's talk for a moment about our second amendment. Many of you, and the people you write for, and the people you write to, think 2A should at a minimum be decimated. And on a good day, abolished. I say no. Abolishing the second amendment is a horrible idea. It's a horrible idea to take the protection and security provided by firearm ownership away from responsible, law-abiding citizens while leaving illegal firearm possession in place for non-law-abiding citizens. You say no one is advocating we do this. But if we make lawful firearm ownership illegal or unduly restrictive, it is exactly what we would be doing. It would be an unfortunate, unintended consequence. And it would lay the groundwork for greater gun violence by those who do not obey nor fear our laws.

"Once we head down the slope of watering down the rights our founding fathers saw fit to grant the citizens of this country, it is the beginning of losing those rights. For better or worse, the right to bear arms is embedded in our culture. If today we were starting this country over, we would use different language in our new second amendment. Language to account for the societal and cultural forces in play today. But we cannot start over, nor would we want to. Our second amendment is foundational to what makes this country great. What makes us the envy of the world. There has never been a country which has offered greater freedoms and greater opportunities for prosperity to its citizens. It serves to remind those in government who would be inclined to abuse their power, they may want to reconsider. Decimating our second amendment against the will of the people is the recipe for a reckoning we do not want to face.

"But the year is 2017, not 1776. Our society and our culture are nothing like they were two hundred forty-one years ago. Today, our societal constructs and value systems are both deteriorating. And, it has led to a wave of violence which cannot and should not be tolerated.

If we are not to tolerate it, then we must address it. The question inevitably debated and contributing to our inability to effectively address and quell this violence is, is the gun or the person at fault?

"Ladies and gentlemen, this is the wrong question. We have always had people with firearms, but not this brand of senseless violence. The question we must answer for ourselves to address the matter is, what is in our midst which compels an individual to take a firearm to a killing field and randomly murder innocent people posing no threat? What compels an individual to put a victim in his sight and pull the trigger to end that person's life? This is what we must endeavor to understand. This is what we must endeavor to address. And, in parallel, we must recognize certain individuals have forfeited their rights to firearm ownership. We must understand the profile of an individual who poses a threat to society and rescind their rights. And we must more effectively enforce our current laws to keep people who pose a threat to others either off the streets or without firearm access. Somehow, we must thread this needle."

Jon took a brief pause, letting his last words hang in the room. The press briefing room was perfectly quiet.

"What contributed to the level of desperation and despair which compelled Stephen Paddock to take the action he did last evening? I can't fathom it. Can you? Betty? Jamie? Peter? Any of you?"

Jon gave the room a moment to respond. It did not.

"There is something most definitely wrong in a country, in a society, where we must confront whatever would possess an Adam Lanza, or a Dylann Roof, or an Eric Harris, or a Dylan Klebold, to randomly murder innocent victims. In many cases, the victims being children. Something is most definitely wrong. Why are we not studying the situations, the motivations, the emotional state of the people who commit these acts? I haven't been offered any clinical data. Have you?"

Jon gave the room a chance to respond. It did not.

"What are we as a society doing to these people? Why don't we know? Is it the medications we prescribe to alter their behavior? Is it a brand of or lack of parenting? Is it over-exposure to violence in games, movies, television? Is it the hateful rhetoric permeating social media? Why don't we know? We need to know."

Jon's anger was now clearly evident. No one in the room stirred. A single cough was heard from the back of the briefing room.

"Can we make the senseless, random violence stop? Honestly, I'm not sure. We don't know what's causing it yet. How can we know if we can stop it if we don't understand what it stems from? But starting now, we're going to do what's within our capability to gain understanding. The Braxton administration, with an effort led by Jeffrey Claymore, from this day forward will work every day to understand what possesses an individual to do what has brought us together in sorrow today. And to pass those insights to the Congress so they can deliberate, author, and pass thoughtful and effective legislation to put on my desk for signature.

"In closing, my message to the Republican and Democrat leadership in Congress is the legislation you put on my desk must not impede nor restrict responsible law-abiding citizens from owning firearms to protect themselves, their families, and their property. We will not desecrate the second amendment. Your legislation must leave your tired and useless political rhetoric at the door, and it must address the executive branch's findings and strongly consider our recommendations.

"My message to you, my esteemed colleagues in the Congress, is you have a job to do. For the sake of the country and for all the victim's families who have suffered from this brand of senseless violence, put your political differences aside, function as human beings, and communicate. Let compassion and dignity be your guiding principles. Attend your committee meetings with one purpose in mind, finding common ground to hammer out thoughtful and intelligent legislation to solve the nation's violence problem and not your fund-raising agenda.

"My final message to you in the media. Tell the story, not a story. And leave your bias at the door."

Chapter 26

Let's Stay In Our Lane

T hey started at dawn. The former president stepped out of the Vice President residence and into a Black Yukon SUV. He instructed his driver to proceed to the Frederick, Maryland, home of Mark Parker. He had asked Mark for a day of his time to travel with him to New York to meet with Sidney to collaborate on their plan.

Wil had not yet discussed with Mark any of the details which led to his urgency for this meeting. When Mark entered the vehicle, he was unaware of the conversations Wil and Sidney had with the President. To his knowledge, everything was going well with their enterprise.

Wil was dreading the imminent conversation with Parker. And even less so, the four-hour drive with the soon-to-be informed former decorated Army Ranger credited with multiple kills in Afghanistan. The ball was in his court to break the news to Mark that their deeds had been discovered, Braxton had them cornered, and it was not outside the realm of possibility they could go to prison for a long time.

Thirty minutes after collecting Parker, the SUV entered Interstate 95, heading north for the drive to New York City. Their destination was the Law Offices of Matthews and Hathaway for consultation with Wil's former Harvard classmate and longtime friend, Sheldon

Matthews. Sidney would meet them there. Once the Yukon reached the interstate, Wil raised the security panel separating them from his driver. Mark took the gesture it was now OK to speak.

"It's been a while since I've been to New York City. It will be good to see Sidney again. Where are we meeting him?"

"Uh Mark. Listen, there are things that have happened over the last two weeks which you need to be updated on. I don't imagine you're going to be happy with what you hear, but hear me out and know we're going to New York to fix things."

"Is all the technology still working well? I haven't heard from you in weeks. I assumed if something weren't right, you would have called me."

"The technology is not working well. In fact, it's not working at all."

Parker was perplexed. "Then why are we going to New York? If anything needs to be fixed, I need to do it here."

Wil decided not to give Mark any details about his ill-advised comments to Heather, which inadvertently alerted her sensitivities. "Mark, Heather's Blackberry. It started making strange noises. Hissing sounds. And the battery life was degrading. She mentioned it to Braxton, and he had his tech guys look at it. They found the receiver and transmitter. They also uncovered the added software code."

"Who do they suspect did it?"

"What do you mean? They suspect us," Wil answered, surprised by the question.

Mark was surprised at the response. "Why do they suspect us?" He started to get anxious. His heart rate picked up, as did the speed of his speech. "How did they come to that conclusion?"

"I don't really understand the tech jargon, but if I remember correctly, they hacked the phone and tracked the transmissions to the satellite. And then to another relay server. And then to the file server at State storing the recordings. They pulled the logs from the file server and saw transmissions to Sidney's IP address."

"Not yours too? You were listening in."

"Braxton didn't mention mine. Only Sidney's."

Mark was now agitated, and he amplified the volume. "You've been talking to Braxton about this," he responded in disbelief. "What are you doing? Fingering me? Trust me, if I'm going down, you're coming along."

"No, Mark. No one's fingering anyone. We're all on the same side here. Sidney and I think Braxton's been toying with us. We believe he knows everything except for your involvement. He indirectly offered Sidney and I, in separate conversations, an opportunity to come clean and provide him all the recordings and any copies. Said if we did, he'd bury the whole thing."

Parker found it hard to believe what he was hearing. "Indirect separate conversations? And he's only mentioning Sidney's IP address? He's got to be playing you. Why else would he not bring up your IP? Or did he mention your IP to Sidney, trying to get you to finger one another? If they found Sidney's IP in the logs, yours would be there too. Braxton said he'd bury everything? You trust he means it? Why would he offer to sweep everything away if he knows you're spying on your wife and his VP?"

"I asked him the same question. He said to protect Heather's legacy and keep her path clear for 2020."

"Yeah right. Maybe save his own ass too? You really believe he'll bury everything?"

"I, uh, yeah. I do."

Parker was unconvinced. "What about Heather? What does she know?"

"I'm not sure. She's not talking to me."

Parker lost all inclination of formality. "Fuck Wil. I can't believe this. You're a former President. Your wife is the current Vice President. And this is where we are? How did we end up here?"

"Maybe I should ask you, Mark. If the Blackberry didn't take a shit, we'd still be in the game. But look, starting a pissing contest isn't doing either of us any good. We can all end up in prison if we don't play this right. We need to talk about what we're doing when we get to New York."

"I'm listening."

"We're meeting with an attorney I can trust. An old acquaintance. You, Sidney, and I. And we're going to get guidance on what we need to do to make this go away."

Parker was still defiant. "I still don't understand why I'm in this. Braxton hasn't connected it to me. The only way he knows of my involvement is if you told him. Did you?"

"Like I said, he mentioned nothing of your involvement, but Braxton made it clear this is not going away for Sidney and I unless we deliver the recordings and all copies to him. He knows Sidney and I are not techie enough to have set this up and he knows the person who did is connected to State."

"Yeah, well, maybe I don't need to say anything," responded a skeptical Parker.

Wil was frustrated. "Well Mark, maybe you do. Because if you don't, then Sidney and I will do your talking for you. At this point, I'm not telling any stories to protect you or anyone else. It seems to me you'll be better off if you come clean. You might get mercy."

"Are you threatening me?"

"Mark, listen to me. We can get out of this. All three of us. All you have to do is deliver all the recordings to Braxton and convince him there are no copies. Can we give Braxton what he wants?"

The reality of the situation was settling in for Parker. "Yeah. I can produce a history of all the files. We can show them being offloaded one time and then deleted. If his tech guys are smart enough, they'll sign off on our file history documentation."

"Good. We should be OK assuming we can get our immunities in place to the satisfaction of my friend Shelley Matthews. If we do, then Sidney and I are going to confess. We'll let Braxton know it was our idea, and you're only involved because we pulled you in."

Jackrabbit arrived ninety minutes early for the Fall 2017 meeting of the Bombay Council. As was custom, the meeting was happening at the exclusive Metropolitan Club in downtown Chicago. Abbott strode into the main bar where he would consume three snifter helpings of forty-year aged Glenfiddich while awaiting his four fellow pharmaceutical company CEOs.

Twice each year, the CEOs of the five largest U.S. pharmaceutical corporations would covertly gather to discuss the ongoing protection of their businesses, their brands, and their reputations against any outside threats. The meetings were held with the utmost secrecy. All reasonable, and some unreasonable, precautions were taken to ensure the five CEOs were the only ones to know of these meetings. They understood should word of these gatherings become public knowledge, it would bring them all under scrutiny for market manipulation and anti-trust activities.

Two CEOs traveled to the meeting from outside the Chicago area. Bradley Donnegan, from Milwaukee, the CEO of Jamison and Jamison. And Dalton J. Talbot, from St. Louis, the CEO of Jzerk Pharmaceuticals. Donnegan and Talbot traveled to Chicago on separate chartered jets, instead of customary corporate jet accommodation. They traveled alone. Reservations for the chartered aircraft were made under aliases and paid for by separate vendors of their respective organizations. The vendors had no knowledge of who was traveling or why. They were instructed it would be 'a good idea' to provide this transportation if they valued their lucrative business relationships with their pharmaceutical mega customers.

For good measure, in case their travel to Chicago was discovered, the two CEOs had separate alibis for the evening. Upon separate arrivals, both Donnegan and Talbot were picked up at DuPage Airport by separate chartered limousines. The limo rides were set up by two separate vendors of Costello, each instructed they discreetly do so to maintain their preferred vendor status with Jack Abbott's organization. Donnegan and Talbot were driven to separate downtown area hotels for which they had a reservation for the evening. At each hotel, they checked into their rooms and then made their way outside through side exit doors, avoiding all security cameras which could jeopardize the alibi they stayed in all night, to catch a cab to take them to their alternate alibi. They were both dressed to obfuscate their identity. Donnegan in a suit with a hat and scarf to limit the view of his face. Talbot in a sweat outfit and oversized baseball cap. He brought a bag to change into his business attire at the Metropolitan.

Two CEOs, like Jackrabbit, were from the Chicago area. Randolph Richardson, the CEO of Jamgen and Associates. And Bartholomew Stein, the CEO of Brizer Inc. Both Richardson and Stein also had alibis for the evening and had their corporate car and driver take them to a location, providing them with plausible deniability to any suggestion they visited the Metropolitan Club on the evening of the Bombay Council meeting. From there, they would each catch a taxi to a location two blocks from their final destination. Stein and Richardson would walk the last two blocks.

Abbott was the only one of the five who was a member of the Metropolitan. His four guests for the evening were all registered under aliases. When each arrived, all except Talbot were escorted to a private dining room reserved solely for their meeting. Talbot would change into his business suit in the locker room before joining his four colleagues for dinner. A dinner where no business would be discussed until the meal concluded and the wait staff cleared all the tables and set up a coffee service in a corner. There would be no business discussion in the presence of wait staff to avoid potentially tipping off anyone serving them as to the identity of Abbott's four guests. With dinner concluded and the coffee service in place, staff was instructed to not reenter the dining room until the meeting had run its course, the guests had all left, and Jack Abbott gave the 'all clear.'

This semi-annual ritual had been repeated in March and October for the last six years. The October 2017 gathering was the twelfth secret meeting of the Bombay Council, and Jack Abbott had never been as concerned for the health of their businesses as he was now.

The assault on their industry being formulated by the Braxton administration was beginning to take shape. Each of the five organizations represented had sizable stakes in the diabetes and antidepressant markets. Each would suffer sizable potential losses should the Braxton administration be successful in their efforts to find the cure for Type 1 diabetes. And each could be significantly affected should Jon's interest in researching correlation between antidepressant medications and random mass murder shootings prove linkage or causation.

Abbott watched the last of the wait staff leave the room. "Let's start our meeting. First, let's review last quarter's numbers for your organizations." He summarized the public filings for the second quarter for each of the five corporations represented. "Gentlemen, congratulations on an outstanding second quarter. We all exceeded analyst expectations by a wide margin."

"Here, here," Abbott's four guests voiced in unison.

Abbott continued. "Dalton, Jerzk had the best quarter of all. Your earnings per share were seven-fifty, exceeding expectations by two dollars. To what do you attribute your success?"

The CEO of Jzerk responded enthusiastically. "Our growth was the result of a new advertising campaign we launched for Crolac in July of last year. And from a new outreach campaign to psychologists and public health agencies. These efforts worked well in tandem and significantly increased our market share for antidepressants."

Abbott responded. "Nice job, Dalton, though I'm not so sure Randolph would think so. From the numbers, it's evident your increased market share came from Jamison. Randy, you want to say anything?"

Richardson was deferential and good-natured. "I'm not surprised. Dalton's running a tight ship. And we've got issues in our businesses. Our marketing department on antidepressants has been lackluster for years. But we're now addressing it. We just made significant personnel changes to refresh our branding. I'm sure Dalton hasn't heard yet, but last night we signed on a team from Jzerk. We'll be back. And Dalton, we'll be coming for you to take back our market share."

Abbott jumped in to limit any bickering. "But overall, the five of us did exceptionally well in the second quarter. The number of new diabetes diagnoses in 2016 was significant and increased all our therapeutics and treatments businesses. And the mental health crisis we're experiencing in this country is helping all our bottom lines. So again, congratulations." The five CEOs all smiled and nodded.

"But all is not so rosy as we look forward," Abbott abruptly noted. The still smiling CEOs suddenly changed their demeanor and looked at Abbott, puzzled. "What do you mean, Jack?" asked Bradley Donnegan from Jamison and Jamison.

"I know you all are aware of the Braxton administration's intent to sell thirty million vials of American insulin to North Korea, a country often identified as one of this country's most dangerous adversaries. A country which has threatened the nuclear annihilation of the United States. And I know you are all aware the administration will soon release requests for proposal from each of our organizations for this purchase. In fact, Costello has already received its RFP and has responded with a 'no bid'."

This revelation created a murmuring amongst the CEOs. Randall Richardson of Jamgen responded. "When did you receive it, Jack? We've yet to see ours. Anyone else seen theirs?" The three CEOs shook their heads no. "Seriously, you 'no bid'? You didn't counter?"

"Yes, we 'no bid', Randy. And did so for a number of reasons. First, I'm not agreeable selling our products to a mortal enemy on which we have a trade embargo. Who the fuck does this Braxton think he is? Second, the terms were so preposterous, we did not want to give the RFP any legitimacy by tendering a counteroffer. We have no intent of offering our insulin for sale to North Korea," Abbott lied.

"What were the RFP terms you were concerned with?" Richardson inquired.

"I'm not going into specifics. You'll see the terms the administration is requesting soon enough. But to summarize, the price was too low, and the risks of liability were way too high. I raise this issue as our first order of business this evening because I'd like to see us all respond to the administration in a coordinated manner. The actions the administration is taking pose a serious threat to our diabetes treatments and therapeutics businesses. While the administration is working in opposition to our interests by launching a targeted objective to find the cure for T1D, at the same time they are working to drive our profits down from the sale of insulin by putting pressure on our pricing models. Trust me gentlemen, when you see their targeted price, you will understand my position. I've been led to believe their targeted price for each of us will be different. Their task force has researched each of our five organizations to determine our costs to manufacture, and their asking price is a markup from their cost estimates. To give you an idea what to expect, the price they want offered by Costello is twelve dollars per vial."

The four looked at Abbott unemotionally. They were all aware of Jon's and Angela's efforts to find the cure for Type 1 diabetes, and Jon's recent comments on the Las Vegas shootings presented potential new challenges to their antidepressant businesses. But none of the four had expressed any abnormal reactions or abnormal concerns prior to this meeting of the Bombay Council. They were all industry veterans and accustomed to threats on their businesses from Washington newcomers looking to make a name for themselves. And from organizations which sprung up from time to time to advocate for one cause or another detrimental to their bottom lines. Their experience told them they could wait these threats out by not overreacting, continuing their investments in lobbying, continuing their sizable advertising spend with mainstream media, and continuing to clandestinely sponsor scientific studies friendly to their cause. Efforts which had all proven highly effective in the past. They saw the administration's efforts as nothing more than the latest bureaucratic attack which they would repel using their standard arsenal. Abbott saw things differently. He saw Jon Braxton as an existential threat.

"Gentlemen, for the first time I can remember the executive branch of our government poses a significant menace to our businesses. We must take notice of the Braxton administration working in areas potentially leading to changes in market landscapes which could impact our revenues and bottom-line profits to significant degrees. Given recent conversations with Bob Krueger, I'm questioning if all the efforts we've made over the years to build relationships and establish beachheads in Washington to protect our industry from such market landscape shifts will prove effective against this threat. Krueger has always been a friend to our industry but seems impotent against this administration. In a way, he also seems reluctant to take on the fight. He's been attempting to rally his troops in the Senate to help us mount a defense against Braxton's agenda but has not been able to build a strong coalition. Frankly, he seems both unwilling and incapable of protecting us. In any event, we must act forcefully and aggressively to defeat Braxton's agenda. This must be the focus of our meeting tonight."

Abbott paused for a moment to gauge the level of concern in the eyes of his colleagues. What he saw alarmed him. He was not seeing or feeling a consensus on the threat level.

Abbott continued. "I had my team take the liberty of running revenue and income projections on each of our five organizations." He reached down into his briefcase and pulled out four file folders. He handed one to each of his colleagues.

"In the folders are numbers for each of our companies modeling profit-and-loss profiles with reductions in both our diabetes and antidepressant revenues. Each of our organizations derive considerable revenue from both those lines of business. It's only prudent we consider the risk to those lines the Braxton agenda poses. To study the risks, my team ran models projecting twenty, thirty, and forty percent declines in revenues for both lines. As you can see from our projections, the impact of such reductions on each of our organizations is significant."

Abbott paused, letting the CEOs examine the numbers in front of them. He then continued to lobby his colleagues to his way of thinking. "Given the risks we are facing, it would be prudent of us to discuss how we protect our organizations. First, let's discuss the likelihood of Braxton being successful with his cockamamie ideas. Second, let's discuss strategies to offset the risk. Bart, we'll start with you. What's your assessment?"

Bartholomew Stein, the CEO of Brizer for the last fifteen years, had stewarded the company's exponential growth to become the world's second largest pharmaceutical corporation behind Costello. He was bright and articulate, and the most respected CEO on the Bombay Council. Though he and Abbott were polar opposites in personality and demeanor, they had competed for years and had developed a healthy level of mutual respect. If there was anyone on the Council who could influence Abbott, it was Stein.

"Jack, are you blowing this Braxton concern out of proportion? I don't hear his rhetoric any differently than what we've heard from all the other new politicians over the years who've come to Washington on a crusade to hurt our industry. This will blow over as long as we execute our defenses efficiently and not amplify his words."

Abbott anticipated his colleagues would not be as aggressive as he wanted them to be in countering Jon's and Angela's efforts. He asked Stein to speak first, knowing he would put up the best argument of the four. He wanted to take on the debate with his colleague from Brizer first. If he won the war of words with Stein, he was confident the others would quickly fall in line and suppress any thoughts running counter to Abbott's. If Abbott could convince Stein to join him in taking a strong, proactive approach against the Braxton administration, the council would unanimously agree.

"Come on Bart. Don't you believe Braxton has more tenacity and guile than the other imbeciles in Congress we've had to contain? Are you following his poll numbers and his popularity on the hill? Krueger can't put a coalition together to stop him. The threat he poses is unlike any other we've encountered. If we rely on the strategies we've used in the past, even though they've been successful in keeping the barriers for entry into our industry high and our margins high, I'm concerned we're up against a more formidable opponent this time."

Stein was not swayed. "Sorry Jack. I'm not convinced he's going to make any headway against us. And he's on record, saying he's only staying for one term. And didn't he do our work for us by setting up Heather Carrington as his successor? If she runs and wins in 2020, good friend Wil Carrington will be back in the White House. The way I see it is we sit tight. Not do anything stupid. Play nice. Say the right things. And 2020 will be here before you know it. He'll be gone. She'll be in. Things will get back to normal."

Abbott was not surprised by Stein's words. He'd known him for fifteen years and anticipated his response. "Bart, you're willing to undertake the risk? There's no guarantee Braxton leaves after one term. Second, there's no guarantee Heather runs in 2020. Third, even if both happen, and she is POTUS in 2020, there's no guarantee she doesn't take on the fight Braxton started. I know what's going on between Wil and Heather, and he doesn't have the influence over her you might think he does. If we don't take a more aggressive approach, we're leaving too much to chance. It's a risky bet. If Braxton is successful in moving the ball down the field for a Type 1 cure and exposing the things we know about antidepressants, he could change the landscape on us. Public opinion could turn sharply. It's possible it won't matter who the POTUS is in 2020. We will have missed our opportunity to turn back his agenda and we will be screwed."

Stein pushed back. "Come on Jack. We've faced these kinds of obstacles before. We've repelled them every time. As long as we all keep up our advertising spend on the major networks, we're good. We might need to produce different messaging for them to report this time around, but we know how to motivate the media and we're good at it. I'll grant you Braxton's formidable, but he's still on his honeymoon. It won't last." Randy, Brad, and Dalton all nodded in agreement.

Abbott changed course. "Bart, have you met Angela Braxton yet?"

"No, I haven't."

"I have, and you need to be ready. After she saw our 'no bid' response, she came to see me. She's a ball-buster. I have a sense now of who she is and what she's capable of and am concerned she will make headway towards a cure. She's got game. I'm concerned about their progress and the awareness around Type 1 and the insulin business they're bringing into the sunlight. And my contacts at the FDA tell me she's been asking lots of questions about insulin pricing. They feel she's going to convince her husband to introduce legislation for some kind of price control. These efforts are not in our interests. And now Braxton has antidepressants in his crosshairs. This is a different kind of threat. We need a different kind of response."

A silence descended over the room. Abbott broke it. "Let's get back to the insulin RFP for North Korea. Lady Braxton shared with me we would each have different target prices based on their projections on each of our costs to manufacture. Her response to our 'no bid' was to threaten us with negative PR. There's no doubt in my mind she will be playing all of us against each other to drive the price down. I suggest we all respond with 'no bid'. This will move them to change the RFPs."

Stein countered. "Jack, you're talking about this administration being a threat to us, and then you suggest we antagonize them by refusing to bid? Just because they list an asking price, it does not mean we have to meet it. We can each bid whatever we want, right? We can bid what we consider acceptable. The same with liability concerns. They can't force us to accept a terrible deal. We haven't seen our RFP yet, so I don't know what their asking price for us is. But I assure you we will not 'no bid.' We'll counter."

"That's unfortunate, Bart. I was hoping we could work together so we all get a piece of better action," Abbott again lied. "If we coordinate responses, we can move Braxton to higher price points and better liability protection." Abbott wasn't interested in sharing his plan to win the order outright, nor had he contemplated any scenario where he would share his true intent. Instead, he endeavored to sell the Bombay Council his idea to 'no bid' in unison. He moved the conversation back to Braxton.

"Let's put the RFP discussion aside for a moment and get back to the Braxton agenda. Are we in agreement we must execute new strategies to counter it?"

Stein spoke up. "All right Jack. Let's, for discussion's sake, assume you're right and we need to take a different tack to oppose him. What do you propose we do?"

"Our best chance to push back against Braxton's agenda is to discredit him and his character. If we can dirty him up, his agenda will lose support. Our best shot is to lay a scandal on him."

Stein was skeptical. "What makes you think we'll find a scandal? I haven't seen or heard anything which even remotely smells. Dalton, Randy, Brad. You guys heard anything?" His three colleagues shook their heads no. "Jack, you're tight with Wil Carrington. What does he think of Braxton? If there's anything out there scandalous about the guy, knowing how Wil operates, I'm sure he's working on a portfolio. Have you discussed your concerns with him?"

"I have and though he hasn't said it, my sense is he's waiting for 2020. He's not interested in seeing Braxton soiled. He's not interested in anything coming close to hurting Heather's chances."

"But does he have anything on Braxton we should try to find out about?"

"As far as I know, he doesn't."

Stein was losing patience. "Let's say there's nothing out there that works for us. What then?"

"Then we fabricate something," Abbott responded instantaneously.

Dalton Talbot decided to be heard. "I don't like it, Jack. The guy is doing good things for the country. If he's successful in his efforts, we lose profits. It's all right. We'll recover in other areas. We've got new drugs in the pipeline at Jzerk, which are promising additional sources of revenue. And we still don't know if his efforts will impact our businesses. It's all your perception. Anything we do outside of our sweet spot is too risky. And I'm certainly not going to endorse smearing the guy. I say we hold the line."

Abbott was disappointed. "Brad, Randy?"

Randall Richardson spoke first. "I agree with Dalton. We've done shady things in the name of business over the last dozen years. I haven't always been proud of what we've done, but always justified things to myself by thinking we're just doing our jobs for our shareholders. But making up a scandal to smear the President? I can't get there, Jack. I won't be a party to it and agree with Bart. We should do what we've always done. Lie low. Play our game. Wait it out."

"Brad, anything to offer?" a disgruntled Abbott asked with an air of desperation.

"I'm afraid I'm with Dalton and Randy, Jack. Let's stay with what we know works and not stick our neck out. Especially since we don't know for sure if we are at risk."

Chapter 27

Battle Lines

The President approached a darkened Oval Office at six a.m. Motion sensors turned on the lights the second he opened the door from the attached dining area and before he reached his desk. The thought crossing his mind as he entered was why had he not taken Abby up on her offer to send him Captain Crunch. He felt he could use his trusted advisor's insights for the upcoming nine a.m. meeting with Wil Carrington, Sidney Rosenberg, Mark Parker, and Sheldon Matthews. Instead, he would query the Vice President on her thoughts about what was on his mind. She arrived at seven-thirty.

"Good morning, Jon."

"Thanks for coming in early. Want some coffee?" The President sprang out of his chair and shuffled over to the two sofas adjacent to his desk. There was a pot of freshly brewed dark roast on the table separating the two. He poured himself a cup and sat. Without a word, she did the same and sat across from him.

She took a small, guarded sip of the hot beverage and uttered the words on her mind the last few days. "Is Wil going to prison?"

"I hope not. Have you and he discussed how he's going to play today?"

"No. He wanted to, but I told him to save his words for you. I can't even look him in the eye."

Jon nodded. "I can understand how you feel, even if I don't agree with it."

"What do you mean you don't agree with how I feel? How could you say such a thing to me, Jon? Perhaps when the one you felt you could always trust betrays you, you would agree with how I feel."

Jon tried to console her. "Heather, you haven't given Wil the chance to apologize. Or the opportunity to explain himself. There's nothing he can say to diminish what he's done, and you have every right to be angry. And it's possible what he tells you might not be the truth, justifying your anger. But to not take the opportunity to better understand the situation? The dynamics? It's not how you normally operate. I see your anger in the way of your judgment. In the way of your critical thinking. And in the way of effectively managing your relationship with your husband. I'm not saying to ignore what he's done. I'm only saying better understand what was behind it."

"Unbridled ambition is what's behind it," she muttered to herself, but loud enough for Jon to hear. Her anger towards Jon subsided the second those words left her lips, words festering in her psyche since she learned of her husband's betrayal. She moved the conversation in a different direction. "What's your plan for this meeting and why did you want me here for it?"

"You don't have to stay for the meeting. Up to you. I wanted to see you before it started to ask you about Sheldon Matthews. Your husband, Sidney, and Mark retained his legal services. Do you know him?"

"A little, not well. Never really cared for him. Wil has lots of friends I never really cared for."

"They're friends?"

"Not good ones. Why the interest?"

"Just wanted to understand who's going to be in the room. I understand why your husband wants an attorney present today, but I'm not thrilled with the idea. I'm not interested in negotiating anything. If their counsel starts dictating terms, I expect I'll lose my patience and the meeting will be over well before their counsel would like. Back to your question about Wil going to prison. I'd say Mr. Matthews is in the driver's seat on that one."

Heather nodded. "I think I'll stick around to see what he has to say."

At nine, the four visitors were escorted into the Oval. Heather and Wil made expressionless eye contact. Mark and Sidney were nervous. Matthews, professional. "Mr. President, it's an honor to meet you."

Jon responded cordially. "Mr. Matthews, welcome to the White House. To help you plan your time, consider we only have one hour. The Vice President and I are entertaining the Prime Minister of Sri Lanka at ten. I trust we can move this meeting along quickly and to a successful conclusion. Let's all sit, shall we?"

Jon extended his arm to the two sofas. He and Heather chose one, leaving the four visitors to the other. "Mr. Matthews, your clients requested this meeting, so please fill us in on why we're here."

The President's cavalier attitude unnerved Wil, Sidney, and Mark. Sheldon Matthews was amused. "Mr. President, we're here today because my clients wish to protect their constitutional rights in light of the accusations your office has made. Accusations for which we have not heard nor seen any evidence of the alleged wrongdoing. And the manner in which my clients have been brought to the point of being threatened with prosecution in return for an admission of guilt is highly unusual coming from the Office of the President. It is our position you are overstepping your authority in issuing threats against my clients, and may be violating their civil rights."

"I see," the President responded, masking his annoyance. "What would you like to suggest, Mr. Matthews? How should we proceed?"

"Mr. President, given the accusations you have leveled for which we have seen no evidence, and the unusual way you are prosecuting your case, it is our position we are within our rights to ask that you discontinue your current course of action and grant my clients immunity from any prosecution related to this matter. In return, my clients will sign a non-disclosure statement agreeing to never discuss these events nor anything relating to them with anyone not currently in this room."

"Mr. Matthews, exactly what are the accusations troubling you?"

"Mr. President, as I understand from my clients, you have accused them of tampering with Mrs. Carrington's cell phone and recording her conversations. Again, accusations for which we have seen no evidence."

"Mr. Matthews, the reason you and your clients have seen no evidence is because we are not accusing your clients of anything. I have not spoken with Mark Parker for almost three years. In my one conversation with Sidney, I showed him Heather's phone and asked for his help in identifying potential suspects. And as for Wil, I shared with him the information we had gathered about the tampering. In no instance did I accuse or threaten anyone with anything. So exactly what is it you're taking exception to?"

"Mr. President, did you not disclose to Mr. Carrington you had evidence of Mr. Rosenberg's IP address being included in your information gathering."

"I did," Jon replied nonchalantly.

"We have seen no such evidence," Matthews responded swiftly.

Jon slapped his knees and stood. He extended his hand to the attorney. "Mr. Matthews, slight change of plans. The Vice President and I must excuse ourselves so we can have a little more time to prepare for our visit with the Sri Lanka Prime Minister. This meeting is over. As for this matter, I'll back out of these conversations and have the Attorney General contact you regarding how the Department of Justice will proceed. Now, let me show you out."

Matthews stood. He refused to shake the President's outstretched hand. "Mr. President, can we discuss this a little further?"

"No, Mr. Matthews. I'm afraid not. Wil, Sidney, Mark. It was good seeing you again." The President moved to the Oval entry door leading to Rosemary's desk. He opened it and turned to his guests, showing them the door. "Now gentlemen, if you will excuse the Vice President and I."

Wil, Mark, and Sidney stood, nervously anticipating the response from their attorney. After ten seconds without one, Wil cleared his throat. "Jon, would you be willing to give us ten minutes? I'd like to have a private word with Mr. Matthews."

"Sure, if ten minutes is enough, you can excuse yourself to the dining room."

"Thank you, Jon." Wil motioned for Mark, Sidney, and Shelly to follow him.

Five minutes later, Wil, Sidney, and Mark returned to the Oval.

"Where's your attorney?" Jon asked Wil.

"He is no longer our counsel and won't be returning. Mark Parker has the proof you requested that all recordings from Heather's phone have been destroyed and there are no copies. This whole idea was mine. Sidney and Mark only participated at my request." Wil handed Jon a full file folder with documents and a thumb drive.

"Thank you, Wil, for your transparency. Both the Vice President and I are highly disappointed you took the actions you did, and the three of you should be prosecuted. But if we can validate Mark's documentation, in order to protect Heather's legacy and her future, I'm willing to put a lid on it. I'll have my team review Mark's evidence and, assuming they concur with your understanding that all the recordings have been destroyed, we can drop this matter and put it behind us. If there's a problem with the information, I'll let you know."

"Thank you, Jon. If you have another few minutes, there's something else I need to discuss with you. It has to do with Jack Abbott, Costello Labs, and North Korea."

"Not now Wil, the Vice President and I are running late for our Sri Lanka meeting. Some other time."

It had been thirty years since Jackson Raymond Abbott last dined at Bruna's Ristorante in Chicago's lower west side. It was located in the working-class neighborhood where he grew up known as Little Italy. He didn't frequent the cozy hangout of his adolescence and young adulthood once he ascended beyond his uneventful 'blue-collar' upbringing. Little Italy was also the neighborhood where Jackrabbit made the acquaintance of Dante Palmieri during their high school years. An acquaintance which developed into a brief friendship through college and then slowly devolved as they went their separate ways. Abbott into the pharmaceuticals industry. Palmieri into the Chicago mob underground.

Bruna's opened in 1933 and had maintained its old-world Italian charm through three ownership changes. The low-ceilinged dining room was modestly appointed with small tables, all with red and white checkered tablecloths and empty chianti bottles serving as flower vases. Adding to the quaintness were large volumes of plastic grapes growing from lattices affixed to the lowered ceiling.

Abbott arrived first and was seated in the back of the dining room, facing the front door. He was accompanied by a full bottle of chianti and an empty one housing white plastic roses. Five minutes after he arrived, Palmieri walked in. He scanned the room before he saw Abbott seated, looking directly at him. Palmieri nodded and walked slowly to greet the man, once his friend, he had not seen or heard from in twenty-five years. Palmieri was well aware of Abbott's professional success and followed his career. Abbott had not been as interested in Palmieri's existence and was unsure if he still held a position of influence in the powerful Giancarlo Cambretta crime syndicate.

"Dante," Abbott declared as the short and thin Palmieri approached the table. The contrast in physical stature between the two was striking. Abbott rose to hug the impish Palmieri, engulfing his slight frame. Abbott's embrace was powerful, and Palmieri was intimidated by his sheer size. An intimidation which quickly brought back Palmieri's memories of their not always pleasant times together.

"Hello Jack," Palmieri replied nervously as he slithered out of Abbott's embrace.

"Sit, let's enjoy some chianti." Abbott barked.

"I was surprised to hear from you, Jack. It's been what, over twenty years?" Palmieri meekly inquired.

"I know. I know. It's my fault. I'll use the job as my excuse, but it's a lousy one. So, I'll just apologize for not being a great friend and ask for forgiveness," Abbott chuckled amused at his feeble attempt at humor. Palmieri was uncomfortable in Abbott's presence and sat emotionless. "What have you been up to, Dante?"

"I'm still working for the same company. Recently got a promotion to CFO. Managing a team now. The business has been growing," Palmieri hesitatingly replied.

"Congratulations. I'm glad things are going well for you. What's the company involved with these days?"

"You know I can't talk about the details of our business, Jack."

"Right, right. The only reason I asked was I might be interested in doing business with your firm. Just wanted to get an idea if they might be interested in what I have in mind."

"You need to be talking to business development, Jack. That's not my domain."

"Of course. Of course. But say I had a business proposition I wanted to discuss with your firm. How would I go about it? Could you set up a meeting with the right person for me?"

"I can let the right people know you want to meet. But if your proposition has anything to do with pharmaceuticals, legal or otherwise, they won't be interested. Don Cambretta has been adamant the firm stay clear of drugs."

"I can assure you. Nothing to do with drugs, legal or otherwise."

"Good morning from Washington DC. It's October 29. I'm Wallis Kriss and welcome to Big News Sunday. We have a special show for you this week. Our full hour will be devoted to four distinguished visitors from the White House, including the President who will join us for our third segment. In our first segment, we'll interview our culture czar, Jeffrey Claymore, again. And we'll meet for the first time, the Secretary of Education, Ms. Connie McIlroy. We understand they have exciting news to share with you. In our second segment, we'll again welcome the First Lady, Angela Braxton. But first a word from our sponsors. We'll return in two minutes."

When the broadcast resumed, Jeffrey and Connie had taken seats across from Kriss. The red light came on and the broadcast resumed.

"Mr. Claymore, welcome back to the show. And Secretary McIlroy, welcome as well for your first appearance on Big News Sunday. I understand you two are collaborating on specific pieces of the President's agenda and have updates you want to share with our viewers. Jeffrey, let's start with you. It's been three months since you were here last when you discussed your recent appointment as the country's first culture czar and presented your thoughts and ideas. Please tell us how you are doing with fixing our culture."

"Thank you for having me back, Wallis. Your viewers will be pleased to know we've been working diligently on fulfilling the President's vision. With the goal of improving our culture in the United States, we've defined a primary objective of helping people in our country find more meaning and purpose in their lives. We believe much of our cultural decline can be addressed and reversed by giving people tools and information they can use to live better. Our initial efforts are targeting the country's twenty largest urban areas. Areas we feel need our help the most. In each target city, we are approaching the business community in search of sponsorships. We're asking not only for financial assistance but also active participation. We're looking for local business communities in the urban areas where we're establishing LABEL campuses to host a variety of events, while encouraging and motivating their employees to engage in the activities taking place on campus. We're using a blueprint President Braxton used during his years running his business in Los Angeles, and the response thus far has been overwhelmingly positive. It's easy to make the case that our efforts will provide a significant return on investment to these businesses who engage with us as we develop more well-educated and motivated potential employees and customers. Businesses are responding favorably with grants to augment the funding provided by Congress. And we are in various stages of building our first LABEL campus in each of our twenty target cities. By the spring of next year, we should have operations underway in ten of them."

Jeffery continued. "In parallel, we have been collaborating closely with Secretary McIlroy to develop curriculums and initiate training for our instructors. We know finding and training quality instructors is key. Besides colleges and universities, we have also been pursuing another avenue for finding and developing instructors. We are working closely with all four branches of our armed services. The instructor opportunities we are creating will appeal to members of the armed forces who fulfill their obligations but do not have the desire to remain in the military. The personality traits which led these individuals to military service are the same traits to enable their success and career satisfaction in teaching the curriculums the Secretary is creating."

Kriss responded. "Very impressive Jeffrey. Secretary McIlroy, again welcome to Big News Sunday. Please tell us more about your efforts in this endeavor."

"Thank you, Wallis. I'd love to. Since the majority of your viewers don't know me, first I'd like to share my resume."

"Of course, Secretary McIlroy. Please."

"The first thing your viewers should know is I spent the majority of my adult life in public education. I worked as a teacher, principal, and executive administrator for forty years in California in the Ventura County public school system. Our area was lower demographic. We worked primarily with disenfranchised minority children, many of whom lived near or below the poverty line. The six years of my adult life not spent in public education were spent in private education. After I retired from the Ventura County Office of Education in 2007, I went to work for Jon Braxton at his personally funded Win-The-Day foundation as the Managing Director. Win-the-Day was established as an after-school program by Jon and designed specifically for children on the verge of failing or dropping out of public school. Our mission was to take these children who were not motivated to learn and provide that motivation. These children were never shown the connection between education and living a better life. Or if they could see the connection, their low self-esteem left them believing they were undeserving. At Win-the-Day we helped young people build the connection. We worked to build appetites within these individuals to learn. We taught them insights and perspectives to enable them to break through their negative self-perceptions as unworthy of a better life. And replace those negative perceptions with positive dreams, possibilities, and beliefs. We led them to self-reflection and the reasons they should apply themselves. We showed them what was possible if they chose to learn. If your viewers followed Jon's career in Congress, they know of the legislation he authored and passed in 2013 to bring the Win-the-Day concepts and curriculums into public schools nationwide. Legislation which is proving extraordinarily successful in improving test scores and lowering dropout rates across the country."

Kriss interjected. "Yes, we are familiar with Jon's STYLE legislation Madam Secretary. He shared his visions with us here on the show before he introduced his groundbreaking legislation. Now please tell us more about your efforts with Jeffrey Claymore and his 'FIX THE CULTURE' initiative."

"Wallis, what we are striving to do is take the concepts proven successful with younger people at Win-the-Day and with STYLE and modify them to resonate with adults. As with younger people, quality of life for adults can be improved by changing thought patterns and malformed beliefs. When we look at the cultural decline in this country, we believe it is rooted in those same human behaviors and frailties we saw in the young people we worked with at WTD. My two roles supporting Jeffrey's efforts are one: to build curriculums to be offered on the LABEL campuses to correct faulty thought patterns and extinguish malformed beliefs. And two, to recruit and train instructors."

"Those are tall orders, Madam Secretary. How are those efforts coming along?"

"Slowly but steadily, Wallis. As Jeffery shared with you on his last visit, the LABEL campuses will offer a wide variety of instruction. We have people in the various departments of the Executive branch engaged in building our curriculums, which I'm overseeing. As for recruiting and training instructors, we are enlisting the help of the psychologist and psychoanalyst communities. Next week we are hosting a symposium at the White House with members of those communities. We are seeking their insights on how we may remodel their work with clients in a one-on-one clinical environment into a format which would be functional in a classroom environment led by an instructor who does not hold a clinical license. We realize we must make tradeoffs, but also feel we can make considerable progress with the right curriculum taught in the right environment. It has proven successful with young people at Win-The-Day. There's no reason to believe we can't be successful with adults. We are not so naïve to believe this will happen immediately. This level of instruction will take time for tuning and refining. But over time, we're confident we can become proficient in training these concepts."

"Impressive, Madam Secretary. Do you have a plan for recruiting and training instructors? And also explain to us how the LABEL campuses will be managed. Who or what agency will have the responsibility for oversight?"

"Of course, Wallis. Besides recruiting within the four branches of our armed services, we're now also working with colleges and universities around the country with strong social sciences departments. We are looking for young people interested in social service careers. There are college students in the country who are looking for opportunities to work within their communities to help others. We believe the career path we are offering will appeal to young people seeking these kinds of community service career opportunities. Our instructors will offer people opportunities to improve their lives. They will see how rewarding the position will be."

Jeffrey interjected. "Wallis, you asked about oversight. We just made the final decision last week to place the LABEL campuses under the direction of the Department of Education, and Secretary McIlroy. We've been debating whether it should be Health and Human Services or Education. And Connie lost the coin flip," Jeffrey offered humorously. "It will be her baby."

"Well," responded Kriss, "it sounds like your hands are now quite full, Secretary McIlroy. Did you have any idea this would become one of your responsibilities when the President offered you the job?"

"No, but it's OK. Remember, I've already done this work for Win-The-Day. We know what concepts we need to teach to achieve our objectives and we are going to learn how to teach them to adults. In my estimation, it will be easier than working with young people. We believe adults who have life experiences and a level of maturity will initially be more receptive to our concepts than younger people. The on-ramp will be shorter. This endeavor will require significant effort, but the President and Jeffrey are committed. I've been promised I'll have access to all the resources we need. I share Jeffrey's vision on this. It's the best effort we can make to improve life in America."

Kriss turned to look directly into the camera stage left. "We'll be back in two minutes with the First Lady."

When the broadcast resumed, it was Angela alone, facing Kriss.

"Madam First Lady. Welcome back to Big News Sunday."

"Thank you, Wally. It's nice to be back."

Kriss bristled at the First Lady now choosing to use Jon's nickname for him. "I understand there have been recent developments within the TYPE 1–YOU'RE DONE Project. I'm sure our viewing audience, which now includes hundreds of thousands of members of the T1D community, is anxious to hear what you have to report. Please, fill us in."

"Wally, do you ever listen to yourself speak?"

"Not as I'm speaking. Doing so would interfere with my thought processes on conducting my interviews. Why do you ask?"

"You and I should share beers like you do with the President. You always seem so stiff and formal when we meet."

"I'm sorry Madam First Lady. It's hard to break old habits. I imagine it's because of my thirty years of conducting these interviews. It's how I roll. But please, tell me how you'd like me to interview you."

"Take off your coat and tie and roll up your sleeves. You are now officially recruited into the project. It's time you and I started working more closely together to fight for the cure. It's time for you to get busy."

Kriss was unsure how to verbally respond to Angela's tongue-in-cheek commands, but found himself following them. A moment later he was coatless and tieless. His bare forearms were exposed as he sat in his chair, uncomfortable and confused, looking at Angela. He realized he had lost total control of the interview and felt powerless to attempt a recovery. "What is it you need from me, Madam First Lady?"

"First, stop calling me madam. We're out of time for formalities. Let's go with Angela. Second, hand me your coat and tie." He did so without hesitation. She stood, draped the coat and tie over her right arm, and walked off the set with them. She returned a second later with a notepad and pen, which she set in front of Kriss. "Wally, take some notes."

He looked at her in a total state of confusion. She wryly smiled at him and then turned her attention to the camera stage right. The cameraman understood her intent and zoomed in on her as she started addressing the eight million people tuned in.

"Ladies and gentlemen, I have considerable good news to report about our progress towards the cure for Type 1 diabetes in the **TYPE 1-YOU'RE DONE** Project. And I have other not so good things you need to know."

"First, the good. All four of our research teams have made noteworthy progress in testing their hypotheses. All have made significant advancements in their research endeavors. And all have conveyed the primary reason for their successful, accelerating paces in research and testing being the improved levels of collaboration the project established. And all have reported the additional levels of structured funding also being a contributing factor. Research decisions are now being made on efficacy and probabilities, not money. It is allowing our teams to be more aggressive in their research. And this new aggressiveness has led to amazing discoveries.

"When we first conceived the project, it was our expectation that spirited collaboration among research organizations with like-minded thinking, and better structured funding, leading to acceleration in the development of the cure for Type 1. Now, we can report our expectations are being exceeded. We are on our way to meeting our objective to see a cure within our three-year timeline.

"As I mentioned during my last visit with you, one of our four teams was making significantly more progress than the others. Our

Blood Stem Cell research team. Today I'm pleased to report we are projecting we will be ready to go to clinical trials with their hypothesis early next year. Currently, Dr. Jonas Shapiro from CanadaDRI and his team, while continuing to evaluate their hypothesis on lab animals, are modeling different age groups for phase one human clinical trials. Factors are age, length of time with the disease, and severity. At this point, we are leaning towards individuals who are between ages thirty and forty, who have been living with Type 1 for at least fifteen years, and who are having abnormal difficulty controlling their blood sugar levels. If any of you watching today fit our criteria and would like to be part of this trial, please go to the project's website and apply for consideration.

"On another note, there are troubling not-so-good things happening with our mission. While our four research teams are working every day to bring us the cure for T1D, there are powerful forces working against us. Over the last three weeks, eighteen lawsuits have been filed in federal courts to shut our project down. The plaintiffs of fourteen of these lawsuits are all recently formed organizations, each providing anonymity and covering for the identity of the individuals behind these efforts. These fourteen lawsuits are seeking to shut us down based on commerce violations. They claim the executive branch of our government cannot unduly force private companies to sacrifice their research and their investments and to share their intellectual property against their will. We see these lawsuits as frivolous and believe we will prevail. If you recall, no research organization has been forced to join our project. It is true we disclosed we would withhold future research grants if they did not, and our position is the federal government has the latitude to determine who is worthy of being provided funding grants, and who is not."

Off camera, Kriss noticed the show's producer was frantically trying to get his attention. When he noticed her, she made a slashing motion across her neck. She spoke into her headset. He heard her clearly. "Wallis, you need to interrupt her. We can't have her go near where the President went last time. You can kiss our big sponsors goodbye if you let this continue." Kriss raised his left hand to his earpiece, wagged his index finger at it and shook his head as if he couldn't make out what she was saying.

Angela continued. "The other four lawsuits have been filed by the ACLU claiming we are violating the civil rights of investors and stakeholders of the research organizations which joined the project. We also have reason to believe there are corporate interests behind all these lawsuits. We fully expect when we have the cure for T1D, there will be seismic shifts in the lines of profit of the diabetes industry. It is not without precedent to have corporate interests fight to preserve their profit centers through the court system.

"Other troubling occurrences the project is facing are threats of physical harm against the Braxton family. The President has received three direct threats against his life in recent weeks. There are forces working against us as we march to the cure. None of which we will allow to stop us, but ones we must recognize and push back against."

The show's producer screamed into Kriss' earpiece. "Interrupt her. Stop her." He ignored her.

Angela continued. "The reason I bring these troubling facts to you is we are asking for your help. As viewers of the Big News Network, we ask you to ask this network to investigate and bring to light the forces working against the project. The best way to push back against whomever is behind these efforts is to expose them. We know this network has the resources and contacts to shine a light on who is attempting to stop the people living with Type 1 diabetes, including my son, from seeing a cure."

Angela turned her gaze away from the camera and back to Kriss. The cameraman zoomed out to bring them both on screen. Kriss looked nervous and uncertain. Angela addressed him. "Wally, thank you for the opportunity to speak directly to your viewers. I hope you took copious notes so we can collaborate on how to expose those who have placed obstacles in the path to the cure."

"Uhh, yes Madam, uhh Angela. I did take notes." He realized it was time for a commercial break. He looked into the camera. Tieless. Coatless. Clueless. "We'll be back in two minutes; I think with the President. And your host, for the remainder of our show, could be anybody."

When the broadcast resumed, it was Kriss with coat and tie back in place, and Jon. There was a pitcher of root beer and two frosted mugs in front of the President.

"Good morning Mr. President. Welcome back to the show."

"Ready for a beer? I'm buying."

"I think I'd like something a little stronger."

"Yeah, I feel you. Mrs. Braxton can make you forget who and where you are when she goes into ninja mode. Have I ever mentioned she's a double black belt in karate?"

"No, you never have. But it doesn't surprise me."

"Well, nothing stronger for you today, my friend. We don't want you drinking and driving."

"Are you saying you're going to let me drive our interview, or will you be carjacking the show as the First Lady did?"

"Wally, I am here for you. Ask me anything."

"Very well. Let's follow up on a couple of things the First Lady mentioned. She said there have been threats against your life. Are you concerned?"

"There have, but the Secret Service does not deem them credible. I'd say were not so much concerned as cautious. Threats against the first family are nothing new. We're well protected. We won't be intimidated. And we're certainly not backing away from any of our positions."

Kriss was getting his mojo back and pressed the President. "The First Lady used the term dark forces and mentioned newly formed organizations being behind the lawsuits filed to shut down the **TYPE 1-YOU'RE DONE** Project. Organizations which have obfuscated the individuals behind them. Care to comment? Any inside baseball on who the people are attempting to shut down the Project?"

"No comment," offered the President.

An awkward pause followed. Kriss hesitated to follow up. The irritated look on Jon's face moved him to change the subject.

"Mr. President, we understand you are considering executing executive orders related to your 'FIX OUR WELL-BEING' agenda. Can you share your thoughts?"

The President obliged. "Last time on your show, we touched briefly on the benefits of micro-dosing natural psychedelics in a clinical environment. I had just tasked Health and Human Services to go deep into reviewing all the research conducted in the country prior to Richard Nixon signing the Controlled Substances Act of 1971. Unfortunate legislation which classified natural psychedelics as Schedule I substances and made it illegal to continue the research and the clinical trials taking place. Clinical trials showing tremendous promise using these compounds to treat a variety of mental illness conditions. But I stress in a clinical environment. Ingesting these substances, in large doses, unsupervised, on a whim or a binge, is not advised. It's important to understand the distinction. Four months ago, I instructed HHS to reopen the research. And we have uncovered a mountain of evidence leading us to conclude these treatments offer tremendous potential to address our country's problems with depression, addiction, anxiety, suicide, trauma. Potential to improve one's well-being if they suffer from any number of mental health conditions. The executive orders we're considering would throw the Controlled Substances Act into the garbage and lay the foundation to bring these therapies into the mainstream of health care in this country. It is long overdue. There's too much potential in these treatments to not place resources of the federal government behind this effort. These compounds will help us fix the nation's wellbeing."

"Mr. President, I see parallels between this effort and your efforts to discover the cure for Type 1 diabetes. Am I seeing this clearly?"

"You are. There are parallels. Both efforts require us to fly in the face of established bureaucracies and political alliances. As with the **TYPE 1-YOU'RE DONE** Project, we expect significant opposition from organizations and individuals whose profit streams would be disrupted by the treating and curing of mental health conditions by compounds provided by nature and not by pharmaceutical company laboratories."

"From whom exactly, Mr. President, are you expecting this opposition?"

"Wally, are you watching the clock? Isn't it time for a word from one of your pharmaceutical sponsors?"

Chapter 28

Oh Canada

J ack Abbott had his driver drop him off along Chicago's Lakefront Trail at the Monroe St. intersection. From there, it was a short walk to the Chicago Yacht Club and the docks comprising Monroe Harbor. Abbott arrived at the reception desk in appropriate attire wearing white casual slacks, red t-shirt, blue blazer, and a Chicago Cubs baseball cap atop his shiny bald head.

"Good morning, sir. How can I help you?" the young female receptionist chirped.

"I'm here to see the *Lucky Lady*."

"Oh yes. She's here today. Have you ever been aboard? She's a beauty."

"No. I've never met her."

"You're in for a treat, then. Let me walk you over to her."

She moved from behind the desk to a door leading to the docks. "Follow me, please."

A moment later she and Abbott were standing beside an immaculate fifty-eight-foot sailing vessel glistening in the early morning sun shining off the calm waters of Lake Michigan. The Lucky Lady's captain emerged from the below deck quarters and the receptionist made Abbott's introduction to Marco DiMarco. She then left the two to return to her post.

"Come aboard Jack. Are you a sailor?"

"No Marco, I'm not. I live on the shore of Lake Michigan, but don't care much for boats."

DiMarco was only slightly offended by Abbott's mention of the word boat. "Your aversion extends to ships as well, I imagine. It's too bad you're not a fan of sailing, Jack. Its serenity provides one with a much-needed respite from the pressures of everyday life. Particularly in my line of work."

"Yes. I can understand that," Jack responded nervously.

Abbott stepped aboard and DiMarco directed him to a set of seating cushions at the forward.

"I know it's still early, Jack, but you want a drink?"

Abbott was still unsure of his emotional footing in the presence of the Director of Business Development for the Giancarlo Cambretta crime syndicate. A man he knew was responsible for the sudden disappearance of upstanding, and otherwise, members of Chicago's illegitimate business community. "No thank you, Marco."

DiMarco sat down across from Abbott. "I don't have much time this morning, so let's cut to the chase. I understand you approached our CFO with an interest in presenting us with a business proposition. Given your standing in the community, we felt we should hear what you have to say. What do you have in mind?"

Abbott was starting to have second thoughts, but closed them out. "Marco, there are some threats against my business I'd like to counter."

"Are these threats against Costello Labs or some other business I'm not aware you're involved in?"

"Costello."

"OK, what kind of threats?"

"There are some things happening in our industry which could, if they come to fruition, significantly degrade highly profitable lines in our business."

"If they come to fruition? So, these events haven't happened yet?"

"No. But there's a distinct possibility they could in the next year."

"And you want to buy some insurance in the event they do."

"In a manner of speaking. What I really want is to ensure these events never happen."

"Where are these threats coming from? I assume your competitors?"

"Not exactly."

"OK Jack," DiMarco was tiring of the Abbott's indirectness, "just spill it. I don't have time for this. Exactly what and from whom?"

"The federal government," Abbott blurted, relieved he finally said it.

DiMarco was surprised. "We don't do lobbying in the traditional sense, Jack. We stay as far away from Washington as we can. We don't trust those motherfuckers and we certainly don't want to attract any attention."

"I'm looking for something untraditional."

"As in illegal or illegitimate?"

"Possibly," Abbott retorted.

"Jack, what makes you think we're interested in that kind of business? We run a clean, legitimate operation."

"Good luck today, puke."

"Same to you, Dar-kashian."

"What did you just call your sister?" Angela said with feigned disgust as she walked into the residence dining room, finding her two teenagers engaged in a friendly match of name-calling over breakfast.

She was fussing with her left earring as she breezed past them on her way to the kitchen to find a cup of coffee.

"Dar-kashian," he yelled loud enough for her to hear him in the other room.

"What?" she yelled back.

"Dar-kashian, as in Darla Kardashian."

Angela walked back into the dining room. "Really Luke? You're old enough to be an international Type 1 warrior superhero, but not old enough to stop teasing your sister?"

"She called me puke," he answered with manufactured annoyance, causing Darla to giggle.

"Yeah, well, maybe you deserve it," Angela responded causing Darla to break into all out laughter. "You have your bag ready? We're leaving in fifteen minutes." She retreated back to the kitchen to make a call.

"Yes, mom." He turned his attention back to his sister. "So, what are you doing today?"

"Bowling cage match in the famous White House bowling alley."

"With who?"

"Me and dad against Abby and Eric."

"Oooooohhh, Darla and Eric Martin sitting in a tree. K-i-s-s-i,"

"Puke! Stop teasing your sister," Angela yelled from the kitchen.

"Sorry mom," he yelled back.

Angela poured herself coffee, retrieved her cell phone from its cubby, and dialed Canada. "Melissa, hey it's Angela." She listened to the response, then concluded the brief conversation. "We're leaving in fifteen minutes. Should be touching down in Edmonton in five hours. Looking forward to seeing you again."

Melissa Hubbard was the operations manager for CanadaDRI. She had traveled with Dr. Shapiro to Washington each time Angela invited him to the White House to participate in the project's formation and team selections. Melissa and Angela hit it off immediately and became close friends. They shared something in common. Both were raising teenage boys suffering with Type 1. The fact Melissa had two teenage Type 1 sons made her a rock star in Angela's eyes.

The efforts of the **TYPE ONE–YOU'RE DONE** Project had significantly expedited the work of CanadaDRI. Prior to the kickoff of the project in May, Dr. Shapiro's research was under-funded, and their progress inhibited. Their hypothesis held great promise and was chosen amongst those of the five organizations within the project's blood stem cell team. With the funding and collaboration set in motion by Angela's efforts, their research accelerated and the possible validity of CanadaDRI's hypothesis was becoming evident.

By September, the team was successfully extracting blood stem cells from animals and utilizing Dr. Yamanaka's twenty-eight-day reversion protocol and re-injecting newly created insulin-producing cells edited from the lab animal's own blood. The injected cells were successfully producing insulin with only minor noticeable rejection from the animal's immune systems. The time for human clinical trials was approaching. Candidates needed to be selected and blood samples extracted. The samples would be subjected to Dr. Yamanaka's protocol and, after twenty-eight days, evaluated for their insulin-producing properties. If successful, and after accelerated approval processes already promised by the President and the Canadian Prime Minister, human trials would commence.

Angela escorted Luke to the South Lawn to board Marine One. They helicoptered to Andrews Air Force base and boarded Air Force One for the three-and-a-half-hour flight to the airfield at CFB Cold Lake, a Canadian Forces Base outside of Edmonton. On the plane ride to Edmonton, Angela mentioned to Luke she felt Dr. Shapiro would not be in favor of him participating in the first round of clinical trials. A suggestion he had recently raised to his mother.

"Yeah, I have the same feeling," he responded.

Melissa was on the tarmac to greet her visitors as they deplaned AF1 at Cold Lake AFB. She and Angela embraced warmly. As did she and Luke. She was coordinating the onboarding of all the clinical trial volunteers and made the arrangements for today's distinguished visitors, even though Luke had not been considered for participation. And Dr. Shapiro had not yet been informed of Luke's request.

"Let's go. We have a three-hour drive to campus. And only a small window to meet with Dr. Shapiro this afternoon."

The Canadian Diabetes Research Institute (CanadaDRI) operations were based in a modern research facility on the University of Alberta campus in downtown Edmonton. Dr. Jonah Shapiro, a pioneer in islet cell transplantation, was leading the research. His past efforts led to a successful pancreatic islet transplantation technique in 2002, which became known as the Alberta Protocol. While these efforts proved impactful for many Type 1 diabetic patients around the world, the protocol was limited in scale as it required donated pancreatic cells. And required immunosuppression therapy to keep the patient's immune system from attacking the foreign transplanted cells. Dr. Shapiro attracted worldwide notoriety for his breakthrough research but was not satisfied. The technique would not scale to meet the worldwide needs of the Type 1 diabetes community. Nor mitigate the risks to the patient posed by a lifetime of taking immunosuppression pharmaceuticals.

In response to these limitations, Dr. Shapiro set out to improve the efficacy and scalability of Type 1 diabetes therapeutics in search of a cure. Utilizing Dr. Yamanaka's protocol and energized by the boost in funding and collaboration resulting from the efforts of the **TYPE 1–YOU'RE DONE** Project, the CanadaDRI team had proven in lab animals Dr. Shapiro's recent conclusions that blood stem cell therapy utilizing the animal's own gene-edited blood could potentially eliminate the need for donated stem cells, donated pancreatic cells, and immunosuppression drug therapy.

Dr. Shapiro greeted his guests as they joined him in a conference room at the Institute. This was the fourth meeting between Angela and Dr. Shapiro, the first one not in the White House. "Mrs. Braxton, it's great to see you again. And Luke, you as well. How are you feeling these days?"

"I'm good, doctor. How are you feeling these days?" he responded sarcastically.

"I'm good as well," the doctor replied cordially. He knew from their two previous conversations that Luke was not comfortable with any reference to his condition.

He returned his glance to Angela. "Melissa told me yesterday you were coming to Edmonton today, but did not explain why. And I was not expecting Luke to join you. Is everything OK with the project? Is there anything I need to be concerned with?"

"Everything with the project is fine, doctor. Before we begin discussing our reason for coming to see you, can you give Luke and I a briefing on any recent developments since our last conversation?"

Shapiro was curious to learn the reason why the First Lady and her increasingly popular son traveled from Washington to Edmonton, but granted her request. "Our update is positive. We injected twenty-six more lab animals over the last month with edited blood stem cells, and thus far, they are all showing no signs of rejection. And all are showing increased insulin production."

Angela was pleased. "What great news. It sounds like everything is coming into place for human trials. I know the President is anxious to work with Trudeau to fast-track approval. Is there anything we can do to assist you with your filing? And are we still on track, given your PM follows through on the commitment he made to Jon?"

Shapiro chuckled. "Our filing is almost complete and ready to be submitted to the Minister of Health. And yes, last I heard, Trudeau is still on board."

There was an awkward pause followed by Dr. Shapiro. "Mrs. Braxton, we spoke two weeks ago and today you flew five hours to meet with me. I don't mean to be short, but I am really terribly busy today. Why exactly are you here?"

Luke answered for her. "It was my idea to come. I wanted to talk to you."

Shapiro looked at Luke and raised an eyebrow. "OK. What are we talking about?"

"Your phase one human trial."

"What about it?"

Even though he had written out and practiced delivering his appeal, Luke was intimidated by Dr. Shapiro and stammered before expressing his question. "Why do the volunteers for the first trial have to be between thirty and forty and diabetic for over fifteen years?"

"There are a few reasons, Luke. One is we need to narrow the age range in our test group so we can eliminate a patient's age being a variable in measuring efficacy. And second, we felt the thirty-to-forty age range would be the most appropriate for the initial trials. Luke, what we are proposing has unknown potential side effects. It's risky. We decided against selecting individuals older than our initial test group because we cannot be dismissive of the fact that the longer the patient lives with the disease, the more compromised their health might be.

And the riskier the trials might be. As for selecting younger patients for phase one, we ruled out younger age groups because therapeutics have improved dramatically over the last few years. We expect their health to be better because of all the recent advancements in treatments, because their blood sugar levels are being monitored with more accuracy than ever, and because insulin delivery systems are improving. Young children diagnosed in the last few years have access to better care options upon diagnosis, and their expectations for a long and healthier life are greater than they have ever been."

Luke was not convinced. "Yeah, but their daily life with the worrying and the carb counting and living the down days/up days roller coaster still sucks."

"Believe me Luke. I understand what life with Type 1 is like. Trying to find the cure has been all I have thought about for the last twenty-five years. And right now, we are concentrating on delivering a cure for the thirty-to-forty age range we can be confident in first. No one on our team would be comfortable having younger patients involved in the first human trials. But trials for children and adolescents won't be far behind if we have success with our first group. We had to pick one age range to be first. To minimize our risks and the risks to younger patients, it made the most sense for us to go with thirty-to-forty-year-olds."

Luke cleared his throat. "How long before kids can be included in testing?"

"I'd say one year following successful results with our first group."

Luke looked at his mother. She nodded to assure him. He looked at the doctor.

"Dr. Shapiro, I'd like you to make an exception."

"OK. What do you have in mind?"

"Include me."

Shapiro looked at Angela. "Mrs. Braxton, are you aware of what your son is asking and the risks associated with it?"

She responded. "I am."

"And you're in favor?"

Luke answered for her. "She doesn't want me to do it, but I feel I have to."

Shapiro was puzzled. "Why, exactly?"

"If I was included in the first trial and it was successful, would it speed up the treatment being available for kids?"

"It's not that simple. This is a new treatment, and we don't know exactly what the future holds for it. But generally speaking, I would say yes. If this first phase trial produced successful outcomes in your case, it could decrease the amount of time to start trials on younger patients. But we're talking here in generalizations. We don't have enough data to definitively answer your question."

Luke was feeling more assured. "Doctor, why do I want to be included in the first group? Because of our project, it seems like all the T1D kids out there are now following me. And I feel a responsibility to them. I'm getting over two hundred letters every day from around the world. Kids and their parents writing, wanting to know more, praying for us, encouraging us. But many of the letters express how kids with T1D are losing hope. They write they don't closely monitor their blood glucose levels after years of doing so. They don't eat right. They write their hopelessness is getting in the way of their taking better care of themselves. I know this is true because sometimes I have those same feelings. And I've only had the disease for four years. Some kids my age have lived with T1D since they were two or three. They need hope. They need a reason to do better. To fight harder to keep their blood sugars controlled until we have the cure. I can give them a reason. I can set the bar. If they see me in the trial, they'll feel hope and they'll take better care of themselves. We can't wait another year. I know there are risks and I'm willing to accept them. Put me in coach."

Shapiro turned to Angela. "Mrs. Braxton?"

"It's your call, Doctor."

"All right. I'll speak with our board."

The motorcade, consisting of three heavily armored Canadian government Cadillac Escalades and eight Edmonton PD motorcycles, each with a heavily armed police officer in the saddle, rolled out of Alberta University at a quarter past four. Angela and Luke were in the back seat of the middle SUV. Two secret service agents were in the front seat, and two each were in the front seats of the lead and trailing SUVs. Four motorcycle officers rode in front of the lead, and four behind the trail.

The motorcade was two hours outside Edmonton on its way back to Cold Lake and Air Force One, traveling along the inside northbound lane. Trailing the motorcade by one mile, also in the inside northbound lane on a desolate stretch of highway AB-28, was a black Honda Accord. It suddenly began a steady acceleration. The two motorcycle officers at the back of the motorcade, responsible for surveilling approaching trailing traffic, eyed the vehicle in their rear-view mirrors. The recent model Accord with blacked out tinted windows approached the motorcade at a reasonable speed. Though it was slowly gaining ground, it presented no cause for alarm. The two motorcycle officers at the rear reacted as if nothing was unusual. They glanced at one another and then turned their attention forward.

When the Honda was three hundred yards behind the motorcade, it made a casual lane change and increased speed. At first, gradually, and then fifty yards behind the motorcade, the pedal was put to the metal. The two officers in the rear became aware and changed lanes to block the Honda's path to the SUVs. The Honda slowed and maneuvered back to the inside lane and pulled alongside the two officers now in the outside lane. The rear driver's side window lowered three inches and a shotgun's front site and barrel emerged. Two shots were fired. The two officers were dead before they hit the ground, only ten seconds after changing lanes.

The two motorcycle officers directly behind the trail SUV heard the shots. By the time they checked their mirrors, they were four hundred yards beyond their two dead comrades. The Honda was in pursuit. It changed lanes again to the outside and had a clear path to the side of the First Lady's vehicle. The two officers directly behind the trail SUV and still ahead of the Honda changed lanes to the outside to block their path. The Honda quickly swerved back to the inside lane to avoid hitting the two motorcycles. It pulled even with the officers attempting to pull their handguns. The sharpshooter in the Honda took them out.

The Secret Service officers in the trail SUV heard the shots. The driver checked his mirror. His partner turned his head and radioed 'mayday' to the other two SUVs. The Secret Service agent riding shotgun in the First Lady's vehicle dove over the front seat and into the back. He grabbed both Angela and Luke and compressed them beneath him.

The Honda now had a clear path to the trail SUV. The sharpshooter fired at its tires, blowing them out and sending the vehicle into a tailspin. The driver of the First Lady's SUV radioed the lead to change lanes. The lead complied and slowed to get into position to ram the Honda as the First Lady's SUV accelerated and roared past.

The driver of the Honda saw the Secret Service maneuver and peeled out to a conveniently placed off ramp exiting AB-28. Ten minutes later, the airspace was flooded with helicopters from Cold

Lake. Thirty minutes later, Air Force One was airborne with Luke and Angela aboard and unharmed.

Chapter 29

It's How He Rolls

The meeting had just started in the Oval when Rosemary's voice burst through the intercom speaker. *"Mr. President, Prime Minister Trudeau for you."*

"About time. Thanks Rosemary. Put him through. Good morning, Justin. What have you got?"

"Unfortunately, Jon, no suspects yet. At first, we believed the ambush was the work of a violent climate extremist group active in Canada over the past three years and becoming more brazen each time they surface. They have always been vocal and harshly critical of the energy partnership between our two countries. The attack on your wife's and son's motorcade fit their profile of escalating violence, and correlated to what we calculated their next act might look like. But new intel uncovered yesterday leads us to believe they may not be involved. And the attack may have been orchestrated and/or coordinated in the U.S."

The President was angered. "OK. You're on speaker with Donovan Granger. I assume you know him."

"No Jon. I've never had the pleasure of meeting your CIA Director. Good morning Mr. Granger."

"Mr. Prime Minister. Please tell us what you know."

"Rogers Telecom reported a significant increase in encrypted message traffic crossing their network for three days before the ambush. While we haven't been able to decrypt any of the messages, we have been able to decipher pieces of the metadata. The encrypted traffic was bouncing between Edmonton and Chicago."

Granger responded without hesitation. "Mr. Prime Minister, it's imperative you keep a tight lid on this. No public disclosure. No leaks. Close ranks on it internally. No one who might be involved in the attack can know we have this intel. Only your closest inner intelligence circle needs to know. And I'd like to engage with your team to get more detail. I assume this is OK with you?"

"It is" responded the Canadian Prime Minister."

The following day, four members from the House's intelligence committee, and four members from the Senate's, were summoned to the White House. The contingent included one Senator Robert Krueger from the great state of Illinois. He was the ranking member on the Senate committee.

The attack on the First Lady's motorcade and the murder of four Edmonton PD motorcycle officers, despite futile and hopeless efforts by Canadian security agencies to kill the story, had leaked and was now widely reported dominating news cycles across the globe. This meeting, coordinated in secrecy and conducted in the White House situation room, was requested by Donovan Granger to brief selected members of Congress on all intelligence collected to date. Including the intelligence on the flurry of encrypted messages exchanged between Edmonton and Chicago prior to the incident. Besides members of Congress, also in attendance were the Director of the FBI, the NSA Director, the DNI and the Director of the Secret Service.

Jon never interacted with Krueger during his two terms in the House. Nor since he moved to the White House. But he was well aware of the Chicago-based Senator's long-standing ties to the pharmaceutical industry. The President studied Krueger's entry to the 'sit-room,' and continuously focused on him during the briefing. It was Jon's first meaningful encounter with Krueger and, in watching the Senator, he formed immediate suspicions of his integrity as Donovan Granger summarized what was known to date. And what the CIA would be doing to identify those responsible. The briefing concluded with no words, but numerous glances exchanged between the President and the Senator.

When Krueger returned to the Senate chambers, he went immediately to his office. There, he instructed his office manager to initiate a call to Jack Abbott's office and officially invite him to a Senate briefing regarding new industry legislation being considered to assist pharmaceutical companies avoid crippling FDA regulatory controls and speed up drug approval processes. He asked his office manager to clandestinely date the call in their logs from two days before. In reality, there was no such briefing scheduled. The call was a signal to inform Abbott he was needed in Washington immediately.

Abbott and Krueger met briefly in the Senator's office to provide an air of legitimacy for their encounter. Krueger was well versed in Washington's intelligence apparatus and now paranoid after learning of the possibility there was a Chicago connection to the attack on FLOTUS. He wanted all his activities, including his interactions with Abbott, to appear as nothing out of the ordinary as he suspected he may be under surveillance. A suspicion amplified from noticing the eyes of the President blazing upon him during the intelligence briefing.

Following fifteen minutes of conversation, Krueger and Abbott headed to The Palm on Dupont Circle for lunch and private conversation. The Senator chose a popular DC hangout so if spotted, their congregating would be inconspicuous. Everything related to their time together needed the appearance of 'business as usual.'

After ordering drinks, Krueger filled Abbott in on the Canadian intelligence. "I'm not believing you had anything to do with this, Jack. Tell me I'm right."

"Of course, you're right, Bob. Four motorcycle cops dead? Jesus."

"You said you were going your own way on stopping Braxton's diabetes agenda. You remember that conversation?"

Abbott feigned indignation at the implication. "Really Bob. You think I set up a hit on the First Lady? You think I'm crazy? What the hell good would that have done? Make Braxton a martyr? How does that help my business? The answer is it doesn't. So, you're right Bob. I had nothing to do with it."

Krueger wasn't convinced. "OK, then who else have you been talking to? What else are you considering?"

"Why would I tell you?" Abbott snickered.

"Depending on what you say, so I can either provide cover or try to talk you out of what you're planning."

"Look Bob, I appreciate the heads up on the intel, but relax. I had nothing to do with what happened in Edmonton."

"Do you happen to know what the First Lady and number one son were doing there?" Krueger inquired.

"No. Should I?"

"Maybe. They were visiting a research team getting close to clinically trialing a cure for T1D."

"Mrs. Martin, the North Korea Foreign Minister is here for his appointment."

"Thank you, Barbara. Show him in."

A moment later, Foreign Minister Ri was sitting across from Abby. "Madam Assistant Secretary. Thank you for inviting me to the State Department. It's my first visit, and I believe the first visit to the United States State Department for anyone from the North Korea government."

"Well, Mr. Ri Yu-Song, then this moment calls for a celebration. Have you ever enjoyed a root beer float?"

"I'm sorry, Mrs. Martin, a root beer float?" Ri answered slowly and uncertainly to ensure he repeated the pronunciation back accurately.

"Excuse me Minister," Abby said as she flashed a smile and hit the intercom button on her phone. Barbara responded. *"Yes, Mrs. Martin?"*

"Barbara, I brought in vanilla ice cream and root beer this morning. Would you be so kind as to go into the kitchen and make the Foreign Minister and I two root beer floats?"

Her secretary took the request in stride. It was not uncommon for Abby to have something unusual delivered to her first meeting with a foreign diplomat.

Ri was curious. "I have heard the term root beer before. But I don't remember where. Oh yes, now I remember. I think from the President when he's on the cable news talk show with his friend. Isn't root beer what they drink?"

"Very good Mr. Foreign Minister. You're familiar with Wallis Kriss. Yes, they do drink root beer, but not root beer floats. When you add vanilla ice cream to root beer, you make magic."

"Ahhh," the Minister responded as Barbara walked in with two full mugs and set them down on Abby's desk.

Abby reached for one and motioned to Ri to take the other. "Ri, let's drink to our partnership and the improvement of the lives of the people in North Korea suffering with Type 1 diabetes." They clinked their mugs.

Ri nodded. "Yes, let's have a toast." He downed a good-sized gulp. "Mrs. Martin, I agree with you. This is magical. It is unlike anything I've ever tasted. But I'm sure you invited me here for reasons other than to introduce me to root beer floats, though I'm pleased you did. What are we going to speak about?"

Abby was still savoring her float. "You know Ri, if you want to really jazz up a root beer float, try putting three pinches of cinnamon on top. You must try it when you get home. Please tell me you have root beer, vanilla ice cream, and cinnamon in North Korea."

"Ice cream and cinnamon, yes. Root beer? I don't think so."

"No worries. I'll ship a few cases to your office in Pyongyang. Now let's get down to business. First, you should know we are close to finalizing a contract for your review with our country's largest insulin producer, Costello Labs. The contract will call for Costello to sell North Korea thirty million vials of their highest quality insulin. The negotiated price will be less than one half of what you currently pay China for their product, which we know to be inferior. As a side note, their offering includes the brand of insulin Luke uses."

"I am happy to hear this, Mrs. Martin. How is Lucas? It's been three months since he and I have spoken. And I was horrified by the news from Canada. I hope he was not injured."

"He was not hurt at all and is doing fine. I'll let him know you asked about him."

"I'm very relieved. Thank you. As you may know, I have developed something of a special relationship with the President's son. Now please continue with the discussion of this contract."

Abby nodded. "The contract calls for Costello to deliver three million seven-hundred and fifty thousand vials every three months to Pyongyang for two years, starting the end of the first quarter of next year. And in preparation for the deliveries, it also includes initiatives the U.S. government will fund to ensure the insulin, once delivered, can be stored efficiently, delivered efficiently, and successfully administered by your health care network. The President was insistent these initiatives be part of our offer. I worked with Jon for over twelve years before he entered politics. He's always on top of the details to ensure his ideas are successful. This is how he rolls."

"How he rolls Mrs. Martin?" Ri asked slowly.

"Yes. It's a saying we use to describe how one acts. Even the President of the United States rolls."

"Oh. I see. This is extremely gracious of the United States. I'm sure our Supreme Leader will roll as well."

"Good. Let's hope so. Negotiating this deal with Costello has been a real ball-buster."

"A ball-buster?" Ri asked slowly and uncertainly.

Abby took Ri's response in stride. "Yes. A difficult negotiation. Costello Labs had concerns doing business with your government. All valid and all addressed in the contract by our government. We are guaranteeing your payments and accepting responsibility for any future product liability litigation issues which may arise. We are confident our arrangement will result in improved health for diabetic North Korean's and your cost savings will be so substantial that payment will never be an issue. And we are completely confident in the quality of Costello's product and willing to accept any risk. It is our desire for the People's Republic of North Korea to know how serious we are to build a lasting relationship of trust between our two nations.

Chapter 30

Diabetes Diplomacy

T he production set was primed. The camera stage right zoomed in on Kriss.

"Good morning from Washington DC. It's Sunday, November twenty-third. I'm Wallis Kriss and welcome to Big News Sunday. It's been eight weeks since we last had the President on the program and so much has happened since his last visit, we asked he and the First Lady to join us today. As you all know, the First Lady and the President's son were ambushed outside Edmonton, Alberta three weeks ago in a brazen kidnapping attempt. An attempt which thankfully failed. We understand the President and the First Lady have news for us on the investigation, and other matters of interest."

The camera zoomed out to show Jon and Angela sitting at a forty-five-degree angle to Kriss behind a glass desk. There were no footballs or pitchers of root beer. "Mr. President. Madam First Lady. Welcome back to Big News Sunday."

They answered in unison. "Thank you, Wally."

Kriss dived in. "First, Mrs. Braxton, tell us how you and Luke are doing. Are there any lingering effects from your traumatic experience outside Edmonton three weeks ago?"

And we hope once your government reviews the contract, they will see our desire reflected in the terms."

"I see, Mrs. Martin. I understand and appreciate your efforts. But I have a question. Why is Costello focused on liability protection? Is there anything we should be concerned with?"

"Not at all. The price we negotiated on your behalf was aggressive. Costello's profit margins are small. They looked at the first draft of a deal through a risk-reward calculation lens and perceived their risk to be high. Before we introduced the President's provisions, they doubted your storage and distribution operations were sufficient to protect the integrity of their product. They were uncertain how capable your network of doctors and practitioners would be in prescribing new insulin correctly. They were unsure if the outcomes of our mission would be positive, potentially tarnishing their brand. If we all agree to the deal to launch the President's initiatives, I'll need information from you. Documentation on all your current insulin storage facilities and distribution infrastructure. Also, I'll need you to put together a task force of your doctors and health care practitioners to come to the United States. Once the contract is approved, we want to quickly train your people on Costello insulin so they can train the people in your country on the front lines delivering and administering. Can I count on you to work with me?"

"You can Mrs. Martin. I'll report this ball-busting to our Supreme Leader and be, how would you say, back in touch."

"Thank you for your concern, Wally. Lucas and I are both fine. We were a bit shaken up for a short while, but everything returned to normal quickly. Our Secret Service detail managed the situation perfectly, and we were never in any proximate danger. Lucas shook everything off and is back to living his life and focusing on our project."

Kriss commiserated. "I know I speak for all our viewers when I say how grateful we are you and your son were not hurt. Now, Mr. President, I understand you have new intelligence on the ambush. Anything you can share with us?"

"Sure Wally. We learned these details yesterday, and they should be formally announced momentarily. The Canadian government has arrested eight individuals associated with an activist climate extremist group. They have definitive evidence this group was behind the attack on the First Lady and my son. Those activists are now off the streets and will not be engaging in any further mayhem for the foreseeable future. From what I understand from Prime Minister Trudeau, this group is fully incarcerated and out of business."

"That's welcome news, Mr. President. We are all relieved. And thank you for the brief exclusive."

"You're welcome. Another reason you should have me on more often. Maybe I should have my own desk."

"I don't see that happening while you're still in office, sir. But maybe after you leave office in three years, we might be able to accommodate you."

"Three years may be the case, Wally. But as I've said previously, my decision to not seek re-election will hinge on the success of the **TYPE 1-YOU'RE DONE** Project. And on the subject of success, the First Lady has breaking news on her progress to share. It may be indeed time to start looking for desks for me."

"Very well Mr. President. I'll go desk shopping tomorrow. Now,"

Jon cut Kriss off. "But first I'd like your viewers to know, on a re-lated note, yesterday we learned the People's Republic of North Korea and Chicago-based Costello Labs, with assistance from the First Lady, have verbally agreed to terms on a historic trade agreement. Beginning in the second quarter of next year, Costello will be delivering large volumes of quality insulin to improve the lives of Type 1 diabetic North Koreans. And in response to the signing of this agreement, Kim Jong-Un has signaled he will undertake continued drawdowns of his nuclear arsenal. And he has expressed a willingness to discuss formally ending the North's state of war with South Korea. We will have a formal signing ceremony in Chicago next week. Thanks to the tireless work of the First Lady and her diabetes diplomacy, the world is safer today than it was yesterday."

Kriss looked at the First Lady. "Diabetes diplomacy? That's an artful catch phrase."

Angela deflected gracefully. "We can thank Abby Martin, my good friend in the State department for that one."

Kriss was impressed. "You and the President are on the verge of achieving something this country has been attempting for almost sev-enty years. It appears you are on the precipice of historic progress in the name of world peace. Amazing. Have you spoken to Kim Jong-Un since the verbal agreement was reached? And should we be expecting another delivery of roses on the set from him?"

"Yes, Wally, we have spoken. His tone has changed dramatically from the first time we met during our visit with the Vice President in March. He seems grateful for the work of the President and excited for the prospects ahead. And no, I'm not expecting more roses."

"Congratulations again Madam First Lady. Now let's move on. What's the latest you can share with us on the **TYPE 1-YOU'RE DONE** Project?"

"Wally, we're proud to announce that one of our four teams, our Blood Stem Cell therapy team, is in the final stages of finalizing their initial animal testing phase. We should soon be ready to seek approval from both our FDA and the Canadian Ministry of Health to begin human trials on a treatment which could eventually develop into a viable and scalable cure. If everything continues on plan, we expect the trials would begin at the CanadaDRI facilities in Edmonton in the second quarter of next year."

"Again, congratulations Mrs. Braxton. This is also tremendous news. What will the human trials look like?"

"We are going to start with a test group of fifty individuals between the ages of thirty and forty, and who have been living with Type 1 for at least fifteen years. Each participant will have blood drawn and run through a process to revert their own blood stem cells into insulin-producing cells. Dr. Jonah Shapiro and his team in Edmonton have been experiencing positive results on lab animals with their latest blood stem cell reversion protocol, and feel it is almost ready for trial on human patients. The doctor is currently working on one last protocol adjustment to improve the results of lab animal testing. He hopes to have that completed shortly, and then put his stamp of approval on human testing. In addition to the fifty trialists in the thirty-to-forty age group, there will be one person outside that age range. A seventeen-year-old young man who has been living with the disease for four years."

Kriss' tone shifted from admiration to suspicion. "That's interesting. Someone similar to your son? Why would someone so similar to your son be participating? Please don't tell me he is being sacrificed as a test case."

"Agreed. I won't tell you that," an annoyed Angela replied.

"Then why is there only one person outside the thirty-to-forty age group participating? And the profile of that one person matches your son's?"

"There are risks, but Lucas requested he be included to provide hope to all the young people living with the disease and to speed up the timeline to have the treatment approved for younger patients."

Kriss was stunned and embarrassed to learn Luke had volunteered for the trial. "Excuse me, Madam First Lady. I had no idea you were referring to your son. He's a brave young man, so it should be no surprise to anyone he would take a personal risk to advance the cause." Kriss shifted his glance to the camera stage right. "We'll be back with the President and the First Lady right after these messages."

When the show resumed, Kriss had questions for the President.

"Now Mr. President, as I understand the Costello transaction, we will be selling North Korea large volumes of high-quality insulin at the exceptionally low price of twelve dollars per vial. Yet for patients here in the U.S. the price of a vial of insulin can be twenty to thirty times that price. How do you feel Type 1 diabetic patients will perceive this transaction once they learn about it? I assume American Type 1 diabetic patients will not be pleased to see the North Korea government buying American insulin at a fraction of what it costs them."

"You're right Wally. They will be unhappy. And they should be. Type 1 diabetics in this country, as well as everyone else buying over-priced medications for a variety of maladies, are being ripped off by the pharmaceutical industry. Why is insulin so expensive in this country? Let's look at our North Korea transaction. Anything about the transaction stand out to you?"

"Uh, no. I'm not sure what you mean, sir," replied a puzzled Kriss.

"Well, let's start with insurance companies. Any of them in our North Korea deal?"

"No, not that I can tell."

"Right. And what about advertising companies, and doctors, and regulatory agencies, and hospitals? Any of those in our North Korea deal?"

"No sir. Not that I can tell."

"Any other outside lobbyists? Influencers? Special interests?"

"I don't know. I can't see that far into the deal."

"If you could see into it, you'd see the North Korea deal had no undue complexity. It was a clean negotiation. This is why North Korea got a great price and why it was good enough for Costello to accept despite the low profit margin. Costello had the capacity, the economies of scale and the value to their brand to offset a less than attractive price. This deal is happening because of unbridled free market enterprise with no unnecessary layers of bureaucracy. And one other reason North Korea got such a great deal? They had the First Lady negotiating on their behalf."

"Yes, I can see she would be formidable across a negotiating table."

"You have no idea, Wally. But you and the country will soon have the idea. Everyone in the country overpaying for medications will soon have Mrs. Braxton negotiating for them. As you know, having fired Tom Price, our administration is looking for a new Secretary of Health and Human Services. Angela told me she wants the job. I learned not to say no to her and her martial arts black belts long ago. I'll be putting her name up for confirmation by the Senate tomorrow."

"Wow. This is certainly breaking news, Mr. President. Madam First Lady, are you aware of what you're asking to step into? Having no experience running a government bureaucracy, are you confident you can be effective in the job?"

Angela glanced over at Jon and then back to Kriss. "The President had no experience running a government bureaucracy when he took office and I'd say he's doing a rather respectable job. Wouldn't you agree?"

Kriss shrugged. "Yes, of course."

Angela continued. "I couldn't have a better role model. So, yes, I'm confident. And I'm confident Jon and I will be successful doing what needs to be done to improve our health care system and improve the well-being of Americans. Being immersed in the **TYPE 1–YOU'RE DONE** Project for the past six months has given me an inside look at how our health care system at the federal bureaucratic level operates. And it does not operate in the best interests of its customers. We're going to change things around to where HHS is working in the interests of the people, not industry."

"Do you have anything specific you're considering you can share with our audience?"

"We're going to put a big emphasis on mental health. Jon mentioned to you during a previous visit the promise shown by psychedelic-assisted therapy to treat PTSD, addiction, and depression. We're going to research this heavily. As part of the President's 'FIX OUR WELL-BEING' initiative, HHS will explore every avenue available to fully understand the opportunities natural psychedelic compounds offer to improve the mental health of Americans. Our goal is to see Americans move away from addictive and dangerous pharmaceutical products into clinically administered, psychedelic-assisted therapies. We want to see more nature-based treatments and therapies, and fewer lab produced drugs in the well-being toolbox for our citizens. HHS will be strongly focused on developing programs and protocols to fully utilize these non-addictive and promising solutions which nature has so generously provided us to combat the mental health crisis in this country."

Kriss stirred uneasily in his chair. The comments of the President and the First Lady did not sit well with the pharmaceutical sponsors of Big News Sunday. After the President's previous visit discussing psychedelics, three of the show's largest sponsors requested a meeting with the network and threatened to pull all advertising spending if the show again discussed the topic. The First Lady communicated her support for psychedelic-assisted therapy so quickly that Kriss had no opportunity to intervene. The only thought in his head as she finished her comments was his career at Big News Sunday was now over. "We'll be right back after a word from our, I imagine very unhappy, sponsors."

Kriss walked off the set, saying nothing to Jon, Angela, or the show's producers. He headed to his dressing room for the three-minute break. Ten seconds before the broadcast resumed, Kriss had returned to his perch to begin the next segment on what he had concluded would be his final show.

"We're back with the President and the First Lady. It's been most informative as we have learned the latest developments on the case involving the kidnapping attempt on the first family. We've learned the promising progress of the **TYPE 1-YOU'RE DONE** Project. And we've learned Angela Braxton is likely to become the country's next Secretary of the Department of Health and Human Services with an agenda of reshaping the influence of the country's pharmaceutical industry over the health and well-being of American citizens. And as a result, she is likely to end my career as a broadcast journalist. Madam First Lady, or is it now Madam Secretary, did I do a decent job of summarizing the first thirty minutes of our show?"

Angela responded affirmatively and asked to add more color to her plans on how she was going to move the country's health care system to embrace psychedelic assisted therapy.

Kriss knew resistance was futile and was resigned to his fate. "By all means, Madam First Lady. Nothing you say can destroy my career to any further degree, so have at it. Let's hear your plan to decimate the pharmaceutical industry and send the Big News Sunday show into oblivion."

Angela countered. "Wally, don't be sure we aren't propelling you to more fruitful and greener pastures. You're attached, like it or not, to the Braxton administration's efforts to improve the lives of its citizens. As our programs roll out and the positive results roll in, you, my friend, will be more valued than ever before. If mainstream broadcast or cable media cannot recognize the value of your brand, there is an emerging broadcast medium which will."

Kriss was not convinced. Cable news was all he knew. "I presume you're referring to internet streaming and podcasting?"

The President intervened. "Wally, I believe you're right. This could be your last broadcast for Big News Sunday. We've got thirty minutes left. Let's make the best of it. And while we're at it, get you positioned for your next career opportunity."

At that moment, a stagehand came out with a pitcher of root beer and three frosted mugs. He set them in front of Jon, who began pouring for the three of them. "It's fitting we drink a toast to your retirement from the Big News Network."

The three of them raised their mugs. The President proposed a toast. "On behalf of the nation, the First Lady and I thank you for giving us the platform you have to help the Braxton administration communicate its plans, and dreams, and desires for improving the lives of all Americans. We will be forever grateful for the opportunities you have provided us. And whatever the future holds for you, you will always be in our thoughts. And in our minds, always a true patriot. Given everything you have done for this nation since we first started drinking beers together, should this network make the unintelligent and ill-advised decision to fire you, we'd like to talk to you about a position in the White House."

"Thank you, Mr. President."

Angela moved the conversation back to psychedelics. "Wally, I know we only have a few more minutes and I'd like to fill you in on a few more details about how HHS will be taking psychedelic-assisted therapy to the mentally ill."

"Sure, why not?" said Kriss sarcastically. "I should know more. The way things are going today, I may be first in line for treatment."

Angela ignored the comment. "The therapies were referring to must be administered properly for any chance of success. Dropping acid or digesting shrooms at a weekend party is not therapy and will not be endorsed by us. The compounds and treatments we will endorse must be administered in micro-doses in a clinical environment. Natural compounds such as ibogaine, ayahuasca, 5-Meo-DMT, all require both pre-work and post-work assessments and counseling to be effective. The healing promise of these nature-based compounds does not come easy, but research concludes they can be highly effective when administered in the right doses and in the right environment. This is what we'll be researching starting the day I'm confirmed."

She continued. "To bring these therapies to the people, we will be following a model similar to what Jeffrey Claymore is using to fix our culture. We will build out and open community treatment centers in urban areas around the country. Our first targets will be cities where there are large VA medical facilities. We're going to help our veterans first. These heroes gave themselves to this country and are paying a tremendous price for having done so. The numbers of veterans suffering with mental illness and PTSD are staggering. And we lose between thirty and forty veterans a day to suicide. Our vets deserve to be first, and these treatments will be covered one hundred percent by their VA benefits. These treatment centers will be built to provide patients with the optimum healing environment for psychedelic-assisted therapy. We have a prototype facility design almost completed and will be posting it and other relevant information online at www.fixourwellbeing.gov. This website will be live shortly after I'm confirmed by the Senate. Once we have constructed the facilities needed to serve our veterans, we will focus on assisting the private sector to build facilities in other parts of the country to address the issue of mental health decline in so many Americans. Thank you again, Wally, for allowing us the time on your show to share our vision with your viewers."

Kriss had thirty seconds to wrap the show. He looked across the table at Jon and Angela. "Thank you, Madam First Lady, and Mr. President. I wish you the best of luck in all your endeavors." He then turned to face the camera stage right. "To our viewing audience, we hope you enjoyed what is very likely our final show. I'm Wallis Kriss. Goodbye."

The speed at which the television remote control was hurled at the seventy-two-inch smart TV was impressive for a sixty-three-year-old man in overstuffed, suboptimal, physical condition. The sound of the remote smacking the glass startled Sadie and Maxine lying at the feet of their daddy. They scurried out of the den, leaving Jackrabbit staring at the cracked screen.

Chapter 31

Do What You Need To Do

Ever since the details of the compromising of the Vice President's cell phone came to light in the Oval Office, the Carrington's relationship resembled an iceberg. Frosty was the term Heather used to describe the state of their union to Angela. Wil's invasion of her privacy left Heather hurt, bitter, and wanting space. In the first few months following the disclosure of her husband's plot to spy on her for his personal gain, she had no time, nor patience, nor interest in Wil's constant pleas for forgiveness and appeals for reconciliation. Heather insisted they keep their distance. They were never seen in public together. Never ate meals together. They slept in separate bedrooms.

Wil abandoned any idea of dispatching Jon from the White House so he and Heather could move back in. The manner in which Jon exposed the eavesdropping scheme, protected Heather's reputation, contained the story, and allowed he and Sidney to elude any consequences, other than the implosion of his marriage, convinced him to temper his ambition. At first, he decided his best use of time and experience would be supporting his wife in executing her expanded duties as the most powerful Vice President in the history of the country, if she would let him. She would not. Without her trust and willingness to accept his help, he faded from her orbit. He would let 2020 take care of itself. For now.

Despite her indifference, Wil wanted to rebuild his marriage and made difficult choices. He broke off all communications with Sidney Rosenberg and Mark Parker. And for good measure, Jack Abbott as well. Against his nature, he disappeared from the Washington, DC scene and stayed clear of the media. Wallis Kriss was relentless with requests for Wil to appear on his show but was always politely rejected. He concluded his best chance to return to the White House in three years as the First Gentleman was maintaining a low profile. Braxton's arc was rising, and Heather's was in tow. Wil decided to not screw things up.

Initially, Wil's withdrawal from public life placated Heather. She knew it was hard on him and served as a fitting punishment. The anguish she saw in his demeanor satisfied her desire to return the pain and embarrassment his scheme had inflicted on her. But as time passed, she realized she missed her husband and found herself wishing he would fight harder to make his way back to her.

Wil was watching Big News Sunday, and the Braxton's ending the broadcasting career of Wallis Kriss, from his study at the Naval Observatory. He surmised Heather was down the hall in her home office, watching as well. When the show concluded, he walked to her office, opened the door, walked in, and slammed it behind him. He stood and hovered over her, sitting at her desk. She was working on her laptop. He said nothing. Last week, she would have confronted him for disturbing her. Today, she felt a sense of hope he was retooling his mojo. She was pleased by the forceful nature of his intrusion but not yet ready to lower her guard. She ignored his presence, continuing to stare at her screen and dance on the keyboard with her fingers. Wil waited ten seconds for an acknowledgement of his presence. When he realized none was forthcoming blurted forcefully, "get us a meeting with Jon and Angela tomorrow, without fail." Heather nodded without making eye contact.

Wil turned and walked out, again slamming the door behind him. It was only after he left the room did she take her eyes off the screen and manage a hint of a smile.

The retirement luncheon for the long-serving Senate Sergeant at Arms, Wilson Davis, was starting in the Senate dining room. Davis had been serving as the Senate's chief law enforcement and protocol officer for the last seventeen years. In June, Davis informed Mitch McConnell he was retiring at the end of the year. This luncheon was to recognize his years of service and proficiency in fulfilling his duties. Sixty senators were in attendance with members of their office staff, including Senator Krueger.

The Senate dining hall serving team was delivering luncheon salads when an eighteen-year-old Senate page approached the back of Krueger's chair. He leaned over the Senator's shoulder, whispered in his ear, and handed him a sealed envelope marked on the outside with Krueger's name. The senator opened the envelope to find a brief typewritten note— *'Call Me ASAP. -Bernie'*.

Krueger folded the note, put it back in the envelope and slid it into the inside breast pocket of his suit coat. He raised his head and scanned the room, looking for Bernie Sanders. He saw his friend and colleague sitting across the room next to Elizabeth Warren. He mused the note came from Sanders, and not Jack Abbott, who was asking to him to call.

"Gentleman, thank you for accepting my invitation on such short notice. This special meeting of the Bombay Council is now in session." At Jack Abbott's urgent request, the CEOs of the country's five largest pharmaceutical corporations gathered on the shores of Lake Michigan at the magnificent estate of the CEO of Costello Labs. There was no one else in attendance other than Claude, Abbott's trustworthy valet, and Sadie and Maxine, his personal eight-legged security force. They were all seated in a large den with an unobstructed view of the lake. The doors and windows were closed as a persistent light snowfall had started three hours earlier. A large fire burned in a gold-ordained fireplace. Bradley Donnegan, Dalton Talbot, Randolph Richardson, and Bartholomew Stein were each enjoying their cocktail of choice, thanks to Claude. Sadie and Maxine were enjoying the presence of their master, both lying at his feet.

The meeting was timed for a six-p.m. start. As was the custom for the Bombay Council, Donnegan and Talbot traveled by air to Chicago. Richardson and Stein were from Chicago and traveled to Abbott's estate by limousines arranged by Costello. As did Donnegan and Talbot once they arrived at DuPage Airport. No one from their staff or families knew where they were. The plan was for all to be back home in their own beds within five hours of arriving at the Abbott estate.

Abbott reinforced the need for their utmost secrecy, disclosing how uncomfortable Krueger was from his meeting in the White House following the ambush in Edmonton. And from the disclosure of encrypted online messages between Chicago and Edmonton in the few days prior. Abbott led his colleagues to believe the White House considered the pharmaceutical industry a 'person of interest' in the ambush, it was possible they were being surveilled, and they should take every reasonable precautionary measure to insure no one knew where they were this evening. No one.

"Gentleman, I trust you all watched Braxton and his wife on the Kriss show last weekend. Did any of you miss it?"

The four CEOs acknowledged they watched the broadcast.

Abbott continued. "Is there any doubt in any of your minds this man's agenda is taking square aim at our businesses and if he is successful, our diabetes-related revenues will be significantly affected?"

The question was followed by silence. Given the note on which the council's last gathering ended, Abbott was not surprised. He went directly into his presentation. He had a laptop, a new large screen TV, and a power point deck prepared.

"Gentlemen, I've had our accounting analysts at Costello do forward looking forecasting for each of our organizations based on assumptions stemming from the President's recent comments about our industry. One assumption is Braxton, and his wife are successful in driving a cure for Type 1. We used 2019 as the baseline year the cure would be available on the market and forecasted gross insulin revenues for each of our organizations out to 2024, covering the first five years the cure was available. We calculated two sets of numbers. One forecast was based on a fifteen percent patient adoption rate. The second one on a thirty percent patient adoption rate."

Abbott projected a slide. "As you can see from our numbers, each of our businesses would see an immediate decline in insulin revenues in 2019. And the decline would increase each year. Using the fifteen percent adoption rate, the total insulin revenue declines our five organizations would sustain in 2024 is forty percent, starting with a small decline of five percent in 2019 and increasing yearly to forty percent in 2024. With the higher estimated adoption rate, we would see insulin revenue loss in 2019 of eight percent, increasing to sixty percent in

2024. These numbers are simply guidelines. Adoption rates could be higher and our revenue losses greater depending on how well the cure works and if there are any side effects."

Abbott reached for his tumbler of scotch, allowing the numbers to sink in. Each of the CEOs did calculations in their head of exactly how much a drop of sixty percent in their insulin revenues would affect their overall business. Abbott didn't allow the calculating and the murmuring to go for long.

"Gentlemen, if you watched Kriss on Sunday, you saw Braxton also talk about shredding our antidepressant business."

Dalton Talbot, the CEO of Jzerk Pharmaceuticals, interrupted. "Come on, Jack. Aren't you being somewhat melodramatic? I certainly didn't hear that."

Abbott responded. "Well, what did you hear, Dalton? I heard clinics all over the country dispensing psychedelics to veterans and the homeless. I heard intense focus on mental health and how it is treated. I heard big government money invested in research to uncover new ways to treat depression, addiction, PTSD. All medical conditions for which we offer treatments. All medical conditions which contribute handsomely to our bottom lines. Everything I heard was a direct threat to our antidepressant businesses."

He projected another slide. "Gentlemen, here is a slide similar to the previous one forecasting the loss in total revenues to this side of our businesses." The projected decline in total antidepressant revenues for the five organizations was equally impactful.

Abbott projected a third slide. "And now, gentleman. Here are our projections for the combined hit to our businesses, considering significant declines in both insulin and antidepressant revenues." The slide broke down, by each organization, the cumulative loss of both insulin and antidepressant revenues in 2024. Abbott read the numbers.

"Dalton, Jzerk will be down six billion in 2024. Randall, Jamgen down four billion. Bart, Brizer will take the biggest hit since you generate so much revenue from Slojak. You're down twelve billion. And Bradley, Jamison and Jamison will be down five. For good measure, Costello will be down eight billion in 2024."

Now it was Bart Stein from Brizer punching back. "Jack, you're fear mongering. Five years is a long time for us to react and respond and retool. We encounter threats to our business from Washington all the time, and we have our ways of protecting ourselves. You're not giving any weight to the talents of the men in this room to run our businesses, even in the face of changing landscapes. But I'll grant you we'll suffer consequences with Braxton's agenda, so what do you have in mind as a response the Bombay Council can get behind? But I, for one, will not be a party to anything amounting to personal attacks on Braxton or his family."

Abbott pressed on. "Bart, since the Council has been in existence, have we ever encountered anything remotely as damaging as Braxton's agenda could be to us? When we face extreme threats, it calls for extreme responses. We must get ready to face the fact the President and his administration are taking dead aim at our industry. For chrissakes, his wife is going to be the Secretary of HHS. We must have a coordinated response and we must be bold to counter this threat. Even if it means taking actions we might be uncomfortable with."

The silence in the room was deafening. Abbott looked each in the eye and saw fear. Not of him, but fear of going to war against the President. "Randall, what are your thoughts?"

"Jack, I'm not sure if you're aware, our most influential board member had a son who served in Iraq from 2005 to 2008. Came home in 2009 with serious PTSD. Was under the care of the VA. They pumped him so full of antidepressants he lost the will to live and committed suicide three months ago. Our board member watched Braxton on Sunday. He called me right after asking what our company could do to work with the White House and advance the research into the use of psychedelics to treat depression. He sees Braxton as a savior. I guarantee you will get no buy in from our board to do anything along the lines of what you likely have in mind."

Abbott continued pursuing his agenda. "Bradley?"

"Jack, our board has expressed a concern about how dependent Jamison is on insulin profits. Our other lines of business have been struggling, and the board is mandating we be more aggressive in diversifying. I doubt they will have any appetite to do or spend to protect insulin profitability. They want us doing and spending on new lines of business."

"Bart?"

"You already know my personal position. From our board's perspective, they see the popularity of Braxton's positions and are concerned about the public opinion of our industry. In the conversations I've had with our board members since Sunday, the consensus is they want us to take actions to get into alignment with the administration. My sense is any ideas of Brizer going counter-trend would be swiftly rejected."

"Dalton?"

"Jack, there's something bothering the four of us yet to be mentioned, but needs to be aired out. At our last meeting, you were adamant we all band together and reject any response to the administration's request for proposals to supply insulin to North Korea. Then we hear from the President you're doing a deal with them for the whole enchilada. You're getting all the money and all the goodwill. There's sentiment in this room to not trust you."

Sadie and Maxine, sensing the budding animosity towards their master, raised their heads from the floor and growled. Abbott patted both their heads. "It's OK ladies. Settle."

Talbot looked at the two Dobermans. They watched him back with suspicion. He continued in a slightly more conciliatory tone. "We all see the positive PR your agreement has generated for Costello. We can't help but wonder if you intentionally misled us as to your intentions."

Abbott had anticipated his North Korea deal being brought up. None of his colleagues were aware of his true intentions, and he was of no mind to share those with them. "Dalton, you're aware we agreed to the administration's price of twelve dollars. None of you four could manufacture under twelve. Costello was the only one who could take this deal and not lose its ass. And when we started talking to them, the administration expressed a preference for going with only one supplier so they could better monitor and control outcomes. You know your different insulin products, as do ours, all have different results based on the characteristics of the patient. If we didn't agree to their terms, it's possible they would have gone shopping in Europe or initiated some kind of emergency powers act to take over our production. Who knows what would have happened if we didn't come to terms with them?"

Talbot looked at his other three colleagues. They all shared the same expression of disbelief. "Bullshit Jack. The RFPs had different buy prices for each of our companies based on the administration's estimate of our cost to produce. And the thought of Braxton going to Europe to buy is ridiculous. That makes no sense whatsoever. If you truly had our industry's interests at heart, you would have had us join together and each take a piece. As for different insulin products, the administration told us during our first conversation, they were in favor of multiple flavors of insulin so their doctors would have options prescribing the one best suiting the patient. Currently, with the Chinese insulin product, they don't have this option."

Thirty minutes later, the last and final meeting of the Bombay Council concluded.

Sadie and Maxine were stretched out on Jack Abbott's bed as he awoke. As he opened his eyes and stirred, both Dobermans rearranged their torsos so their tongues were in range. Once they saw Jackrabbit's eyes open, they began licking his bald head with abandon, enhancing its shine.

"Ladies," he shouted. The two monsters jumped from the bed and out into the bedroom's adjoining hallway. Abbott, now fully awake, put his hands behind his saliva-lathered cranium and stared at the ceiling. His thoughts went to what he needed to do. The gathering the previous evening ended with all four of Abbott's Bombay Council colleagues communicating their decision to abdicate their membership. They all expressed an interest in working with the Braxton administration and suggested Jack reconsider his acrimony. A suggestion he had no interest in considering.

Claude walked in with a tray of poached eggs, rye toast, pastries, and coffee. He set the tray on the bed.

"Claude, take a seat." His faithful valet turned around and moved to a sitting chair on the opposite side of the room. Abbott began eating, as usual, with veracity. After inhaling his breakfast, he moved the tray off his lap. Claude stood to retrieve it.

"Wait," Abbott instructed his valet. "Sit. I want to ask you your thoughts about last night. You heard the conversations. You know I'm trying to solve a problem in the business. I'm struggling to find the solution and I don't have anyone I can talk to anymore. Carrington,

Krueger, Price, Stein, Talbot, Donnegan, Richardson. We're not on the same page. All the others I put in place at the FDA. They're either dead, retired or just not interested anymore. All my VPs at Costello? They're stupid. I can't depend on their opinions. Claude, it feels like you're the only one I can trust, but I've never really asked you your opinions. You heard the conversations. You heard my position, and you heard theirs. Any thoughts?"

Claude knew exactly what his boss wanted to hear. "Sir, you need to do what you need to do."

Chapter 32

Perfectly Understandable, Jack

K rueger waited three days before calling Jackrabbit with 'bernie.' He knew what Abbott wanted to discuss and knew he had nothing to offer to placate his largest campaign donor and long-time ally. He hoped the space in time would dial down Abbott's expectations and the reaction he would have to Krueger's inability to build a firewall in Congress to separate Jon and Angela Braxton from their pharma agenda.

Abbott was in his office on Thursday at Costello HQ when the call came in. He decided to play nice to mask his frustration. "Bob, thanks for calling me back," he said cheerfully. "It took you three days. You must be busy rolling up to your holiday break," he chuckled, alone.

"We've got a full plate of matters to address in the next week. Yes. It's been hectic. What's up, Jack?"

Abbott was steamed by the question. The niceties were over. He knew Krueger knew exactly what was up. "Did you watch Kriss on Sunday?"

"I missed it. I was golfing."

"Really Bob? What was it? Twenty degrees over the weekend in DC?"

"I was invited to Palm Beach by Rubio for the day. Flew down. Played well. Was back in time for Monday's retirement luncheon for Wilson. What about Kriss?"

"Jesus Bob. You gotta be kidding me. If you had watched Kriss on Sunday, you would be as convinced as I am the Braxtons are set on destroying our two most profitable lines of business. Given all the fucking money Costello sends your way, the question is what are you going to do to help us?"

"Not much I can do, Jack. The man is a popular President amongst the people. Not so much in Congress, but only a dwindling few on Capitol Hill are ready to die on that hill."

"What about his wife's HHS confirmation? Can you at least block her? Or at least dirty her up? Isn't there impropriety in a President nominating their spouse for a cabinet position? What is he, a fucking dictator?"

Krueger decided it was time to end the call. "I'll talk to Senator Stenson. It's his committee overseeing the confirmation. I'll see what I can do, but don't get your expectations up."

"And that's it, Bob? That's all you got?"

"Goodbye, Jack."

The meeting Wil requested with the Braxton's was delayed. Both Jon and Angela had travel and limited availability in the week following the last Kriss appearance. They were both back in town the following Saturday when Jon reached out to Heather and suggested they meet on Sunday.

The activity in the White House was muted, but still more active than Wil or Heather remembered their Sundays in the office to be. A recognition which invigorated Heather, but annoyed her husband.

The Carrington's arrived in the Oval at ten. Jon and Angela were waiting.

"Hey guys. Come on in. Sit down." Jon directed them to one of the two sofas adjacent to his desk. "Want some coffee?"

"No thank you, Jon," Heather offered. Followed by Wil's, "no thanks," as they took their seats. Jon and Angela were seated across.

"Wil, good to see you again. It's been a while."

"Yes, it has. Four months, I think," the subdued former president replied.

"Well, it's long overdue we chatted. Glad you reached out. What's on your mind?" an upbeat President Braxton inquired.

"Jon, I've been trying for a while to tell you some things I know about Jack Abbott. Things even Heather doesn't know, and I doubt you know as well. Every time I've tried to raise the subject, I've been asked to save it for later." Wil turned his head to look at Heather to make his point. She pursed her lips and nodded acknowledgement. He continued.

"Jon, have you met Jack Abbott yet?"

"I haven't. I've left the Costello negotiations to Angela."

"Right, well, you need to meet him."

"Why is that?"

"The man is dangerous and untrustworthy. Your Costello insulin deal for North Korea is not what it seems."

Jon and Angela looked at one another and then in unison turned their gaze back to Wil. "Go on," Jon invited. Wil stood and started pacing the room. He walked to the wall at the far end of the Oval opposite Jon's desk. He stood under a portrait of George Washington and tilted his head up to stare at it while he gathered his thoughts.

There was a momentary silent pause before Heather expressed her frustration with her husband's theatrics. "Why are we here Wil," she demanded.

He returned to the seat beside his wife. "Angela, I was surprised but nonetheless impressed you decided to go for the HHS job. It's not an easy department to shepherd. There's lots of, how should we say, distractions. Lots of outside influences. Lots of illogical constructs. Lots of money flying around and lots of weak-minded people ready to put those ill-begotten dollars in their pockets. Have you started looking around to see what you're getting into?"

"I'm digging in. Starting to learn the ropes a little," Angela responded cautiously.

Wil nodded. "It's good Barnhardt's out at FDA. He's responsible for a good deal of the shit lying around over there. Have you met with Martin Roberts yet?"

"I have. Seems like a talented guy," she answered.

"Did you have an exit interview with Price after Jon canned him?"

Angela joined in Heather's frustration. "No. Get to the point, Wil."

"What I'm going to tell you I did not know when I was in office, though I always had suspicions. If it's not already apparent to you, within HHS, the FDA and the NIH are corrupt beyond your wildest imagination. The decision making is profoundly flawed and highly influenced by the pharmaceutical industry and the food processing industry. And the amount of money flowing to the people in power in those bureaucracies would astound you. Jon, I'm guessing you may have already been exposed to this, which is why you canned Barnhardt, but I don't think you know just how bad it is."

"How bad is it, Wil?"

Wil stood again, walked to windows behind Jon's desk, and looked at the lightly falling December snow dusting the grounds just outside the Oval Office. He turned to face the three of them.

"Angela, have you had a chance to get familiar with NIH?"

"Wil, can we dispense with the questions and have you just tell us what you want us to know?"

The former president shrugged. "The NIH is symbolic of the corruption within the nation's health care system. A system consisting of both private industries and government bureaucracies. The NIH employs over fifteen thousand people, and its annual budget is close to forty billion. They have one particular practice reflective of the entire culture of corruption in the bureaucracy you're now in charge of. That practice enables royalty payments to flow personally to scientists and administrators from private industries and foreign governments who license patents researched by NIH and then issued to the Federal Government. Patents paid for with tax dollars. You need to review information released by the NIH from Freedom of Information requests between 2009 and 2014 to get a taste. You'll see administrators like Tony Fauci receiving twenty-three royalty payments, Francis Collins receiving fourteen royalty payments, and Clifford Lane receiving eight royalty payments. The amounts of the payments were redacted by the NIH when responding to the FOIA requests. Why? Maybe because estimates peg each payment with six figures? Why do these guys get paid this big money? They're not the scientists doing the research. And why do they hide it? Maybe because they are the guys who control the funding and dole out the research grants which run in the hundreds of millions annually. And this is just one example. If you look deeper, you'll find others. And keep a keen focus on the FDA. What they're doing with big pharma and big food is unconscionable."

Angela took it in stride. "I'm not surprised. What I've learned working on our T1D project has opened my eyes to the corruption. It's another reason I want the HHS job. We're going to clean it up."

Jon added in. "Disheartening, but I'm not surprised either. It's consistent with other garbage we've learned over the last year."

"One other thing, Jon, Angela," Wil offered. "Your new business partner, Jack Abbott, might be the dirtiest and most complicit of all the non-government players. He got his paws dug in so deep at the FDA he can dictate any outcome he wants. Whether its legislation designed to destroy the ability of new competitors to threaten any of his lines of business, or drug approval shortcuts to speed his time to market, he has the connections and the leverage to make it happen."

Angela was only half-kidding. "Maybe you should join my cleaning crew once I'm confirmed."

"Maybe I should. But one thing for sure is the next time you see Jack Abbott, let him know your FDA will do strict quality control testing on the insulin he produces for North Korea."

Jon and Angela looked at one another curiously before Jon replied. "You know something else we should?"

Wil dismissed the question and responded with his own. "Are you looking at anyone for FDA Director? Is Martin Roberts on your list? If he is, he shouldn't be."

There was another burner cell phone in Washington, DC, supplied by Jackrabbit. It was in the hands of his insurance policy at the FDA, Martin Roberts. Abbott had been lax in contacting Roberts since Tom Price's firing. Before that occurrence, Roberts was in line to take over for Stanley Barnhardt as the Director of the FDA. Now it was unclear to Jackrabbit who'd land the job and be instrumental in helping execute his intent for the insulin he would deliver to North Korea.

"Hello," Roberts answered cautiously from his office. He rarely received calls at his burner number. Only the infrequent calls from Abbott and the daily dose of spam.

"Martin, is it you?"

He recognized Abbott's voice. "Hello Jack. Give me a minute and let me walk outside."

A moment later, the conversation resumed. "Jack. I was wondering why I hadn't heard from you lately with all the fireworks going on around here. I was actually going to call you today with news I just got this morning."

"Sorry I haven't been in touch, Marty. We have a lot going on at Costello as well."

"I can imagine. Your new deal with North Korea must be keeping you busy," Roberts responded innocently. He had no idea of Abbott's insulin-tainting intentions.

"You're right, Marty. Very busy. Now, fill me in on what's going on there since Price was canned. I'm sure you know Braxton is nominating his wife to take over at HHS. How is your tenure looking? Still think you have a shot for FDA Director?"

"Yeah, Jack. About that. The news I had for you? I'm on my way out. Was fired this morning."

Air Force One was in the air on the way to Chicago. Jon and Angela, thanks to the conversation two days ago with Wil Carrington and now understanding the true motivations of their new partner, decided it was time to give Costello Laboratories Chairman and CEO his moment in the sun. It was time to properly thank him for his patriotism. Time to have a contract signing ceremony within one of

Costello's insulin production facilities, attended by the President, the soon-to-be confirmed Secretary of the Department of Health and Human Services, and the North Korea Foreign Minister. Time for the country, and the world, to be fittingly introduced to Jackson Raymond Abbott.

Upon arriving at DuPage Airport, Jon, Angela, and Ri were whisked away via motorcade for the forty-five-minute ride to Costello HQ. Along the way, Jon informed Minister Ri of what they recently learned from the former president, and their plan to address it. Ri was uncomfortable to learn of Abbott's depravity on the verge of the signing of the historic agreement, but put his faith in Jon's plan. He would play his part.

They arrived at Costello HQ for the pre-signing meeting Angela requested the evening before from Abbott's team. It was agreed they would meet at Costello HQ two hours before proceeding to the Costello insulin production facility in Joliet, Il. for the historic formal signing ceremony and press conference.

Once in the secured parking garage at 55 Monroe St. in downtown Chicago, Ri and the Braxtons were escorted to an executive conference room on the thirty-seventh floor. The same conference room where Angela and Heather met with Abbott seven months earlier. They were all seated as Abbott ignored the President and addressed the North Korean Foreign Minister. "Minister Ri, welcome to Costello Labs. We're honored to have you."

Despite the information Ri was just presented, he presented a façade of graciousness. "Chairman Abbott, on behalf of the North Korean people, I extend our deepest gratitude for your offering to partner with us to improve the health of so many North Koreans who suffer with Type 1 diabetes. We know you make an excellent product and replacing the insulin we receive from China will benefit our people."

Abbott had nothing to say to Jon, and Jon could only look at Abbott with masked contempt, creating an awkward pause. Angela sensed the tension and cheerily addressed Abbott. "Jack, I'm assuming you and your team received the latest amended draft of the contract we sent last night. Since we haven't heard anything from your team, and given you agreed last week to the signing ceremony with the press coming from around the world, we assumed it met with your approval. We've gone forward and drafted the final agreement for the signing today. This is a tremendous moment for you, Jack, and for Costello. We did make a few minor changes on the last draft and since we have heard no objections, I assume everything is still a go on your end."

Jon had yet to say a word and continued to gaze at Abbott. His emotionless stare and the smugness of the First Lady's remarks had Abbott on edge. To Abbott's thinking, something was not right.

Suddenly, one of Abbott's legal advisors approached the conference room. With urgency, he requested entrance from the Secret Service detail outside the closed conference room's double doors. Abbott saw his advisor out of the corner of his eye. One of the Secret Service agents began a thorough pat down. When he was satisfied the lawyer had no weapons on him, the agent entered and addressed the President. "Sir, this gentleman is requesting to meet with Mr. Abbott."

Jon said his first words to Abbott. "Who is that, Jack?"

"He's a lawyer on my team who's been the lead on the review of the North Korea contract."

Jon was not surprised by the interruption given the changes he and Angela unilaterally made to the agreement and incorporated in the draft submitted the previous evening. Changes Minister Ri was now aware of. "Do you want to talk to him before we proceed?"

"Yes." Abbott stood and stormed out of the room. His instincts now had him on high alert.

Jon addressed the Secret Service agent. "Jerry, escort Mr. Abbott and his attorney to a room where they can talk and then escort Mr. Abbott back when he's ready."

"Yes, sir."

Twenty minutes passed before Abbott returned to the Conference Room escorted by two secret service agents. He was livid as he walked in while staring at Jon. A signature-ready copy of the agreement with the previous night's changes was now lying on the table in front of Abbott's seat. He looked at it with disdain as he sat. He then looked at Jon.

"Mr. President, I thought you were a man of integrity."

"And I you," Jon calmly replied.

Abbott's temper began to seethe. "Just what are you implying?"

"I imply nothing. We modified the agreement, with the consent of Minister Ri, because we came into added information not previously disclosed to us. We've addressed this information in the latest draft. As the First Lady asked, are you ready to sign?"

Abbott was indignant. "Absolutely not. You want to drop the price to nine dollars? You want us to take a ninety million dollar hit? And you want us to agree to remove critical liability protections we agreed on to satisfy our board? And you want us to agree, and pay for ul-tra-strict FDA quality control increasing our costs to manufacture? This is preposterous. I will not sign it."

"All right, Jack. Perfectly understandable." Jon rose. Angela and Minister Ri followed suit. "Angela, Minister Ri, and I will be on our way. We'll head back to Washington and start planning a little fireside chat where President Carrington and I will detail to the world the latest information he disclosed to Angela and I about you and your intentions to deliver North Korea tainted insulin. We'll explain our deal fell apart because you rejected the revisions we required to protect the people of North Korea from your intentions. We'll give special thanks to your four largest insulin-manufacturing competitors for stepping up and filling the void you are leaving. And we'll talk about the Department of Justice and what their role might be in your life going forward."

Hearing Wil Carrington's name triggered Abbott. As did mention of the DOJ. The veins in his neck started to protrude, and his large bald shiny head became flushed. Perspiration suddenly formed on his face and began dripping onto his shirt collar. He was consumed by the combination of rage and fear.

Jon noticed his distress. "I believe you know President Carrington and collaborated with him while he was in office. He seems to know much about you."

Abbott sat silent, not knowing what to say or do. Jon reached into his jacket pocket and pulled out a pen. He stood and walked over to Abbott's seat and put the pen on top of the North Korea insulin agreement in front of him.

"Sign this one, Jack, and then let's go to your facility in Joliet to sign one in front of the press and tell the world what a great philanthropic, patriotic man you are."

Chapter 33

Setback

J on hit the intercom button on his phone. "Rosemary, check with Jeffrey Claymore. Ask him to meet with me now if he's available."

"Yes, Mr. President."

The morning after his return from Chicago, Jon started thinking about his first State of The Union address. He was to deliver it in six weeks.

"Mr. President, Jeffrey is here for you."

"Send him in."

Jeffrey walked in with a broad smile. "Jon, good to see you. Congratulations my friend. I've been reading the positive comments from around the world about your masterpiece in Chicago yesterday. You hit a massive home run. All the goodwill you created towards the people of North Korea. And towards Angela's project. God certainly knew what he was doing when he called on you."

Jon motioned Jeffrey to a seat on a sofa adjacent to his desk. He sat across from him on the other. "Thank you, Jeffrey. We accomplished quite a bit, especially considering the late obstacles we ran into. But Angie deserves all the credit. And speaking of God, how does he view a man like Jack Abbott?"

"You can give Angela the credit if you like, but you two are a team. And a great one, I might add. I say we split the credit down the middle. As to your question about how God and Jack Abbott get along, let's just say God has a way of leveling the playing field. Mr. Abbott will face a reckoning down the road."

"Not soon enough to my thinking. And on the credit, ok, fifty-fifty it is. I won't disagree with you on this one. But on what I want to talk to you about, we may end up disagreeing quite a bit."

"And what is that, Jon?"

"Abortion."

"I see. No wait, I don't see. Where is this coming from? We've never discussed it before."

"I'm delivering a speech about the state of our union in six weeks. There's no shortage of things to cover, but none divides our union more than this issue. We are split right down the middle, and the sides are so dug in they can't see beyond the edge of their positions. I imagine the slavery issue prior to the Civil War felt a little like this. The divide is poisoning this country, and no one is talking about a way to bridge it. I've got a position to lay down. I don't think you're going to go along with it, but I want to debate it with you. Hear your thoughts."

"Taking a life is a sin, Jon. It clearly violates one of God's ten commandments. To sanction abortion is a position impossible to accept."

"I don't disagree with you on either point. But I also don't disagree with the position on the left that, in a free society, one has the choice to do with one's body as they choose. Even if one makes the argument, it's immoral. What I do disagree with is the position of the right that it is the responsibility of our government to legislate morality."

"All right Jon. If one is free to choose to abort a child, and it is not the responsibility of our government to legislate against it, you must be advocating to remove any obstacles to abortion. In essence, legalize it. Is this where you're going? I hope not."

"I'd prefer to say abortions should not be in violation of federal law. It is not the responsibility of the federal government to call balls and strikes on this. Instead, we should return the issue to the individual. The individual is their own umpire. They make their own decision."

"And you feel people who find themselves in the position of carrying an unborn child they believe they don't want will be good umpires," Jeffrey inquired.

"Who are we to judge their umpiring skills? Isn't it God's role to judge?" asked the President.

"Granted, but taking another's life is still a sin."

"Noted. And one of the foundations of your belief system is forgiveness, right?"

"Yes."

"If one of the kids you mentored in Philadelphia twenty years ago went off the rails, became a career criminal, committed immoral acts, and came to you asking you to lead them to God for forgiveness, what would you do?"

"It happened more times than I care to count. I show them the way."

"OK. What about a woman who aborted a child twenty years ago seeking you out looking for forgiveness? What would you do?"

"The same, Jon."

"Jeffrey, what causes someone to emerge from darkness, see the light, and ask for redemption?"

"It could be any number of things. A revelation comes to them without any provocation or pretext. They witness something which triggers a new perspective. They suddenly become remorseful and seek understanding and guidance."

"They seek guidance and understanding from someone like you."

"Yes."

"Has a young pregnant woman undecided in her choice ever come to you asking for guidance?"

"Many times."

"What's been the result?"

"I don't keep a scorecard, Jon. Sometimes I was successful counseling a young woman against abortion. A majority of time I was not."

"The times you were unsuccessful, would the results have been different if you had more resources? Say you had the tools to communicate all the reasons, not just the moral ones, to not abort. Fully explaining adoption options, for example. Meeting with other young women who faced the same decision and chose life. Would your results have been different if you had a better game?"

"I don't know, Jon. I was working for God and not doubting how he was guiding me."

"Jeffrey, when you and I first met, you told me to go forward with advocating for pluripotent stem cell research despite the spiritual inconsistencies. You told me if I headed down the wrong path, God would let me know. He's never let me know. We talked about Luke's illness and how it was God's way of sending both you and I down this road. And here we are. Still working together to improve the lives of others. I strongly believe the role of government on this issue is not to dictate, but to educate. Not judge, but guide. This is what will serve young women the best. And serve the soul of this nation the best. We should steer people in this predicament away from both the agenda of Planned Parenthood and the tenants of religious dogma. Be sensitive to the situation while maintaining the separation of church and state. Respect the rights of individuals but ensure informed decisions. This should be the federal government's role on abortion. Provide women the information they need to make the best decision for themselves. Provide the information in an unbiased, non-judgmental manner. And if that young woman chooses to make what others believe to be an immoral or sinful choice, they take it up with God when judgment day comes. Not with a legal system run by flawed, biased, judgmental human beings."

Jon stood and walked over to his desk, and hit the intercom. "Rosemary, can you bring in coffee for Jeffrey and I?"

"Yes, sir."

The President returned to where he was sitting and eyed Jeffrey sitting across from him. There was an awkward silence as Jon gave Jeffrey the chance to speak next, but he was deliberate in processing the President's idea.

There was a knock on the Oval Office door, followed by Rosemary coming in with a tray holding two steaming cappuccinos. She set the tray down on the coffee table between the two sofas. Jeffrey hardly noticed. His mind was elsewhere.

"Thank you, Rosemary."

"You're welcome, sir." She looked at Jeffrey, who had his head bowed and looked to be in prayer. She left the room, shutting the office door behind her.

Jon leaned forward to fetch his drink. He took two sips, then returned the cup to the table and leaned back. Jeffrey opened his eyes and lifted his head. "Jon, I cannot sanction an idea or a policy which suggests abortion is not a sin."

"I would never expect you to. And would never ask you to do so. Seven months ago, I asked you to help me fix this country's culture. I believe building a bridge to cross the divide on abortion will be a great leap forward towards repairing it. The LABEL campuses you're building are perfectly suited for this purpose. Adding unbiased, non-judgmental abortion education to the other education tracks you and Connie are developing will enhance these centers and give them a positive reputation in the community. And I know you, Jeffrey. You'll design a curriculum which will have a tremendous impact. You will build a platform to help countless young women who, without guidance would do otherwise, choose life. And help heal the country by bringing compassion and understanding to the issue. I'm convinced if you do this, you save more babies' lives than we could ever hope to without building the bridge. I don't know God as you do, but I imagine he would welcome your efforts."

Jeffrey looked up. "Let's hope so."

Abby's intercom came alive. *"Mrs. Martin, Foreign Minister Ri is here to see you. He recognizes he doesn't have an appointment and has a gift for you. Said he only needs ten minutes. What would you like me to do?"*

"Send him up, Betty."

The door to Abby's office was opened by an assistant. Ri carried in a gift-wrapped box he gripped with both hands. It was three feet across and weighed twenty pounds. He set it down on her credenza to the left of her desk. In his familiar Korean accent, he offered, "good morning, Mrs. Martin."

"Mr. Foreign Minister, what a pleasant surprise. What brings you here today?"

"You should know it is not lost on the people of North Korea how instrumental you were in bringing quality American insulin to us. I wanted to show our appreciation."

"Well, we haven't delivered anything yet. Perhaps we consider postponing this little celebration until we actually have something to celebrate."

"Perhaps you are right, Mrs. Martin, but we anticipate only good things in light of the events which took place in Chicago two days ago."

Though Abby was not present for the signing ceremony fireworks in Chicago, she was fully aware of the backstory. Jon had discreetly read her in on Jack Abbott's clandestine intentions and the administration's last-minute maneuvering to counter. She made the changes to the contract Jon insisted on after his conversation with Wil Carrington.

"What's in the box?"

"A gift for you, Mrs. Martin. Please open it."

Abby pulled a pair of scissors from her desk and walked over to the credenza. She cut the ribbon and then the wrapping paper. She peeled it all away.

"Well, well, Mr. Foreign Minister, what do we have here?" Abby asked as she examined the now unwrapped case of twenty-four aluminum cans with Korean writings she could not decipher.

"It's a brand-new soft drink we recently started manufacturing in North Korea. It is called Tanzanio Abby."

"Oh my. I have a drink named after me in North Korea? Is it any good? What does it taste like?"

"Root beer."

Jon was in the Oval early the next morning. He called his Chief of Staff. Lance Reibus was already an hour into his day. *"Good morning, Jon."*

"Good morning, Lance. Come in when you're free."

Five minutes later, the two of them were facing each other.

"Lance, I want to address the country from my desk in prime time as soon as possible. Have all the networks cover it. How long for you to set it up?"

"At least a week. What do you want to talk about?"

"Taxes and politics."

"You sure? Congress isn't making meaningful headway with campaign finance reform or your income tax initiatives. I think we should wait until we move the ball a little farther down the field. The holidays have never been a good time for political theater. Given we're only five weeks away and folks will be holiday shopping in prime time next week, we should use your State of the Union address for the points you want to make."

"Overruled. Set it up for next week."

—⊛✦⊛—

"Luke?"

"Yeah mom?"

"Dr. Shapiro wants to speak with us. Can you be in my office after school around three?"

"What does he want to talk about?"

"Not sure. We'll find out soon enough."

—⊛✦⊛—

Though he was demeaned and embarrassed by the events which took place in the Costello executive conference room prior, Jack Abbott artfully leaned into his moment in front of the world press at the North Korea contract signing ceremony. He smiled and said all the right things in response to the praise Jon, Angela, and Minister Ri showered upon him. Praise which portrayed him as a true patriot and T1D warrior for playing his part in assisting the Braxton administration execute its diabetes diplomacy efforts. Efforts successfully transforming North Korea from a rogue nuclear adversary into a trusted diabetes research partner. Efforts successfully convincing Kim Jong-Un to draw down his nuclear ambitions, end hostilities with South Korea, and shepherd his country into the brotherhood of nations.

Underneath the grateful and humble exterior Abbott projected at the event was a wounded man raging with anger and hate. Based on Jon's rapidly advancing 'FIX OUR WELL-BEING' agenda and its projected impact on pharmaceutical industry profit streams, Abbott developed a healthy dose of contempt for the President prior to meeting him. After being humiliated and intimidated into signing an unfavorable agreement within thirty minutes of their first face-to-face engagement, Abbott had become all consumed with a desire to get even.

Besides his unbridled loathing of the President and, to only a slightly lesser degree the First Lady, Abbott was irritated by the crumbling of his influence network. Senator Krueger abandoned him after a successful thirty-year, mutually beneficial association. The Bombay Council disbanded, isolating Abbott from the other power players in the pharma industry. Relationships Abbott consistently parlayed into lobbying and manipulating Congress to bend to his will had vanished. His influence at the FDA, a key component of Costello's grip on the industry, had disintegrated with the firings of Stanley Barnhardt and Martin Roberts. And with the nomination of Angela Braxton as the new Secretary of HHS, Abbott's invaluable connection to the Executive branch, at its height during Wil Carrington's two terms in office and continuing through the Obama administration, had rotated from favorable to toxic.

Jack Abbott was backed into a corner. All he had built and accomplished was at risk. His company's diabetes business, in the Braxton crosshairs with the advancing efforts towards the cure for Type 1 diabetes, would be hamstrung by the distasteful agreement he was coerced into signing. And his antidepressant business was next in line for the President to target. Without his influence network and having his diabolical plan to taint the insulin he was conspiring to sell to North Korea neutralized, he sensed he was powerless to control the future profitability of Costello Labs. A feeling which left him both depressed and livid. He was not accustomed to sitting on his hands and letting others steer the ship. His isolation left him consumed with thoughts of how to destroy Jon and Angela Braxton.

"Wil, Jack Abbott here."

"Hello Jack. You haven't called me in months. How have you been?"

"Plowing ahead. Still grinding it out every day. You'd think after all these years things would get easier. Unfortunately, it's not the case. How have you been?"

"I'm doing fine, Jack. What do you want?"

"Is that any way to treat an old friend? I just called to let you know how much I miss the days when you and Heather roamed the White House. Things certainly seemed to run better than they are these days. And, by the way, how is Heather? Is she enjoying the VP job?"

"She seems to be," the former president responded nonchalantly.

"What's on her mind for 2020? Is she going to run if Braxton isn't?"

"You'll have to ask her yourself. Give her a call. I'm sure she'd like to hear from you."

"Very funny, my friend. But seriously, is she still entertaining aspirations for the job? I'd like to help her if she does. All this goodwill I now have as the diabetes ambassador to North Korea, I'm sure we could use to her advantage. And if by circumstance she ends up in the Oval, just where is her head? Is she onboard with the Braxton's agenda?"

"You know, Jack, you used to be better at obfuscating. Let me roll this out for you. Heather is one hundred percent on board with the Braxtons. If he opts out and she succeeds him, it will be exactly like a second Braxton term. You're screwed, my friend."

"This is Dr. Shapiro, calling for the First Lady. She's expecting my call."

"Hold one moment. I'll connect you."

The First Lady was at her desk. Luke was seated across from her. She punched line 1 and the speakerphone button. *"Dr. Shapiro. It's good to hear from you. I have Lucas here with me."*

"Hi Doctor."

"Hello Luke, Mrs. Braxton. Thank you for being available. I felt I should call you to bring you up to date on our research. Particularly given our recent discussion in Edmonton about Luke participating in our first human trials."

"Thank you, doctor. Yes, please fill us in."

"Unfortunately, Mrs. Braxton, the news is not good. Since our last conversation, eight of our lab animals who were injected with their own edited blood stem cells in our third trial set six weeks ago have developed cysts on their liver. As of now, they are all benign, but they are of concern. Because of this development, we are taking a step back and reevaluating all our protocols. At this point in time, we are unsure when we will be ready to start human trials. I know this is a tremendous disappointment for you and Luke, as it is for us. But we have come to expect the unexpected on our journey to the cure. Our utmost priority is minimizing risk to our trial volunteers. This, of course, includes your son. If you have questions, I'll answer them as best I can."

Angela looked at Luke, who had bowed his head before asking one. *"Doctor, you say the cysts are benign. What is the danger they pose to a patient?"*

"If they remain benign, the danger is minimal. We can surgically remove them. What causes our concern is they may be pre-cancerous. If they are, even if we remove them, there is an elevated risk for the lab subject to develop more aggressive cancerous cells."

"I see. How long will it be before you can determine if the cysts on the lab animal livers are benign or pre-cancerous?"

"We estimate we will know within eight weeks. But whether they are benign or not, we are taking a step back and reevaluating our protocols. The emergence of cysts following our last modification signaled to us we may have crossed a trip wire of some sort. We will only finalize a protocol when we have no instances of cysts forming anywhere in the lab animal patient. Again, I'm sorry I do not have better news."

"Doctor, what happened? Last we spoke, you were so optimistic."

"We're not yet sure, Mrs. Braxton. On each trial set, we measure the recalcitrance rate. It's a measurement of what percentage of the lab animals in the set experience abnormal or troublesome side effects from the injections. We've set a level of three percent to move on to human trials. Our first set of lab animals experienced a ten percent recalcitrance rate. We revised our protocols to bring the rate down and were successful in getting the recalcitrance rate on our second set down to five percent. Hence, our optimism we were on the right path. Unfortunately, on our third set, our rate jumped to twenty percent. Something we did in our last protocol revision reversed our progress. We've must backtrack and learn the reasons. It's going to take time."

Luke and Angela looked at one another, stunned by the unexpected development. *"Doctor, the best-case scenario to bring your recalcitrance rate down to three percent,"* the First Lady asked, apprehensive of the answer.

"Likely one year."

Chapter 34

Personal Policy

J ack Abbott needed another meeting with Marco DiMarco. He had no number for DiMarco and felt showing up in Monroe Harbor with no warning was not a sound move. He had been given instructions should he want to speak with DiMarco again; he was to go through Dante Palmieri.

"Dante," Abbott exclaimed enthusiastically when Palmieri answered his call.

"Hello Jack," Palmieri responded less than enthusiastically.

"I'm sorry to bother you at home, but I just had a quick and easy request."

Palmieri couldn't hide his annoyance. *"What is it, Jack?"*

"Can you arrange another meeting for me with Mr. DiMarco?"

Palmieri was now even less enthusiastic. *"Jack, you sure? Whatever it is you want to talk to him about, I don't think it's a good idea to involve yourself with this organization."*

"What do you mean? They're businesspeople. And I have a lucrative business proposition for them. I think they'll be grateful for the opportunity I want to present them with it."

"What I mean is I've seen and heard guys like you involve themselves with these people, and it won't end well for you if you step one inch out of bounds. You're already remarkably successful. I'm saying it's risky for you to do business with the guys I work for."

"I appreciate the heads up, Dante. I'll keep what you said in mind, but I need to talk to DiMarco as soon as possible."

Three days passed before Jack heard anything. The response arrived as a note in a sealed envelope marked personal and confidential and delivered by special messenger to Costello HQ.

Jack—We'll meet after the first of the year. On January four at ten p.m. go down to the fifth underground level in your parking garage. The far west end. I'll be in a Black Lincoln Navigator. Come alone. Make sure all your pockets are empty except for your phone, but have it powered down. This better be important. -Marco

Lance Reibus tried only half-heartedly to talk Jon out of delivering his version of a fireside chat on national TV three days before Christmas. His automatic response was to push hard on Jon to not do this, but he stood down once the memory of the promise he made to himself just prior to Jon stepping on stage at the RNC Convention in Cleveland last year reemerged. His promise to himself to never again question his boss's instinct for stage management. Reibus witnessed on numerous occasions Jon's uncanny knack for knowing what to say, how to say it, and when to say it. He concluded to himself, *'we're speaking to the nation on December 22, holiday or no. Got it.'*

The Oval was decked out in holiday cheer. A Christmas tree could be seen on camera, just to the left of Jon's desk. The desk itself was adorned with wreaths and two poinsettias. A string of colorful lights ringed the window curtains behind it. Jon was not one to decorate or be decorated and was uncomfortable with the setting. If it wasn't for

Angela gently scolding him to lighten up and enjoy the good cheer, there may have been no decorations whatsoever.

The White House, in a show of reconciliation, offered the Big News Network the opportunity of exclusivity to broadcast the speech. And the lucrative opportunity to syndicate it to other networks which wanted to show the broadcast live. They declined, and it was a CNN camera in the Oval. They would syndicate the President's address to forty-eight other networks around the world. Though networks were told the President would only address domestic issues this evening, because of the worldwide appeal of the **TYPE 1-YOU'RE DONE** Project, any news or press conferences now coming from the White House were of keen interest internationally.

At eight p.m. eastern standard time, Jon was at his desk and the broadcast was underway.

"To all of you choosing to spend time with me this evening instead of doing your holiday shopping or partying, I'm grateful. Thank you. To those of you who had nothing better to do or are simply watching me as the show you normally watch at this time was preempted, I hope to make our time together worthwhile for you.

"Normally Presidents use these opportunities to discuss public policy matters. Things like regulations, rules, conventions, concepts, protocols, guidelines, and laws. The things which local, state, and federal governments adopt and execute to keep social order and ideally make your lives better. And we will do a little talking about public policy shortly. Specifically, taxes and campaign finance reform.

"But before we do, I'd like to share concepts which should be more important to you than public policy. I'm referring to your personal policy. Your personal policy should be front and center for you as it interacts with your lives every minute of every day. Public policy does not. Your personal policy has a direct impact on your quality of life.

Public policy does not. Your personal policy affords you the freedom and opportunity to make changes, tweaks, and adjustments as you see fit to improve your daily lives. Public policy does not.

"During my eleven months in office, you've heard me often discuss, as a matter of public policy, things government can do better to improve the quality of life for Americans. This thinking had led us to a Culture Czar and a keen focus on improving and strengthening our nation's social fabric. And we have initiatives underway to improve our collective physical and mental health. But the fact of the matter is public policy has limits on what it can do for you. Without you having a personal policy designed to improve your own life, dependence on public policy is futile. We can attempt to leverage public policy to provide Americans things we would put on a list of items to improve our lives. More money, improved well-being, more and better career opportunities, shedding unhealthy habits, losing weight, learning new skills, mending a broken relationship, learning an art form, being more philanthropic, learning to play a musical instrument. Unfortunately, public policy is not efficient in delivering the real things which can make your lives better. Throughout history, political constructs have tried to provide for what their architects refer to as the common good. These constructs, usually created by an autocratic dictator to hold on to the grip of power and enrich themselves, rarely deliver on the promise of improving the common good. In the vast majority of instances, the execution of invasive public policy, despite its true intentions, good, bad, or otherwise, fails to improve the lives of those under its rule. Inevitably, as history teaches us, its execution leads to greater poverty and despair.

"In 2017 America, it is the job of our governments, local, state, federal, to manage, monitor, and execute public policy. To prevent us from forgetting the tragic lessons of the past, we must always be aware of history. And we should all be eternally grateful to our founding fathers who gave us the U.S. Constitution, the framework to keep our governments from succumbing to attempts to impose invasive and dangerous public policy which have destroyed societies throughout history. If we look for public policy to solve problems for which it is incapable of doing, it is a dangerous oversight which ultimately leads to tyranny and autocracy. Public policy will not solve your problems. Will not make your lives better or more fulfilling. Only personal policy can do so.

"I bring you these words tonight because I have a vision of how to make life in our country better. I know the struggles Americans face every day. As a young child growing up in a foster care environment, I too struggled. I struggled just to be a normal kid. But it was hard because I couldn't understand why my parents were killed in a tragic accident and left me to live with people who did not love or genuinely care about me. And this was four years after I was told they were OK and coming back for me. Nobody ever explained why I was misled for four years by the system. How to perceive it. How to deal with it. It made life hard. Throughout my childhood and adolescence, my inability to understand why I was dealt the hand I was prevented me from developing meaningful personal relationships. I got into more fights with other kids than I care to remember. I was always alone and angry. I lacked a personal policy to get me on the road to happiness and a fulfilling life.

"Fortunately, I learned my first lessons about personal policy when I was sixteen and my life took a turn onto a road which has dropped me in front of you tonight. In my case, those first lessons came from a book. They were lessons which taught me my thoughts and beliefs controlled my life. I learned I can be, and will be, whatever and whoever I believe I am. Lessons which taught me the distinction between our conscious and subconscious minds. Lessons which taught me how to use my thoughts to bring me whatever it was I told my subconscious mind I wanted. Lessons how to program my subconscious mind with thoughts, visualizations, and attitudes with the understanding our subconscious can be programmed for both good and bad outcomes based on the thoughts I fed it.

"The day I was introduced to the book *'Psycho Cybernetics'* was the day my new life started. A life I could live understanding I had the power to bring home my dreams. I wanted to share my experience with you this evening in the event you are looking to start something new. The new year is the perfect time for new beginnings. Understanding the power you have to bring yourself happiness, success, and well-being is a gift. A gift you should treasure forever. A gift you should pass along to the ones you love. It is you who has this power. Government does not. The day you come to this realization will be the day you find yourself on the road I turned onto when I was sixteen.

"A great desire of mine is years from now for you to look back on this moment as I look back to age sixteen and my moment of enlightenment. I desire tonight you adopt a new mindset of crafting your own personal policy. And those of you listening tonight who have an interest in holding public office will come to Washington recognizing the limits of public policy. And the great promise in helping your constituents set their own personal policy.

"I mentioned when we started this evening, we would talk about a few of our administration's public policy positions. I've reconsidered. Not tonight. We'll discuss those with you in the new year. Allow me to just leave you with the thoughts I shared about my experience and how you can build yourself a better life. Accept it as a holiday gift from the Braxtons. From Angela, Luke, Darla, and I, we wish you all a joyous holiday season. Good night."

⸺❈⸺

Chicago was frozen on January four. The daytime temperature hovered around ten degrees. At eight p.m., it had dropped to fifteen below.

Jack Abbott was still in his office, mindlessly scrambling paperwork as he contemplated for the umpteenth time how he would present his offer to Marco DiMarco. The Costello HQ offices were empty except for the CEO and his trusted valet, Claude. Abbott ordered a massive gourmet dinner to be delivered at eight thirty and wanted Claude to receive the meal and serve it to him.

At eight forty-five, Claude notified Abbott his meal was ready in the conference room. It included five courses from his boss's favorite downtown French restaurant, Bistro Campagne. The feast included French onion soup, quiche Lorraine, coq au vin, ratatouille, and boeuf bourguignon. The aromas emanating from the conference room served as a magnet for Abbott's insatiable appetite, drawing him as if in a trance to his awaiting indulgence.

It was Abbott's intent to finalize in his mind his presentation to Di-Marco as he enjoyed his favorite French cuisine. But once he reached the conference room, took his seat, had his napkin stuffed into his shirt collar, and his soup served, there was no time for contemplation. All thoughts were now centered on the feast before him, a feast which existed for fifteen minutes before Abbott, in his inimitable style, inhaled every morsel of every dish. A bottle of 2014 Chateau Pontet-Canet Bordeaux blend endured the same fate. After swallowing the last bite of beef, he raised his head and tilted his wine glass to gulp the last swallow. To cap off the demolishing of his dinner, he unleashed a thunderous belch which could be heard and sensed throughout the thirty-seventh floor of 55 Monroe St. Fortunately for the sixty people who inhabited the thirty-seventh floor during the day; they had all vacated by six p.m.

Having finished, Abbott stood. "Claude, the meal was magnificent. Please pass along my compliments to Chef Campagne. Stay here while I take my ten-p.m. meeting. I should be back well before midnight, and we can head home." He floated back to his office to put the final mental touches on how he would present his offer to Cambretta Enterprises.

At nine-fifty, Abbott entered an elevator to take him from the thirty-seventh floor to the lobby. He was still in his business suit sans necktie and was wearing a heavy woolen overcoat to account for the possibility he would be outside in the freezing night during his meeting with DiMarco. He had nothing in his pockets but leather gloves and his cell phone. It was powered off.

Once in the lobby, Abbott transferred to a parking level elevator to take him down to five. Level five was empty except for one vehicle he saw two hundred feet in the distance at the far west end. He walked in that direction. When he was within thirty feet of the vehicle, DiMarco's muscular and immaculately dressed driver opened the front driver's-side door, stepped out, and began walking menacingly towards Abbott. The left rear driver's side window lowered. It was DiMarco.

"Jack, thanks for being on time. Anthony's going to check you out before you get in the car. I'm sure you understand."

Anthony approached Jack, grabbed his left arm, and escorted him to the side of the Navigator. "Face the car, put your hands on the roof, and spread your legs," he ordered. Abbott complied.

Anthony gave Abbott a thorough pat-down search and pulled the cell phone from Abbott's overcoat pocket.

"He's clean, Mr. DiMarco," Anthony declared as he handed him Abbott's cell phone.

"Come around the other side and get in, Jack."

Five minutes later, the Navigator exited the parking structure and headed east on Monroe St. toward Lake Shore Dr.

"All right Jack. You've got thirty minutes. What are we talking about?"

"When we last talked, Marco, I mentioned I had a problem I was hoping you could help me take care of. I'm one hundred percent serious and willing to put my money where my mouth is."

"Very nice, Jack. It really is. You certainly have a big mouth and could shove lots of dough in there if you wanted. You're down to twenty-nine minutes."

Jack nodded his head and continued. "I know you mentioned last time we spoke that Cambretta Enterprises doesn't do business in Washington. How long has that been the case?"

"Jack, I suggest you ask no more questions because I won't be answering them and you're wasting time. If you have something you want from me, I suggest telling me what it is."

Everything Abbott prepared in his head to say to lead up to his request seemed inappropriate given DiMarco's instructions. "Marco, just one more question. Was the Chicago mob involved with JFK's assassination?"

DiMarco took the question in stride. "Really Jack? By the way, who's JFK? You've got twenty-five minutes and if you don't tell me what you want with the next words out of your big fucking mouth, we're done."

Abbott's palms became sweaty, and his knees shook. His voice cracked as he stuttered. "OK Marco, here it is. I've got one hundred million dollars for you, and I need four people dealt with."

"Really. Four people, huh? Dealt with? And what do we mean? Give them haircuts? Walk their dogs? Take the air out of the tires of their cars? Convince them to leave you alone? Motivate them to take some kind of action on your behalf? What Jack?"

"Eliminated."

DiMarco didn't respond immediately. The resulting awkward silence preceded by the word 'eliminated' hung in the air, becoming more ominous with each passing second. DiMarco's silence unnerved Abbott, who became more anxious and more unsure of what he was doing. "I see. You want us to kill four people for you. That's pretty intense, Jack. What makes you think we're in that business?"

"JFK and Jimmy Hoffa."

DiMarco bowed his head and shook it. "I knew Jimmy Hoffa. Poor bastard just disappeared one day. Feel sorry for his family. And again JFK? Who is that?"

"Marco, I'm offering Cambretta one hundred million dollars. Is it not enough to at least have you consider my proposition?"

"It is an impressive number, Jack. Remind me again who we are talking about eliminating."

"The President, and the Vice President, and their spouses."

DiMarco suppressed any expression and again refrained from responding. The Navigator was now twenty miles outside of downtown traveling north on Lake Shore Dr. They drove for another five minutes before DiMarco uttered another word, instructing Anthony to pull over and stop. He reached into his pocket for Jack's cell phone and handed it to him. "Get out of the fucking car."

"What," Abbott responded.

"You heard me. Get out."

"But it's freezing cold. You can't leave me out here."

DiMarco reached under his coat and pulled a Glock handgun from his shoulder holster. He set it on his lap for Abbott to see. "You don't get out of the car right now, you'll end up next to Hoffa. You've got a phone. Call someone to fetch your sorry ass."

Chapter 35

Christina

J ack Abbott was out of options. His spheres of influence outside Costello Labs had all disintegrated, along with the implosion of the variety of relationships he had cultivated in Chicago and Washington over the last thirty years. His diabolical plan for North Korea was exposed and held over him, serving as a shackle on his ability to operate as he had become accustomed. His last hope, contracting the Cambretta crime syndicate to conduct his desperate final act, died alongside Lake Michigan in the freezing cold as he waited for Claude to come for him. The thought of operating his organization while isolated, encumbered, and accountable was not to his liking. He contemplated his next move, but nothing took root as viable or possible. As the days passed, he resigned himself to his new reality.

One week after his fateful meeting with DiMarco, Abbott received another envelope marked personal and confidential, delivered by a special messenger. Inside he found a formal invitation to a sweet sixteen birthday party, and a handwritten note.

Jack, we'd welcome having you join us for my daughter Christina's sixteenth birthday party this coming Saturday evening. We're having the party at the Omni Hotel. When Christina heard you and I will be doing business together, she insisted I invite you. Please don't disappoint her.—Giancarlo Cambretta

Abbott read the note three times. It didn't help resolve his confusion.

'Why would his daughter want me to come to her party?'

'Why would Cambretta want to do business with me, given how DiMarco responded to my proposal?'

The cautionary words of Dante Palmieri crossed his mind. He contemplated calling him in search of clarity. Twice he started dialing. He aborted both times.

Abbott arrived at the Omni at seven and approached the Picasso Ballroom. He was met by a pretty, twenty-something receptionist asking for his name.

"Jack Abbott."

"Yes, Mr. Abbott," she responded cheerfully. "Mr. Cambretta asked I escort you to his table. Please follow me."

She led Jack past six tables to the one where Cambretta was seated, entertaining five guests. As soon as they were table-side, Cambretta stood and extended his hand. He was as tall as Abbott, but a little older, much thinner, and this evening much more assured. In contrast to Abbott's shiny dome, Cambretta's head was adorned full of long, whitish hair combed straight back and curling atop his white suit coat collar. His shirt was jet black and his tie silver.

"Jack, thank you for coming. It's good to meet you," Giancarlo greeted his guest with a thick Italian accent, shaking Jack's hand vigorously.

"Thank you for inviting me, Mr. Cambretta."

"It's Carlo. Come, let's go to the bar and get you a drink."

They made their way to the back of the ballroom. "Jack, what are you having?"

"Glenfiddich."

"Make it two," Carlo instructed the bartender.

With drinks in hand, Carlo led Jack to a standing cocktail table at the far end of the bar area where they could speak out of earshot of the two hundred guests in attendance. They set their drinks on the table. Jack waited for Carlo to speak. Carlo waited for Jack to start sweating. It took only thirty seconds as Carlo stared relentlessly at Jack with a hint of a smile. Jack unsuccessfully tried to relax. He came to the party curious and hopeful. After two minutes with Giancarlo Cambretta, he was petrified.

"Jack, Mr. DiMarco shared your proposition with me. It's the type of opportunity were not usually presented with. What's behind it?"

Abbott cleared his throat. His fear obstructed his instinct. He struggled for the words to explain his desperation. "Carlo, I believe we have much in common. We both run large, complex, and profitable businesses. And we both have potent adversaries to contend with. Adversaries who wield tremendous power in the name of governance. I've been fighting government overreach and regulation for thirty years and I've always been successful thanks to strategic relationships and partnerships I've been fortunate to build. But over this past year, things have been happening which lead me to believe I need a new game plan. All of my defenses, which have always been solid, are now crumbling."

"Because of Braxton?" Carlo inquired.

Jack paused, uncertain how to answer. Finally, "yes."

"I know your reputation, Jack. You are very resourceful and have been for thirty years. Your business prowess is well recognized in Chicago. It's hard for me to imagine you have no other avenues available to address your dilemma other than what you shared with Mr. DiMarco."

Abbott started to relax. He felt Carlo was sympathizing. "Without going into too much of the backstory between Braxton and I, I believe if he sticks around and cranks up his agenda, the profitability of Costello Labs and the entire pharmaceutical industry is in peril."

Cambretta acted surprised. "And you say this having recently been awarded a two-hundred-seventy-million-dollar contract? Plus, the opportunity to put a nice shine on your personal brand? And the goodwill your deal will generate for Costello? All coming from the people you say are out to harm you?"

"It's a shit deal for Costello, Carlo. No profitability and lots of government oversight. Was three-hundred-sixty-million until Braxton pulled a fast one at the end."

Carlo nodded. "Jack, you recognize the tremendous risks to us for taking your project on, yes?"

"Of course, Carlo. I recognize the risk to your organization, and I believe my offer is commensurate with that risk. If not, and you feel you want to negotiate, I'm open. And I would understand if you turned me down. If you do, if there's anyone you might refer me to who would be a better fit for this project, I would be appreciative."

Carlo tried to talk him down. "You're truly serious about going through with this? You've thought it all out? What happens if you're successful? What happens if you're unsuccessful? You've considered all the consequences? Once you go down this path, there is no turning back. You're absolutely sure you want this to happen?"

"I've considered everything. I want it to happen."

Carlo took his eyes off Jack and scanned the room. "I see Christina. Come, let me introduce you."

Carlo led the way to a group of four teenagers standing and talking. As they were walking, Jack's confidence was building. He felt Carlo was considering his offer.

"Christina, are you having a good time?"

"Yes dad. Thank you for throwing the party for me." She looked directly at Abbott.

Carlo noticed her stare. "Honey, this is Jack Abbott."

"I know, dad. I recognize him from the North Korea ceremony." She extended her hand to Jack. "Mr. Abbott I'm so glad you came. I really wanted to meet you and say thank you for all the good things you're doing to help Type 1 diabetics."

Jack was momentarily confused. *Why would Carlo's daughter bring up diabetics?*

He then noticed the continuous glucose monitor affixed to her sleeveless upper left arm, just below her shoulder. His confidence collapsed, and the terror returned. Carlo noticed Jack's change in demeanor.

"Jack, I'm sure you recognize the CGM. Christina was diagnosed with Type 1 when she was three and until we found your insulin five years ago, she was having serious difficulties with blood sugar control. We spent more hospital time together than you can imagine. But thanks to your product, she's doing so much better."

Without a hint, Christina rushed into Abbott's arms and gave him a big hug. She held him tightly, barely able to get her arms around Abbott's bulky frame. He returned the gesture and held her in place, looking sideways at Carlo, terrified. She put her head on his chest and began weeping. After twenty seconds, she released her grasp. Her eyes were filled with tears. "Thank you for making my life better, Mr. Abbott."

Carlo put his hand on Jack's shoulder. "Honey, Mr. Abbott and I are going to leave for a bit to talk business. I'll be back before the party's over. Now go have some fun."

Christina nodded, wiping tears from her eyes. Carlo moved his grip from Abbott's left shoulder to underneath his left bicep and led him towards the ballroom exit. They were immediately joined by Anthony, Marco DiMarco's muscular driver, and a second, equally fit, associate.

Dante Palmieri's cautionary words rushed into Jack's head. "Where are we going, Carlo?" he fearfully uttered as he was ushered out of the ballroom.

"Let's go upstairs and talk about how we're going to work together, yes?"

Carlo tightened his grip on Abbott's arm. The four of them, walking casually to not draw attention, left the ballroom for an elevator which took them to the sixteenth floor. They exited to the left and entered a hotel room at the end of the hallway. The furniture in the room had all been moved to the room's outer edges. All except one chair in the middle of the room sitting on a sheet of plastic, which covered the entirety of the room's carpeting. Additional sheets of plastic covered the furniture.

Upon entering, Carlo handed Abbott off to Anthony and Fausto. Fausto took a towel from his pocket, stuffed it into Jack's mouth, and then duct-taped it in place. Jack screamed for help, but the towel muffled his cries. Anthony and Fausto then each took one of Jack's arms and pulled him to the chair. They pushed him down into it. Fausto took two zip ties from his pocket. "Put your hands behind your back, Jack," Anthony ordered.

Fausto took Abbott's hands and secured them with the two zip ties. Carlo brought a second chair to face Abbott and sat in front of him. "Jack, isn't Christina a beautiful young lady?"

Abbott screamed, but to no avail. He could not be heard outside the room.

"Jack, besides you, do you know who Christina really admires?" Abbott's eyes opened wide. "She loves Angela Braxton. And, of course, the President. And especially Luke. She has a serious crush on the President's son. She's been following him and the project since they moved into the White House. They've given her so much hope they are going to find a cure and one day soon she'll be able to live her life without the effects of what the disease is doing to her."

Carlo stood and moved the chair away from in front of Abbott. Anthony moved in and reached into his coat pocket. He pulled out a set of brass knuckles and slipped them onto his left hand. Without warning, he delivered a crushing punch to the right side of Jack's face, causing his cheekbone to buckle and blood to squirt from his right eye, his nose, and a now split lip. Jack let out a muted moan as his head dangled to the left.

He was still conscious as Carlo brought his chair back in front of Jack and sat to face him. Abbott's right eyelid had swelled shut from the punch. He looked at Carlo with only his left. Blood dripped from his right eye, nose, and lips.

"Now Jack, Mr. DiMarco has informed me you have one hundred million dollars for us. And we will gladly accept it. But you should know no one is going to kill anyone. Unless, of course, you don't follow my instruction, in which case we will kill you."

Carlo let those last words hang for effect, then continued. "My first instruction is what you are going to do with your generous offer. When you leave the hospital, which is where you'll be going after our chat, Costello Labs will donate fifty million dollars to the **TYPE 1-YOU'RE DONE** Project. Just think, Jack, you're going to be loved by everyone in the Type 1 community even more than you already are.

How proud you must be. As for the remaining fifty million, Cambretta Enterprises will accept those dollars as payment for our services. We will give you wiring instructions when you're feeling better."

"Second, you will never again make any threats or trouble of any kind for the Braxton's. No more proposals to anyone like you made to Mr. DiMarco. If we ever learn of any funny business from you or your company to hurt the Braxton's in any way, you can bend over and kiss your fat ass goodbye. Capito?"

"Third, because you have such a wonderful relationship with the first family, you are going to set up an opportunity for Christina to meet Lucas Braxton in the White House. Soon. Yes? And fourth, you will never mention our little meeting in this room to a soul. Should anyone inquire about your injuries, you can tell them you were mugged on the beautiful streets of Chicago tonight. If anyone is told otherwise, well, about that fat ass of yours."

"I know it's a lot to take in, Jack, especially in your current condition. But I assume we have an understanding. Confirm it for me if you would. Blink once for yes and two for no."

Jack blinked his left eye.

"Good. Boys, put ice on Jack's face, stop the bleeding, put the room back together, and then get him out of here."

Thirty minutes later, Fausto, Anthony, and a semi-conscious Jack Abbott were in the Lincoln Navigator heading to Northwestern Memorial Hospital. When they were three blocks away, Fausto pulled into a deserted alley. Before Anthony helped Jack out of the car, he asked him if he could recall Carlo's instructions. Jack's face was disfigured and his head hurting. He softly uttered, "yeah."

Anthony helped Jack out of the Navigator and sat him down against a wall in the alley. "Jack, stay right here. I'll call the hospital to let them know there's a guy alone in this alley who needs immediate medical attention. Fausto and I will stay hidden and watch, so no one fucks with you until the ambulance gets here."

Chapter 36

'Soulidarity'

The camera stage right zoomed in on Kriss.

"Good morning. It's February fourth, two thousand eighteen, and time for Big News Sunday. I'm Wallis Kriss."

The production set was completely redesigned thanks to a lucrative new contract Kriss was offered shortly after Jon and Angela's last visit in December. A contract which included significant studio upgrades. Kriss and his producer were prophetic in assessing the show would lose all their pharmaceutical advertisers, but the network was soon after flooded with new sponsorship opportunities. All new opportunities conditioned on Kriss being retained. And the President and First Lady having the right of first refusal for any future show dates. Jon made his first request to appear on February fourth.

After Kriss' intro, the camera zoomed out to show Jon sitting across the new and overly stylish glass desk. In front of Jon were six aluminum cans with writing the show host could not make out, and two frosted mugs."

"Mr. President, welcome back to Big News Sunday."

"Thank you, Wally. It's nice to be here and nice you're here too. It was touch and go for a while whether we'd again be drinking beers with our seventeen million friends on Sunday mornings. But you pulled it out. And, whew, what a contract you landed. The biggest in the industry my sources tell me. We might have to call you the comeback kid. But the First Lady and I are not surprised. We knew you would prevail if you wanted to stay. So, our sincere congratulations to you. And let's go with Jon for this show."

"Uh yes sir, Jon. Thank you. I couldn't have done it without you and the First Lady. And tell me, what's the story with those cans?"

Jon grabbed one, popped it open, and poured the contents into a mug. He picked up the mug and set it in front of Kriss, grabbed a second can, popped it open, and poured it into a second mug. He held his out to his host for a toast.

"What are we drinking today, Jon?"

"It's a brand-new soft drink being produced in North Korea. They named it Tanzanio Abby after Abby Martin, our assistant Secretary of State. She's been instrumental in our efforts to improve our relations with the PRNK. And the new drink was a way of their showing appreciation. Salud."

"Hmmm. Tastes like root beer. Not bad," Kriss offered with a hint of surprise.

"OK. Wally. What are we talking about today?"

"Well, sir. Let's start with your performance two weeks ago in front of both Houses of Congress."

"Yes. Of course. The State of the Union address. What did you think?"

"Well, sir. Uh Jon. My first thought was, what were you thinking? I mean throwing footballs into the House chamber during your speech?"

"Yeah Wally. If I had the chance for a do over, I wouldn't be balling in the chamber. Even if they were foam balls and no one was going to get hurt. I can promise we won't be doing it next year. I got quite an earful from Reibus with his promise to resign if I didn't leave the footballs home next year. But you have to admit it loosened things up a bit. Kept everyone on their toes. I didn't notice anyone falling asleep. And what about Senator Grassley's one-handed, over-the-shoulder grab of the 'FIX OUR CULTURE' football? You must admit, it was a helluva catch."

"I'll grant you it was very impressive for someone his age. But you did take a serious beating in the media for your stunt."

"I'd rather focus on the fact we had seventy million viewers, the highest viewership ever for a State of the Union address. And most public opinion polls had the address at eighty percent approval. The fact the American public is approving of what we're doing is most important to me. I couldn't care less what the media thinks other than you, of course."

Kriss nodded approvingly. "Your highest approval among the viewers during your address was for your plans to improve the mental health of Americans while reigning in the influence of Big Pharma. And thanks to our sponsorship changes, I can say that freely now. I know you covered it in your address, but for the benefit of our viewers who didn't tune in, please tell us what to expect from the Braxton administration in its relationship with the pharmaceutical industry."

"Wally, are you aware there are only two countries in the world today which permit direct-to-consumer pharmaceutical advertising on television?"

"No sir. I was not aware that is the case."

"It is the case. Only the U.S. and New Zealand permit it. Every other country on the planet bans pharmaceutical television advertising. Ok for me to summarize the reasons for our seventeen million friends?"

"Who am I to say to no?"

"There are six primary reasons every country in the world other than the U.S. and New Zealand ban this form of advertising. First, it's widely accepted direct-to-consumer advertising leads to overmedication. These ads encourage patients to request medications they may not need or are harmful to their individual situation."

"Second, pharmaceutical advertising does not always provide accurate information. It's difficult to determine if the information contained in the advertising is accurate and equally difficult to control using traditional truth in advertising statutes. It's impossible to ensure the integrity of the information in the advertisements."

"Third, some countries believe allowing direct-to-consumer pharmaceutical advertising increases the cost of health care as advertising costs are passed along to the consumer."

"Fourth, this form of advertising undermines the doctor-patient relationship as doctors are pressured by their patients to prescribe these medications against their better judgment. With added pressure coming from drug manufacturers."

"Fifth, countries with public health care systems have concerns advertised medications are not made available to patients covered under government provided health care programs because the costs are inflated. They have concerns advertising is used by big pharma to reserve certain medications for an upscale market of individuals who have the means to afford the higher prices. And in doing so, these medications are priced out of reach for public health system consumers."

"Sixth, most countries believe the promotion of life-style drugs, those for weight loss or erectile dysfunction as examples, are not appropriate for their culture. They also pose potential public health issues, as their side effects are not always understood or communicated effectively. Advertising creates a strong demand for these products despite the potential negative consequences associated with their use."

"Bottom line, Wally, the world does not consider allowing pharmaceutical companies to push their products on TV as good for public health. It's easier and more effective for these countries to ban these advertisements than take responsibility for the arduous task of ensuring compliance with ethical and legal standards. In our country, for a consumer to access these medications, they need a prescription from a licensed physician. There's a reason. Building demand for these products with advertising has too many consequences, unintended or otherwise. The First Lady and I share the belief that we and New Zealand have it wrong. Over the coming year you can expect HHS, under Angela's direction, to limit the pharmaceutical industry's ability to market drugs requiring a doctor's prescription directly to consumers."

Jon paused to allow Kriss to respond.

"Jon, having collaborated with our previous pharmaceutical sponsors for years, I can tell you this will not be received well by those in power in the pharmaceutical industry. They will put up hurdles for you in your efforts to block their ability to advertise. I'm certain your efforts will be labeled as censorship."

"I'm sure that will be the case, but we're on the right side of this debate. Big Pharma will certainly claim infringement of one right or another, but the First Lady and I are convinced the overmedication of Americans is one of our nation's most serious problems. And television advertising is primarily responsible for the demand. It's an unhealthy association, and incompatible with the objectives of a Department of Health, which is in place to serve our citizens, not the pharmaceutical industry. Unfortunately, it's only one of many pharmaceutical industry practices making our nation unhealthy."

The President reached for his root beer and took a swig. Kriss filled the gap.

"Speaking of the First Lady, she's been leading HHS since the beginning of the year. How is she enjoying managing a government bureaucracy?"

"Well Wally, one thing I can say for sure, unfortunately, is she is no longer surprised by the degree of corruption within HHS. What goes on inside the bureaucracy is wrong on so many levels. Unfortunately, it's not unique to HHS. After a year in office, I've witnessed so many things wrong with how our country operates. The fact we are still a functioning constitutional republic in spite of how screwed up our federal agencies and bureaucracies are is a testament to the wisdom of our founding fathers. If we did not have a document as well-constructed, insightful, and forward-looking as our U.S. Constitution to guide us, I'm certain we would have imploded by now."

"Jon, I've never heard you sound so pessimistic. Let's take a quick break." Kriss turned his eyes from Jon to the camera stage right. "Time for a word from our sponsors. We'll be back with the President in three minutes."

As the commercial break started, Kriss disconnected his microphone and motioned to Jon to do the same. He spoke softly, almost whispering. "Jon, I feel I should mention to you how dangerous it might be for you and your family to get in the way of Big Pharma. Having been associated with them for twenty years, I know how ruthless they can be. I'm not convinced they weren't somehow involved in the incident with your wife and son outside Edmonton. Be cautious."

The broadcast resumed and Kriss reconnected with his audience. "We're back with President Braxton. Sir, your comments before the break were both enlightening and troubling. It sounds like the First Lady will have no shortage of matters to address at HHS. And you sir, given what you described to us, how will your observations impact your coming year in office? What else can we expect from the Braxton administration in 2018?"

"First Wally, in no way am I pessimistic about the U.S. Yes, our nation has problems. But they can all be addressed. We have to start somewhere and the best place to start is to identify them in terms our citizens can understand. Our problems are intentionally obfuscated by politicians and seen as too complex for solutions to be crafted and articulated. We don't see our problems clearly, so the feeble, misguided solutions we come up with aren't relevant, or effective, or compelling enough to build bipartisan consensus around. Add partisan politics into the mix and we have a recipe for gridlock. It explains why we're trying to solve the same problems we've been working on for years and years. If we're going to fix what's wrong with this nation, even though our problems are complex, it's critical to simplify the way we see them. Only then will viable solutions be seen in a light where we can get past what stands in our way."

"When you say we should simplify the way we see our nation's problems, what do you mean? And why do you feel simplification is a good strategy?"

"OK Wally, two things. One, what do I mean? Here's an example. Our nation is in serious debt. We have no federal budget and have borrowed and continue to borrow beyond our means to pay our bills. We're staring at massive future unfunded entitlement liabilities. Social security. Medicare. Federal employee pensions. If we continue at our current pace, the problem is going to get worse and become disastrous. Before we moved into the White House, little was being done to address these unfunded liabilities. Remember, I chaired House Ways and Means for a year.

"I had a bird's-eye view of our fiscal ineptness. With the Braxton administration's executive branch cost-cutting measures we implemented early last year, we started addressing our looming monetary crisis. But the fact remains it's the first sincere effort to reduce our debt since 9/11, and it's only making a small dent in spending. The years of neglect have brought us to a precarious place. The reason we are where we are is because of the caliber of the people we send to Washington. Most have a lust for power and an interest in owning a campaign war chest. Both of which result from where and how they spend the taxpayer's money. They have little motivation to be sensible or responsible."

Jon continued. "But the fact remains we are in serious debt is simply because our government spends too much. Politicians will say no, it's a revenue problem. We need to raise taxes. But the root cause of the problem is not revenue. The solution, simply stated, is to reduce spending. Once we look past all the political BS and see the problem clearly, the simple solution presents itself."

"Second, why is simplification a good strategy? The primary reason is it enables the voters to engage. In general, our citizens are apathetic to the country's issues which don't directly affect them. The reason for their apathy is not because they don't care. It's because it's hard to truly understand the issues thanks to intentional obfuscation. Bureaucrats have learned to describe our problems in terms which leave voters with the idea that it's not the politician's fault we don't solve them. Washington paints a picture that the problems are too complex, and we somehow need to live with them. Our architected ineptness is working according to plan. Our political machinery has done an outstanding job framing our problems in complex terms, making it difficult for the average American to fully comprehend. By simplifying how we view our issues, more Americans will understand them and engage in the political process to solve them. The end result will be the public will be more aggressive holding their representatives accountable."

The President took a breath and reached for his root beer. Kriss did the same before responding.

"Jon, you're not concerned simplifying the way we see our problems could lead to oversimplification, which could lead to ineffective or destructive policies?"

"It's a possibility, Wally, no question. But until we get better people coming to Washington to do the people's work, we need better mechanisms to hold our current cast of characters accountable. If we pay a price for being too simplistic, it will be a small price compared to what we pay for our current way of operating. Remember, we're thirty trillion in debt."

"Anything specific the Braxton administration has in mind to get us where you want to take us?"

"The Braxton administration has adopted a mantra. We're here to solve problems. In many cases, our solutions will be to take our hands off the steering wheel and let the free market drive. In other cases, our solutions will entail shifting priorities where we move funding from an initiative not needed or not effective over to one which is. We're establishing a clear process for this year, starting with identifying the problems we want to address.

"Second, we classify them in a manner which allows us to see them more clearly. Third, we establish firm objectives and timelines for solving them. Identify, classify, address. And our efforts will also include pulling the covers back so the voters can see what their representative's voting priorities are."

Kriss was skeptical. "Do you really feel this simple approach can be effective?"

"I do. Identification will be straightforward. We'll establish two sets of focus groups. One from the public at large and the other from a variety of think tanks. This effort will give us a list of prioritized issues our citizens face in their everyday lives. And a second list from people more informed of the inner workings of our government.

"Next is classification. This will not be as straightforward as classifications require nuanced judgment calls. We will classify all our problems by root cause. It's not always evident what a true root cause may be, but we need to start somewhere. And we will start by classifying the problems we want to address into four buckets. Some of our problems are caused by government behaviors and result from either excessive government involvement or deficient government involvement. And some are caused by the public's behaviors, again either excessive or deficient. With the list of identified problems we want to address in 2018, each classified in such a way we can identify solutions, we can make headway in addressing them."

Jon paused for a gulp of Tanzanio Abby, allowing Kriss to ask a question.

"Jon, this sounds like you want to take over the work of Congress and redesign our policy-making processes. Have you considered this might be an overreach for the executive branch?"

"Could be. But one job of the departments of the executive branch is to craft solutions. We'll let the courts and the American people decide with their votes if they don't like what we're doing. Having been in Washington for four years now, I understand why we don't get things done. It's not so much the processes as the people. As I've said to you before, our campaign mechanisms with all the dirty money attract the wrong people to Congress. I only have three years left in office and our campaign finance reform will take longer to have any impact, so while I'm here, and now understanding what's wrong, I'm going to move things along."

"All right. How is this identifying and classifying actually going to work and who will do the work?"

"Good questions Wally. We're shifting a few positions around in the White House. Sandra Seracin, our Press Secretary, will take on a new role. She'll become the nation's first Solutions Czar. And Abby Martin from the State Department will move to the White House to take Sandra's position."

Kriss picked up an empty root beer can. "Abby Martin, of Tanzanio Abby fame, will be your new Press Secretary?"

"That's right."

"And Sandra Seracin is your new Solutions Czar?"

"Right again."

"And exactly what will be the Solutions Czar's responsibilities?"

"Sandra will conduct the orchestra. She'll be the liaison between the focus groups, the executive branch departments, and the legislative branch committees. Once she and I have prioritized the list of problems we want to tackle in 2018 from our focus groups, she'll classify them. When we have classification, she'll then work with the executive branch department responsible for the issue and work with the department's policy staff to craft a solution. Once the solution is approved by the Vice President and I, she'll manage the interactions with Congress for budgetary requirements. If she runs into any roadblocks, Abby Martin and the White House press apparatus will inform the voters who or what is in the way. Wally, give me an issue you think is worthy of our time and effort to solve?"

"Let's go with infrastructure for four hundred."

"Good. Infrastructure. I agree, this needs attention. OK, first, how would you classify the infrastructure challenges our country faces given our buckets?"

"Uh, we don't spend enough on rebuilding and repairing it?"

"Exactly right Wally. It's a government caused issue, and it's from lack of action. If we want to fix our infrastructure, we need more government action."

"But Jon, the federal government has attempted to address infrastructure many times over the last two decades, and those attempts have always failed. It's a political hot potato. What's going to be different with what you're proposing?"

"Climb out of the rabbit hole, Wally. Remember, we're simplifying our problems so we can more easily identify potential solutions. The direct reason our infrastructure is failing is because of government inaction. The reasons why could be the topic for an entire show, so I won't get into them now. But the fact remains, our federal government has neglected our aging infrastructure for too long. What's going to be different this time is we will find the money and identify the projects before any bills are written. Second, we'll be mobilizing the public so they participate. We'll do this by using language in the bills and through messaging coming out of the White House press office the public can understand. And through occasional executive branch visits with you throughout the year."

"Sounds like I might be spending some of my Sundays with the woman responsible for Tanzanio Abby this year."

"Count on it. And you can expect your ratings to go even higher."

"Jon, you say you will find the money before you write the bills? What does that mean?"

"It means we're going to act responsibly. If upgrading our infrastructure makes it onto our list of priorities to address in 2018, we'll first determine how much we want to spend in the next year or two. Then we look for the money within current budgets allocated but not yet earmarked for specific problems. Our first option will be to always use always be using existing funding for projects we prioritize. Being around Washington for as long as you have, you know there are billions of dollars allocated for pork. That practice will stop while there is a Braxton administration.

"There's no shortage of things we can cut to pay for infrastructure upgrades once we've identified and classified the project. Once we have a target issue and the funds identified, Sandra will go to the Department of Interior and work with their policy team to build out projects which fit within our budget parameters. Will we solve all the nation's infrastructure issues with this first effort? Of course not. But what we will have done is identified a genuine problem in the country, identified a viable solution, reallocated funding from pork and put people to work on something worthwhile. Perfect process? No. Better than we're doing today? I think so."

Kriss shook his head. "Is that all there is to it?"

"Don't understate our communication strategy. We will be openly communicating everything we're doing with the American people. And we'll ask our citizens to contact their elected representatives in Congress with their thoughts. Abby Martin will use her platform as Press Secretary to communicate everything Sandra and the executive branch departments are doing to solve the nation's problems and make life better for all Americans. Knowing Abby as I do, this should make for entertaining press briefings in the White House this year. And for some entertaining Big News Sunday shows when she joins you."

"Well, Mr. President, it sounds like it's going to be a busy year for the Braxton administration in 2018. We'll look forward to your progress. Let's move on to the **TYPE 1-YOU'RE DONE** Project. I understand the most promising research in the project had a serious setback. Can you give us any details?"

"You're understanding is correct. We did incur a setback. Our blood stem cell team, which was getting close to human clinical trials, had to make a course correction after failing to achieve a targeted benchmark on what we hoped would be their final round of animal trials. We were planning for human trials to start by the end of March, but as of now, it looks like the earliest possibility is November."

"That must be tremendously disappointing, especially for Angela. And for Luke. He was going to be included in the initial trial," Kriss offered remorsefully.

Jon remained upbeat. "He disappointed, as you expect. He lives with the disease every day and feels he has an obligation to the world-wide T1D community to lead the way. The delay has upset him. On the other hand, our other three teams are each making noteworthy progress on their hypotheses and the possibility remains by the end of this year we will have four potential cures or preventive options in human trials. We're down, but not out."

Kriss was ready to wrap the show. "OK. Last topic for today. Abortion. It was the part of your State of the Union speech with the least favorable reactions. Your position received considerable attention in the press and stimulated intense debate and criticisms from both sides of the aisle. You are taking the position that the federal government should not be involved in legislating abortion in either direction. You advocate Roe v. Wade should be reversed, and the matter returned to the states. In doing so, you have drawn fire from both sides. There are many in your party upset and already calling for you to be primary challenged in 2020. And others who feel you should be impeached for advocating reversing what has been considered law since 1977. Care to respond?"

"Sure, Wally. Was hoping we might go for infrastructure for six hundred. But let's address this. First, I do not belong to the Republican Party. As for those in the party suggesting I be primaried in 2020, it seems they haven't been listening to me discuss my future plans. They're going to need to come up with some candidates anyway as there's a strong possibility I won't be running.

"Now let's dive in. Abortion is a complex subject for our country to navigate because it is viewed through many different prisms. There's a moral prism. Is it right or wrong? There's a legislative prism. Should it be legal or illegal? There's a freedom prism. Does the individual choose or does the state? There's a Constitutional prism issue. Abortion is not identified as a responsibility of the federal government, leaving the matter to the states. We have a judicial prism. The Supreme Court's Roe v. Wade decision. And we have a biology prism. When does life begin? It's no surprise the country is so divided. With so many prism combinations to see this issue through, it's impossible for the country to come to any semblance of a consensus. The country will never adopt a policy to satisfy both camps. That ship has sailed. But this doesn't mean we can't build a bridge of understanding. This is what my position strives for. Allow everyone to be aware of the multiple views of this issue and present the arguments on both sides so women can become informed before they choose life or death for their unborn child. Shall we go into detail about our prisms?"

"I don't believe we have enough time. We'll make sure to come back to the prisms the next time you're on. With the few minutes we have left, can you give us your closing thoughts?"

"Sure Wally. Let's agree abortion is not something anyone looks forward to or wants. When a couple engages in sex, they are not doing so with the intent of having an abortion. When a woman chooses to terminate a pregnancy, she does not do so out of malice towards the life growing inside her. Abortions are chosen for other reasons. Desperation, uncertainty, fear. A choice usually made under duress. Often by the mother alone and in fear of sharing her situation. And other times under pressure from those around the mother who feel they will be inconvenienced or shamed by the birth of the child. But in the aftermath, the mother is alone, often wracked with remorse and guilt. Often left with lifelong scars and mental health repercussions. These decisions are of great consequence yet are often made under circumstances which make it impossible for the mother to make her best decision. What we're hoping to do with our position is to create 'soulidarity' with our position."

"Soulidarity? I'm not sure I'm familiar with that term," Kriss interjected.

"Do you like it? I just came up with it last week. To bridge the divide, we must find a position both sides can accept, even if neither endorses. And we must do so without sacrificing the soul of the nation. As a civilized society, we must always advocate life. And as a constitutional republic, we must respect our doctrines. In the U.S., the federal government's legislative reach is limited by the Constitution. Any powers not explicitly granted to the federal government are the responsibility of the individual states. If one accepts this interpretation of the Constitution, as I do, then one recognizes Roe v. Wade was flawed. It is not the responsibility of the federal government to legislate abortion. Does this mean the federal government recuse itself from the issue? No. This issue speaks to the heart of freedom and religious liberty and is harshly dividing us.

"In the case of abortion, I believe our federal government's role should be to give our citizens all the information they need to make their best personal individual decision, in a non-judgmental, unbiased manner. What the states do with abortion is their business and the federal government should not be interfering. But this should not preclude the federal government from taking a stand on the side of freedom and liberty while at the same time use its resources to promote life. Promoting life will be a core tenant of 'FIX OUR CULTURE,' but at the same time the federal government should not act in any manner to interfere with a state's decision."

"You've chosen to climb a slippery slope, Mr. President. Are you confident you can navigate it?"

"For the sake of the nation and for so many young lives being terminated because of ill-formed decisions, let's hope so."

Chapter 37

Call A Fireman

Sadie and Maxine were sound asleep at Jack Abbott's feet when they were awakened by a conversation in the kitchen. In unison, they lifted their heads and perked up their ears. They recognized Claude's voice and stirred only slightly, not wanting to wake their master. They laid their heads down. Their eyes were open as they stared at one another.

Abbott was in a light sleep on his left side when Sadie repositioned herself and brought him out of his slumber. He had been home for three weeks following his month-long hospital stay recovering from a serious concussion, light bleeding on the brain, and a broken face. Despite the severity of his injuries, his prognosis was good. He would fully recover within four months. He painfully rolled to his right when he heard Claude down the hall engaged in a friendly conversation in French with another man.

"Claude!"

His trusted valet walked briskly towards Abbott's bedroom and entered the open door. "Good morning, sir. How are you feeling?"

Abbott propped himself up, sitting with his back against the head-board. "Thankfully, no headache this morning. Who were you talking to?"

"It's my brother, Alain. He arrived from Paris three days ago. He would like to meet you. May I bring him in?"

"OK, but just for a minute. I'm not in the mood for conversation."

"As you wish, sir." Claude left the room and returned a moment later with his taller and younger brother. Sadie and Maxine lifted their heads and growled.

"Ladies. Quiet." The Dobermans whimpered momentarily and returned their heads to the bed.

"Sir, this is my not so little brother Alain Renault. Alain, this is Mr. Jackson Abbott."

Alain approached the bed and extended his hand. Abbott ignored it.

"What brings you to the U.S., Mr. Renault?"

In his heavy French accent, Alain responded. "You do, monsieur."

"Hmm. I don't recall we've ever spoken. What have I done to give you that impression?" Abbott responded while wracking his aching brain to remember if it was true.

"Monsieur Abbott, I would very much like to work for you."

"And what is it you would do for me, Alain? Claude does not need any help. He's managed my affairs for years superbly, without assistance."

"Monsieur Abbott, the work I would like to do for you would be outside of your home."

"Oh? What kind of work is it you do?"

"Among many talents I am a fireman, Monsieur."

"Well Alain, I'm afraid I don't need to put out any fires at the moment."

"No Monsieur. I do not put out fires. I create them."

"I see."

"Yes Monsieur. I build great fires. They burn extremely hot, and they burn extremely fast. And they leave behind no traces or evidence or DNA."

Abbott was confused. He looked at Alain's brother. "Claude, what's this all about?"

Instead, Alain responded. "Monsieur Abbott, have you read the newspaper or watched your television yet today?"

Abbott looked at Claude with anxiety. His trusted valet attempted to reassure him. "It's OK sir." Abbott then looked warily at Alain.

"Monsieur, when you read or watch your local news, you will see a large mansion in Hinsdale burned to the ground yesterday. It was the home of Christina and Giancarlo Cambretta. Christina Cambretta no longer lives there. Giancarlo Cambretta and your one hundred-million-dollar liability no longer live. And monsieur, I would very much like to move to Washington in your employ."

NEXT IN BRAXTONS AMERICA

www.ingramcontent.com/pod-product-compliance
Lightning Source LLC
Chambersburg PA
CBHW070616260626
47161CB00007B/2451